A Buccaneer at Heart

"A young lady—well, not *that* young, I suppose, but young enough, if you catch my drift. She turned up and was searching for her brother—a naval lieutenant by the name of Will Hopkins. She was asking questions." Sampson drew in a deep breath. "I didn't think that was wise and I tried to warn her off."

Robert grimaced; the last thing he needed was a gently bred but determined female complicating his simple and straightforward mission. But that she was in the settlement at all, let alone determinedly asking questions, argued that convincing her to meekly step back, return to England, and leave the investigating to him wasn't going to be any easy task.

Still, he had no intention whatever of allowing anyone—male or female—to interfere. The lady might be determined, but so was he; he was determined to allow nothing to get in the way of him finishing this assignment in the shortest amount of time.

He wanted it done so he could put it behind him and concentrate on following the lure that, increasingly, drew him.

The need for a hearth. The need for a home. The need of a wife to be his anchor.

Other titles from Stephanie Laurens

Cynster Series

Devil's Bride
A Rake's Vow
Scandal's Bride
A Rogue's Proposal
A Secret Love
All About Love
All About Passion
On a Wild Night
On a Wicked Dawn
The Perfect Lover
The Ideal Bride
The Truth About Love
What Price Love?
The Taste of Innocence
Temptation and Surrender

Cynster Sisters Trilogy

Viscount Breckenridge to the Rescue
In Pursuit of Eliza Cynster
The Capture of the Earl of Glencrae

Cynster Sisters Duo

And Then She Fell
The Taming of Ryder Cavanaugh

Cynster Special

The Promise in a Kiss
By Winter's Light

Cynster Next Generation

The Tempting of Thomas Carrick
A Match for Marcus Cynster

Medieval

Desire's Prize

Novellas

"Melting Ice"—from *Scandalous Brides*
"Rose in Bloom"—from *Scottish Brides*
"Scandalous Lord Dere"—
from *Secrets of a Perfect Night*
"Lost and Found"—from *Hero, Come Back*
"The Fall of Rogue Gerrard"—
from *It Happened One Night*
"The Seduction of Sebastian Trantor"—
from *It Happened One Season*

Bastion Club Series

Captain Jack's Woman (Prequel)
The Lady Chosen
A Gentleman's Honor
A Lady of His Own
A Fine Passion
To Distraction
Beyond Seduction
The Edge of Desire
Mastered by Love

Black Cobra Quartet Series

The Untamed Bride
The Elusive Bride
The Brazen Bride
The Reckless Bride

Other Novels

The Lady Risks All

The Casebook of Barnaby Adair Novels

Where the Heart Leads
The Peculiar Case of Lord Finsbury's Diamonds
The Masterful Mr. Montague
The Curious Case of Lady Latimer's Shoes
Loving Rose: The Redemption of Malcolm Sinclair

Regency Romances

Tangled Reins
Four in Hand
Impetuous Innocent
Fair Juno
The Reasons for Marriage
A Lady of Expectations
An Unwilling Conquest
A Comfortable Wife

The Adventurers Quartet

The Lady's Command

A Buccaneer at Heart

Recycling programs for this product may not exist in your area.

ISBN-13: 978-0-7783-1940-5

A Buccaneer at Heart

For questions and comments about the quality of this book, please contact us at CustomerService@Harlequin.com.

www.MIRABooks.com

Printed in U.S.A.

First printing: May 2016
10 9 8 7 6 5 4 3 2 1

A Buccaneer at Heart

CAST OF CHARACTERS

Principal Characters:

Frobisher, Robert	Hero
Hopkins, Aileen	Heroine

In London:

Family:

Frobisher, Declan	Robert's younger brother
Frobisher, Lady Edwina	Robert's sister-in-law

Staff in Declan & Edwina's town house:

Humphrey	Butler

Government:

Wolverstone, Duke of, Royce, aka Dalziel	Ex-commander of British secret operatives outside England
Wolverstone, Duchess of, Minerva	Wolverstone's wife
Melville, Viscount	First Lord of the Admiralty
Dearne, Marquess of, Christian Allardyce	Ex-operative of Dalziel's, now functioning in some unspecified capacity in government intelligence
Carstairs, Major Rafe	Army liaison in matters requiring discretion
Hendon, Lord, Jack	Ex-operative, now owner of Hendon Shipping

In Aberdeen:

Frobisher, Fergus	Robert's father
Frobisher, Elaine	Robert's mother
Frobisher, Royd (Murgatroyd)	Eldest Frobisher brother

In Southampton:

Higginson	Clerk, Frobisher Shipping

At sea:

Frobisher, Caleb	Youngest of four Frobisher brothers
Frobisher, Catrina (Kit)	Female cousin
Frobisher, Lachlan	Male cousin

In Freetown:

Dixon, Captain	Army engineer, missing
Hopkins, Lieutenant	Navy, West Africa Squadron, missing
Fanshawe, Lieutenant	Navy, West Africa Squadron, missing
Hillsythe	Ex-Wolverstone agent, governor's aide, missing
Holbrook, Governor	Governor-in-Chief of British West Africa
Holbrook, Lady, Letitia	Governor's wife, now absent
Satterly, Mr.	Governor's principal aide
Eldridge, Major	Commander, Fort Thornton
Decker, Vice-Admiral	Commander, West Africa Squadron, currently at sea
Richards, Captain	Army, Fort Thornton
Hardwicke, Mr.	Anglican minister
Hardwicke, Mrs. Mona	Anglican minister's wife
Sherbrook, Mrs.	Local lady
Hitchcock, Mrs.	Local lady
Winton, Major	Commissar of Fort Thornton
Winton, Mrs.	Wife of Major Winton
Babington, Charles	Partner, Macauley & Babington Trading Company
Macauley, Mr.	Senior partner, Macauley & Babington Trading Company
Undoto, Obo	Local priest
Sampson	Old sailor
Lashoria	Vodun priestess
Fortescue, Katherine	Missing governess from the Sherbrook household
Wilson, Mary	Missing shop owner/assistant, Babington's sweetheart
Muldoon	Naval Attaché

On board The Trident*:*

Latimer, Mr. Jordan	First Mate
Hurley, Mr.	Master
Wilcox	Bosun
Miller	Quartermaster
Foxby, Mr.	Steward
Benson	Experienced sailor
Coleman	Experienced sailor
Fuller	Experienced sailor
Harris	Experienced sailor

One

May 1824
London

Captain Robert Frobisher strolled at his ease along Park Lane, his gaze on the rippling green canopies of the massive trees in Hyde Park.

He'd steered his ship, *The Trident*, up the Thames on the previous evening's tide. They'd moored at Frobisher and Sons' berth in St. Katherine's Dock, and after he'd dealt with all the associated palaver, it had been too late to call on anyone. This morning, he'd dutifully gone into the company office in Burr Street; as soon as the customary formalities had been completed and the bulk of his crew released for the day, he'd jumped into a hackney and headed for Mayfair. But rather than driving directly to his brother Declan's house, he'd had the jarvey let him down at the end of Piccadilly so that he could take a few minutes to drink in the green. He spent so much of his life looking at the sea, being reminded of the beauties of land was no bad thing.

A self-deprecating smile curving his lips, he turned the corner into Stanhope Street. Barely ten o'clock was an unfashionably early hour at which to call at a gentleman's residence, but he felt sure his brother and his brother's new wife, the lovely Edwina, would welcome him with open arms.

The morning was fine, if a touch crisp, with the sun intermittently screened by gray clouds scudding across the pale sky.

Declan and Edwina resided at Number 26. Looking down the street, Robert saw a black carriage pulled up by the curb farther along.

Premonition swept cool fingers across his nape. Early as it was, there was no other conveyance waiting in the short residential street.

As he continued strolling, idly swinging his cane, a footman perched on the rear of the carriage saw him; instantly, the footman leapt down to the pavement and moved to open the carriage door.

Increasingly intrigued, Robert watched, wondering who would descend. Apparently, he wouldn't need to check the house numbers to discover which house was his goal.

The gentleman who, with languid grace, stepped out of the carriage and straightened was as tall as Robert, as broad-shouldered and lean. Sable hair framed a face the features of which screamed his station.

Wolverstone. More precisely, His Grace, the Duke of Wolverstone, known in the past as Dalziel.

Given Wolverstone was plainly waiting to waylay and speak with him, Robert surmised that Wolverstone's status as commander of British agents outside of the isles had, at least temporarily, been restored.

Robert's cynical, world-weary side wasn't all that surprised to see the man.

But the gentleman who, much less elegantly, followed Wolverstone from the carriage was unexpected. Portly and very precisely attired, with a fussy, somewhat prim air, the man tugged his waistcoat into place and fiddled with his fob chain; from long experience of the breed, Robert pegged him as a politician. Along with Wolverstone, the man turned to face Robert.

As Robert neared, Wolverstone nodded. "Frobisher." He held out his hand.

Robert transferred his cane to his other hand; returning the nod, he grasped Wolverstone's hand, then shifted his gaze to Wolverstone's companion.

Releasing Robert, Wolverstone waved gracefully. "Allow me to present Viscount Melville, First Lord of the Admiralty."

Robert managed not to raise his brows. He inclined his head. "Melville." *What the devil's afoot?*

Melville curtly nodded back, then drew in a portentous breath. "Captain Frobisher—"

"Perhaps," Wolverstone smoothly interjected, "we should adjourn inside." His dark eyes met Robert's gaze. "Your brother won't be surprised to see us, but in deference to Lady Edwina, we thought it best to await your arrival in the carriage."

The notion that consideration of Edwina's possible reaction held the power to influence Wolverstone even that much... Robert fought not to grin. His sister-in-law was a duke's daughter and thus of the same social stratum as Wolverstone, yet Robert would have wagered there were precious few who Wolverstone would even think to tiptoe gently around.

Curiosity burgeoning in leaps and bounds, at Wolverstone's wave, Robert led the way up the steps to the narrow front porch.

He hadn't previously called at this house, but the butler who opened the door to his knock recognized him instantly. The man's face lit. "Captain Frobisher." Then the butler noticed the other two men, and his expression turned inscrutable.

Realizing the man didn't know either Wolverstone or Melville, Robert smiled easily. "I gather these gentlemen are acquainted with my brother."

He didn't need to say more—Declan must have heard the butler's greeting; he appeared through a doorway down the hall.

Smiling, Declan strode forward. "Robert—well met!"

They grinned and clapped each other on the shoulders, then Declan noticed Wolverstone and Melville. Declan's expression shuttered, but then he looked at Robert, a question evident in his blue eyes.

Robert arched a brow back. "They were waiting outside."

"Ah. I see."

From Declan's tone, Robert gathered that his brother was uncertain whether Wolverstone and Melville's appearance was good news or bad.

Yet with assured courtesy, Declan welcomed Wolverstone and Melville, shaking their hands. "Gentlemen." As the butler shut the door, Declan caught Wolverstone's eye. "The drawing room might be best."

Wolverstone inclined his head, and the butler moved to throw open the door to their left.

Declan waved Wolverstone, Melville, and Robert through; as Declan started to follow, Robert heard the butler ask, "Should I inform her ladyship, sir?"

Without hesitation, Declan replied, "Please."

Sinking into one of the numerous armchairs spread around the cozy room, Robert was surprised that Declan hadn't even paused before summoning his wife to attend what was clearly destined to be a business meeting—although of what business, Robert couldn't guess.

Declan had barely had a chance to offer his guests refreshments—which they all declined—before the door opened and Edwina swept in, bringing all four men to their feet.

Fetchingly gowned in cornflower-blue-and-white-striped silk, she looked happy and delighted—glowing with an uncomplicated enthusiasm for life. Although her first smile was for Declan, in the next breath, she turned her radiance on Robert and opened her arms. "Robert!"

He couldn't help but smile widely in return and allow her the liberty of an embrace. "Edwina." He'd met her several times, both at his parents' home as well as at her family's, and he thoroughly approved of her; from the first, he'd seen her as precisely the right lady for Declan. He returned her hug and dutifully bussed the smooth cheek she tipped up to him.

Drawing back, she met his eyes. "I'm utterly delighted to see you! Did Declan tell you we planned to make this our London base?"

She barely paused for his answer—and his quick look at Declan—before she inquired about *The Trident* and his immediate plans for the day. After he told her of his ship's position and his lack of any plans, she informed him that he would be staying for luncheon and also to dine.

Then she turned to greet Wolverstone and Melville. The ease she displayed toward them made it clear she was already acquainted with them both.

At Edwina's gracious wave, they resettled in the armchairs and sofa, and the next minutes went in general converse, led, of course, by Edwina.

Noting the quick smiling looks she shared with Declan, and noting his brother's response, Robert felt a distinct pang of envy. Not that he coveted Edwina; he liked her, but she was too forceful a personality for his taste. Declan needed a lady like her to balance his own character, but Robert's character was quite different.

He was the diplomat of the family, careful and cautious, while his three brothers were reckless hellions.

"Well, then." Apparently satisfied with what Wolverstone had deigned to share about his family's health, Edwina clasped her hands in her lap. "Given you gentlemen are here, I expect Declan and I had better tell Robert about how we've spent the last five weeks—about the mission and what we discovered in Freetown."

Mission? Freetown? Robert had thought that, while he'd been on the other side of the Atlantic, Declan and Edwina had remained in London. Apparently not.

Edwina arched a brow at Wolverstone.

His expression impassive, he inclined his head. "I daresay that will be fastest."

Robert didn't miss the resignation in Wolverstone's tone.

He felt sure Edwina didn't either, but she merely smiled approvingly at Wolverstone, then transferred her bright gaze to Declan. "Perhaps you had better start."

Entirely sober, Declan looked at Robert and did.

Between them, Declan and Edwina related a tale that kept Robert transfixed.

That Edwina had stowed away and joined Declan on his run south wasn't really that much of a surprise. But the puzzling situation in Freetown—and the consequent danger that had stalked them and, beyond anyone's ability to predict, had reached out and touched Edwina—was a tale guaranteed to capture and hold his attention.

By the time Edwina concluded with a reassurance that she'd taken no lasting harm from the events of their last night in Freetown, Robert no longer had any doubt as to why Wolverstone and Melville had been waiting on the doorstep to waylay him.

Melville huffed and promptly confirmed Robert's assumption. "As you can see, Captain Frobisher, we are in desperate need of someone with similar capabilities as your brother to travel to Freetown as fast as may be and continue our investigation."

Robert glanced at Declan. "I take it this falls under our…customary association with the government?"

Wolverstone stirred. "Indeed." He met Robert's eyes. "There are precious few others who could do the job, and no one else with a fast ship in harbor."

After a second of holding Wolverstone's dark gaze, Robert nodded. "Very well." This was a far cry from his usual voyages ferrying diplomats—or diplomatic secrets of whatever sort—back and forth, but he could see the need, could appreciate the urgency. And he'd sailed into Freetown before.

He looked at Declan. "Is this why there were no orders waiting for me at the office?" He'd been surprised to learn that; the demand for his services was usually so great that *The Trident* was rarely free for more than a few days, and Royd and his *Corsair* often had to take on the overload.

Declan nodded. "Wolverstone informed Royd the government would most likely need to call on another of us once *The Cormorant* got back, and fortuitously, you were due in. I received a missive from Royd, and there's one waiting for you in the library—we're free of our usual business and are to devote our services to the Crown."

Robert dipped his head in acknowledgment. He tapped his fingers on the chair's arm as he sifted through all Declan and Edwina had revealed, adding in Wolverstone's dry comments and Melville's few utterances. He narrowed his eyes, in his mind studying the jigsaw-like picture he'd assembled from the facts. "All right. Let's see if I have this straight. Four serving officers have gone missing, one after another, along with at least four young women and an unknown number of other men. These disappearances occurred over a period of four months or more, and the few instances known to have been discussed with Governor Holbrook, he dismissed as due to those involved having gone off to seek their fortune in the jungle or elsewhere. Some such excuse. In addition, seventeen children from the slums are also missing, apparently disappearing over much the same period, with Holbrook brushing their vanishing aside as children running off—nothing more nefarious.

"Currently, there is nothing to say if Holbrook is trying to suppress all interest in this spate of missing people because he's involved, or whether his attitude springs from some other entirely noncriminal belief. Regardless, Lady Holbrook has proved to be definitely involved, and it's doubtful she'll still be in the settlement, but you would like me to verify whether Holbrook himself is still at his post. If he is, then we presume him innocent—or at least unaware of whatever is driving these kidnappings." Robert arched a brow at Wolverstone. "Correct?"

Wolverstone nodded. "I haven't met Holbrook, but from what I've been able to learn, he doesn't seem the type to be involved. However, he might well be the type of official who will refuse to react until the unpalatable truth is staring him in the face—until circumstances force him to it."

Robert added that shading to his mental jigsaw. "To continue, in the case of the missing adults, there are reasonable grounds on which to believe that they're being selected in some way and that attendance at the local priest Obo Undoto's services in some way facilitates that. We know nothing about how the children are taken, other than that it's not through any connection with Undoto's services."

Declan shifted. "We can't even be sure the missing children are being taken by the same people or for the same reason as the missing adults."

"But given that young women have been taken as well as men," Edwina put in, "there has to be a possibility that all the missing, children as well as adults, are being...used in the same way." Her chin firmed. "By the same villains."

Robert paused, then said, "Regardless of whether the children are going to the same place, given the priestess's claims—none of which have yet proven unfounded, so let's assume she spoke true—Undoto and his services are clearly the obvious place to look for the beginnings of a trail."

No one argued. After a second of considering the picture taking shape in his mind, Robert went on, "If I've understood correctly, the vodun priestess Lashoria, Reverend Hardwicke, and even more his wife, an old sailor named Sampson, and Charles Babington are people you"—he glanced at Declan and Edwina—"consider safe sources."

Both nodded. Declan stated, "They're potential allies and might well be willing to play an active hand in helping you learn more." He met Robert's eyes. "Babington especially. I believe he has a personal interest in one of the young women who has gone missing, but I didn't get a chance to pursue that or him further. But he can command resources within the settlement that might prove useful."

Melville cleared his throat. "There's also Vice-Admiral Decker. We have no reason to imagine he has any involvement in whatever heinous crime is under way in the settlement." He all but glowered at Declan. "I gave your brother a letter enabling him to call on Decker's support. I believe I worded it generally, so it will apply to you as it would have to him."

Declan dipped his head. "Decker wasn't in port while I was there. I still have the letter—I'll give it to you."

Robert wasn't fooled by Declan's noncommittal tone; he wouldn't be tripping over his toes to ask any favors of Decker, either. Indeed, he hoped the vice-admiral remained at sea throughout his visit to the settlement.

"Regardless," Wolverstone said, "I cannot stress enough how critical it is that whatever occurs while you're on this mission, you must not at any point do anything to alert the perpetrators to any level of official interest. We must protect the lives of those taken—sending in a rescue team who find only dead bodies isn't something any of us wish to even contemplate. Given that we cannot be certain who of those in authority in the settlement is involved, and conversely who is safe to trust, every action you take must remain covert."

Robert nodded curtly. The more he heard—the more he dwelled on all he'd learned—remaining covert first to last seemed his wisest choice.

"So, Captain," Melville said bracingly, "we need you to go into Freetown, follow the trail your brother has identified, and learn all the details of this nefarious scheme."

Melville's expression was a blend of belligerence and something much closer to pleading. Robert recognized the signs of a politician facing a threat beyond his control.

Before he could respond, Wolverstone softly said, "Actually, no." Wolverstone caught Robert's gaze. "We cannot ask you to learn all the details."

From the corner of his eye, Robert saw Melville's face fall as he stared at Wolverstone, who, in this matter, was effectively his mentor.

As if unaware of the angst he was causing, Wolverstone smoothly went on, "From what your brother has said, and from all I've learned from others over recent days, given that those effecting the kidnappings are slave traders, then I gather that in Freetown, as generally in that region, the slave traders will be operating out of a camp. They will hold their captives at that camp until they have a sufficient number to take to whoever they're supplying. Further, the camp will almost certainly be outside the settlement's borders, somewhere in the jungle, possibly some distance away."

Wolverstone glanced at Declan, who, his expression impassive, nodded.

Imperturbably, Wolverstone continued, his gaze returning to Robert's face, "Consequently, this mission is highly unlikely to be accomplished in only two stages. There will be however many stages we require to learn what we need to know, all without alerting the villains involved. Your brother"—he paused, then inclined his head to Edwina—"and Lady Edwina got us the first vital clues. They identified Undoto's services as being a part of the scheme and gave us the connection to the slave traders. They also confirmed that those in high places in the settlement are involved, something we must strive never to forget. If Lady Holbrook was suborned, almost certainly others will have been as well."

Wolverstone's gaze cut to Melville, but although he looked dejected and, indeed, disgruntled, the First Lord made no attempt to interrupt.

"Therefore," Wolverstone continued, "your mission must be to confirm the slave traders' connection to Undoto and, by following the slavers, to identify the location of their camp. Your orders are specifically that. Locate the slavers' camp, then return and report. You must not follow the trail further, no matter the temptation."

Wolverstone paused, then added, "I appreciate that, very likely, that will not be an easy directive to follow—it's not one I take joy in giving. But in order to mount a rescue of all those taken, it's imperative we learn of the location of that camp. If you go further and are captured yourself...put simply, all those missing can't afford that. If you are taken, we won't know until your crew return to tell us. And once they do, we'll be no further forward than we are now—no nearer the point of knowing enough to effectively rescue those taken."

Wolverstone glanced at Melville; when he looked back at Robert, his features had hardened. "Running a mission in successive stages may seem like a slow way forward, but it is a *sure* way forward, and those taken deserve our best attempts to successfully free them."

Robert met Wolverstone's gaze; two seconds ticked past, then he nodded. "I'll locate the slavers' camp and bring the information back."

Simple. Straightforward. He saw no reason to argue. If he had to sail to Freetown and do this mission, he was glad enough that it should have such a definite and definable endpoint.

Wolverstone inclined his head. "Thank you." He looked at Melville. "We'll leave you to prepare."

Melville rose, as did everyone; he offered Robert his hand. "How long before you and your ship will be ready to depart?"

Robert gripped Melville's hand. "A few days." As hands were shaken all around and they moved toward the door, Robert thought through the logistics. He halted at the doorway and spoke to all. "I'll send *The Trident* to Southampton to provision from the stores there. I imagine I'll be able to set sail in three days."

Melville humphed, but said no more. From his expression, Robert surmised that the First Lord was even more deeply troubled by the situation in Freetown than Wolverstone.

Then again, Wolverstone had no real responsibility to shoulder in this instance, while Melville…as Robert understood it, as First Lord, Melville had his neck metaphorically on the block, at least politically, and possibly even socially.

Robert returned to the armchair opposite the sofa. While Declan and Edwina farewelled their unexpected guests, he swiftly reviewed all he'd been told.

When Declan and Edwina reentered the drawing room and resumed their seats, he looked from one to the other. "All right. Now tell me all."

As he'd assumed, the pair had a great deal more to impart to him of society in Freetown, of all the characters who had played even small parts in their own drama, of the sights, sounds, and dangers of the slums, and so much more that, he knew, could well prove helpful, and perhaps even critical, once he was on the ground in the settlement.

The hours slid by unnoticed by any of them.

When the clocks struck one, they repaired to the dining parlor and continued their discussions over a substantial meal. Robert grinned when he saw the platters being brought in. "Thank you," he said to Edwina. "Shipboard food is good enough, but it's nice to eat well when one can."

Eventually, they returned to the comfort of the drawing room. Having exhausted all the facts and most of the speculation applicable, they finally turned to the ultimate question of what purpose lay behind the strange kidnappings.

Slumped in the armchair he'd claimed, his long legs stretched out before him, his booted ankles crossed, Robert tapped the tips of his steepled fingers to his chin. "You said that Dixon was the first to vanish. Given he's an engineer of some repute, assuming he was chosen for his known skills, I agree that that suggests the enterprise our villains are engaged in is most likely a mine."

Lounging on the sofa beside Edwina, Declan nodded. "At least in those parts."

"So what are they mining?" Robert met his brother's blue eyes. "You know that area better than I. What's most likely?"

Declan twined his fingers with Edwina's. "Gold and diamonds."

"I assume not together, so what's your best guess?"

"If I had to wager, I'd go for diamonds."

Robert had a great deal of respect for Declan's insights into all matters of exploration. "Why?"

Declan's lips twisted. He glanced at Edwina. "I've been thinking about why those behind this have chosen to take young women and children—what uses they might have for them. Children are often used in gold mines to pick over the shattered ore—they'd be just as useful in mining for diamonds, at least in that area. But young women? They have no real role I can think of in gold mining. But in mining for diamonds in that area?"

Gripping Edwina's hand, Declan looked at Robert. "The diamonds there are found in concretions, lumped together with other ore. Separating the ore from the stones is fine work—not so much precision as simply being able to work on small things. Young women with good eyesight could clean the rough stones enough to reduce their size and weight so that the final product, while keeping its value, would fit into a relatively small space—easy to smuggle out, even by mail."

Declan held Robert's gaze. "If I had to guess, I would say our villains have stumbled on a pipe of diamonds and are busy retrieving as many stones as they can before anyone else learns of the strike."

* * *

Later that same day, in a tavern in Freetown located on a narrow side street off the western end of Water Street—an area frequented by clerks and shopkeepers and others more down at heel—a man rather better dressed than the other denizens sat nursing a glass of ale at a table in the rear corner of the dimly lit taproom.

The tavern door opened, and another man walked in. The

first man looked up. He watched as the second man, also better dressed than the general run of the tavern's clientele, bought a glass of ale from the man behind the counter, then crossed the room to the table in the corner.

The men exchanged nods, but no words. The second man drew up a stool and sat, then took a deep draft of his ale.

The sound of the door opening reached the second man. His back was to the door. He looked at the first man. "That him?"

The first man nodded.

Both waited in silence until the newcomer had bought an ale for himself and approached the table.

The third man set his glass down on the scarred surface, then glanced around at the others in the taproom before pulling up a stool and sitting.

"Stop looking so damned guilty." The second man raised his glass and took another sip.

"All very well for you." The third man, younger than the other two, reached for his glass. "You don't have an uncle as your immediate superior."

"Well, he's not going to see us here, is he?" the second man said. "He'll be up at the fort, no doubt busily sorting through his inventory."

"God—I hope not." The younger man shuddered. "The last thing we need is for him to realize how much is missing."

The first man, who had silently watched the exchange, arched a brow. "No chance of that, is there?"

The younger man sighed. "No—I suppose not." He stared into his ale. "I've been careful to keep everything we've taken off the books. There's no way to see something's missing if according to the books it was never there."

The first man's lips curved without humor. "Good to know."

"Never mind that." The second man focused on the first. "What's this about Lady H? I heard through the office that she's decamped on us."

The first man flushed under his tan. His hands tightened about his glass. "I was told Lady H had gone to visit family, and for all I know, that might still be the case. So yes, she's gone, but as she knows nothing about my connection to our operation, she didn't see fit to explain her reasons to me. I asked around—indirectly, of course—but apparently Holbrook doesn't know when she'll be back."

"So we might have lost our ability to vet our kidnapees?" The second man frowned.

"Yes," the first man replied, "but that isn't what most concerns me." He paused to take a sip of his ale, then lowered the glass and went on, "Yesterday, I heard from Dubois that Kale claims he lost two of the three men he sent to the governor's house to fetch some lady Lady H had sent word to them to come and get."

The third man looked puzzled. "When was that?"

"As near as I can make out, it was fifteen nights ago. Three days before Lady H sailed. I spent the evening in question dealing with dispatches, so I knew nothing about it at the time." The first man paused, then more diffidently went on, "From what I could gather, it was Frobisher's wife, Lady Edwina, who came to see Lady H that evening, but I can't be certain Lady Edwina was the lady Lady H called Kale to come and get, and I see no point in asking too many questions of the governor's staff.

"According to Dubois, Kale said that the lady his men picked up was drugged and asleep. All his man—the one who survived—could tell him was that the lady had golden hair. In their usual team of three, Kale's men wrapped her in a rug and carried her out through the slum behind the house, but then they were attacked by four men—sailors, according to the survivor. The sailors killed two of Kale's men and took the lady back. Kale's third man ran, but then doubled back and trailed the sailors to the docks. He saw them get into a tender and be rowed off, but in the dark, he couldn't tell which ship they boarded."

The second man continued to frown into his glass. "If I'm remembering aright, Frobisher's ship was in the harbor that night. It wasn't there the next day—they must have left on the morning tide."

The first man humphed. "Word is that they—Frobisher and Lady Edwina—were on their honeymoon and were headed to Cape Town to visit family there. If that's so, then even if it was Lady Edwina who Lady H drugged—God alone knows why the silly bitch would do such a thing, but if she did—I can't imagine we'll hear any more about it."

The third man stared at the first. "But…surely Frobisher will lodge some sort of official complaint with Holbrook?"

The first man grinned. "I doubt it. Lady Edwina's the daughter of a duke—very highly placed within society in London. I really can't see Frobisher wanting to draw attention to his wife being in the hands of the likes of Kale's men, in the night, in the slum, no one else about. Not the sort of thing he'd want known about his wife."

"I agree." The second man nodded. "He's got her back, and by the sounds of it, no harm done. He'll leave it at that." He paused, then added, "If Frobisher had wanted to make anything of it, he wouldn't have sailed without pounding on Holbrook's desk. He didn't, so I agree—that's that." He cut a glance at the third man. "No need to borrow trouble on that account."

The first man leaned his chin on one hand. "And I don't think we need to fear Lady H giving us up to anyone, either. She has far more to lose than we do. The only reason she agreed to Undoto's suggestion was for the money—that's really all she cared about. And if it was Lady Edwina she tried to drug and send off to Kale, then once she learned that Lady Edwina had been rescued, I can quite understand Lady H wanting to make herself scarce. I would, too. But if that's the case, it's better for us that she's taken herself off—we wouldn't want her to be waiting here to be asked any awkward questions if any are ever directed this way."

The second man grunted. "She doesn't know enough to point the finger at us, anyway."

The first man dipped his head. "True. But she might have pointed at Undoto, or given up her contact with Kale, and that might have started things unraveling… No. Overall, we should be glad she's gone. But if she has done a flit for good and all, then the one thing we do need to work on is how to cover for her expertise." The first man looked at the other two and raised his brows. "Any notion how we're to vet those we take to make sure their disappearance doesn't set off any alarms?"

Silence ensued.

Finally, the second man raked his hand through his thick black hair. "Let's leave that for now, but keep alert for any possible other way. As of this moment, Dubois has enough men for his needs."

"But he says he'll need more," the first man countered. "He said Dixon's not far from opening up the second tunnel, and once he does, if we want to increase production like we've promised our backers, then Dubois will need more men."

"So he'll need them soon, but not immediately." The second man nodded. "No need to panic. We'll find a way."

"What about women and children?" the third man asked.

"Dubois said he has enough of both for now." The first man turned his glass between his hands. "He won't need more until they start hauling rock from the second tunnel."

The three fell silent, then the second man humphed. "I hope Dixon can be trusted to do what's needed."

The first man's lips quirked. "Dubois was very confident that in order to keep Miss Frazier safe and unmolested, Dixon will perform exactly as we wish."

The second man grinned. "I have to say that Dubois's notion of using the women's safety to control the men has proved nothing short of inspired."

The first man grunted and pushed away his empty glass. "Just as long as the men don't think ahead and realize that, when we have all we need from them, it's all going to come to the same thing in the end."

★ ★ ★

A gray dawn was breaking far to the east as Robert steered *The Trident* down the last stretch of the Solent. The day was overcast and blustery, the waves a choppy gray-green, but the wind gusted from the northeast, which made it damned near perfect sailing, at least to him.

He'd risen in the small hours and had jockeyed *The Trident* into position to be one of the first ships to heel out on the surging tide. With the way clear before the prow, he'd called up the sails in rapid succession. Ships like *The Trident* were best sailed hard, with as much canvas flying as possible; they were designed to race over the waves.

The buoys at the Solent's mouth came into view, rising and falling on the swell. Robert corrected course, then, as the first of the Channel's rolling waves hit, swung the wheel. He called rapid sail changes as the ship heeled; the crew scurried and shouts flew as the sails were adjusted, then *The Trident* was shooting into the darker waters of the Channel, prow unerringly on the correct heading to take them out into the Atlantic on the most southerly tack.

Once the ship steadied, he checked the sails, then, satisfied, handed the wheel to his lieutenant, Jordan Latimer. "Keep her running as hard as you can. I'll be back for the next change." That would come when they swung even further to the south to commence the long haul to Freetown.

Latimer grinned and snapped off a salute. "Aye, aye. I take it we're in a hurry?"

Robert nodded. "Believe it or not, *The Cormorant* made the trip back in twelve days."

"Twelve?" Latimer let his disbelief show.

"Royd put a new finish on the hull and fiddled with the rudder. Apparently, if running under full sail, it shaves off nearly a sixth in time—Declan's master reported *The Cormorant* was noticeably faster even on the run from Aberdeen to Southampton."

Latimer shook his head wonderingly. "Pity we didn't have time for Royd and his boys to doctor *The Trident* before we set out. We'll never make it in twelve days."

"True." Robert turned to descend to the main deck. "But there's no reason we can't make it in fifteen, as long as we keep the sails up."

If the winds held steady, they would. He went down the ladder to the main deck, then paced along the starboard side, checking knots, pulleys, and the set of the spars, listening to the creak of the sails—the little things that reassured him that all was right with his ship.

Halting near the bow, he glanced back and checked the wake, all but unconsciously noting the way the purling wave broke and the angle of the hull's cant. Seeing nothing of concern, he turned and looked ahead to where, in the far distance, the clouds gave way to blue skies.

With luck, when they reached the Atlantic, the weather would clear, and he would be able to cram on yet more sail.

The ship lurched, and he gripped the rail; as the deck righted, he leaned against the side, his gaze idly sweeping the seas ahead.

As he'd predicted, it had taken three days for *The Trident* to sail from London to Southampton and to be adequately provisioned from the company's stores there. Add fourteen more days for the journey south, and it would be eighteen days since he'd agreed to this mission before he sighted Freetown. Fourteen full days before he could start.

To his surprise, impatience rode him. He wanted this mission done and squared away.

The why of that had been difficult to define, but last night, as he'd lain in his bed in the large stern cabin—his cold, lonely, and uninspiring bed—he'd finally got a glimpse of what was driving his uncharacteristically unsettling emotions.

After three full days spent with Declan and Edwina, he wanted what Declan had. What his brother had found with Edwina—the happiness, and the home.

Until he'd seen it for himself, until he'd experienced Declan's new life, he hadn't appreciated just how deeply the need and want of a hearth of his own was entrenched in his psyche.

Put simply, he envied what Declan had found and wanted the same for himself.

All well and good—he knew what that required. A wife. The right sort of wife for a gentleman like him—and that was definitely not a sparkling, effervescent, diamond-of-the-first-water like Edwina.

He wasn't entirely sure what his wife would be like—he had yet to spend sufficient time dwelling on the prospect—but he viewed himself as a diplomat, a man of quieter appetites than Royd or Declan, and his style of wife should reflect that, or so he imagined.

Regardless, all plans in that regard had been put on hold. This mission came first.

Which, of course, was why he was so keen to have it over and done.

He pushed away from the side and headed for the companionway. He dropped down to the lower deck and made his way to his cabin. Spacious and neatly fitted with everything he needed for a comfortable life on board, the cabin extended all the way across the stern.

Settling into the chair behind the big desk, he opened the lowest drawer on the right and drew out his latest journal.

Keeping a journal was a habit he'd acquired from his mother. In the days in which she'd sailed the seas with his father, she'd kept a record of each day's happenings. There was always something worthy of note. He'd found her journals as a boy and had spent months working his way through them. The insight those journals had afforded him of all the little details of life on board influenced him to this day; the impact they'd had on his view of sailing as a way of life was quite simply incalculable.

And so he'd taken up the practice himself. Perhaps when he had sons, they would read his journals and see the joys of this life, too.

Today, he wrote of how dark it had been when they'd slipped their moorings and pulled away from the wharf, and of the huge black-backed gull he'd seen perched on one of the buoys just outside the harbor mouth. He paused, then let his pen continue to scratch over the paper, documenting his impatience to get started on this mission and detailing his understanding of what completing it would require of him. To him, the latter was simple, clear, and succinct: Go into the settlement of Freetown, pick up the trail of the slavers, follow them to their camp—and then return to London with the camp's location.

With a flourish, he set a final period to the entry. "Cut and dried."

He set down his pen and read over what he'd written. By then, the ink had dried. Idly, he flicked back through the closely written pages, stopping to read entries here and there.

Eventually, he stopped reading and stared unseeing as what lay before him fully registered. Unbidden, his gaze rose to the glass-fronted cabinet built into the stern wall; it contained the rest of his journals, all neatly lined up on one shelf.

The record of his life.

It didn't amount to much.

Not in the greater scheme of things—on the wider plane of life.

Yes, he'd assisted in any number of missions, ones that had actively supported his country. Most had been diplomatic forays of one sort or another. Since his earliest years captaining his own ship, he'd claimed the diplomatic missions as his own—his way of differentiating himself from Royd and Declan. Royd was older than him by two years, while Declan was a year younger, but they were both adventurers to the core, buccaneers at heart. Neither would deny that description; if anything, they reveled in being widely recognized as such.

But as the second brother, he'd decided to tread a different path—one just as fraught with danger, but of a different sort.

He would be more likely to be clapped into a foreign jail because of an unintended insult exchanged over a dinner table, while his brothers would be more likely to be caught brawling in some alley.

He was quick with his tongue, while they were quick with their swords and fists.

Not that he couldn't match them with either blades or fists; growing up as they had, being able to hold his own against them had been essential—a matter of sibling survival.

Thoughts of the past had him smiling, then he drew his mind forward, through the past to the present—then he looked ahead.

After a moment, he shut the journal and stowed it back in the drawer. Then he rose and headed for the deck.

Given how boring his recent life had been—more like existing than actively living—perhaps it was a good thing that this mission was not his usual diplomatic task. Something a little different to jar him out of his rut, before he turned his mind to defining and deciding the details of the rest of his life.

A fresh and different challenge, before he faced a larger one.

Climbing back onto the deck, he felt the wind rush at him and lifted his face to the bracing breeze.

He breathed in and looked around at the waves—at the sea stretching forever on, as always, his path to the future.

And this time, his way was crystal clear.

He'd go to Freetown, learn what was needed, return to London and report—and then he would set about finding a wife.

Two

"Good morning." Miss Aileen Hopkins fixed a polite but determined gaze on the face of the bored-looking clerk who had come forward to attend her across the wooden counter separating the public from the inner workings of the Office of the Naval Attaché. Located off Government Wharf in the harbor of Freetown, the office was the principal on-land contact for the men aboard the ships of the West Africa Squadron. The squadron sailed the seas west of Freetown, tasked with enforcing the British government's ban on slavery.

"Yes, miss?" Despite the question, not a single spark of interest lit the man's eyes, much less his expression, which remained impersonal and just a bit dour.

Aileen was too experienced in dealing with bureaucratic flunkies to allow his attitude to deter her. "I would like to inquire as to my brother Lieutenant William Hopkins." She set her black traveling reticule on the counter, folded her hands over the gathered top, and did her best to project the image of someone who was not about to be fobbed off.

The clerk stared at her, a frown slowly overtaking his face. "Hopkins?" He glanced at the other two clerks, both of whom had remained seated at desks facing the wall and were making a grand show of deafness, although in the small office, they had to have heard her query. The clerk at the counter wasn't deterred, either. "Here—Joe!" When one of the seated clerks reluctantly raised his head and glanced their way, the clerk assisting her prompted, "Hopkins. Isn't he the young one that went off God knows where?"

The seated clerk shot Aileen a quick glance, then nodded. "Aye. It'd be about three months ago now."

"I am aware that my brother has disappeared." She failed to keep her accents from growing more clipped as her tone grew more severely interrogatory. "What I wish to know is why he was ashore, rather than aboard *H.M.S. Winchester.*"

"As to that, miss"—the first clerk's tone grew decidedly prim—"we're not at liberty to say."

She paused, parsing the comment, then countered, "Am I to take it from that that you do, in fact, know of some reason William—Lieutenant Hopkins—was ashore? Ashore when he was supposed to be at sea?"

The clerk straightened, stiffened. "I'm afraid, miss, that this office is not permitted to divulge details of the whereabouts of officers of the service."

She let her incredulity show. "Even when they've disappeared?"

Without looking around, one of the clerks seated at the desks declared, "All inquiries into operational matters should be addressed to the Admiralty."

Her eyes narrowing, she stared at the back of the head of the clerk who had spoken. When he refused to look around, she stated in stringently uninflected tones, "The last time I visited, the Admiralty was in London."

"Indeed, miss." When she transferred her gaze to him, the clerk at the counter met her eyes with a wooden expression. "You'll need to ask there."

She refused to be defeated. "I would like to speak with your superior."

The man answered without a blink. "Sorry, miss. He's not here."

"When will he return?"

"I'm afraid I can't say, miss."

"Not at liberty to divulge his movements, either?"

"No, miss. We just don't know." After a second of regarding her—possibly noting her increasing choler—the clerk suggested, "He's around the settlement somewhere, miss. If you keep your eyes open, perhaps you might run into him."

For several seconds, her tongue burned with the words with which she would like to flay him—him and his friends, and the naval attaché, too. Ask at the Admiralty? It was half a world away!

Thanking them for their help, even if sarcastically, occurred only to be dismissed. She couldn't force the words past her lips.

Feeling anger—the worst sort, laced with real fear—geysering inside her, she cast the clerk still facing her a stony glare, then she picked up her reticule, spun on her heel, and marched out of the office.

Her half boots rang on the thick, weathered planks of the wharf. Her intemperate strides carried her off the wharf and up the steps to the dusty street. Skirts swishing, she paced rapidly on, climbing the rise to the bustle of Water Street.

Just before she reached it, she halted and forced herself to lift her head and draw in a decent breath.

The heat closed around her, muffling in its cloying sultriness. The beginnings of a headache pulsed in her temples.

Now what?

She'd come all the way from London determined to learn where Will had gone. Clearly, she'd get no help from the navy itself...but there'd been something about the way the clerk had reacted when she'd suggested that there was a specific reason Will had been ashore.

Her older brothers were in the navy, too. And both, she knew, had served ashore at various times—dispatched by their superiors on what amounted to secret missions.

Not that she or their parents—or even their other siblings in the navy—had known that at the time.

Had Will been dispatched on some secret mission, too? Was that the reason he'd been ashore?

"Ashore long enough to have been captured and taken by the enemy?" Aileen frowned. After a moment, she gathered her skirts and resumed her trek up to and around the corner into Water Street, the settlement's main thoroughfare. She needed to make several purchases in the shops lining the street before hiring a carriage to take her back up Tower Hill to her lodgings.

While she shopped, the obvious questions revolved in her brain.

Who on earth was the enemy here?

And how could she find out?

* * *

"Good morning, Miss Hopkins—you've been out early!"

Aileen turned from closing the front door of Mrs. Hoyt's Boarding House for Genteel Ladies to face its owner.

Mrs. Hoyt was a round, genial widow and a redoubtable gossip who lived vicariously through the lives of her boarders. Her arms wrapped around a pile of freshly laundered sheets, Mrs. Hoyt beamed at Aileen; with frizzy red hair and a round face, she filled the doorway to her rooms to the left of the front hall, opposite the communal parlor.

Having already taken Mrs. Hoyt's measure, Aileen held up a small bundle of brown-paper-wrapped packages. "I needed to buy some stationery. I must write home."

Mrs. Hoyt nodded approvingly. "Indeed, dear. If you want a lad to run your letters to the post office, you just let me know."

"Thank you." With a noncommittal dip of her head, Aileen walked on and up the stairs.

Her room was on the first floor. A pleasant corner chamber, it faced the street. Lace curtains screened the window, lending an aura of privacy. Before the window sat a plain ladies' desk with a stool pushed beneath it. Aileen laid her packages and reticule on the desk, then stripped off her gloves before unbuttoning her lightweight jacket and shrugging it off. Even with the window open, there was little by way of a breeze to stir the air.

She pulled out the stool and sat at the desk. She opened her packages, set out the paper and ink, and fixed a new nib to the pen, then without allowing herself any further opportunity to procrastinate, she got down to the business of informing her parents where she was and explaining why she was there.

She'd been in London staying with an old friend, with no care beyond enjoying the delights of the Season before returning to her parents' house in Bedfordshire, when she'd received a letter from her parents. They'd enclosed an official notification they'd received from Admiralty House, stating that their son Lieutenant William Hopkins had gone missing from Freetown, and that he was presumed to have gone absent without leave, possibly venturing into the jungle to seek his fortune.

Her parents had, unsurprisingly, been deeply distressed by that news. For her part, Aileen had considered it ludicrous. To suggest that any Hopkins would go absent without leave was ridiculous! For four generations, all the men in her family had been navy through and through. They were officers and gentlemen, and they viewed the responsibility of their rank as a sacred calling.

As the only girl in a family of four children, Aileen knew exactly how her three brothers viewed their service. To suggest that Will had thrown over his position to hie off on some giddy venture was pure nonsense.

But with both her older brothers at sea with their respective fleets—one in the South Atlantic, the other in the Mediterranean—as Aileen had been in London, her parents had asked if she could make inquiries with a view to discovering what was going on.

She'd duly presented herself at Admiralty House. Despite the family's long connection with the navy, she'd got even less satisfaction there than she had at the naval office here.

Goaded and angry, and by then seriously worried about Will—

he was younger than she, and she'd always felt protective of him and still did—she'd gone straight to the offices of the shipping companies and booked the first available passage to Freetown; as she'd brought ample funds with her to London, cost had not been a concern.

She'd arrived two days ago. She'd had plenty of time on the voyage to plan. Although her station and family connections meant that there was almost certain to be some family from whom she could claim support and a roof over her head while she searched for Will, she'd decided on a more circumspect approach. Hence, Mrs. Hoyt's Boarding House, which was located on Tower Hill, the province of local British society, but below the rectory rather than above it. The houses of those moving in what passed for local society were located on the terraces higher up the hill.

Aileen had no time for social visits. Her sole purpose in being in the settlement was to find out what had happened to Will—and, if at all possible, rescue him.

At twenty-seven years of age and as naturally inclined to command as her brothers, she'd seen no reason not to come to Freetown and see what she could do. She was as capable as her brothers, and the other two were not in any position to help Will at that time.

There was also the underlying niggle of knowing that if she hadn't been the only one of their brood available and, moreover, already in London, her parents would never have turned to her for help.

She was the girl in the family. No one expected her to contribute to anything in any way. She was supposed to be decorative rather than effective, and the only expectation anyone seemed able to credit her with was to make a comfortable marriage and keep house for some husband—most likely another naval officer.

In her heart, she knew that such a future was unlikely to ever come to pass. Aside from all else, her temperament and the odd itch beneath her skin—the same impulsive longing for adventure that had compelled her to set sail for Freetown—made her unsuitable for the position of meek and mild wife.

Even as she sent her pen scratching across the paper, she felt her lips quirk. Meek and mild was not an epithet anyone had ever applied to her.

After outlining her decision to come to Freetown and her intention to discover where Will had gone, she devoted several paragraphs to describing the settlement and where she was staying with a view to easing her parents' minds, then briefly outlined what she'd ascertained from her first inquiries.

Yesterday—her first full day in the settlement—hoping to gain some casual insights before she called at the naval office, she'd sought out the usual taverns around the docks where naval officers were wont to congregate. There were always certain establishments that attracted their custom, and while in general she would never have ventured into a tavern alone, in those places that catered to naval officers, her family's connection to the service—and the Hopkins name was well known throughout the navy—gave her a degree of protection.

She'd relied on that, gone in, and as she had hoped, she'd found several old sailors who knew her brother and had shared drinks and tall tales with him. She'd reasoned that if Will had been sent ashore on some mission that involved the settlement, then these were the men from whom he would have first sought information.

If Will had asked questions, she wanted to know what about.

And she'd been right. According to the old sea dogs, shortly before he'd disappeared, Will had asked questions that circled two subjects. First, an army officer called Dixon, who was stationed at Fort Thornton, which squatted at the top of Tower Hill. That was puzzling enough, but Will's second area of interest had been some local priest who held services in the settlement. Apparently, Will had attended several services, possibly as many as three.

Of all her brothers, she knew Will the best, understood him with the greatest clarity. That he'd voluntarily attended a church service meant he'd gone for some reason that had nothing to do with religion.

She lifted her pen and read over all she'd written. After a moment's deliberation, she decided against sharing her intention to rescue Will; there was no need to add to her parents' anxieties. Instead, she concluded with a less stressful repetition of her intention to discover where Will had gone. She ended with a promise to be in touch in due course.

While she sanded the sheet, then sealed her missive, she debated her options.

She set aside the letter, then glanced at the small clock on the mantelpiece. Lips firming, she pushed back from the desk and walked to the low chest that served as a dressing table. In the mirror above it, she considered her reflection, then grimaced and started unpinning her hair.

As she did, she considered the image the clerks at the naval office had seen. A gently bred English rose with pale skin and roses in her cheeks. Her face was close to oval, her nose unremarkable, her forehead wide. Her bright hazel eyes were her best feature, large and fringed with long brown lashes and well set under finely arched brows; other ladies might have used them more, but she rarely thought of it. Her lips were well enough—pink and softly plump—but they were usually set in a firm if not uncompromising line above her distinctly determined chin.

Her hair was a pleasing but unusual and distinctive shade of copper brown. It normally fell in glossy waves, but at the moment, her tresses were frizzing almost as badly as Mrs. Hoyt's in the unrelenting humidity.

With her pins removed, she wielded her hairbrush with grim determination. Eventually, she managed to rewind and refasten her hair in a passable chignon.

She put down the brush, twisted side to side examining her

handiwork, then she nodded to herself in the mirror. “Good enough.”

Good enough to pay a call at the rectory.

She resettled her skirts of pale bone-colored cotton, then put the matching jacket on again, but in a concession to the heat, left it open over her neat white blouse. After sliding the cords of her reticule over her wrist, she picked up the letter and headed for the door.

From Mrs. Hoyt, she’d learned that the Anglican minister’s wife was a Mrs. Hardwicke, and that Mrs. Hardwicke could be found most mornings at the rectory. Aileen felt sure that the minister’s wife would know about the other priest’s services.

Pausing with her hand on the doorknob, she hesitated. “There’s also the army officer, Dixon.” As far as she knew, Will had no friends in the army.

For a second, she debated—rectory or fort? Then she firmed her lips and opened the door.

She would post her letter and then call at the rectory.

One question at a time. Step by step, she would hunt Will down.

And then she would get him back.

* * *

Two days later, Aileen filed out of the rustic church in which the local priest, one Obo Undoto, conducted his services. Hemmed in between two other ladies, she was carried forth on the tide of the emerging congregation, which then spread across the dusty area before the church.

As matters had transpired, she hadn’t had to ask Mrs. Hardwicke for information; when she’d called at the rectory, she’d found a small gathering of ladies taking tea. At Mrs. Hardwicke’s invitation, she’d joined the group. After the introductions had been dealt with, the conversation had turned to events occurring in the settlement—and a Mrs. Hitchcock had mentioned that Undoto’s next service would be held at noon two days hence.

Later, Aileen had left the rectory with Mrs. Hitchcock and had asked for directions to the church, which Mrs. Hitchcock had readily given, along with a recommendation that she would find the service diverting.

When Aileen had walked into the rectangular church just before noon, she'd had to hunt to find a seat; she'd been astonished by how full the church had been. People of all races and of a wide range of social classes had crammed the pews—Europeans of all nationalities primarily to the left, with local natives and others of the African nations mostly to the right.

Her surprise had lasted until she'd heard enough to appreciate the tenor of Undoto's offering. In a voice full of thunder and brimstone, with a showman's zeal, he delivered something more akin to a stage performance than a conventional religious experience. Given the dearth of entertainment she had by then noted in the settlement, the crowd packing the church wasn't such a wonder. Anything to fill the boredom that many, of necessity, had to bear.

None of which explained why Will had attended. Most likely more than once. She knew beyond question that Undoto's performance wouldn't have appealed to her younger brother as a way to pass his time.

She'd spent the majority of the service surveying the congregation and everything else she could see, searching for some sign of what might have drawn Will to the place, but she'd seen nothing and gained no clue to that mystery.

As she slowly wended her way through the crowd now thronging the forecourt, she noticed an old man—a grizzled old tar if she'd ever seen one—ponderously stumping away from the church. He leaned heavily on his cane; he had lost one leg and had an old-fashioned wooden peg leg.

Instantly, Aileen knew who among all the congregation Will would most likely have approached. Her younger brother had always been fascinated with old tales of the sea.

She changed tack and went after the old man. As she drew level, she glanced at his face and discovered he was one-eyed, too. "Excuse me," she said. "I wonder if I might speak with you."

The old sailor glanced at her in surprise. But the instant he took in her face and her attire, he halted, politely raised his cap, and, planting his cane, half bowed. "Of course, miss." His eyes crinkled at the outer edges as he set his cap back on his head. "Old Sampson at your service. Always happy to have a chat, although what a lady like you might want with an old sea dog like me, I can't imagine."

She smiled. "It's quite simple, really. My brother was here"—with a wave, she indicated the church—"some months ago, and I'm quite sure he would have spoken with you. He's mad for tales of seafaring, and you look like you could tell quite a few."

The old sailor folded both hands over the head of his cane. "Aye." He nodded. "You have that right. I've sailed all of the seven seas in my day. Ain't nothing I like better than to remember those days. Rip roaring, they were. But what's your brother's name?" Before she could answer, he added, "I pride myself on learning the name to go with every face I see, at least among the Europeans."

Excellent. Aileen's smile brightened. "His name is William Hopkins. He's a lieutenant currently serving with the squadron here."

"Will Hopkins? Sure and I remember him. Interesting lad—keen to hear my stories."

She beamed. "I was sure he would have asked."

"So how can I help you?" Sampson arched his bushy brows. "Young Will hasn't been by for some time, and truth to tell, I never did understand why he came. Lads like him can usually find enough to interest them in the settlement without resorting to Undoto's histrionics."

"I can imagine." With three brothers, she certainly could. "But Will has disappeared, it seems, and I'm here to see if I can find any trace of where he might have gone, or why." She saw a frown form in Sampson's eyes. She tipped her head, regarding him more closely. "I gathered that Will came to more than one service."

"Aye." Sampson nodded, but his expression had grown absent-minded, as if the news that Will had disappeared had triggered thoughts of something else. "He came three times."

"Do you recall if he met with anyone after the service—perhaps some young lady? Or was he watching someone?"

Sampson shook his head and answered in a distracted fashion, "Not that I saw. And I sit on a stool in the back corner, so I see most things."

With the obvious excuse discounted, Aileen concluded that Will's purpose in attending the services—three of them—had to have been connected with his mission. Whatever that mission had been.

But how?

She raised her gaze to Sampson's face, only to discover he'd refocused on her and was now regarding her with some concern. "What is it?" she asked.

He frowned. "It's possible I shouldn't tell you this, but there were others asking questions—a captain and his crew, not navy, but I got the impression they was...authorized, if you get my drift. A couple of weeks ago, they were here asking about people—officers—who'd apparently attended Undoto's services and then...vanished. They didn't mention your brother by name, but if I recall aright, they said there were two navy lieutenants among the missing."

Her heart leapt. "This captain and his crew—are they still here?"

The worried look in Sampson's eyes increased. "No. I heard they'd sailed off in something of a rush. Some say to Cape Town, but others as saw them go say they left under oars at night, and the tack they took out of the estuary lay to the north."

For a second, Sampson searched her eyes, then he drew himself up. "If you'll pardon the liberty, miss, this Captain Frobisher was a sharp sort, and he and his crew knew what they were doing. They came asking questions about people who'd gone missing, and they must have found something—something of the sort to send them packing, possibly back to London."

Sampson glanced swiftly around, then shifted closer and lowered his voice. "It's true there's something havey-cavey going on in the settlement. Seems there's more missing than a handful of officers. But whatever's going on, it's dangerous enough to have a captain of the likes of Frobisher playing cautious. You need to take that on board. Asking questions about those who've gone missing might end with you going missing, too." He shifted back and looked her in the face. "Trust me, miss, you need to back away and leave this to those trained to handle such things."

The possibility that, contrary to all appearances, someone—most likely someone in authority in London—was pursuing those missing, Will included, came as a huge relief.

However, they—whoever they were—weren't here, and she was.

And Will was still missing.

She'd held Sampson's gaze while those thoughts flitted through her mind; his worry remained plain to see. She drew breath, hesitated, then inclined her head. "Thank you for the warning, Mr. Sampson. Rest assured, I'll pay it due heed."

No need to tell him that learning that Will had, indeed, been on some mission and had subsequently disappeared, and that others had disappeared as well, had only made her more determined than ever to find her missing brother and, if possible, rescue him, too.

★ ★ ★

The obvious first step was to learn more about the mission Will had been pursuing.

Other than attending Undoto's church, the only oddity she'd

heard of in Will's behavior before he'd disappeared had been his interest in Dixon, the army officer stationed at the fort.

Given the time-honored tensions between army and navy, Will's interest in Dixon had to have been work related—ergo, mission related. Presumably, he'd gone to speak with Dixon, which made Dixon an obvious person for her to speak with, too.

Her hopes of gaining some insight into the nature of Will's mission were riding high as she toiled up the final stretch of road that led to the open gates of the fort, with its guardhouse built against the palisade to one side of the entrance.

On gaining the cleared area before the gates, she paused and looked back. Perched on the crown of the hill above the harbor, the fort commanded an arresting view over the settlement and the ships clustered before the docks to the wide blue sweep of the estuary beyond. She took a full minute to savor the sight.

Three days had passed since she'd spoken to Sampson outside Undoto's church. She'd spent those days alternating between vacillation and action. On the vacillating side, she'd found herself entertaining nagging doubts along the lines that perhaps Sampson was right, and she and her family would be better served by her retreating and then waiting to hear through official channels…

Every time she'd got to the "waiting to hear through official channels" part, her thoughts had come to an abrupt halt, and she hadn't been able to follow that line any further.

She would never convince herself that waiting for someone else—especially someone with official authorization—to rescue Will was a viable alternative.

Her actions had been more to the point; she'd gone back to the taverns she'd previously visited and tried to learn more about Dixon. She'd reasoned that the more she could learn about him before she faced him, the better placed she would be.

Unfortunately, that tack had proved futile. For the same reasons she hadn't expected Will to be acquainted with an army officer, none of those he had drunk with knew much of Dixon, either.

Just that he was stationed at Fort Thornton.

And now she was there.

She turned away from the vista and walked the last yards to the guardhouse and the pair of middle-aged guards taking the sun at their ease beside it.

They straightened as she neared. Both respectfully touched a hand to their hats.

"Miss," said the younger with a nod.

"Ma'am," said the older, straightening even more.

Aileen halted before them and smiled. "Good morning. I would like to speak with an officer by the name of Dixon. I understand he's quartered here."

Both guards looked at her, then to her surprise, the pair exchanged a sidelong glance.

The older refocused on her. "I'm afraid, ma'am, that that won't be possible."

She blinked.

Before she could formulate an appropriate response, the younger guard blurted, "He's not here, you see. Gone off to seek his fortune in the jungle, they say."

The older guard cut his junior a chiding look. "Don't believe—much less repeat—everything you hear." Looking back at Aileen, he said, "Captain Dixon was here—he should still be here—but he went missing some months back, and no one's seen hide nor hair of him, nor heard anything about him since."

"He's vanished?" She fought to rein in her shock. Battled to keep her expression uninformative.

Nevertheless, the older guard frowned in concern. "Why did you wish to speak with him, ma'am?"

She met his shrewd eyes. She couldn't think of any reason to lie. "I believe my brother, a lieutenant in the navy, came to speak with Captain Dixon. This would have been some months ago—possibly three months or more."

"I remember that!" The younger guard beamed at her.

"Thought it odd that one of the navy bas—ah, officers wanted to speak with one of ours."

"So he—my brother—and Dixon met?"

The younger guard shook his head emphatically. "Couldn't. Dixon was already gone. Would have been a good five weeks before. I remember we told your brother that. Had quite a jaw about it, now I think back. About what Dixon vanishing like that might mean."

The older guard was regarding her closely. "Why don't you ask your brother about Dixon—about what he was after him for—when the squadron sails in? Should be in a week or so, I gather."

Aileen met his eyes, then grimaced. "Would that I could. Sadly, my brother has vanished, too."

"Cor!" The younger guard's eyes rounded. "Mercy me! Whatever's going on?"

The older guard narrowed his eyes on his junior. "Told you. Don't know what's going on, but it's not what it looks like."

★ ★ ★

A week later, late in the afternoon, Aileen threw a shawl about her shoulders and left the confines of the boardinghouse to walk in the public gardens behind the rectory. She'd found the little oasis of civilized peace just a few yards up the road and down a short lane six days ago, and it had quickly become her favorite place for thinking.

As the sun began its final descent toward the western horizon, a cooling breeze often lifted off the harbor and estuary beyond, sweeping up the hill with gentle grace, refreshing and renewing the air after the stifling, muggy heat of the day.

Pacing along the lightly graveled path, Aileen made for her favorite bench. Situated beneath the spreading branches of a tall, shady tree, the bench was unoccupied, as it usually was. She'd seen only a handful of people using the gardens, and most of those were nursemaids or governesses with their charges; at this time of day, they were busy elsewhere, doing other things.

Amid the leaves of the old tree, long brown seedpods hung, dry now, and in the stirring of the breeze, they added their soft rustle to the evening's chorus. She found the already familiar susurration welcoming. She sat, letting the fine shawl fall to her elbows so she could better enjoy the coolness on her skin.

She scanned the short stretch of lawn below and saw only a single couple who were already heading home. She watched them go, then she raised her gaze to the wider vista of the harbor and its ships, and the estuary beyond. From there, she could even see the opposite shore, so distant it was nothing more than a thick band of jungle green edging the water.

This was a very foreign land.

She told herself that. Told herself it was no real surprise that finding any trace of Will months after he'd disappeared would take time. More, that any trail wouldn't easily be uncovered.

In search of that trail, she'd returned to sit through two more of Undoto's performances. She'd spent both observing closely, searching for some hint of what had sent Will there—desperately hoping for some inkling of what he had gone there to find. Other than feeling faintly disturbed by the tenor of the services, she'd learned nothing more.

She'd spoken with Sampson again, but perhaps unsurprisingly given his earlier concern, he'd been discouraging.

His attitude had only added to her welling despondency.

She'd expected to get *somewhere* by now.

Glumness dragged at her. Instead of giving in to it, she focused on the scene before her. A ship—sleekly hulled and sporting three towering masts—was sliding gracefully up the estuary. Even from this distance, she could make out the tiny figures of sailors scrambling high on the spars, furling a quite staggering array of sails.

The sight of the ship held her transfixed. As she watched, it smoothly slid past the mouth of the harbor and continued up the estuary, still well out from shore.

She wondered why the ship wasn't turning in. As far as she knew, there was no other settlement—certainly not a settlement of the size to which such a ship might sail—farther along the estuary's shores.

She continued to trace the stately passage of the ship. Watching it was curiously soothing.

Courtesy of her brothers' incessant obsession, she was more than passingly acquainted with the latest designs in sailing vessels. In the sleek lines of the ship nosing down the estuary, she thought she detected the telltale shape of the new ships out of the Aberdeen shipyards. Clippers, as people were starting to call them, because under full sail—which was how they were designed to be sailed—the hull rose and sped across the water, clipping the waves.

She imagined how fast the ship before her might go if all the sails she could see were set before a good wind.

It would fly.

Will would have loved it.

"Will *will* love it one day." She frowned at herself, at the unintentional surfacing of her deepest fears.

The best way to eradicate fear was to face it. She didn't want to, yet she forced her mind to consider the unthinkable.

She still couldn't believe it. *Will isn't dead.*

He'd gone missing, but he was somewhere, and still alive.

He was findable. In turn, that meant he could be rescued.

She *would* do it.

She would not give up—she would never give up—on Will.

Finally, the ship she'd been watching turned its prow toward shore. It came in a short way, then anchored just inside a cove two bays to the east of the harbor.

She wondered why the captain had chosen to avoid the harbor proper. "Perhaps they're only anchoring for the night, or to take on water."

Regardless, she'd seen enough; she had more pressing matters to address.

Eschewing the sight before her, she turned her thoughts inward. Doggedly, she retrod—yet again—all she'd learned. Now that she'd worked out why Will had gone to see Dixon—because Dixon had already disappeared and Will had wanted to learn more—that left Will's attendance at Undoto's services as the one peculiarity she had yet to explain.

She decided that was a clear enough sign. Either something happened at the services that Will had seen but that she had yet to notice, or…

She couldn't think of anything that *or* might be.

Frowning, she refocused on her surroundings and realized the light was fading. In the tropics, night descended like a curtain falling on a stage—with brutal finality and quite surprising abruptness.

She rose. The temperature had started dropping with the setting of the sun. She flicked her shawl about her shoulders and set off at a brisk walk for the lane, the road, and Mrs. Hoyt's Boarding House.

As she entered the lane, her senses came alert. Pure habit; she didn't expect to meet with any difficulty in that area.

Nevertheless, as she emerged onto the road by the rectory, she recognized that, with the falling of night, the atmosphere in the settlement changed.

It wasn't only the view, the surroundings, that grew darker.

She set off along the rough pavement toward the boardinghouse. Lights were already burning on the front porch, and a welcoming glow shone through the parlor curtains.

Then she nearly tripped as her mind connected her recent thoughts. She halted and stared ahead as she realized…

"I might have been looking in the right place, but at the *wrong time*." She breathed the words as the possibilities firmed in her mind.

In this place—as in any other rough and dangerous place in which predators lurked—time of day made a very real difference to what anyone watching might see.

Her heart lifted. She stepped out, her stride firmer, more decided—even more determined.

She'd been watching Undoto during the day. She needed to watch him during the evening and night.

True evil walked in darkness, after all.

Three

Robert stepped out of *The Trident*'s tender onto a rickety pier constructed of old spars lashed together with vines. Better than slogging through the waves, he supposed, and definitely better for the swift execution of his plan than sailing into the harbor proper.

With its usual abruptness in these climes, night had fallen some hours before. *The Trident* had been in position by then, but he'd deliberately held off and waited until the bustle of early evening activities had faded before coming ashore.

He directed a searching look into the darkness beyond the pale sand, but there were few people to witness their landing—an old man slumped with a bottle in his hand in front of a ramshackle hut, a young man sitting on a stool and frowning over some nets, several women and children flitting like wraiths through the shadows; none seemed to be paying any great attention.

No doubt they knew better than to stare too openly at men like his party, white men who came ashore under the cover of darkness and well away from the lights of the settlement.

With a few quiet words, he and the four men he'd handpicked to accompany him hoisted their bags, then moved silently and swiftly off what was plainly the local pier of a small fishing village huddled around a pocket of the shore of the wide-mouthed bay two bays farther east from Kroo Bay and the main port of Freetown.

Robert led the way up a stretch of deep sand. He paused where the sand gave way to firmer ground and the shadows of listing palms created a pool of deeper darkness and waited for his men to join him.

As they trudged toward him, he looked past them at the tender steadily pulling out through the shallow waves. *The Trident* herself was a dark, somewhat indistinct shadow that seemed to hover, gently drifting, on the dark surface of the water farther out in the cove.

The four men reached him. With a tip of his head, he indicated that they should follow him; resettling his seabag over his shoulder, he walked on in the direction of the settlement.

He took whatever path offered, tacking this way and that as he steadily led the way westward through the straggling shantytown of crude dwellings that bordered the settlement like lace on a woman's petticoat.

He'd left all his officers on board; they couldn't merge into the population of Freetown in the same effortless, unobtrusive way the four men he'd brought with him could. Benson, Harris, Fuller, and Coleman were all sailors, plain if experienced seamen for whom no one in a port city would spare a second glance. All four were also highly experienced fighters, whether on deck or on land. For what Robert imagined he would need to complete this mission, the four possessed the best collection of requisite skills.

Jordan Latimer, his lieutenant and second-in-command, hadn't liked it, any more than his ship's master, Hurley, and his quartermaster, Miller, had, but they'd held their tongues. They were accustomed to being the ones by his side; that, this time, he'd chosen others for that role simply illustrated how very unlike his usual missions—which often involved drawing rooms and even ballrooms—this particular mission was.

He'd left his officers to manage the ship and hold her ready to depart at a moment's notice. He'd given instructions that once the tender was re-stowed, they should let the ebbing tide draw them farther out from shore, back into the estuary proper, and then anchor where, through a spyglass, they could see the rickety pier, yet where their position made it clear they were not intending to engage with—or threaten—anyone.

He paused to glance back—to see if the tender had been hauled in and if *The Trident* was drifting out again—but the stands of palms that lined the shore, and the black shapes of the village houses with their palm-frond-thatched roofs, blocked his view.

His men milled behind him. Cloaked in darkness, he turned and strode on.

He'd been to Freetown before; his memory of the settlement's geography was rudimentary but sufficient, and Declan and Edwina had spent hours describing the various areas of the town as they now were. So while he didn't have anything resembling an accurate map, he had a fair idea of where he was heading, and the pulsing throb of many lives lived at close quarters drew him steadily on.

They entered the settlement proper—the area defined by recognizable streets, even if the surfaces were merely beaten earth—from the east and made their way toward the nearer edge of the commercial district. There, traders' stores, smaller warehouses, and inns and taverns catering to various types of travelers congregated between the end of Water Street and the shore.

Robert halted in the middle of a dark street that in one direction led to Water Street and in the other to the wharves the local fishing fleet used. He looked around, then glanced at his men. "Let's see if we can find an inn—one catering to merchants should suit. I want something not too far from this spot. Meet back here in ten or so minutes."

With nods, the men spread out, drifting down this alley, that lane. Robert himself walked on toward Water Street, but found only stores and offices.

He was walking back to where he'd parted from his men when Benson came trotting out of a lane on the side of the street away from the harbor.

He fell in beside Robert. "Nice little place just along there,

Cap—sir." With a tip of his head, Benson indicated the lane he'd come out of. "Could be our place."

Robert halted. "Let's see what the others turn up."

Gradually, the other three drifted back. Harris had found another inn, but was dubious about its quality. "Bit too run down and leery, I'm thinking. We're supposed to be respectable, right?"

Robert nodded and jerked his head toward the lane. "Let's take a look at the place Benson found."

Benson's find proved to be perfect for their needs. Only a few doors from the street connecting with Water Street, the inn was small, unassuming, and run by a stalwart couple, who, by their careful manner, clearly strove for security and respectability, and therefore also offered a degree of privacy to their guests.

Posing as a trader visiting the settlement to determine what prospects for goods for Europe and the Americas the region might provide, Robert hired three decent-sized bedchambers—one for him and two for his four men to share.

His men knew how to slip into the supporting roles he'd assigned them, bobbing respectfully to the landlady and dismissing with relaxed thanks the landlord's offer to have their bags carried up.

After reassuring the landlady that they wouldn't be putting her to the trouble of making up a meal for them at such a late hour, Robert accepted a lighted lantern from his host and followed his men up the scrubbed wooden stairs.

His room was neat and clean, the bed a touch more solid than a cot, with decent linens and a fine net looped over a metal circle suspended over the well-stuffed mattress. The room also contained a simple desk and a single straight-backed chair. Robert swiftly unpacked the few clothes and other items he'd brought with him and tossed his seabag into the narrow armoire.

After discussing his options with Declan and Edwina, he'd decided to avoid the port and enter the settlement on foot, and subsequently to assume an identity and a purpose that would keep him well away from—essentially out of sight of—all the various local authorities. And even farther from local society.

Declan had been here mere weeks ago, and too many would recognize the similarity between them. Robert's hair was a darker shade of brown than Declan's, and his features were a touch more austere, but they both had blue eyes and in so many other ways echoed each other physically that Edwina had been adamant that even if people didn't recognize him as *Robert* Frobisher, they would definitely recognize him as a Frobisher.

While Declan's appearance in the settlement, explained by being on a honeymoon cruise with Edwina, would have passed muster well enough not to raise any suspicions, a second Frobisher turning up a month later would certainly make any villain with links to the authorities…twitchy, at the very least.

Luckily, Robert wasn't the least averse to what was—compared to where his usual missions landed him—slumming it. Posing as a trader meant he didn't have to call on anyone, didn't have to play the gentleman-diplomat-captain—didn't have to do the pretty by anyone at all. He could simply get on with this mission—get started immediately on picking up the slavers' trail, finding their camp, then heading back to England.

In pursuit of that goal, he returned downstairs. His men were waiting just inside the inn's door. At his nod, they all filed outside.

Robert paused under the narrow porch that ran along the front of the inn. Looking into the darkness, listening to the distant yet raucous sounds emanating, no doubt, from the taverns lining the docks, he confirmed his bearings, then looked away from the harbor toward the now largely silent streets that terraced the slope of Tower Hill.

All was quiet up there.

"Time to learn the lie of the land." Lips quirking, he glanced at his men and tipped his head toward the quieter quarter. "Let's take a walk." At this time of night, they could go all the way up to Fort Thornton itself, then descend and walk the length of Water Street, through the heart of the commercial district.

In a loose group, they strode down the lane, then up the road to Water Street. They crossed the thoroughfare and started up the slope into the residential streets, dimly lit by flickering flares, beyond.

They weren't out to take the air. All of them scanned the streets, taking note of landmarks, occasionally turning to look down at the settlement and the harbor beyond. Sauntering along, Robert slid his hands into his pockets. "We'll save the docks for last."

That was where the greatest danger of him—or even his men—being recognized lay, but by then, most of those sober enough to trust their eyes would have gone back to their bunks, and those remaining would pose no real threat.

When they reached the precinct of the fort, a jumble of buildings squatting behind a timber palisade, they hugged the shadows, careful to avoid the sentries keeping watch from the flare-lit area before the gates.

"How they expect to see anyone with all that light about, God only knows," Coleman muttered.

"Oh, they'll see 'em," Fuller replied. "Just too late to save themselves."

Robert's lips twitched at the sneering comments. Even though his men weren't navy, they had a seafarer's contempt for those who served on the land.

As they headed down the hill again, Robert felt satisfied with the day's progress. By the time they returned to their beds, they would have a working knowledge of the settlement, enough to see them through their mission.

Enough to be able to start investigating properly tomorrow.

The inn would provide a safe base. Undoto's church and the tavern the old sailor Sampson frequented were a little farther up and around the hill—easy to walk to from the inn. The slum where the priestess Lashoria lived also lay in that general direction, but farther away from the settlement's center.

While they ambled down the length of Water Street, noting the shops and offices along the way, Robert reviewed his potential contacts—Lashoria, Sampson, and Babington. Of the three, Babington was the one Robert felt least confident about asking for help. He knew Babington better than Declan did; they'd crossed paths several times. Babington was a shrewd negotiator, more so because he didn't appear to be outwardly aggressive—much like Robert himself. In Robert's opinion, Babington was not properly appreciated by his own family. He was largely wasted here, essentially playing nursemaid to Macauley—who, heaven knew, needed, and would accept, no one's help.

Babington might prove to be a valuable ally, but attempting to recruit him might also be a big mistake, depending on where his loyalties lay. Robert had no intention of revealing any of the mission's more pertinent details—such as their belief that there was a diamond-mining operation involved—unless he could first satisfy himself as to what Babington's priorities truly were.

Given that dealing with Babington might not be straightforward, Robert decided to call on Sampson first. Declan and Edwina had suggested that interviewing Lashoria would be best done in the evening, so he'd start his day with Sampson and see where the trail took him from there.

He'd been following the direction his men had been taking without any real thought. Refocusing, he discovered they'd circled around and down to the end of Government Wharf.

His men halted at the steps leading down to the wharf itself; they glanced his way as he joined them.

To their left, Government Wharf extended into the harbor. While there appeared to be no navy frigates moored there or anywhere else in sight, Robert studied the long line of merchant vessels tied up and slowly rising and falling on the gentle swell. "Not along the wharf."

Too dangerous. Too many merchant captains knew his face.

He looked ahead, along the main quay and the row of buildings fronting it. Most were government offices, agencies, harbormaster's quarters, and the like. The now diminishing sounds of revelry drifted from lanes and alleys that ran back from the quay. There were no taverns directly facing the water.

He started down the steps. "Along the quay to the end. We can get back to our inn that way."

And tomorrow he'd make a start on finding the slavers' trail. The sooner he did, the faster he'd learn where their camp was hidden, and then he would be on his way back to London and the challenge of finding a wife.

As he imagined was the case for most men, a large part of him instinctively recoiled from even contemplating that final task. Yet as he stretched his legs and strolled through the humid dark, he discovered that one small part of his mind was already cautiously questing, imagining and envisioning his ideal wife.

* * *

The morning after the epiphany that if she wanted to discover any nefarious dealings, she would need to watch Undoto in the dark hours rather than in the full light of day, Aileen stood in her bedchamber and surveyed the items she'd spread on the chintz counterpane.

Clothing came first. She'd left the bulk of her wardrobe with her friend in Russell Square, so she had limited choices. But she'd had time between booking her passage and her departure from London to purchase four simple outfits—skirts with matching jackets—in lightweight cotton. The modistes had only just started to create such garments for the English summer, and they'd cost a pretty penny, but since arriving in the settlement, she'd been glad of her foresight.

The most useful outfit for any nighttime excursion would be the one in deep blue twill. Although the ensemble was intended to be worn with an ivory blouse, she'd bought a silk blouse in the same shade of dark blue with some thought of possibly needing to pass herself off as a widow.

She hadn't had to employ the subterfuge, but that had left her with a dark-colored outfit she'd yet to don; the unrelenting heat of the days had dissuaded her from wearing the darker shade.

"With a hat and veil…" She grimaced and looked at the bureau, at her one and only hat, a villager style in straw, sitting perched on the bureau's top. She wrinkled her nose. "Entirely unsuitable."

But she'd seen a small milliner's shop tucked in a side street off Water Street. She glanced again at the clothes she'd laid out, then down at what she was wearing—one of the jacket-and-skirt ensembles in a soft lemon yellow with an ivory blouse. She wouldn't need the hat or the darker clothes until the evening; if she accomplished what she hoped to by midafternoon, she would have plenty of time to call in at the milliner's and find something more appropriate. "Along with a good swath of black netting for a veil."

She felt sure any milliner would have black netting to hand; no doubt the settlement had funerals enough.

With her clothes and headgear decided, she turned to her open suitcases, located her gloves, and discovered she'd packed a pair of mid-length black gloves. "Perfect." Laying the pair aside, she looked down. Raising her skirts, she regarded her dusty half boots. "More than adequate for creeping about in."

She released her skirts and smoothed them down. Sartorially speaking, she had everything she needed.

"Next—equipment." She reached into one suitcase, underneath her clothes at the very back, and drew out what appeared to be a jeweler's box, along with a silk roll of the sort ladies used to carry pearls.

She crossed to the small desk and placed both items on the surface. Smiling to herself, she sat on the stool, opened the jeweler's box, and surveyed the tiny American-made pistol her eldest brother had given her for her last birthday. She'd already known how to shoot a pistol, but she'd practiced diligently with the smaller weapon and now counted herself an excellent shot, at least at appropriate range.

Just to check, she untied the cords about the jewelry roll and spread it open, revealing a pair of sharp daggers and a whetstone. Satisfied she had everything she would need, she returned her attention to the pistol; after gently easing it from its velvet bed, she hefted the familiar weight in her hand.

Carefully, she put it down, lifted out the cleaning supplies that had been nestled alongside it, and settled to clean the weapon.

The exercise, something she'd done many times in the past, freed her thoughts to wander. She was convinced Will's disappearance was somehow connected with Undoto; she intended, therefore, to watch the priest, evening and night, until she saw whatever there was to be seen.

Her lips firmed; her gaze was fixed on the pistol in her hands, her eyes not truly seeing. "There has to be something." Something about Undoto that had caused Will to haunt his services. Some link that would lead from Undoto to Will.

After reassembling the pistol, she laid it aside and picked up the whetstone and one of the knives.

As the sound of the whetstone passing along the blade filled her ears, she forced herself to face the fact that she had no idea if she would find anything—would stumble upon anything pertinent—by watching Undoto, but she had no other clue, no other avenue to follow.

So she would follow this one and see where it led.

The resolution had her reviewing the practicalities of what she'd planned. "First—find out where Undoto lives."

That would be easy enough, but she would need transportation.

* * *

Robert found Sampson exactly where he'd expected him to be—in the taproom of the tavern above which he lived.

The old sailor was seated at a table in the corner; head down, he was scanning a news-sheet and didn't look up when Robert and his four men entered the low-ceilinged room.

Despite the relatively early hour, Robert bought a round of ale for his men, himself, and an extra for Sampson, then carrying Sampson's drink as well as his own, he crossed to the table at which the old man sat.

When Robert halted before the table, Sampson deigned to look up. And up.

When Sampson's gaze found Robert's face, the old tar blinked, then sat back, the better to view him.

Robert smiled and gestured with the mugs of ale. "Mind if we join you?"

Sampson glanced at the other four hanging respectfully back; he identified them as fellow seafarers and grinned. "Not at all." He nodded at the four in welcome, then his gaze returned to Robert's face as Robert placed the mugs of ale on the table and pushed one toward him. "Thank ye. Looks like me mornin' just became more interesting."

He scrutinized Robert as he settled on the stool opposite. "Was it your brother who was here before, then? Cap'n Frobisher?"

Robert nodded. "Yes. My younger brother."

Sampson studied Benson, Fuller, Harris, and Coleman as they pulled up stools, sat, and sipped their ale. He looked back at Robert. "You're another Cap'n Frobisher, then?"

Robert dipped his head in assent and took a long pull of his ale. The taste was distinctly different, but it was recognizably ale. Lowering the mug, he met Sampson's inquisitive eye. "We're here to follow the trail my brother blazed."

Sampson sobered. "Aye. Good thing, too. I'd noticed people not turning up to Undoto's services even before your brother came, but I don't go farther afield in the settlement, so I just thought they'd growed bored with it and hadn't bothered coming back. But your brother and his men said people had vanished, and I gather that's still true."

"Indeed. We're trying to find out where they've gone, with a view to staging a rescue. My brother suggested you'd be amenable to helping us out with information."

Sampson nodded. "Happy to help any way I can." His lips twisted wryly. "And these days, supplying information is about my limit."

"Nevertheless, we appreciate your help." Robert sipped, then said, "What can you tell us about any changes in behavior of those you see regularly? Especially any changes since my brother was here."

"Hmm." Sampson's brow creased in thought. He lifted the mug of ale and sipped, absentmindedly savoring the taste before he swallowed and said, "The most notable change would have to be her ladyship—Lady Holbrook. She stopped coming to Undoto's services some weeks back. Thinking on it, her stopping would have been just after your brother sailed." Sampson flicked Robert a shrewd glance. "Bit abrupt, that seemed—he and his ship were here one day and gone the next."

Robert acknowledged the point with a nod. "He had his wife with him."

Sampson nodded readily. "I remember her—pretty little thing."

Robert's lips eased. "In her case, you don't want to be fooled by the prettiness. But she and my brother ran into strife courtesy of his—their—investigations, and they had to draw back. I'm their replacement—the next stage of the investigation."

"Aye, well, there haven't been any other major changes in those I see, other than Lady Holbrook not coming to Undoto's services anymore, and for all I know, she might just have lost interest, or taken to her bed ill, or have too much to do."

"Do you know if Holbrook himself is currently in the settlement?"

"Far as I've heard—or rather, I've heard nothing about him sailing off anywhere." Sampson grinned. "But I don't exactly swan about in those circles, so I can't rightly say what the governor's been up to."

Robert nodded. "I'll check with others." He would have to; Wolverstone and Melville would be waiting to learn which way the wind blew with Holbrook. He watched Sampson down a large mouthful of ale. "Have you heard any whispers of people going missing recently, or of any other odd happenings?"

Sampson pursed his lips. After a moment, he said, "Haven't heard anything about anyone on Tower Hill being gone, but I did hear about the docks that some navvies didn't turn up where they were expected. But hereabouts, no one can say if they've vanished like those others, or if they just upped stakes and went off to some better prospect, or took work on some ship." Sampson shrugged his heavy shoulders. "No way to know, is there?"

"Indeed." That was half the problem in this case; in this sort of place, so many people were disconnected drifters.

Sampson shifted on his bench. "Howsoever, in terms of odd happenings, there was one I hadn't expected." His voice had grown stronger, more definite. "A young lady—well, not *that* young, I suppose, but young enough, if you catch my drift. She turned up...ooh, must be going on two weeks ago now. Showed up at one of Undoto's services and spent the whole time looking sharply about. She spotted me, and after the service, she came up and asked to speak with me. She was searching for her brother—a naval lieutenant by the name of Will Hopkins. I'd seen him at the services, months back. And she—the lady—was right. Young Will had come up and had a jaw with me. He liked to hear my stories."

Robert frowned. He was acquainted with the older two Hopkins brothers. "This lady. Did she mention her name?"

Sampson's brow furrowed as he clearly thought back, but then he shook his head. "No." He met Robert's eyes. "I suppose she'd be Miss Hopkins, but she was more than old enough to be married, and widowed, too, so she might have another name now."

Before Robert could comment, Sampson continued, "Anyways, she was asking questions, obviously trying to figure out what had brought her brother to the services. Asked if it were some young lady, but I put her straight about that. But she was right—a lad like Will Hopkins had to have had some reason to come to the services. He wouldn't have just wandered up to waste his time, not on three occasions at least."

"He was sent to track Dixon, the army engineer who had already vanished." Robert saw no reason to conceal that fact.

"Aye, well—Miss Hopkins, or whatever her name is, hadn't tumbled to that, but she knew as well as I did that there had to be something behind Will coming to the services. She was asking questions, trying to learn what." Sampson drew in a deep breath. "I didn't think that was wise, and I tried to warn her off." He met Robert's gaze. "I told her about your brother and how he'd been asking questions about the officers who'd gone missing, including her brother, most like. I also told her that your brother had to withdraw quickly—that he'd sailed from the settlement and just might have headed back to London—and I pointed out that people who asked questions about people who've gone missing tended to wind up missing, too. I did me best to get her to back off and leave the investigating to those qualified to do it."

Robert arched a cynical brow. "Did you succeed?"

"I'm not hopeful. She's been back to two more services, and anyone who thought to watch her would know she weren't paying attention to Undoto's thunderings."

Robert grimaced; the last thing he needed was a gently bred but determined female complicating his simple and straightforward mission. "Do you have any idea where she's staying?"

"Not precisely. She'll be up on Tower Hill somewhere, would be my guess."

"What did she look like?" It was Benson who asked.

Sampson took a moment, plainly calling up a picture in his mind. "Brassy-brown hair—sort of bright brown and glossy, not dark. Hazel eyes. Average height. Good figure, but well laced. Very English looking, and if I had to guess, used to getting her own way. Wouldn't say spirited so much as forceful."

Unease trailed tauntingly down Robert's spine. Damn! He was going to have to act to effectively deflect the woman. He couldn't risk her popping up at some crucial moment and interfering with his mission. More, if she was Hopkins's sister, then given his acquaintance with her older brothers, he should definitely do his best to send her packing all the way back to England.

Sampson humphed. "I made it clear she was dabbling in dangerous waters, and while she listened, I'm damned sure she's not going to pay my warning much heed."

For a moment, all were silent. Sipping the last of his ale, Robert considered what would have brought a lady like Miss Hopkins all the way to Freetown. Sibling devotion, clearly, but it would have to be strong to have driven a gently bred lady to take ship and brave the dangers of a place like Freetown, a settlement on the outer fringes of civilization. That Hopkins's sister was in the settlement at all, let alone determinedly asking questions, argued that convincing her to meekly step back, return to England, and leave the investigating to him wasn't going to be any easy task.

That she'd found her way to Undoto's services and Sampson—and it sounded as if she was concentrating her efforts around Undoto and his church—suggested she was intelligent, too.

Robert drained his mug. He would need to remove the lady from the situation, and soon. Before matters became any more complicated.

He set his mug on the table and glanced at his men, then looked at Sampson. "I need to speak with the vodun priestess, Lashoria. My brother told me she lives in the slum on the hillside to the east of here—is that still the case?"

Sampson nodded. "Far as I know." He drained his mug.

"There's a gentleman by the name of Babington—Charles

Babington. I'll probably need to speak with him, too. Do you know where he lives?"

"He's the one that's Macauley's junior partner, aye?" When Robert nodded, Sampson said, "That's easy, then. He lives in the apartment above the company's office. On Water Street, that is. You can't miss it."

Robert nodded. He'd noted the Macauley and Babington office during their walk the previous night.

He'd call on Lashoria that evening and decide what he wanted to do about Babington after that.

He refocused on Sampson. All the men had finished their ales. "Our landlady mentioned that Undoto is holding one of his spectacles at noon today."

"Aye." Sampson nodded his shaggy head. "I planned on heading up there about now."

"Do you mind if we join you?"

"Not at all." Sampson grasped his cane and levered himself to his feet. He beamed at Robert and his men. "Glad of the company."

They rose and left the tavern. Robert waved his men ahead and adjusted his pace to Sampson's halting one. Robert looked about him as in companionable silence they progressed slowly up the hill.

He doubted he needed to ask Sampson to point out the notables in the congregation; if Robert was any judge, the old man thoroughly enjoyed having his knowledge plumbed, his observational skills put to use.

But when they halted at the edge of the forecourt before what was obviously the church, Robert murmured, "If you see Hopkins's sister..."

Sampson nodded. "I'll point her out." He surveyed the people streaming toward the open doors. "Can't see her, but she might already be inside." With his cane, he waved toward the door. "Let's go in."

The forecourt stretched across the front of the rectangular church and extended down both sides, wider to the left than the right. To the left, several benches sat beneath a row of trees large enough to cast some shade. Carriages were drawn up in a long line opposite the front façade; ladies and gentlemen descended and strolled across the forecourt to the doors, most smiling and chatting, nodding to each other as if they were attending a social event.

As they walked forward and Robert refocused his attention on the church itself, a frisson of awareness—the sort of awareness he recognized very well—swept tantalizingly across his senses.

Glancing around, he looked back at the carriages. Most were simply black. Dusty, anonymous, and unremarkable.

Anyone could be sitting inside one and looking out.

It was hardly the first time he'd been the recipient of an assessing glance. If the lady had noticed his reaction, she probably wouldn't show herself until after he'd gone inside.

Mentally shrugging—he certainly wouldn't have time to follow it up, distractions of that ilk being indisputably the very last thing he needed—he returned his attention to those before him.

As they joined the throng streaming inside, Sampson added, "I hope you'll be able to make the lady see sense."

"I'll give it my best shot." Robert hadn't expected to have to use his diplomatic talents on this mission, but he could be very persuasive when he wished.

Curious, he looked around as they moved into the church, noting the disposition of people to cluster in their own groups. His men had gone in ahead of him and Sampson and had sat in the last pew. Robert followed Sampson to a stool in the rear left corner.

The old man settled on the stool, his peg leg braced at a comfortable angle. Then he surveyed those seated.

Robert remained standing, leaning against the wall as several other men had elected to do.

Sampson grunted. "I can't see her. She's not here yet."

His gaze sweeping the room, Robert shrugged. "Let me know when you spot her."

As soon as he got a bead on her, he intended to seize the first chance that offered to warn her away from the investigation—and he was prepared to be a great deal more definite and effective than Sampson had been.

He had no intention whatever of allowing anyone—male or female—to interfere with his mission. For once, he had a mission whose path was blissfully clear and defined—learn the location of the slavers' camp, then race the information back to London. The lady might be determined, but so was he; he was determined to allow nothing to get in the way of him finishing this mission in the shortest amount of time.

He wanted it done so he could put it behind him and concentrate on following the lure that, increasingly, drew him.

The need for a hearth. The need for a home. The need for a wife who would be his anchor.

* * *

Aileen leaned back against the squabs of her hired carriage as the last stragglers made their way into the church.

She'd debated joining the congregation, but she couldn't imagine that she would see or learn anything she hadn't already by subjecting herself yet again to Undoto's version of fire and brimstone. Much better to sit and conserve her energies. She'd rolled up the flaps on the carriage windows, and a breeze as faint as an exhalation stirred wisps of hair at her nape.

Her strategy had already yielded one piece of information—the direction from which Undoto approached the church. After leaving Mrs. Hoyt's, she'd walked down to Water Street and had hired a driver for the rest of the day; she'd had him drive her up to the church at just after eleven o'clock and draw his carriage to a halt at a spot toward the end of where the line of carriages would form. She'd been inside the carriage watching when Undoto had come walking down the street that curved up the flank of the hill.

Most of the congregation came from either below the church or, in the case of the European contingent, along the road from the west. The area from which Undoto had come was not one she'd previously explored.

But she would. Later, when she followed the priest back to his home. For the next hour, however, she had nothing to do but sit in the carriage and cling to her patience.

She'd chosen this spot from which to watch because it allowed her an unobstructed view of the church's forecourt and also the smaller door along one side toward the rear of the building. That was the door through which Undoto had entered the church; others—the choristers and altar boys and several older men—had followed. One of the older men had later opened the front doors.

Patience wasn't really her long suit, but she could, she told herself, manage an hour. In pursuit of Will, she could manage more than that.

With nothing else to do, she reviewed all she'd seen to this point, cataloging those of the congregation she'd seen previously, searching for anything odd or different.

Her mind snagged on the man—a newcomer, at least to her—who had arrived with old Sampson.

There was something about the man that had snared her attention, then effortlessly held it. In the privacy of the carriage with nothing else to occupy her, she could admit that and, via a distinctly vivid memory, indulge in a long, mental perusal.

He was the sort of gentleman commonly described as well set up. Tall with broad shoulders, but lean with the length. Strong, but flexible, too, exuding an aura of reined physical power. That he'd arrived with Sampson, chatting with the old man and clearly accepted by him, suggested the unknown was a sailor, but she would have guessed that anyway. She was accustomed to dealing with seafaring men, and the way he held himself, balanced in a certain fluid way, had instantly registered.

As had the sword at his hip. It wasn't the type of weapon your average sailor sported. If she had to guess, she would say the intriguing stranger was a captain, one who commanded; an ineffable air of command had hung like a cloak about him, something innate that showed in the way he'd stood, in the manner in which he'd looked about him, scanning the surroundings, taking note of the people as well as the place.

Remembering that, she felt certain he'd never been to Undoto's church before.

She hadn't forgotten Sampson's mention of a Captain Frobisher who had come to ask questions about those missing; it was tempting to speculate that this man was Frobisher, come back to take up the hunt, but if he hadn't previously attended the church, that seemed unlikely.

Although courtesy of the distance, she hadn't been able to note anything specific about the man's face and features, she had to admit he'd made an impression.

She realized her lips had curved appreciatively, but there was no harm in such idle admiration. It wasn't as if he and she were likely to meet face to face.

The warmth of the sun lay heavy on the land; the distant hum of the settlement's center and port droned almost below the level of hearing.

Lulled, she felt her lids drooping. After a second, she allowed them to fall.

Her mind wasn't empty; the image of the unknown man still lingered. He hadn't been wearing a uniform; she recalled Sampson's description of Captain Frobisher—not navy, but *authorized*. Most likely, Sampson had meant that the man had some degree of backing from the authorities; despite his lack of uniform, the unknown stranger had exuded the ineluctable sense that he possessed such authority.

So a captain, but almost certainly not of a naval vessel.

The memory of the clipper-style ship she'd seen so gracefully gliding up the estuary the previous evening swam across her mind's eye.

The unknown captain's ship?

Her attention shifted to the ship. Truth be told, she could admit to feeling a certain attraction to the vessel, too—a wish to see her, to examine her, to sail on her. To stand on her deck and experience the sensation of flying over the waves.

Aileen had long known she was no more immune to the siren song of the sea than her brothers.

And it was probably a good deal safer to explore an attraction to the ship than to the ship's captain, even in her mind.

She grinned, then the sound of voices spilled into the forecourt. She opened her eyes and saw that the service was finally over. Undoto stood at the door, farewelling his parishioners.

Aileen sat up, then stretched her arms, easing her spine. She leaned closer to the window, then, realizing she might be seen, sat back in the shadows of the carriage once more.

She watched the congregation leave. She saw the intriguing stranger again. After exchanging words with four sailors—members of his crew?—and apparently dispatching them ahead, the stranger left with Sampson, pacing more slowly beside the one-legged sailor as they followed the winding street down the hill.

There was a courtesy there, in the stranger's attention to Sampson, of which Aileen approved—a recognition that old men like Sampson were by no means worthless.

The stranger and Sampson soon passed out of sight.

She returned her gaze to the church itself and, counseling herself to patience anew, watched and waited while the congregation dispersed. When all were gone, Undoto and one of the older men who helped with the church pulled the doors shut, while two other older men set the woven-rush window panels back in place.

Aileen shifted her gaze to the side door. The altar boys and choristers had already left. The old men came out; calling to each other, they waved and went their separate ways.

Finally, Undoto emerged, shutting and locking the door behind him.

Again, Aileen was tempted to lean forward, but she held herself back; she hadn't yet got her hat and veil.

She watched as Undoto walked along the side wall of the church and into the forecourt. He saw her carriage, but barely gave it a glance and continued across the gravel to the street.

Aileen crossed her fingers, praying he would return to his home and not go wandering elsewhere in the settlement.

Undoto reached the street and turned up it, heading back in the direction from which he'd earlier come.

She let out the breath she hadn't realized she'd been holding. She'd chosen this carriage because it had a small window set beneath the coachman's seat through which she could look out over the horses' backs and see what was happening in front of the carriage. Through that window, she watched Undoto stride up the dusty street. She waited as long as she deemed she could, then rose, stretched up, and lifted the small trapdoor in the carriage's roof.

For all she knew, her driver might have been snoring for the past hour. "Driver?"

The carriage shifted as the driver started. "Yes, ma'am?"

"I was hoping to meet my friend here, but she didn't attend the service. I must have dozed off. I've only recently arrived in the settlement, and as we are here, I would like you to drive slowly—just rolling very slowly along—up the street before us, the one heading up the flank of the hill." The one Undoto had taken; he was almost out of sight. "Just carry on, and I'll tell you when I've seen enough, and we can then return to Water Street."

"Aye, ma'am."

Aileen swayed, then sat as the carriage rocked into motion. The driver followed her instructions well enough and kept their pace nice and slow. Through the small forward-facing window, she could see Undoto well ahead, but as he was striding along at a good clip, the distance between him and the carriage was only slowly decreasing.

The area the street ran through was neither a slum, nor was it Tower Hill. The houses were modest, but neatly kept; most were situated on their own small block. Few plants graced the gardens, but rocks and stones marked entrances and paths. From the few people she glimpsed, it appeared this was the area populated by the equivalent of the lower middle class.

There were still a good fifty yards between the carriage and the priest when Undoto crossed the road, went up a short path, climbed a few steps to a house's porch, then opened the door and disappeared inside.

Aileen shifted to the window on that side and, as the carriage rolled closer, studied the house the priest had entered. As the house neared, she again drew back into the concealing shadows, but with her eyes fixed on the building, she cataloged every identifying feature she could spy.

The carriage rolled on, and the house fell behind. Satisfied, she sat back. She would recognize the house, even by night.

Her afternoon's work—laying the groundwork for her evening's endeavors—was done.

She let the driver steer his horses on for a full minute more, then she lifted the trapdoor again. "I've seen enough for today. Back to Water Street. You can let me out near the middle of the street."

She had a milliner to visit.

And then…

She couldn't be one hundred percent certain that the house Undoto had entered was his own abode, yet there'd been a lack of concern, of even the slightest hesitation, in the way he'd walked up the front path and had opened the door and gone inside. If it hadn't been his house, surely he would have knocked?

Still, tonight would tell. If Undoto was still there when night fell…that was really all she cared about.

As the carriage rocked slowly down the hill and turned toward the center of the settlement, she reviewed her preparations. Once she bought what she needed from the milliner, there was one last issue to address.

To keep watch on Undoto's house, she would need the concealment of an anonymous carriage, much like the one she was presently in. But she couldn't risk hiring just any coachman and trusting him to keep his mouth shut about her peculiar excursions, much less the address from which he picked her up.

Unfortunately, she couldn't see any way around trusting the driver she hired. "Which means," she murmured, "that I'll have to make sure the driver I hire is, indeed, trustworthy."

Hat and veil first; carriage and trustworthy driver second.

Once she'd succeeded in securing both… "Then I'll be ready to keep watch and see who comes calling on Undoto."

Four

Darkness had fallen. The slum area in which Lashoria lived had no lighting to illuminate its winding alleys.

Robert paced steadily up the passageway that Declan had told him led to the priestess's red door. Somewhere in the shadows behind him lurked Benson and Coleman. Both men were past masters at trailing others. Even though he knew they were there, Robert couldn't hear or in any way sense them; if he glanced around, he knew he'd see nothing.

It was a slow climb. Long enough for him to feel the atmosphere of the slum—of such a density of close-packed humanity—close around him. The smells and sounds rifled his senses, tickling and pricking them to higher awareness. The smothering heat, a solid warmth from which there was no escape, didn't help. As most locals did, he'd dispensed with his coat. Unfortunately, in the gloom of the slum, the relative whiteness of his linen shirt made him feel like a walking target.

To distract himself, he thought back to his afternoon, to Undoto's service. Admittedly, he was predisposed not to approve of Undoto, but the man's belligerent, overconfident—almost bellicose—delivery had set his teeth on edge. At least he and his men would now be able to recognize the priest.

After taking a thorough look at the congregation, noting especially the Europeans attending, he'd confirmed via Sampson that Hopkins's sister hadn't been present. Once that was established, he'd spent the rest of the hour thinking of various ways in which he could send the overinquisitive lady packing.

He glimpsed a flash of bright red ahead on the right.

A minute later, he stood facing what was patently Lashoria's door.

Neither Declan nor Edwina had said anything about the brilliant red being splotched with black.

The black looked recent.

There was no light showing through the thick material covering the window of the front room. Neither Declan nor Edwina had mentioned curtains, either; instead, Declan had said he'd been able to look into the alley while seated on the love seat inside that room.

The fine hairs at Robert's nape stirred.

He drew in a breath, climbed the two steps to the front door, and rapped sharply.

He had to knock a second and a third time before he heard shuffling footsteps—too light to be a man's—approaching from deeper inside the house.

Then the door was flung open, and he found himself facing an old woman, her face haggard and worn.

"What do you want?"

The demand was aggressively made, but the woman's voice sounded rusty, scratchy.

Before Robert could reply, her dark eyes drifted over him—then flicked back to lock on his face.

The old woman's eyes narrowed. "You…no, your brother. He was here before. With his pretty wife."

Robert nodded. "Yes. He and his wife spoke with Lashoria. I need to speak with her, too."

The old woman's eyes widened. For two seconds, she stared at him.

Then she glanced furtively down the alley as she reached out, gripped his sleeve, and tugged. "Come inside. Quickly."

Robert needed no further urging. He stepped over the threshold and past her. He watched as she shut the door, then wrestled two heavy bolts across.

She turned and slipped past him. She beckoned. "Come. To the back."

She led him down the corridor Declan and Edwina had described, but instead of going into the room at the end—Lashoria's consulting room, as Edwina had termed it—the old woman turned left and led the way down a flight of crude steps cut into the earth. Robert had to duck to pass under the lintel at the bottom of the steps; straightening, he found himself in a small chamber carved into the ground. A wood oven built into one wall marked it as the kitchen. It was transparently the old woman's domain.

She perched on a stool at one end of the narrow wooden table that took up most of the floor space. "Here." She pushed a low stool his way. "Sit."

A single candle in a holder on the table cast a small circle of golden light.

As Robert complied with her order, taking the place to her left, the old woman folded her hands on the table and met his gaze. "They killed her—the beasts. They killed my Lashoria."

Robert had suspected as much—why else the black on the door?—but the wealth of emotion in the old woman's voice, the virulent hatred he could see burning in her eyes, made him still. Then he drew breath and asked, "Who?"

"The slavers who work with Undoto." The old woman's fingers gripped tight. "They killed her because she spoke of their evil to others."

"Their evil?"

Robert didn't have to ask more questions; just that was enough to fracture the dam wall. The old woman poured out her hatred of those she termed "the beasts." Robert let her rave, let her sob and rail; she remained dry-eyed throughout, as if she had no more tears to shed.

He waited silently, unjudging, just being there. When she finally fell silent and simply breathed, he quietly said, "My brother and his wife had nothing to do with Lashoria's death. They were attacked when they left here."

The old woman waved dismissively. "You think I don't know that? That I would speak to you if I believed...?" She shook her head. "I know it was not them. I was here." She pointed over their heads. "I was in my room upstairs when Lashoria showed your brother and his wife out of the back door. I peeked out and saw them go down the hill. But then there was a pounding on the front door, and Lashoria...she went and opened it. They came in—the beasts. I could hear, but not see. They struck her, then pushed her into her room. They beat her." The old woman exhaled a shuddering breath. "They did not stop until she was dead."

The simple words held a weight of helpless fury.

The old woman's gaze had grown distant, her hands once again gripping tight. "There was nothing I could do to save her—my lovely Lashoria. The beasts did not know I was here, under the same roof, or they would have killed me, too."

Robert heard the guilt. He wondered if he was wrong to do so, yet... "There was nothing you could have done then." He met the old woman's gaze. "But if you know who did this, tell me. I cannot promise swift justice, but justice can be served in many ways."

She considered him in silence for a full minute, then she nodded. "Lashoria spoke, and they killed her. I am a very old woman—now that they have killed her, I have little to live for. So why not speak?"

Robert said nothing; he was far too old a hand at negotiating to push.

The old crone regarded him for several more moments, then she nodded again, this time decisively. "It was Kale and his men. I heard his voice, and I am sure it was he."

"Who is Kale?"

"He is the leader of one band of slavers. I know him from long-ago days. Many years ago now, my husband, he was one of them, so I know of Kale, although he was only a young one then."

"Do you know where Kale's camp is?" Robert held his breath. Surely it wouldn't be that easy.

The old woman shook her head. "Not now. Now Kale is in charge, and he is an arrogant beast. Everything is his way. New ways."

"Tell me what you know of this Kale. What does he look like?"

"He is English, but not just Anglo. A mix. He does not look that much different from many others, not until you look into his eyes or hear him speak. His voice was damaged in the fight in which he killed the last leader of their band. But Kale…he is a snake of a man, quick with his fists and blades, and cunning and clever, too."

"How do the slavers operate? Lashoria told my brother that Undoto was involved."

"Yes!" The word was hissed. "He is a snake of a different skin, that one. But he is not the leader—that is Kale, without any doubt. Undoto is his…procurer. Yes, that is the word. Undoto points and says, 'That one.' And Kale and his men, they take that one. That is how it works."

Robert recalled the point Declan and Edwina had made about those taken being selected, not chosen at random. Facts shifted in his brain. Lady Holbrook had known the background of virtually every English person in the settlement. She told Undoto which ones would fit his bill, and Undoto then pointed Kale their way. But who had told Lady Holbrook or Undoto which types of people were needed?

With no answer to that, Robert set the point aside and turned his mind to the other end of the slavers' operation. "You said your husband used to run with the slavers. What are the steps the slavers take once they seize someone in the settlement?"

"They will take them first to their lair."

"Lair?"

The old woman huffed out a breath. "The slavers do not usually walk the streets during the day. That would be inviting too much attention, and snatching people in daylight is more difficult. More risky. So they wait for the darkness to hunt their prey. But their camps are too far out in the jungle"—the old woman flung out a hand—"for them to come in every night from there. So they have a lair—a place where they can wait during the day. And they gather any they snatch in one night there before taking them out to the camp."

"Do you have any idea where Kale's lair is?"

"No. It will be in one of the slums somewhere. I do not think it is in this one, but I cannot be certain."

Robert reviewed what he now knew, then he looked at the old woman. "What can you tell me about Kale's camp? Anything at all will be helpful."

She pulled a face. "Few who visit a slavers' camp return to tell of it. All I know is from my husband, and that is from years ago. The camps must be out in the jungle a long way. They have to be beyond the areas your soldiers patrol, and also outside any villages' or chieftains' boundaries, or the chiefs will cause trouble." She met Robert's eyes. "The villagers around do not hold with slavery—very few in this area do."

Robert nodded. He knew that some tribes from the north were wont to assist slavers who preyed on natives from deeper in the interior, but with the West Africa Squadron sailing out of Freetown, he'd assumed this area was less troubled by the scourge.

The old woman had been studying his face. "For what it is worth, this business of stealing English men and women is very different from the usual trade."

"How so?" Robert tipped his head, inviting her to explain.

She took a moment to order her thoughts. "Kale has been a slave trader for years and years, yet only now, in this business with Undoto, has he started to take Europeans. That has never been normal anywhere, but especially not here. With the fort so close and the ships, too, why risk the wrath of the governor and his men? So that is one mystery. And the care to pick the people—this one and not that one—is also unheard of. A man is a man—why do they need to choose so carefully?"

So that they took only those whose disappearance would be unlikely to raise any, or at least not too much of, an alarm. Robert didn't say the words, but he was sure enough of that.

The old woman straightened from the table and raised her hands. "There is no rhyme or reason to this. No sense in it at all. It is very peculiar to choose to play this game right under the English governor's nose."

A nose that had been singularly unresponsive to date, but that, Robert was starting to realize, had been very carefully arranged.

He was starting to believe that Holbrook was entirely innocent of any complicity in the scheme.

The old woman looked tired, even more worn out. Robert could think of no more to ask her. He rose. When she looked up at him, he half bowed. "Thank you for speaking with me." He hesitated, then reached into his pocket. "If you will not take it amiss…" Hauling out three sovereigns, he laid them on the table. "For your help."

The old woman's gaze had fallen to the coins. She studied them for a long moment, then she reached out a hand and covered them, and drew them to her. "Beggars cannot be choosers. Thank you."

Robert hesitated. "I don't expect it will be any real consolation, but the help you and Lashoria have given will, in the end, save many lives."

The old woman's head came up. Some of her earlier hate sparked in the darkness of her eyes. "Kale. Be careful of him. He is like a rabid dog—do not take your eyes from him. But if you and your people can end Kale's life, I will die happy."

Robert held her gaze for a moment more, then nodded. "I'll

see what we can do." He stepped back from the table. "I'll show myself out, but please bolt the door once I'm gone."

She nodded.

He didn't wait for more but climbed the rough steps, strode along the corridor, slid back the bolts, opened the door, and stepped outside. He pulled the black-blotched red door closed behind him, then went down the steps.

In the alley, he paused, breathing deep of the air that, although still cloyingly humid, felt much less smothering than the air in that kitchen, weighted as it had been with so much helpless emotion—powerful emotions that had no outlet. When he caught the scrape of the bolts sliding home again, he straightened his shoulders and set off to walk back down the long passage.

He felt nothing more than a stir in the air at his back as Benson and Coleman fell in at his heels.

"Learn anything?" Benson murmured.

"Enough to be going on with." As he strode down the slope, Robert used what he now knew to construct what he thought must be the slavers' operation. Some of the slavers would be waiting in their lair. Undoto, or perhaps Lady Holbrook when she'd been there, would send to summon them, directing them to this victim or that. The slavers waited until night, then seized their victim. They returned to the lair—possibly to report, also possibly to combine their victims—then either on the same night or the next, the slavers ferried said victims out of the settlement and took them to their camp.

It was the location of the camp Robert needed. But clearly, the first step toward finding the camp was identifying the slavers' lair.

★ ★ ★

Night had fallen hours ago.

Seated in the small and entirely plain black carriage she'd finally chosen and hired for the duration of her stay in the settlement, Aileen fidgeted, impatient and restless.

She'd had her new driver, Dave—a cockney who, of the dozen

coachmen she'd interviewed, had struck her as the most trust-worthy—call for her at the boardinghouse at sunset. She'd directed him to drive on a roundabout route to eventually pull up in the tiny lane that joined the street above Undoto's church almost directly opposite Undoto's house.

From their position in the lane, through the forward-facing window beneath the coachman's bench, she could look across the street. The entire front façade of Undoto's house was within her field of vision, along with the extension of the narrow lane that ran down the right side of the house. She suspected—hoped—that meant she would see anyone entering or leaving from either the front or rear of the house.

The tiny lane was the perfect spot from which to observe all comings and goings from the priest's abode. Well and good. But the waiting was getting on her nerves.

She shifted on her seat. She lifted her reticule, feeling the weight of the pistol inside it, then set it back down on the seat beside her. She had no idea if anything would come of this covert surveillance. If she was asked to explain what she expected to happen and what she hoped to achieve, she wouldn't be able to formulate any real answer beyond that this was something she could do, and she had no other viable avenue to pursue.

And, deep down, some instinct—that conviction of the emotions her mother called a woman's intuition—insisted that this was the way to go, the path to follow if she wanted to find Will.

Everything revolved about Undoto. Surely, through watching him, she would see something and learn something more.

Thus far, all she'd seen had been an old woman who had come out of the side gate into the narrow lane and fed table scraps to the neighborhood dogs.

Stifling a sigh, Aileen fixed her gaze on the front of Undoto's house and lectured herself for the umpteenth time to be patient.

She heard the men approaching before she saw them; the tramp of heavy feet coming down the dusty street reverberated through the quiet and reached through the open carriage windows. Eagerly leaning forward, she peered out through the small window; she prayed Dave was following her instructions and pretending to be asleep on the box.

As it happened, the image Dave projected mattered not at all. The four large armed men who appeared from the left and turned off the street onto the path to Undoto's front door didn't spare even a glance toward the carriage. Their arrogant confidence was absolute, demonstrated unequivocally in their swaggering gaits, in the soft laugh they shared as the leader reached out to thump a meaty fist on the door.

The moon was high, casting a silvery light over the scene. Aileen studied the four men. Although all were deeply tanned, the leader appeared English, the others of mixed European heritage. They were at ease, relaxed, transparently at home. This was their territory, and in it, they reigned supreme; they didn't expect to be challenged.

She had the sudden thought that if they'd known she was watching, they would merely have leered and shrugged it off as of no account.

The door opened, and Undoto stood framed in the doorway. Even though the narrow porch was poorly lit, she could make out his smile of welcome. He shook hands with the leader and stood aside to wave him and his three cohorts into the house, beaming and exchanging comments and claps on the shoulders with the men as they filed past.

Close acquaintances, at the very least. Almost brothers-in-arms.

Undoto stepped back and shut the door.

Aileen sat back.

Now what?

She was tempted to get out of the carriage, sneak across the street, and crouch beneath the single window of Undoto's front room. But the house was long and narrow; there was no reason to assume Undoto was conversing with his guests in that particular room, and the risk…

Was too great.

Quite aside from the danger of being discovered by those inside the house, she would be readily visible to anyone in the street and in the houses opposite. Even in her dark clothes, she would stand out.

She huffed and forced herself to remain where she was. In the dark, looking out of the small window at Undoto's uninformative front door.

Impatience and impulsiveness were abiding weaknesses; she had to hold against both.

In search of distraction, she directed her mind back to what she'd actually seen, to replaying the images and studying them for clues.

The four men. What could she deduce about them?

They'd come from farther up the hill. She'd noticed the street looped over and around the squat hill's flank, dipping away into an area of the settlement into which she'd yet to venture. That was the direction from which the four had appeared.

Was that where they lived?

Certainly, nothing she'd seen suggested that they lived with Undoto or even in this quieter neighborhood; they certainly wouldn't have fitted in.

She'd got the impression they were brothers-in-arms. Colleagues, at least. Reviewing the interplay between them only strengthened that conclusion.

So what enterprise did Undoto share with these men?

Other than his ministry, she knew very little of Undoto. Sampson hadn't known much about the priest, either.

That brought her back to the four men. They'd been large, but most of their size had been muscle. Quite a lot of it.

Undoto was tall, well built, and had a commanding presence,

but that presence relied more on the force of his personality, not merely his physical size.

In contrast, the armed group's leader was taller by several inches and was significantly more physically overwhelming. That, too, was not simply due to size but to the menacing way the man moved, the intimidating way he stood.

Adding to the image of danger, each of the four men had carried at least one long-bladed weapon strapped to his side or back, and all four had bristled with smaller knives; she hadn't had to look hard to see that. They wore their weapons openly…

Mercenaries?

The more she thought of it, the more the description fitted.

What connection might lie between a priest and a group of mercenaries?

Was stumbling on the mercenaries why Will had disappeared? And Dixon before him?

Undoto's front door opened. The mercenaries trooped out. The leader was the last to leave. He turned on the narrow porch to speak with Undoto.

Aileen watched the exchange like a hawk. She strained her ears; although she couldn't make out the words, the tone of both men's voices reached her.

The mercenaries weren't happy, but it didn't seem that they were angry with Undoto. For his part, the priest appeared—and sounded—resigned. He didn't seek to appease the hulking mercenary leader, but his responses were grave, as if he shared their… disappointment?

That was the impression Aileen received. That the mercenaries, and Undoto, too, had hoped for something, but had been denied.

The mercenaries turned away from Undoto with no exchange of smiles, waves, or any farewells. They strode up the short path and turned into the street—heading back the way they'd come.

Aileen gave a little jig on the carriage seat. If her luck held…

The trapdoor in the coach's ceiling lifted.

“You want me to follow them, miss?” Dave’s disembodied whisper floated down.

“Please,” she whispered back. “But entirely unobtrusively. Hang well back.”

“I’ll do me best, miss.”

The trapdoor fell shut. The carriage moved forward, then halted. Aileen realized Dave had stopped where he could see up the hill, but he hadn’t yet turned the carriage into the street.

He waited, waited, and eventually gave his horse the office and slowly, ponderously, rolled around the corner and on up the street. Like most streets outside the settlement’s center, this one was potholed and rutted, forcing any driver to ease their conveyance over dips and bumps; a very slowly moving carriage wasn’t as suspicious a sight as it would have been in London.

Aileen peered out of the forward window. There were no streetlights, and clouds had now veiled the moon; she could just pick out the four dark shapes as they moved through the shadows.

The street continued to climb. There was a flare burning at the side of the road at the crest. Beyond lay nothing but the blackness of the night sky as the land dipped on the other side of the ridge.

“Miss.” Dave’s voice reached her. “The street narrows just over that crest ahead. It quickly becomes too tight for me carriage. ’Nother of the slum areas starts about there. Must be where those four are headed.”

Aileen considered their situation. “How far can we go before turning back?”

“Well, there’s a side street ahead, a little way below the crest—we can take that, and it’ll carry us back to the streets of Tower Hill. I wouldn’t want to go over the crest—it’ll be hard to turn the carriage if’n I do. I’ll have to get down to manage it, and if you don’t mind, miss, that’s not something I want to do at this hour in this area with the likes of those four hanging about.”

“No, indeed.” Aileen bit her lip. She didn’t want to pull back, to give up this odd chase, but the danger...and it wasn't just her involved but Dave, too.

Ahead, the four dark shapes walked into the circle of light cast by the flickering flare. The first three trudged on and over the crest, but the leader halted. And looked back.

Directly at the carriage.

He stood bathed in the light from the flare.

Less than thirty yards away, Aileen saw his face—saw the scar slashing across one cheek. Saw the hard, merciless gaze he trained on the carriage.

Even though she knew he couldn't see her, she felt herself freeze like a rabbit before a rabid dog.

"Miss?"

Dave's urgent whisper jerked her into action. Into speech. "Take the side street!"

Smoothly, as if that had been his direction all along, Dave angled his horse slowly to the right, away from the watching mercenary and on into the quiet street leading across the hillside.

Shrinking back into the deepest shadows in the carriage, Aileen stared at the mercenary as the coach turned.

Her second look didn't improve on her first. Instinctive fear closed chill fingers about her throat.

She couldn't take her eyes from the threat. As the carriage continued, she shifted, keeping the mercenary in view.

But with the carriage turning aside, he appeared to lose interest. He turned and continued over the crest, disappearing into the darkness beyond.

Aileen exhaled. She slumped back against the seat, only then realizing her hand had risen to her throat.

She lowered her hand and dragged in a huge breath. Her heart was still pounding.

Minutes later, the carriage reached better-surfaced streets, and Dave urged his horse to a faster pace.

As her breathing returned to normal, Aileen reminded herself that the mercenary wouldn't have been able to see her, that he wasn't following her.

Despite the reassurance, her heart continued to thump faster than it had before.

★ ★ ★

Robert returned to the inn, but couldn't settle; thinking of Lashoria's death at the hands of the slavers left him restless—wanting, needing, to act.

On diplomatic missions, he rarely had to cope with situations like this—when an unnecessary and violent slaying provoked him.

Sleep wasn't going to come soon. Remembering his earlier plan, he told Benson where he was headed, then left the inn.

Cloaked in deep night, he walked to Water Street and on to the office of Macauley and Babington. As befitted the holders of the lucrative trading license between the colony of West Africa and England, the company's office was in a relatively new stone building in the middle of Water Street—in business terms, the beating heart of the settlement. A foray down the alley running alongside the building revealed an exterior staircase leading to an apartment above the rear of the office.

The door on the landing at the top of the stairs was locked, and Babington didn't respond to Robert's knock.

After deciding Babington was most likely out socializing, Robert picked the lock and went in.

The door opened into a living room. Robert stepped inside, quietly closed the door, then listened. Half a minute sufficed for his senses to confirm that he was the only person there.

He relaxed and looked around.

Two well-stuffed armchairs with a small round table between faced a sofa set against one wall. A bureau bearing a tantalus graced the wall opposite the sofa, while a desk stood against the wall a little way from the door. The fourth wall, opposite the door, played host to four long windows; the central panes were French doors giving onto a narrow balcony.

Sufficient moonlight washed through the uncurtained windows for Robert to see well enough. A door in the wall against which the sofa sat stood ajar; a glance beyond showed a bed and the usual appurtenances of a bedchamber.

Robert walked to the bureau, checked the decanters in the tantalus, then helped himself to a glass of whisky. Drink in hand, he angled one of the armchairs toward the door, sat, sipped, and settled to wait.

As the whisky slid down his throat, he found himself pondering his lack of hesitation in breaking into Babington's rooms. Perhaps he had more of his brothers—and his father—in him than he knew.

Or perhaps it was simply his impatience to get on, further fueled by learning of Lashoria's murder.

An hour later, he heard footsteps steadily climbing the outer stair. A key slid into the lock.

Babington didn't realize the door was unlocked, but carelessly opened it and sent the door swinging wide.

He immediately saw Robert sitting in the chair, outlined by the light from the windows at his back.

Babington froze.

Robert remained where he was, but realizing that Babington couldn't see his face, said, "Robert Frobisher." When Babington blinked and the tension that had tightened his frame eased, Robert held up the half-empty glass. "Not a bad drop, but the Glencrae is better."

"Frobisher." After a further second's hesitation, Babington stepped inside and walked to the small table. He lit the lamp upon it; the light flared, and he glanced at Robert—a sharp glance confirming his identity. Satisfied, Babington turned down the wick, set the glass on the lamp, then returned to the door and closed it. He set his cane in the rack beside the door, then went to the tantalus and poured himself a drink.

Only when he had it in hand did he look at Robert. Babington raised his glass, sipped, then asked, "Why are *you* here?"

Robert sent him an unamused grin. "As you rightly suspect, it's connected with Declan's visit. But as you've already realized, my visit is quite deliberately more...private."

"Covert, in other words." Babington crossed to the sofa and sat at his ease, stretching out his long legs. The lamplight played equally over them both. Babington studied Robert, then asked, "I presume you want my help with something. So what's going on?"

Robert had had plenty of time to decide how he wished to proceed. "I understood from Declan that you might have an interest in people who've gone missing."

Babington was too experienced to shift, but he stilled.

Over the rim of his glass, Robert scrutinized Babington's expression, then quietly asked, "Is that so?"

Babington's features didn't give him away, but his color had ebbed. He remained frozen, staring at Robert. After several seconds, in a voice devoid of inflection, he asked, "Why do you want to know?"

Robert shifted his gaze to the glass in his hand. "Because if you do have such an interest, then, presumably, it would predispose you to assist me in my quest." He paused, then glanced at Babington. "However, if you don't have such an interest...then I fear I would be unwise to share with you the details of why I am here."

Babington remained sprawled on the sofa, staring through the lamplight and studying Robert's face.

Then, slowly, Babington sat up. Moving deliberately, he set his glass down on the small table. Leaning his elbows on his thighs, he scrubbed both hands over his face. He stared blindly across the room for several seconds, then he met Robert's gaze. "All right."

Robert fought to keep his expression impassive, unresponsive. Babington looked almost tortured, his eyes shadowed.

"There's—there was a young lady, a young woman in our

terms. A Miss Mary Wilson. Her family was down on its luck, and she came out here for a fresh start, helping her uncle in his store. She was more than an assistant. More like her uncle's heir—a co-owner." Babington drew in a tight breath, then went on, "She and I…we were courting, but of course, I haven't told anyone in the family that. They'd have an apoplexy if they knew I wanted to marry a shopkeeper—that's how they'd see it. See her. They wouldn't even want to meet her."

Robert came from much the same background; he understood Babington's familial situation.

Babington had paused as if ordering his thoughts. He continued, "One day, I called at the shop, and when he saw me, her uncle was furious. He tried to throw me out, but then he realized I hadn't come to tell him that I'd persuaded Mary to give up her place with him and become my ladybird. That I didn't have any more idea of where she was than he.

"We were frantic—the pair of us. We searched. I hired men to hunt high and low through the settlement—but she was gone. Vanished." Babington gestured helplessly. "As if into thin air."

Babington looked at Robert, and now anger lit his eyes. "So if you want to know if I have an interest in people going missing from the settlement, the answer is yes. *Yes!* I'd give my right arm to know what has happened to Mary."

Robert set down his glass and crisply stated, "Then obviously, you'll do all you can to further any venture that might—just might—result in getting her back."

Babington snarled, "Anything. I'll do *anything* to get her back." He lifted his glass and tossed back his drink, then looked again at Robert, hesitated, then asked, "Do you think there's any chance of that? That she's even alive?"

Robert held his gaze, then sighed. "I won't lie to you—I can't be certain. But there is a chance that she's been spirited away by those who've been taking a range of other Europeans, picking them off—men, women, and, it seems, even children—and taking them out of the settlement. The reason behind the kidnappings is a mystery, but as far as we've been able to make out, there's a definite chance those taken are still alive." Robert paused, then went on, "We're proceeding on the basis that they are still alive, and that whatever we do in pursuing them must be done in such a way as to not alert the perpetrators."

Babington was by no means slow. He figured it out in seconds. "So said perpetrators won't risk covering their tracks by killing those they've taken." He nodded. "And you think someone in the settlement is involved."

"Some people, yes. More than one person, but exactly who is involved we can't say." Robert paused, reading what he could now see in Babington's face—stripped of the man's usual debonair mask—and made the decision to trust him. "Pour yourself another drink, and let me tell you what we know."

Babington cut him a glance, then complied. Once he'd resettled on the sofa, a glass of whisky in his hand, Robert proceeded to lay out the entire scenario as they knew it, starting with Declan's mission.

When he got to the part about Edwina being drugged by Lady Holbrook and then passed on to men they believed to be part of the slavers' gang, Babington swore.

"She's gone, you know. Took ship…it must have been a few days after Declan sailed. Holbrook told Macauley she went to help a sister in need, but I later heard the ship she'd sailed on was headed to America." Babington's face hardened. "That seemed odd at the time. Now…"

"Indeed. One thing you can confirm for me—Holbrook's still here?"

Babington nodded. "On deck as usual. No change that Macauley or I have noticed—and the old man would have said if he'd sensed anything amiss."

"So it's likely Holbrook is innocent in all this—but he's not likely to be much use to us, either. Until we know the identity of all those involved, alerting Holbrook might see him react in a way that will alert the villains, which, again, is the last thing we want. Also, as the focus of the investigation lies outside the settlement, it's unlikely Holbrook will be able to provide the kind of help required. That makes telling him a large risk without much chance of reward." Robert cocked a brow at Babington. "At least that was Declan's assessment."

Babington grimaced. "I wouldn't disagree. Holbrook is paranoid about keeping the colony calm, and any hint of white slavers operating within the settlement would cause a panic—and send Macauley's blood pressure soaring." Dryly, he added, "Never a good thing. Especially not for the political classes. And Holbrook's no great poker player. If he knew something disturbing—let alone something as threatening to his well-being as this—he wouldn't be able to hide it."

Robert humphed. After a moment, he resumed his recitation of events—Declan's return to London, his report to Melville and Wolverstone, and Robert's subsequent recruitment to undertake the next leg of the mission.

Babington arched a brow. "Not your usual sort of escapade."

"True, but I'm not averse to the occasional challenge." Robert realized that was, indeed, the truth. "It keeps me on my toes."

"It'll do more than that if there are slavers involved. Normally, they don't operate in the settlement—they give it a wide berth—but I've heard tales aplenty. Enough to know the locals both despise and fear them with good cause." Babington looked at Robert. "So you're here to pick up the slavers' trail."

Robert nodded. "My task is to locate their camp, which I've learned will be out in the jungle somewhere, sufficiently far out to avoid the patrols out of Thornton, and also to steer clear of the surrounding villages and their chiefs."

"That makes sense." Babington met Robert's gaze. "Whatever help I can give, you can count on it."

Robert inclined his head in acknowledgment. "My orders are

to learn the camp's location, then take that back to London. I've been expressly forbidden to follow the trail of the captives any further." He looked Babington in the eye. "In trusting you with the details of this mission, I expect you to abide by the restrictions, too."

Babington thought, then grimaced. "As you say, locating the enterprise—the mine, if it turns out to be that—without alerting whoever the villains have in their pockets here is absolutely vital. If news that London is conducting an investigation leaks out…" He took a swig of his whisky, then bleakly finished, "All the captives will be dead sooner than you can blink."

"Just so." Robert felt his face harden.

"So what do you need me to do?"

Robert reviewed his options. "At present, my men and I are quietly tucked away in an inn in the merchants' quarter. Far enough from the docks that it's unlikely we'll run into anyone who would recognize me—or my men."

Babington frowned. "Where's *The Trident*?"

"At anchor farther down the estuary." Robert paused, then added, "We have false name boards up, and with the squadron at sea, there's no one around likely to recognize her lines."

"Except me." Babington drained his glass. "And I won't tell."

"Exactly." Robert paused, then asked, "Do you have any inkling of who in the settlement might be involved in this? Anyone acting suspiciously?"

Babington snorted. "I hadn't a clue Lady Holbrook was involved, and I met with her and Holbrook regularly." He shook his head. "On the one hand, I can still barely believe it, but on the other, I can. She was always so much more…*grasping* than he."

Robert returned to his earlier line of thought. "At the moment, I have all the help I need. My orders more or less forbid me to engage, so having an extra sword isn't going to make a difference. But thinking ahead, having you on the ground here, keeping your eyes and ears open…at some point, once we have the location of the mine, I imagine a force will be sent in to liberate it. And given the issues in the settlement, that force will almost certainly arrive direct from London. They'll need help—the sort of help you will be perfectly positioned to give."

Babington nodded. "Very well. I'll keep my head down, eyes open, and ears flapping. However..." His eyes narrowed. He tapped one fingernail on the now empty glass in his hands. Slowly, he smiled, although there was no humor in the expression. "One thing I can do that would be entirely in character—all but routine, or at least I could make it appear so—is to run checks on the cargoes being loaded into certain holds. Even when a ship is sailing for some port not in England, we will occasionally run a spot check, just to make sure there are no goods marked to be shipped on."

Babington met Robert's gaze. "I agree with Declan that the most likely enterprise at the bottom of this scheme is a diamond mine. And if it's diamonds, the shipments will be headed to Amsterdam. I can search all ships bound for that area. I'll disguise it as some sort of crackdown due to something or other—easy enough for me to fabricate a cause."

"What about Macauley?"

"He tends to leave the day-to-day business to me, while he massages the politicians and the relevant authorities." Babington's lips twisted. "It's an arrangement that works for both of us and, in this case, leaves me free to make it harder for our villains to clear their ill-gotten goods."

"Interfering with their logistics in such a way..." Robert narrowed his eyes as he contemplated that, then he nodded decisively. "As long as you can make it seem entirely due to some other unconnected reason, putting that sort of pressure on the villains' plans might well unsettle them, might even force them to act in some way they haven't planned, which can only be to our advantage."

Babington nodded. "There'll be no risk to the captives as long as the villains have no reason to imagine their game has been uncovered. They'll merely see my efforts as an annoying and unhelpful nuisance." He grinned coldly. "I'll certainly be doing my best to make that so."

After a moment, Babington asked, "So where do you intend to start your search for the slavers' trail?"

The question brought Robert back to his day. He'd told Babington of Lashoria's claim of the slavers being connected with Undoto. Now he filled Babington in about what he'd found when he'd visited Lashoria.

Babington listened in stoic silence. Robert ended his tale with the old woman's information about the slave trader Kale. Babington nodded. "As I said, the locals hate them, but they're generally too afraid to make any sort of move against them, not even to pass on information."

Robert exhaled and sat up. "So I'm going to start with Undoto, because he appears to be the only lead I have. Can you add anything to what I already know about him?"

Babington shook his head. "I've been to only one of his services—I never saw the point. But Mary liked them—she said it was the drama." Babington's voice had grown cold. "If it turns out it was that—her going to his services—that led to her being taken—"

"He'll pay."

Babington's lips curved menacingly. "Indeed, he will."

Deciding to ignore that, Robert said, "One thing Lashoria's old servant stressed was how very different this scheme was to the usual sort of slavery practiced hereabouts."

Babington nodded. "It is. Normally these days, those seized by the slavers are tribesmen from deep in the interior. The slavers walk them out, then load them onto ships well away from any of the settlements. Coming anywhere near Freetown—well, it's the base for the governor and the squadron, so for slavers, that's akin to asking to be caught and clapped in irons themselves. But in this case, they're taking Europeans, and not just men but young women and children, too, and it seems they're taking them out of the settlement and into the jungle—and, if the assumption of a mine is correct, they're using them here, not shipping them out for sale far away. It's a very different kind of trade."

After a moment, Babington said, "If it's a mine, why take young women and children? I understand Declan's suggestion of how young women and children might be used in a diamond-mining operation, and that might well be true, yet when we're talking about amassing a workforce via slavery, then if there's a choice between men on the one hand and women and children on the other..." Babington shook his head. "If there's a sufficient supply of men, and in a settlement like this there surely is, then taking women, much less children, should have been a less attractive—less efficient—option." Babington met Robert's gaze. "An option of lower return to the slavers as well as the mine operators, yet it's one they've taken, apparently deliberately."

Robert thought of all he'd learned. "When you assess this scheme dispassionately, everything about it has been thoroughly planned by people who know how things operate here. Whoever they are, they foresaw the problems they would face and took steps to counter them. Given that, I think we can be sure that with respect to them taking young women and children, they will have a reason, and it'll be a good one."

Five

The following morning, Robert adjourned with his men to Sampson's tavern. The old sailor had insights into the local population; seated about Sampson's corner table, mugs of ale before them all, Robert relayed what Lashoria's old servant had told him.

"The old woman confirmed all that Lashoria had told my brother and sister-in-law—that Lashoria had seen Undoto with the slavers, and she'd seen him accept money from the slavers' hands. While Lashoria was killed virtually on the heels of my brother and his wife leaving, it seems unlikely that it was Lashoria's contact with them that brought the slavers down on her head."

Robert paused, recalling what else Declan and Edwina had told him. "She—Lashoria—had spoken of Undoto's connection with the slavers to Hardwicke, the minister. He hadn't taken her case to Holbrook..." Robert tipped his head. "As far as we know. We don't know with whom in the settlement Hardwicke might have spoken, but my sister-in-law understood from Hardwicke's wife that the minister was disturbed by Lashoria's claims, so he might have sought advice from others over what to do."

"Perhaps that's something we could check?" Fuller suggested.

Robert nodded. "If we have the opportunity, it might lead us to another of those involved—we have to assume there are others besides Lady Holbrook drawn into and actively supporting this." He pulled a face. "It's possible the person Hardwicke spoke to was her ladyship, but I'll check if I get a chance."

He paused, then said, "More to the point, however, we need

to move forward. If Lashoria's old servant is correct, then the first place we need to find is the slavers' lair inside the settlement." He glanced at Sampson.

The old sailor nodded his grizzled head. "She's right—that's how I've heard they operate. Or, at least, how they used to. As everyone says, the slavers haven't been making away with locals from this settlement for a good long while now. But I've heard they occasionally come in and lurk—no one's ever sure why or what for. But they always have a bolt hole buried somewhere in the slums."

Robert nodded. "So that's our first goal—locate the slavers' lair. The only potential connection anyone's turned up is Undoto, so he's the one we'll watch." He looked at Sampson. "I don't suppose you know where Undoto lives?"

Sampson shook his head. "I know he comes walking down along the road above the church, but I've never seen beyond that or heard tell of his house."

Robert looked at his men. "We need to identify Undoto's house. I'll leave you four to handle that. Once you've found the place, scout around for a spot from which we can set up surveillance. From what the old woman said, we need to watch at night—the slavers don't generally amble about in daylight."

All four men started to raise their hands, then stopped and nodded instead.

"Once you've found a useful spot," Robert continued, "two of you remain on watch. I'll meet the other two back at the inn."

The four nodded again, drained their mugs, set them on the table, and rose. After farewelling Sampson, they headed out.

Sampson watched them go. "You didn't tell them how they were supposed to learn where Undoto lives." Sampson met Robert's gaze. "I'm curious as to how you think they'll do that."

Robert grinned and set down his mug. "They'll start asking around the area—anyone they meet. They'll say they're trying to find the priest to ask him something one might ask a priest about." He smiled at Sampson. "They're good at what they do—I can trust them to get the job done. Quietly."

Sampson grunted. "Like I thought, you're not just a ship's captain, and they're not just sailors."

Robert's smile deepened. "For all that, we're sailors first." He got to his feet, hesitated, then said, "I saw the Office of the Naval Attaché at the end of Government Wharf. Who is the attaché—is he a navy man?"

Sampson snorted derisively. "Not sure he's even a sailor. A bureaucrat of some sort—a trumped-up public servant clerk. An Irishman by the name of Muldoon." Sampson shrugged. "I've never heard much about him. Only time I went into the office, there were three junior clerks pushing papers. That seems all they do."

"Thank you." With a salute for the old man, Robert left him and walked out into the welling heat.

He glanced around, then started walking toward the harbor.

He'd been debating his next move all morning. Being so readily identifiable as another Frobisher meant he needed to avoid any offices Declan had visited; having two Frobishers turn up within a month of each other, both asking questions, would undoubtedly give rise to unhelpful speculation. So the governor's office and residence, and the fort, too, were off limits to him.

But Declan hadn't called at the Office of the Naval Attaché.

Declan had, rightly, been concerned over running into Vice-Admiral Decker or any of his officers, all of whom would recognize a Frobisher on sight and immediately start questioning the reason for their presence, but Robert doubted lowly clerks would pose much of a threat.

Navy men would, but the ships of the squadron were noticeably still absent from the harbor. There wouldn't be any naval officers coming into the office today.

Robert was certain he'd never met Muldoon before, and the chances of the junior clerks knowing him by sight were miniscule.

Eyes narrowing against the sun's glare, he murmured, "And I need to know if Decker's going to hove on my horizon any time soon."

He reached the area near their inn and continued steadily on. He had no idea if Decker himself was involved with the villains and their scheme—even if his involvement was merely to turn a blind eye.

Equally, however, he could see no reason for the villains to involve Decker, not if the focus of their enterprise lay inland in the jungles somewhere. Decker's area of interest—and his arena of influence—lay out to sea, in the sea-lanes he policed.

Robert didn't particularly like Decker—the older man was a rigidly stuffy, indeed, reactionary stickler—but Robert also had difficulty believing that Decker, if he heard of any operation involving slavery, would turn a blind eye; he was simply not the sort to bend in any way at all—which in part fueled the animosity Decker felt toward the Frobishers.

To Decker's rigid mind, the Frobishers were far too...innovative. In the widest sense of the word.

Robert looked ahead. The brilliant blue of the harbor lay beyond the end of the street he was descending. From this direction, he could walk down to and then along the length of the quay fronting Kroo Bay to the office at the end of Government Wharf, but navy men weren't the only ones who might recognize him; there were many who sailed on merchant fleets who might, too.

He turned left into an alley and tacked through the narrower streets and lanes that riddled the area immediately behind the quay. Stepping onto the quay close by the naval office would reduce the risk of being recognized.

As he walked, he ran through various scenarios in his mind—deciding what questions were safe to ask and evaluating which would best lead the junior clerks into revealing what he needed to know.

He needed to know if Decker was expected back in the near future. Although Robert hadn't sailed into this harbor in years—hadn't crossed Decker's bow in even more years—Decker would nevertheless recognize *The Trident* on sight.

But Robert didn't want to walk in and simply ask when Decker was due back. What excuse could he give for such an interest? He certainly didn't want to claim he was a friend asking after the old man—the clerks would immediately demand his name, and giving a false name would alert Decker when he eventually heard about it, and that might jeopardize the mission further along its evolution…

Too complicated.

Robert frowned. He needed a reason to call at the office, some subject that would allow him to get chatting with the clerks, something simple and obvious—so obvious the clerks wouldn't question it or his interest…

Hopkins—or rather, his sister.

Robert halted as he recalled that little complication Sampson had warned him of; in the aftermath of learning about Lashoria's murder, he'd forgotten all about the Hopkins woman.

He grimaced and resumed walking. He should have asked Babington about her; he might have met her socially, might have known where Robert could find her. However, in pursuing his current tack, perhaps the unknown but inquisitive lady might prove useful. If she'd been asking Sampson about her brother… surely her first port of call would have been the squadron's office on shore—namely, the Office of the Naval Attaché.

A minute of deliberation served to convince him that in Hopkins's sister, he'd found the perfect excuse with which to engage the naval office clerks.

A smile on his lips, he stepped onto the quay. Two paces on and he turned in through the open door of the Office of the Naval Attaché.

He'd been into such offices the world over; they were all very similar. The staff was drawn from the Admiralty and often had never served on any vessel; one glance confirmed that all three clerks working behind the long counter were most likely of that ilk. Certainly, none of them showed any sign of recognizing him as he approached the counter and they glanced, briefly, his way.

One clerk rose from his desk and came to the counter.

With an easy smile, Robert leaned against it. There was no other outsider presently vying for the clerks' attention—no one else there to hear their exchange.

Exuding an air of relaxed camaraderie, Robert met the clerk's eyes. "I've just sailed in on *The Filmore.*" That was the name *The Trident* was presently carrying. When the clerk's gaze went to the large window overlooking the harbor, Robert smoothly continued, "She's moored out in the estuary—we're only here for a day or so. But my family asked me to check on behalf of friends of theirs—the Hopkinses. About a lady of that family who's apparently come out here to ask after her brother…a lieutenant, I think?"

Understanding dawned on the clerk's face. "Oh, you mean Miss Hopkins."

"So she made it this far?"

The clerk nodded. "She came in…must have been about two weeks ago now." He met Robert's gaze. "Rather pushy, she was, wanting to know why her brother Lieutenant Hopkins had been ashore and away from his ship when he went absent without leave. But, of course, we couldn't tell her anything."

Robert softly laughed. "Of course, you couldn't." His expression grew commiserating. "Although I expect she didn't take that too well."

The clerk snorted. "Got rather hoity, but"—he shrugged—"nothing we could do for her." He glanced at one of the other clerks and grinned. "Edgar told her she had to ask at the Admiralty for information like that. That went down even better."

One of the clerks still seated at his desk—presumably Edgar—

threw a long-suffering look over his shoulder. "At least that got her to go away."

Robert settled more comfortably, leaning his forearms on the counter. "I know of the family—I'm surprised she didn't demand to see the attaché, or even the admiral."

"She did ask to see Muldoon—the attaché," the clerk at the counter replied, "but he was out. And Decker—vice-admiral in command of the squadron—won't be back in harbor until at least the end of next week."

"I think she's still hanging around—Miss Hopkins." Edgar glanced around. "I've seen her here and there around Water Street. Perhaps she's waiting for Decker to get back so she can demand her answers from him?"

The other two clerks laughed. Robert understood why—the notion of a lady demanding answers from Decker was unquestionably amusing—but he contented himself with an understanding smile.

"Sadly," he said, as the laughter faded, "I won't be here to witness that. We'll be upping anchor soon and heading on." He pushed away from the counter. "But I was badgered to check that the lady had reached here safely. As long as I can report she did, my job is done."

He raised a finger in salute to the clerks; they grinned and nodded back, and he turned to leave—but then stopped and swung back. "Oh—one other thing. Our crew picked up some scuttlebutt on the docks—something about them needing to be careful because there were slave traders operating in the settlement, picking off navvies..." He pulled a face. "Seemed far-fetched to me—slavers inside the settlement, taking navvies—but I thought I'd ask. Any of you heard anything along those lines?"

The three clerks looked at each other, then all three looked at him and shook their heads.

"Haven't heard a whisper of anything like that," the one at the counter said.

From their expressions, Robert suspected that was the truth; none showed even a hint of unease.

He grinned and waved the matter aside. "That's what I thought—that it was a tall tale told to frighten gullible crewmen passing through."

With a last general smile, he walked out of the office, leaving the clerks relaxed and settling back to their work with no inkling they'd just been interrogated.

Robert halted on the wharf, glanced swiftly around, then with rapid strides, got off the quay and into the relative anonymity of the warren of streets behind it. Once he was clear of the immediate area and pacing steadily back to the inn, he allowed himself a satisfied smile.

He'd learned all he'd expected to and a little more. The lady he needed to locate and send packing—persuade to return to London—went by the name of Miss Hopkins. He needed to find her and dispatch her home. In particular, he needed to ensure she left before Decker returned to port, especially if she truly had it in mind to question Decker directly.

But Decker's projected return also meant that he and his crew had only another week to complete their mission. When he'd sailed up the estuary, he'd assumed a handful of days would suffice, and indeed, a handful more might. But they needed to leave before Decker returned and got a glimpse of the ship anchored farther down the estuary.

No matter how little credence he placed in the idea of Decker being involved, he had to assume the admiral—or someone on his immediate staff—was connected with the scheme, and act accordingly.

As he walked, he thought over his plans. Having a deadline imposed, even if it was one that seemed easy enough to meet, focused the mind in a powerful way.

Clearly, the official channels in general knew nothing about the slave traders' activities. If the clerks hadn't heard even a whisper—and Robert felt certain they hadn't been lying—then the slavers and their associates were, indeed, being very clever in ensuring their operation ran beneath official notice.

Robert knew what it took to accomplish that; the knowledge left him with a healthy respect for the intelligence and forethought of those behind the scheme.

He needed to get this mission done. He needed to prioritize.

His men were on Undoto's track. They were better suited to merging anonymously into the populace than he was.

While they were hunting down Undoto and setting up to watch for the slavers, he should take care of the other issue that had forced its way onto his plate.

He needed to find Miss Hopkins and send her, if not home, then out of his area of operation.

★ ★ ★

The following day, Robert returned to the inn at midday; after spending the rest of the previous day and all of the morning in and around Water Street, slouching on corners and keeping his eyes peeled for the elusive Miss Hopkins, all to no avail, he was in no good mood.

He knew her older brothers. He was fairly certain Miss Hopkins was younger than David and Henry; he was fairly good with faces and believed he would recognize her if he saw her. But although he'd wasted hours watching the emporia the European ladies in the settlement patronized, he hadn't seen any woman who might conceivably be her.

Frustration rode him as he stalked into the inn. He'd expected to stumble upon his quarry reasonably easily; there was precious little entertainment for ladies in the settlement, and as she hadn't attended Undoto's last service, presumably she'd given up on that, so where the devil was she?

Even more exercising was the thought of what she might be doing.

Dropping onto the bench at the corner table in the tiny taproom, the table he and his men had made theirs, he scrubbed his hands over his face. Lowering his hands, he found a smile for the landlady as she placed a mug of ale before him without him having to ask. "Thank you."

She nodded. "Will you be wanting a piece of pie, sir? We've some beef stew from yesterday, too."

After ordering a serving of today's beef pie—most likely goat, he knew—Robert took a long draft of the ale.

He put the mug down and stared into the dark liquid. Perhaps he hadn't sighted Miss Hopkins because she'd given up and was already on her way back to England?

The thought lifted his mood, but he couldn't just hope—he would have to confirm that the wretched woman had actually boarded a ship and sailed away.

He was wondering how to make such inquiries when Benson, Coleman, Fuller, and Harris walked in. They saw him and hurried over. Their expressions—eager and enthusiastic—made Robert's pulse kick.

Yesterday, the four had been as frustrated as he, having got nowhere in their efforts to locate the priest's house.

"Finally ran the beggar to earth." Coleman dropped onto the bench to Robert's left.

Robert glanced at the other three as they settled on the benches; he signaled to the landlady to bring mugs of ale for them all.

"His house isn't in the slums," Harris said. "We started too far along that way."

They all fell silent while the landlady distributed mugs of ale, and Robert suggested they all place their orders for food. Once that was done and the landlady had retreated, he said, "Tell me."

The other three looked at Benson, who was the oldest of the group. He swallowed a mouthful of ale, then said, "The priest's house is on that road he walks down to get to the church, most of the way up the first long slope. It's a detached wooden house in good repair, and the area's neat and respectable. The nearest slum lies more than half a mile farther along the road—you have to go over the first crest and down, into a little valley on the flank of the hill."

"That's where we started," Fuller said. "Over the hill closer to the slum. And, o' course, people that way didn't know precisely where he lived, just that it wasn't near them."

"This morning," Benson said, "we came back much closer to the church and started asking our questions, and that's when we struck gold. We watched the house for most of the morning—in shifts, so to speak—but all we saw was women going in and out, along with an old man and five children. And himself, of course. But there was no sign of any men who might be part of a slaving gang."

Robert's orders had been to find some suitable spot to mount surveillance and to leave two men on watch. The fact all four had returned meant… "I take it there's no suitable place to use as a hide?"

"Well, there is, and there ain't," Benson said. "We thought as how midday was the best time to come back and ask as to what you wanted us to do."

The landlady approached with a tray piled with five plates loaded with sections of pie, and they fell silent.

Once she'd handed around the plates and departed, and the men had taken their first bites, Benson resumed, "Like we said, this is no slum area. It's a quiet neighborhood. The houses are well kept, and ordinary folk live in them. A few are from one or other of the local tribes—shopkeepers, warehouse managers, that sort of thing. Most are Europeans of the same ilk, and some are of mixed blood. While one of us watched the priest's house, the others asked around, and we found an old woman has a house across the street and four doors down—and she has a nice big front room to let. We could watch from there—the window looks to have a good line of sight to the priest's door—and staying in the street will give us reason to be out and about in the area. No one glances twice at someone who's staying in the neighborhood."

Robert nodded. "Good work." It had been too much to hope that Undoto's house might prove also to be the slavers' lair. Robert pushed away his empty plate and reached for his ale. "Given the location of Undoto's house, combined with what you've seen of the occupants, it seems certain the slavers' lair will be somewhere else. So yes, we'll rent that room and keep watch from there."

"We thought," Harris said, "that three of us can hunker in there and one stay here in case you need to send for us, but we can rotate whoever stays here, and that way the locals will see all our faces and grow used to us being around."

Robert nodded again and reached for the pouch tucked into his belt. He counted out coins—more than enough for renting a room—and pushed them across the table to Benson. "Take the room. Get anything else you need to make yourselves comfortable. We'll start our watch this evening. When you have everything in place, one of you come back and fetch me. I expect to go out again, but I'll be back before sunset."

"Aye." Benson nodded. "We'll do that."

The four had cleaned their plates. They drained their mugs, then with nods to him, rose and clattered upstairs to fetch their bags.

Robert remained where he was, thinking and weighing his possible actions. After his men had left, he rose and went up to his room. From his bag, he pulled out paper, a tightly capped bottle of ink, and a pen, then sat at the serviceable desk. He laid out his supplies, then settled to write a letter to London, reporting on what he'd already learned.

No point in taking the risk of something happening and London not hearing about what he'd already discovered.

He understood Melville's need to know if Holbrook was innocent, and from all the evidence, that was indeed the case. However, as Robert stressed, there was no way of knowing if someone else in Holbrook's inner circle was involved. Consequently, he advised against anyone trusting the governor's office with any potentially sensitive information.

He related what he knew of Lady Holbrook's departure and confirmed that Babington could be relied upon, both for further information and also for support as required as the mission progressed. He wrote of Lashoria's death at the hands—or, at the very least, the orders—of the slave trader known as Kale, and included all he'd gleaned about how the slave traders operated, explaining that a lair within the settlement was used as a staging point before those kidnapped were taken to the slavers' camp somewhere in the surrounding jungles. He detailed the location of Undoto's house, and his plans for watching and picking up the trail of the slavers.

After some deliberation, he resigned himself to mentioning Miss Hopkins and her campaign to locate her missing brother, but he assured Melville—and therefore Wolverstone—that he would have her on a ship back to England as soon as he could locate her.

He didn't add that locating her was proving far more difficult than he'd foreseen. Again, the hope that she'd already departed floated tantalizingly across his mind.

Satisfied that he'd adequately conveyed his progress to that point, he sealed the letter, wrote Melville's direction on the front—and then realized that posting such a missive wasn't going to be a matter of simply walking into the post office on the quay, handing over the letter, and paying the price.

The post office stood high on the list of places he shouldn't risk entering—there was far too much chance of some other potential customer walking in and recognizing him.

And he couldn't send one of his men, either. An ordinary sailor—an ordinary person of any sort—posting a letter to the First Lord of the Admiralty would inevitably raise eyebrows and draw attention. And sending the letter to Wolverstone House wasn't going to work, either.

"Damn!" He stared at the letter—his carefully scripted missive. He could leave it with his crew on *The Trident*—a fail-safe of sorts—but he would much rather have the information on its way to London by some other, relatively anonymous route. What if Decker returned early and impounded *The Trident*?

Babington? Not a good idea; his mail would go via the company's mailbag, and any attempt to send a letter separately would be noted. And the idea of some Macauley and Babington clerk in London sorting through the mail and finding a letter addressed to the First Lord…definitely not a good idea.

He could send the letter via Declan, but he didn't know if his brother and Edwina had intended to remain in town, and if they hadn't?

Robert tapped a fingernail on the desk's scarred surface. There had to be a way to send the letter straight to where he wanted it to go…

Frustration bloomed. He was almost at the point of destroying the letter when his other source of frustration crossed his mind.

"Salvation," he breathed. If Miss Hopkins was still in the settlement—and despite his vain hope, instinct told him she almost certainly was; if she shared her brothers' sterling trait of stubborn doggedness, she would be—then he could put her to use before he saw her safely aboard some England-bound vessel.

No one would question a lady with a connection to the navy—especially one who'd been told by the naval office to contact the Admiralty—posting a letter to the First Lord.

More, he could couch his request in such a way as to placate the meddlesome Miss Hopkins and make her feel that she was doing something useful with respect to finding her brother.

An exaggeration, perhaps, but not entirely untrue.

Feeling inordinately pleased at the prospect of removing two albatrosses with one stone, Robert rose, tucked the letter into the inner pocket of his loose shirt, and turned to the door.

Now all he had to do was find Miss Hopkins.

The damned woman had to be somewhere. He was determined to hunt her down.

★ ★ ★

By the time the sun set and night washed across the settlement, Robert had reverted to mentally swearing whenever he thought of Miss Hopkins. Where the devil was the infernal woman hiding?

Was she *actively* hiding?

Given the difficulty he was having finding any trace of her, that was no longer an idle question.

Harris had returned to the inn and was waiting to lead Robert to the house in which the men had established their observation post. After eating a quick supper, then collecting a pie and skins of ale for the three men on watch, he and Harris set off on foot.

Without raising his head, Robert scanned the houses as they trudged up the street that curved above Undoto's church. Everything he saw confirmed his men's assessment that the neighborhood was quiet and respectable; few people remained on the streets, while lamplight glowed inside many of the houses, and the distant murmur of voices—male, female, and the piping tones of children—suggested that families resided within.

Not a wealthy area, and certainly not one the upper echelons of local British society inhabited, but neat, relatively clean—to all appearances law-abiding.

Exactly the sort of area in which one might expect a local priest to make his home.

And by the same token, not a place one would imagine slavers lurking.

"Undoto's place is just up there." Harris flicked a hand toward houses farther up the street to their right. "Our place is the browny-colored house coming up on our left."

There was a carriage—one of the anonymous hackneys that could be hired in Water Street—drawn up by the curb on the other side of the street, facing down the slope. Robert glanced at the carriage as they passed. The inside was drenched in darkness; he couldn't see anyone inside, nor did he detect any movement. As for the driver, his head was drooping, and he appeared to be asleep.

Presumably, someone was visiting the house before which the carriage was waiting.

Facing forward, Robert turned left where Harris indicated and followed him up a short path to the browny-colored house's front door.

The house in which his men had rented space proved to be the sort where tenants were given the key to the front door so they could come and go without hindrance while the owner lived at the rear, and privacy was preserved all around.

Walking into the front room, Robert saw two pallets lying against the inner wall, and a lantern perched on a plain table, which stood at the far end of the room with four low stools arranged around it. An old armchair had been angled to face the nearer corner of the wide front window. Long, old, but serviceable curtains had been drawn across the glass.

Coleman and Fuller were seated on stools at the table, playing some card game in the light shed by the lantern, the wick of which was turned relatively low. Closer to the door, Benson was sitting in the armchair, leaning forward and peering past the edge of the curtains.

Robert nodded to Coleman and Fuller. Leaving Harris to hand over the pie and ale, Robert crossed to the armchair. "Let me see."

Benson rose, and Robert took his place, sinking into the cushions. With one hand, he edged aside the curtain as Benson had been doing, leaned forward, and looked out.

"It's the one with white-painted trim and the alley going down the side of it," Benson said. "The one with the alley between the house and us."

Robert studied the house—just another house composed of wooden slats. "Go and have your supper. I'll watch for a while."

"Aye, aye, sir."

Robert heard Benson cross to the table, heard the scrape of a stool as he drew it out. Robert surveyed Undoto's house; he could have wished for a less acute angle, but they did have a clear view of the stretch of street before Undoto's gate, the front path, the narrow porch, and the front door. They wouldn't be able to see past the door, but at least they could see virtually all the area in front of it.

He watched the house while his men ate, and weighed and considered all the possibilities. When Harris came to relieve him of the watch, Robert relinquished the post. On his feet again, he glanced at the others, still sitting about the table. "As I see it, the slavers—assuming they come to call on Undoto—could come down the street from above or up the street from below. Or they might come to the rear of the house via that alley."

Coleman nodded. "Aye—we were discussing that. And there's another alley, too—more or less directly opposite Undoto's house. But if the slavers come from above, below, or opposite, we'll see them."

"And if they come to the rear via the alley?" Robert asked.

Coleman grimaced, glanced at the other men, then looked at Robert. "We were thinking, what with all that you told us about what your brother said, and even what the priestess's old woman said, that these slavers act like bullies around here. Think they're cock o' the walk and no one would dare get in their way, at least not at night. Seems like they'd come to the front door, even here. Wouldn't look right for them to sneak about alleys to knock on the back door."

Robert considered that aspect, then slowly smiled. He nodded to Coleman and the others. "You're right. They'll come to the front door."

He lowered his gaze, set his hands on his hips, and put his mind to assessing how best to proceed. How to most efficiently do what needed to be done.

After several moments of deliberation, he raised his head and looked at the three men at the table. "You know what to do if the slavers come calling."

"Just follow them to their lair," Benson said. "No heroics. See where they go to ground, and then look for a hide from which to watch the place."

Robert nodded in affirmation. "I'm going to leave you to it. There are other matters I can more usefully pursue." He turned to the door. "I'll be back as soon as I've dealt with them—most likely tomorrow. If you need me, or if you see action tonight, leave word at the inn."

To murmurs of "Aye, aye," he left the room and quit the house. He strode back down the street, noting that the carriage he'd seen earlier was still waiting where it had been before.

Half an hour later, he was once more letting himself into Babington's apartment above the Macauley and Babington office.

After another half hour of sipping Babington's whisky, Robert heard Babington arrive.

Babington opened the door, stepped into the room, then jerked in surprise when he saw Robert, once again seated in one of the armchairs.

Babington's lips compressed, and he shut the door. "We need to stop meeting like this. What if I'd brought a lady home with me?"

His gaze on Babington's face, Robert swirled the liquid in his glass. "What about Mary Wilson?"

Babington grimaced. All resistance went out of him, and he waved their words aside. "Why are you here? Or should I say, what do you need?"

Robert acknowledged the point with a tip of his head. "I forgot to ask you last time—have you come across a Miss Hopkins, a relatively recent arrival?"

"Hopkins?" Babington set aside his cane and shrugged out of his coat. He draped the garment over a chair, then crossed to the tantalus. He shot Robert a sharp glance. "I haven't met or heard of any lady by that name. But is she, by any chance, connected to Lieutenant Hopkins—the one who went missing after being sent to find out what happened to Dixon?"

"Indeed. She's his sister." Once Babington had poured a glass of whisky and crossed to the other armchair and sat, Robert went on, "Apparently, she's taken it upon herself to investigate her brother William's disappearance. Her older brothers—at least, I assume they are older—David and Henry, are also in the navy and are, as far as I know, far distant with their fleets."

Robert paused, then, frowning, continued, "The family is navy through and through. If some suggestion of Lieutenant Hopkins being absent without leave was passed back to them…" He grimaced and tossed back a mouthful of whisky.

Babington humphed. "If so, I imagine the elder Hopkinses might have been rather exercised."

"And for whatever reason, Miss Hopkins decided she had to come out here and learn the truth." Robert met Babington's gaze. "Regardless of her motives, having her going around the settlement asking pointed questions is not going to aid our cause."

Babington sipped and nodded. "So you want to find her and persuade her to go home."

"Exactly. I've been searching for her for the past two days, but I haven't yet succeeded in even spotting her."

Babington cast Robert a curious look. "Would you recognize her if you did?"

"I think so. Henry has hair of a particular brassy brown. A coppery brown that's not quite red. According to Sampson, she has the same."

Babington nodded. "I haven't spoken with Hopkins, but he has the same coloring."

"So." Robert drained his glass. "All I need to do is find the damned woman, explain the situation, and get her aboard some ship back to England." He met Babington's gaze. "My only problem is I can't find her."

Babington's lips twitched. "I'll see what I can turn up."

"Just don't ask questions," Robert said. "Or do anything else to draw attention to her." He sighed. "It's possible she's concealed herself or gone to ground—and you'll note I'm trying hard not to entertain the idea that she might have gone the way of her brother and been taken, too. But it's equally possible I just haven't been looking in the right venues, the right places." He looked at Babington. "I came to ask if you know of any particular social engagements the ladies of the settlement have planned for tomorrow. Either day or evening."

Babington reached for his coat and drew out a small black book. He opened it and thumbed through the pages, eventually halting on one. "Tomorrow, I have nothing noted during the day, but that's not unusual. During the day, if the ladies aren't going to one of Undoto's services, they tend to gather in small groups to chat and gossip."

"In their homes on Tower Hill?" Robert asked.

Babington nodded. "Shopping in Water Street and the streets off it is really their only other daytime entertainment, and if you've been keeping watch there…?"

"I have, but if Miss Hopkins is merely visiting briefly to learn about her brother, shopping might not be high on her list of things to do."

"The only event scheduled for tomorrow evening is a soirée to be held at the home of Major and Mrs. Winton. He's the commissar at the fort. Nice couple. Their home is just down the hill from the fort. I won't be going—it'll be pure socializing, no business, and in fact, most of the settlement's ladies are likely to attend." Babington glanced at Robert. "Are you contemplating attending in search of Miss Hopkins?"

"Good God, no!" Robert all but shuddered at the thought. "I intend to lurk in the shadows. All I need is to set eyes on Miss Hopkins—I can follow her to a more suitable location in which to have a quiet discussion."

After a moment, he refocused on Babington. "During the day, what streets are the most likely to host their morning and afternoon teas?"

Babington's lips quirked. "If you're really that desperate." He rattled off three street names. "Houses on those three host the bulk of the ladies' daytime get-togethers."

Robert nodded rather grimly and rose. "Thank you."

Babington rose, too. "I'll keep my eyes and ears open for any hint of your elusive Miss Hopkins. If I learn anything, where should I send word?"

Robert told him the location of their inn. "It's our base, and we'll check there every so often, but we're currently watching Undoto's house." Briefly, he explained their plan as Babington walked with him to the door. Halting before it, he met Babington's gaze. "Once we learn the location of the slavers' camp, I'm under orders to return immediately."

Babington reached for the doorknob. "If you can, send word before you set sail—if you suddenly vanish, I won't know what to think."

Robert paused, then said, "If possible, I'll send word before we go. But regardless, you'll know if I've been successful or not." He met Babington's eyes. "Just look for *The Trident* in the estuary. If she's gone, then I'm on board and bound for London with the location of the slavers' camp in my pocket."

"What if you get taken by the slavers and vanish, too?"

Robert's grin was self-deprecatory. "I can give what orders I like, but my crew won't sail without me. They'll wait until I return—or, more likely, until Royd comes after me."

Babington hesitated, then said, "If I haven't heard from you in over a week and *The Trident*'s still out there, I'll go out and see what the situation is."

Robert thought, then nodded. "If it comes to that, be careful."

Babington snorted and opened the door. "It's not me who's chasing slave traders."

They shook hands, then Robert left, slipping silently out into the shadows.

Six

Aileen sat in the humid darkness of Dave's carriage and stared all but unseeing through the forward window at Undoto's front door.

Four days had passed since she'd seen the small group of heavily armed thugs, possibly mercenaries, come to Undoto's house, then later leave. Four nights since she'd had Dave follow those thugs as far as the crest in the street. Four nights since she'd seen and sensed the menace emanating from the group's leader and had had Dave turn aside and, metaphorically and in actuality, run away.

Although she'd watched diligently over the nights since, no more armed men had come to visit Undoto.

She didn't know what to make of any of it—who the armed thugs were or what their connection with Undoto might be. As for what any of that might have to do with Will disappearing, she had no notion of that, either.

And yet...she felt driven to watch Undoto's house. She continued to believe that the armed men represented some sort of clue as to where Will was.

Cloaked in the shadows, she muttered, "God knows, there's no other trail to follow."

A strange mix of emotions had her in its grip. Frustration was uppermost; she'd wasted most of the past four days sleeping, catching up after fruitlessly spending the hours from sunset to dawn in the carriage somewhere along Undoto's street. But that lingering frustration was now laced with expectation; when she'd woken that afternoon, she'd realized that she'd seen the armed men on the evening following Undoto's last service.

Undoto had held another service that day at noon. If her new hypothesis was correct and the connection was with Undoto giving a service rather than simply Undoto himself, then the armed men should appear that night.

Over and under frustration and expectation ran a thread of apprehension.

Tonight, she needed to go at least one step further. If the armed men arrived, when they left, she'd instructed Dave to follow them as he had before, if anything hanging even farther back, ultimately turning off Undoto's street onto the same road they'd previously taken.

Then, however, she'd ordered Dave to pull up and let her out. She was dressed in her darkest clothes; she had her hat and veil on the seat beside her and was cradling her pistol in her lap. She intended to follow the armed men on foot—at least far enough to establish whether their destination lay in the slum.

Once she'd confirmed that…

She didn't know what she would do next; she would think of that later—one step at a time.

But no men had yet arrived, armed or not.

She'd let down the windows so she would be able to hear the tramp of feet—and so the faint stir of the night breeze might save her from expiring.

An underlying tension—nerves, a sensation she wasn't accustomed to feeling—had her glancing briefly to the right, to the circumscribed section of street she could see.

Over the past nights, she'd had Dave draw the carriage up in different locations along the street—above Undoto's house, below it, on this side or that. All she needed for her purpose was to see the men arrive and later leave; she didn't need to see Undoto himself.

Dave's carriage was as near to anonymous as a carriage could be; even his horse was a plain mid brown.

Yet seeing the stranger—the one she'd pegged as an officer when she'd seen him speaking with Sampson days before—striding along *this* street of all the streets in the settlement had set her nerves on edge.

Over the past evenings and nights, as well as identifying all those who lived in Undoto's house via their comings and goings, she'd also seen the officer and his four men go into and come out of one of the houses along the street.

She hadn't exactly felt threatened, but tonight, she'd directed Dave to pull up in the alley directly opposite Undoto's house again—out of sight of the officer and his men as they came and went from their house.

Minutes ticked past.

Her nerves flickered; they were tense and tight, anticipation plucking at them as if they were harp strings.

She shifted on the seat, then drew patience about her, refocused on Undoto's house—

The carriage door on her left was wrenched open.

She jerked. Her heart leapt to her throat.

The horse shifted, startled; the carriage rocked, then settled.

Before she'd even thought, she'd leveled her pistol at the chest outlined in the doorway.

Outside the carriage, the moon cast a faint glow, enough to see…

What a chest.

She had no idea where such an inappropriate and unhelpful observation sprang from, but…*oh, my.*

As if from a distance, she heard Dave protest. "'Ere—this carriage's taken."

"I know." The voice was deep, laced with tones of overt command. "I want a word with your fare."

Why? And who the devil is he?

Aileen knew such questions deserved immediate attention, but she was still caught by the image before her. Her would-be accoster was wearing a light jacket over a loose ivory shirt; the jacket was open, and his stance displayed the full width of his chest barely screened by fine linen to her now wide-eyed gaze. Her eyes had adjusted to the darkness within the carriage; the light outside was more than enough for her to see, to trace, to drink in…what she had to admit was a very impressive chest.

A distracting, mesmerizing one.

Her heart was thudding in a distracting manner, too.

She blinked free of the spell and realized that he—whoever he was—had glanced in and seen the pistol, and had wisely frozen.

It was tempting to use his fixation to stare some more, but prudence raised its head.

Before she could lay her tongue to any words, the man slowly lowered his head. With one hand braced on the door frame and the other locked about the door's handle, he looked deeper into the carriage. He raised his gaze from the pistol to her face. He studied her for a second; his gaze rose briefly to her hair, then returned to her eyes. His jaw set. "Miss Hopkins, I assume?"

His tone set her hackles rising. "You presume, sir." Her voice dripped icy disdain. "I suggest you shut my carriage door and go away."

The moonlight fell across his features, leaving the austere planes shadowed, yet she could have sworn an expression of frustrated exasperation fleetingly washed over his face. She'd seen a similar expression on her brothers' faces often enough to recognize the emotion from the veriest glimpse.

He shifted his gaze to the pistol; she'd continued to hold it steadily aimed at the center of that quite impressive expanse. "Is that loaded?"

"It wouldn't be much use if it wasn't."

His lips compressed into a thin line. After several seconds of what she sensed was inner debate, he crisply stated, "Captain

Robert Frobisher. I'm acquainted with your older brothers—David and Henry." His gaze rose to her face. "And I believe, Miss Hopkins, that we need to talk."

Her heart was still beating far too rapidly. She focused on his face and opened her mouth to inform him just how mistaken he was…

The words died in her throat.

He was the officer she'd seen with Sampson, the one she'd glimpsed off and on in Undoto's street over recent evenings.

He was *Frobisher.* Sampson had told her a Captain Frobisher had been searching for answers as to where people, including Will, had disappeared.

Sampson had said Frobisher had gone, sailed away, presumably back to London.

Obviously, he'd returned.

Hope made her heart skip a beat.

All manner of questions tumbled through her brain. Rendered giddy by the sudden breadth of possibilities, she drew in a breath—

A flash of movement snapped her attention back to the forward-facing window. It took her a split second to pinpoint what had caught her eye—a reflection in a half-open window of Undoto's house, a window with its glass angled up the street.

The armed men were approaching.

Then she heard the tramp of their feet.

They hadn't yet reached the intersection where the alley met the street—they couldn't yet see the carriage or the large man standing alongside it, plainly conversing with someone inside.

She swung her gaze back to Frobisher—just in time to realize he was leaning into the carriage and reaching for her pistol.

She jerked the pistol up and away from him, simultaneously sank the fingers of her other hand into his sleeve, and yanked as she whispered in a furious tone, "*Get in*, damn you! They're coming!"

Robert had heard the tramp of feet, but focused on her, he hadn't registered what it might mean. Even as he responded to her hissed command and scrambled into the carriage, pulling the door shut, but then easing the latch silently home, his brain was catching up with events—with her. She'd been able to see farther up the street than he; she'd seen and had reacted. Incredibly quickly and decisively.

He fell back on the seat facing her. The carriage was small and narrow; they couldn't easily sit side by side.

Immediately, she pushed at him to shift to his right—out of her way as she peered through a window in the carriage's front wall. He obliged. He would have liked to seize the moment to study her while she was distracted, but he didn't like having his back to the action; he twisted around until he could see through the small rectangular window, too.

Four well-armed men were swaggering up Undoto's front path to his door.

Slavers. Had there been any question of their occupation, the cutlasses and bandoliers hung with knives—and in one case, a long-barreled pistol—that the four were sporting obliterated all doubt. Only outlaws of one stripe or another would walk about a settlement armed like that.

The man in the lead, a heavyset brute, from his skin tone and glimpsed features more English than not, raised a fist and thumped once on Undoto's door.

Seconds later, the door was opened by Undoto himself. Although he didn't smile, the priest welcomed the four men warmly, shaking hands and clapping them on the back as he ushered them into the house, then closed the door.

Miss Hopkins sat back.

Shifting on the seat, Robert looked at her. He and his men had seen the small black carriage arrive every evening and depart close to dawn over the past three nights, all without letting anyone out or taking anyone up. When they hadn't seen the carriage this evening, he'd come out to reconnoiter and check, and had spotted it drawn up in the alley.

Resisting temptation really wasn't his forte. He'd approached from the rear, confirmed there was someone—a female—inside...

Even then, some part of him had guessed.

Any surprise he'd felt at discovering that the occupant was the elusive Miss Hopkins had been submerged by a sense of inevitability.

Despite the dimness inside the carriage, he could see the grim determination in her face—in the set of her lips and her resolute chin.

In the way her gaze remained locked on Undoto's front door.

That she was Miss Hopkins...even in the carriage's dark interior, one glance at her hair was enough to detect the telltale brassy sheen. She was, however, rather older than he'd expected. Her oldest brother, David, was of an age with Royd, and Henry was near Robert's age. He'd assumed Miss Hopkins was the youngest of the brood, but from what he could see—and all he could sense of the considerable feminine strength occupying the seat opposite—she fell somewhere between Henry and William. As a lieutenant, William was most likely in his mid-twenties, so Miss Hopkins must be in her late twenties.

His eyes had adjusted; he could see reasonably well. Well enough to take in her full figure along with her rigidly upright posture, the competent and confident way she held the pistol in her lap, and the naturally commanding set of her head—all hints anyone with skill at reading others would interpret as suggesting an unbending will.

Just what he needed—a determined *and* strong-willed female complication.

His notion of turning on his diplomatic charm and persuading her to pack her bags and head home dispersed like mist before a gale.

As he watched, her eyes, still staring out of the window at

Undoto's house, slowly narrowed in thought. Her expression screamed that she was making plans…

The implications of all he'd learned coalesced in his mind. While he'd been hunting high and low, skulking about streets on Tower Hill, hiding in the shadows watching ladies arrive at their evening's events or lurking in alleys to watch them during the day, she'd been under his nose all along.

Sitting in this carriage, watching Undoto's house.

How much did she know?

How much had she guessed?

"They're slave traders," he murmured and was rewarded with her immediate attention and a thoroughly shocked look.

"What?" For a second, her consternation shone clearly, then it was wiped away, hidden beneath a nearly blank, slightly suspicious expression. "How do you know?" She looked back at Undoto's door. "Not all armed men are slave traders—they can't be. How can you be sure? How—"

She broke off; her knuckles showed white as she gripped the small pistol, then with quite awful deliberation, she dragged in a breath and refocused on him.

He could all but feel her regroup, feel her reharness the wits he'd scattered and redirect them at him.

"Sampson told me you'd been here, in the settlement, some weeks ago, asking questions about people who've gone missing. He said you'd returned to London." She tipped up her head, lips firm as she fixed her gaze squarely on his eyes. "Why have you returned? To follow the armed men? Is that who you think have taken those missing—including my brother?"

Robert regarded her evenly, then sat back and folded his arms across his chest. When she opened her mouth—no doubt to ask more questions—he silenced her with a raised finger. "The Captain Frobisher that Sampson mentioned being here earlier wasn't me. That was my brother Declan Frobisher. He was sent to gain insight into a spate of officers mysteriously going missing. As per his orders, when he encountered active opposition, he returned to London to report what he'd learned to that point."

Her gaze hadn't wavered. "And you're the one London has sent to follow the trail?"

He glanced over his shoulder, confirming that Undoto's door was still shut. He looked back at her. "Where are you staying?"

She'd followed his gaze to Undoto's door. She glanced at him and frowned. "I asked if you've been sent by the Admiralty or one of the offices in London…how does that connect to where I'm staying?"

"It's called reciprocation—tit for tat. I gave you a certain amount of information. Now it's your turn to answer some of my questions."

He saw her jaw firm, sensed her mutinous look. When she showed no sign of obliging, he stated, "Miss Hopkins, instead of being able to concentrate on the purpose for which I was sent here, I've been forced to spend the last three days trawling through this settlement hunting for *you*."

Her frown deepened. "Why?"

"Where. Are. You. Staying?" He'd reined in his temper, but it edged his tone.

She considered him for a long, rather fraught moment. "You truly do know my brothers?"

"Yes."

She met his gaze evenly, giving not an inch, but finally consented to open her lips and say, "I have a room at Mrs. Hoyt's Boarding House for Genteel Ladies. It's not far from the rectory."

He'd seen it. It just hadn't occurred to him that she—who he knew was well connected and not in straitened circumstances—would be staying there.

As if sensing his surprise, she tipped her chin upward. "I deliberately chose to stay there to ensure no one—no well-meaning friend of the family—would attempt to stop me doing what

I need to do to locate William—my younger brother, Lieutenant William Hopkins—and, if possible, rescue him."

Well, that answered his questions about her intentions. He frowned. "How did you know about your brother going missing?"

Briefly, she told him about the letter her parents had received.

He mentally cursed the Admiralty's clerks. The letter must have slipped past Melville's office. He understood all too well how distressed her parents must have been by the supposed news. And he could comprehend why she—a female of the type he was starting to realize she was—had set out to clear her brother's name. "Do your parents know you're here, searching for William?"

She countered with, "Am I to interpret your presence here as a sign that the authorities are finally taking action?"

He debated insisting she answer his question first, but… "Yes, and no. I'll explain in a moment, but first—"

"Oh, my God." Her expression blanked, then her eyes snapped to his face. "Slave traders. You said those men who went into Undoto's house are slave traders. So that's where Will's gone. *Slave traders* have taken him."

For an instant, he feared that his reading of her character had been in error and she was about to succumb to hysterics; like any man, he felt a panicky sense of incipient helplessness.

But then her jaw firmed and her eyes blazed as she shifted her gaze to Undoto's door. "*That's* why Will went to Undoto's services—for some reason, he was looking for the slave traders. And that's why they—the slave traders—only turn up on the evenings *after* Undoto holds a service."

He felt his brows rise. He and his men hadn't realized that.

Without him having to prompt, she went on, "I saw those men—the same four—call on Undoto four nights ago, on the evening following his previous service. The men stayed for nearly an hour, then left—less happy than when they'd arrived, but not angry, as far as I could tell. The men haven't been back for the past three nights—I've been watching every night. But Undoto held a service today, and tonight the men are back."

Her gaze swung his way and fixed on his face with an intensity he could feel. "What does that mean? That Undoto…what? Points the slave traders at people they're supposed to seize?"

Robert debated his response; on the basis of everything he knew, that seemed a sound supposition. "Very likely it's something along those lines."

A second of silence ensued, then he opened his mouth on his next question just as she did the same—but then her gaze whipped to the small window over his left shoulder. Unfolding his arms, he swung around on the seat and looked out.

Undoto's door had opened. The four slavers emerged and trudged straight down the steps. None of them looked happy.

The leader—Robert wondered if he was Kale—turned back and, in a belligerent tone, barked at Undoto, "He wants more men. Find us the right men. That's all you have to do."

Undoto stood framed in his doorway; he gave no reply. For once, his expression was impassive and sober, with not even a hint of a smile.

The leader turned and stalked after his men. Undoto watched him go, then stepped back and quietly shut his door.

Within a few strides, the slave traders passed out of their sight, moving swiftly up the street.

Robert turned back to Miss Hopkins—to discover the lady on her feet, using the end of her pistol's barrel to lift the trapdoor in the carriage's ceiling.

"Whenever you judge it's time, Dave." She whispered the strange order, then let the trapdoor fall.

Before she could resume her seat, the carriage rocked. She swayed, feet shifting as she fought for balance—

Robert seized her about her waist.

A frisson of sensation speared through his hands, up his arms, and across his shoulders, the effect more potent and powerful in the dark.

His hands locked about her, holding her, steadying her.

He heard her breath catch. Felt the lithe shift of her body beneath the fine layers separating his hands from her skin.

His palms, his fingers, burned.

His jaw tensing, he forced himself to ease his hold until he was barely touching her.

She hauled in a strangled breath, pulled out of his grasp, and sat down heavily. Through the darkness, she stared at him; her expression suggested she saw him as some strange species, one she hadn't encountered before.

He returned her regard. For several seconds, it was all he could do to haul back on the reins of impulses that hadn't slipped their leash in years.

In decades.

Why now?

Why with her?

He squelched the urge to shake his head as if he could shake the fact aside—slough reality away.

Then the carriage rocked again and started slowly rolling forward.

He glanced out of the window and realized the driver was turning the corner in the direction the slavers had gone. He looked at the redoubtable Miss Hopkins. "While I appreciate your intentions, you don't need to follow the slave traders."

The narrow-eyed look she bent on him suggested he save his breath, then she redirected her gaze through the window beside his head.

A familiar owl hoot floated through the open window; his men were already on the slavers' trail.

The carriage cleared the corner and continued rolling very slowly up the sloping street in the slavers' wake. Suppressing his natural inclination to reveal nothing of his mission—much less to her—he said, "My men are following the slavers on foot. They're experienced and know what they're doing. They'll follow the slavers all the way to their lair somewhere in the depths of the slums."

The information succeeded in capturing her attention. She considered him, then said, "I take it you intend to join your men."

He shook his head. "I know I can trust them to get the job done, and I can't blend into the local population as well as they can." Through the shadows, he held her gaze. "And neither can you. You'll be spotted the instant you walk toward any slum, no matter how carefully you skulk."

"You're sure the slavers will go to ground somewhere in the slums?"

"So we've been led to believe."

She was silent for a second; the carriage rolled ponderously on, but they were still some way from the crest.

He could hear hoots and soft birdcalls—like gulls softly cawing. His men had spread out and were pacing the slavers to either side, in alleys and lanes running parallel to the street.

Miss Hopkins opened her lips. "What—"

"Miss!" The agitated whisper floated down through the trapdoor. "That big bruiser we're following—he's noticed the carriage. He's stopped, and he's looking back at us."

Before Robert could react, the thorn in his side sprang up and whispered in reply, "Pull into the curb. Now. And just wait."

She dropped back to the seat.

The carriage slowed and angled toward the roughly scored curb.

Robert twisted about and peered through the small window. The upward angle gave him a good view along the dusty street. Three of the slavers were continuing on, apparently oblivious, but the leader—the big bruiser—had turned around and, with one hand on the hilt of his cutlass, was standing, staring down at the carriage.

The carriage rocked to a halt. The muffled clop of the horse's hooves faded.

The man shifted his considerable weight, then he started toward the carriage.

"Miss?"

"Keep your head down," Miss Hopkins quietly directed. "Stay as you are."

Robert wouldn't have said any different; now was not the time to panic.

But the big slaver didn't slow; his suspicions had clearly been aroused, and he wasn't going to go on until he'd reassured himself over who was in the carriage.

And what they were doing.

Robert watched the slaver pace steadily nearer, the man's expression growing increasingly intent.

"He's almost here!"

Robert didn't need the anguished, barely audible warning to realize Miss Hopkins's time had run out. Disaster loomed—six-plus feet and more than three hundred pounds of it.

He had to act.

Swearing beneath his breath, he swung to face her. Time seemed to slow; through the dimness, he met her wide, faintly horrified gaze.

He reached for her. "This is the only way. Don't scream."

It was all the warning he gave her—all he had time for. He seized the feisty Miss Hopkins about her waist, lifted her and deposited her in his lap, hauled her to him, and slammed his lips over hers.

Even as sensation flooded his brain, he reminded himself this had to look convincing.

He wrapped his arms about her, crushed her to him, and devoted himself to kissing her as if ravishment was his immediate goal.

Seven

Sensation crashed through Aileen with a force that left her reeling.

That left her adrift on a sea of surging reactions, of impulses and urges and the giddy sense of having stepped off the edge of the known world.

Her world, at least.

Her awareness expanded, then fractured.

Heat. Hardness.

Lips that demanded.

Limbs of steel surrounding her, that held her so tightly she had no hope of breaking free.

A hard body that made her own stir, that made her pulse race. Thighs like oak beneath hers, and that fabulous chest like a warm wall against which she could lean.

A startling new reality broke over her; she tried to take hold, to grip and steady herself.

Curling her fingers in the fine fabric of his shirt, she clutched and hung on. Tried to make her wits stop whirling, her senses stop waltzing.

What the devil is he doing?

Even as the thought formed, she heard again his words. *No other way.*

He was right—and she should be grateful he'd thought quickly enough…

His lips moved on hers, and her thoughts fragmented, flitting off like butterflies in the sun.

She couldn't call them back, not while his lips supped at hers, coaxed and tempted. Barely aware of what she was doing—driven by an urge too powerful to resist—she straightened her curled fingers and slid her palms up, up the long, hard planes of his amazing chest to his shoulders, solid with muscle and just the right anchor to cling to; she gripped.

And kissed him back.

She needed to play her part in this staged scene. The armed man would look in, and see and think...

As if driven—nay, *goaded*—by her response, Frobisher angled his head and kissed her more forcefully, with a potent demand she felt race down every nerve.

On a smothered gasp—she wasn't sure when last she'd breathed—she parted her lips in invitation, eager, as she'd never been before, for more. More of the heat. More of this headiness.

More of him.

He surged into her mouth and ruthlessly claimed.

And something inside her rose to meet him.

No wilting flower, she. She wanted to experience, wanted to feel—wanted to seize and savor, too.

So she met him and matched him, kiss for kiss, demand for demand—and found herself utterly enthralled.

Never before had she been so captured by a kiss. Truth be told, she'd never been kissed like this before—as if she were a delicious fruit to be devoured, as if her lips and mouth were a succulent delight to be savored.

Some part of her mind understood his motives; to pull off this deception, they had to make the armed thug—the *slaver*—believe that this was why they were there, wildly and obliviously consorting in the carriage on the darkened street. That their hunger for each other was enough to have driven them to such flagrant madness.

Their lips parted for a heated breath. For just a split second, from beneath heavy lids their eyes met, and in that instant, she realized she wasn't calling on any large degree of histrionic ability—and neither was he.

This was all too...*real.*

Then they plunged back into the fiery exchange, melding their lips, their mouths, driven by an unprecedented madness—by a desire too potent to deny.

Passion beyond anything she'd ever imagined all but erupted between them.

She caught and framed his jaw and recklessly returned the fire and molten heat he'd sent streaming down her veins.

From a great distance, she heard a throaty chuckle.

Then a very deep male voice growled, "Wondered what you and your fare was up to, mate."

"Pretty obvious, I'd a thought," Dave mumbled back.

"That it is, and clearly not something I need to worry about. Leastways, not unless I was her husband."

With a distinctly male guffaw, the thug walked off.

Aileen strained her ears, trying to refocus enough of her senses away from the demands of the utterly engrossing kiss to track the man's retreat.

Frobisher's hand firmed about the back of her head, and he relentlessly drew her and her senses back, down, into the still-swirling cauldron of their exchange.

She knew she could stop kissing him now, but she couldn't seem to summon the strength, the will, to pull back, to turn away from the enthralling embrace.

Surely she could rely on *him* to end the exchange once they were safe? She'd draw back when he did—and he wasn't by any means drawing back yet...

"He's gorn, miss. Where'd you want me to take you to now?"

The words rudely jerked her back to the here and now. To full consciousness of what she'd been doing, and with whom.

Where had her wits gone begging?

It was suddenly easy to end the kiss and pull back—assisted by Frobisher having returned to earth courtesy of Dave, too.

They sat wrapped in the warm dark of the carriage; from a distance of mere inches, their gazes met.

And held.

She could feel the rigid rod of his erection against her hip. She was twenty-seven; she knew what that particular circumstance meant.

But then his features hardened. His arms fell from around her; he gripped her waist and lifted her off his lap and set her back on her seat with an alacrity that made her blink.

And question her conclusion. Perhaps he was hiding something else in there…*no! Don't think of that.*

Composing herself—regaining her usual firm mental footing—was going to be difficult enough as it was.

Robert watched the delectable Miss Hopkins blink distractedly several times—as if trying to bring the world into focus. He knew precisely how she felt. While one part of him was pleased to note the first sign of anything like weakness in her—and was tempted to preen—his own inner turmoil wiped out any inclination to smugness.

What the hell just happened?

He knew what it was supposed to have been—hell, he'd instituted it. But somehow the simple act of pretense had metamorphosed into something quite different.

Into something else.

He could barely catch his breath. Him!

And where the devil did she learn to kiss like that?

He mentally shook aside the question; it was something he didn't need to know.

This was his chance to seize the initiative, to claim and keep the upper hand.

Ruthlessly blocking the lingering sensations of having her—all warm feminine curves and sleek limbs—in his arms, he refocused on her—

Just as she leaned forward to peer through the window beside his head.

Her features eased. "They've gone." Immediately, her gaze flicked to his face. "Are your men following them?"

He nodded. He listened, then said, "I can't hear their signals, but they'll already be on the other side of the crest, so that's no surprise."

She sat back and studied him. He got the impression that she'd recovered from the kiss—from its unexpected, unprecedented intensity. Given he was still inwardly scrambling to do the same, he wasn't sure he approved.

Her eyes narrowed on his face. "I know why *I* was following those men—even if I didn't know they were slave traders. But why were you?"

"For much the same reason." He hesitated, but she already knew enough to guess the rest, and probably would. "As you've discovered, this particular band of slave traders is working in conjunction with Undoto, and the people they've been seizing have been Europeans, mostly English—men, young women, and children."

"Good Lord."

"Indeed. That's not the normal pattern of slavery in these parts—and yes, it's been outlawed, yet it does still go on. However, there are several oddities about this particular outbreak, not least that it's been occurring *inside* the settlement under the very noses of the local authorities, apparently without hindrance. But this enterprise is also notable in that they've chosen to kidnap several serving officers—your brother William among them."

"From what I've gathered, Will was following the trail of a Captain Dixon, an army man from the fort."

Robert nodded. "Dixon disappeared first. Hopkins—your brother—was sent to see what he could learn about Dixon's disappearance, and he, too, vanished. Next came a Lieutenant Fanshawe, who was sent to find William, and he also disappeared. There was one other, too, but after that, London called my brother in, and subsequently, I've been sent to pursue the trail."

"What—"

"Are we going anywhere, lady and gent?"

They both looked up at the coachman's faintly exasperated question.

Seize the initiative. Quickly, Robert ordered, "Back to Miss Hopkins's lodgings."

Silence, then the coachman carefully queried, "Miss?"

Robert shackled his annoyance and calmly met the delectable Miss Hopkins's glare. Finally, she looked up and called, "Thank you, Dave. Go by the same route we've taken previously."

"Aye, miss."

Robert heard harness jingle, then the carriage rocked into motion. It picked up speed as it continued up the slope, then veered right into a street that led across the side of Tower Hill toward the more fashionable quarter.

Once they were bowling along, before she could return to her attack, he caught her eye and said, "As I mentioned, I'm acquainted with your older brothers. Given that connection, I must in all conscience insist that you leave the pursuit of the slave traders and the subsequent rescue of those taken—including your brother—to me and my crew, and those who will be sent subsequently."

Her eyes narrowed on his face; he was growing accustomed to the sensation, to being the absolute focus of her keenly attentive gaze. "Why *subsequently*? Why wouldn't you see this…this mission through to its end and rescue those taken by the slavers yourself? Well, you and your men."

Opportunity offered, and he reached for it. "That is one of the difficulties with this particular mission." He paused, realizing he stood on the brink of revealing another secret, yet the potential reward outweighed the risk; he needed to get her to leave the settlement. "There are those in the settlement whom we have yet to unmask who are working with the slavers. We cannot and, indeed, must not risk alerting any of those people, whoever they are, or to escape eventual exposure and justice—to cover their tracks—they might well order the massacre of all those who've been taken. At this juncture, we have no reason to imagine that those taken are already dead. In fact, we believe they're alive and have been specifically taken for some reason—for something they know or something they can do. So at no point must we do anything to jeopardize the safety of those missing."

He paused to study her face; she was listening intently and all but immediately waved at him to continue. He hid his reaction to her imperious, if wordless, command and went on, "Because of that restriction, each…operative sent to look into this business can only remain here long enough to further the investigation to the next stage. Consider—your brother William was the first to be sent in. He was followed by Fanshawe, who was in turn followed by a highly skilled operative named Hillsythe. Your brother, Fanshawe, and even Hillsythe, experienced though he was, each pushed one step too far—and were seized and taken, leaving London no wiser as to what was happening here."

Her frown was definite, her concentration complete, and she gave no sign of wishing to interrupt. He hesitated, considering the wisdom of further revelations, but eventually continued, "My brother came to the settlement openly—he and his wife posed as merely calling in while on their honeymoon cruise to Cape Town. They identified attendance at Undoto's services as a common key in all the disappearances, and also learned of the slavers' association with Undoto himself. But then my sister-in-law was drugged and handed to the slavers—because she asked questions of the wrong person. My brother rescued his wife, but of course, they then had to leave to maintain the covert nature of the investigation and to take word back to London.

"When I arrived here, I learned that the local priestess who had connected the slavers directly with Undoto had been brutally murdered shortly after my brother and his wife had spoken with her, so I had no direct avenue to locate the slavers other than by watching Undoto."

"The priestess was murdered?"

"Yes. This priestess lived among her people, yet the slavers were able to walk into her house and bludgeon her to death." He'd deliberately led her to that fact—the one he felt most clearly illustrated the danger involved in pursuing the slave traders. "As I said earlier, this is not a mission that's safe for someone like you—someone without the requisite training and support—to actively pursue." He had far too much experience with women to say she couldn't pursue it because she was female. "I assure you that you may, with full confidence, leave your brother's safety in my hands and in the hands of those who will follow. London is now fully aware of the delicacy and urgency of the situation here, and the authorities there are fully committed to ending this illegal endeavor and rescuing those taken and seeing them safely home."

The carriage started to slow; they rolled past the church, then Dave drew his horse to a halt.

Robert waited, breath bated, for the thorn in his side to pluck herself out and agree to return to safety on the next vessel bound for England.

She continued to study him, then quietly said, "So this mission is being run in stages, as it were—each with some definable goal?"

He didn't respond.

Her gaze grew more intent. "What's your stage—your goal?"

He inwardly swore. Her brothers were well known for their dogged stubbornness; clearly, that was a familial trait.

She wasn't his responsibility. She was old enough to be her own mistress and clearly was determined to be so; he didn't need to feel that it was incumbent on him to keep her safe at all costs.

He told himself that. Several times, in various ways, increasingly explicitly.

He knew himself well enough to know it hadn't worked.

For whatever godforsaken reason, responsibility for Miss Hopkins and her safety, at least while here, now rested squarely on his shoulders.

He sighed and tipped his head back against the squab.

Her eyes had narrowed on his face; he could tell without looking.

"Are you going to tell me? Or should I start to follow you, or ask at the governor's office for information—"

He swore virulently and didn't care if she heard; she had brothers—he doubted she'd be shocked.

Abruptly, he raised his head and met her gaze.

He wasn't sure what to say—which tack to take, which was the wiser course to pursue. He was an experienced negotiator, an expert persuader; he could usually talk anyone into trusting him with almost anything, but with her…he felt stumped.

He was also well aware that while it might be unwise to tell her too much, telling her too little might potentially be worse.

Telling her anything went entirely against his grain. He compressed his lips against the impulse, but he couldn't not say, "Promise me one thing—that you will not under any circumstances speak to anyone in authority here. Not at the governor's office, not at the fort, not at the Office of the Naval Attaché."

"Why?"

"Because at least some of those involved are connected with those offices." He paused, then added, "The governor's wife was the one who drugged my sister-in-law. After she was rescued and my brother and she sailed for London, the governor's wife took her leave. All those here believe she left to visit family, so please, under no circumstances reveal you know otherwise."

He'd finally managed to stun her.

"The governor's wife? Lady Holbrook?"

He nodded.

Her stunment didn't last long. "What evidence do you have that the Office of the Naval Attaché is involved?"

This was why he hadn't wanted to tell her even that much. "We have evidence to suggest the army as well as the governor's office have been suborned to some extent. We don't as yet have any direct evidence of naval involvement, but we have to assume it exists—as it well might. In this sort of case, we have to assume we can't trust anyone until it's proven that we can."

She humphed; to his ears, it sounded irritatingly dismissive. Then she refocused on him. "You haven't yet told me what your goal in the ongoing investigation is."

He hadn't. He didn't want to.

He still didn't know what he was going to do with her.

"Are you two ever going to get out?" Dave's voice drifted down through the trapdoor. "If we're not headed anywhere else, I wouldn't mind finding me bed tonight."

Saved by the coachman. Again.

Robert shifted forward and reached for the carriage door—the one opposite the pavement, away from her lodgings. No need for anyone happening to glance out to see him leaving her carriage. The movement brought him closer to the irritating female who, her gaze still locked on his face, seemed intent on driving him to his wits' end.

Jaw clenched, he nodded curtly. "I'll call on you tomorrow—at eleven—and we can continue this discussion."

With that, he opened the door and stepped out into the street; with exaggerated care, he shut the door, then stalked into the night.

Aileen watched him go. For just those seconds, she allowed her senses the luxury of drinking in the sight of all that sauntering masculinity; he had a grace of movement she found unutterably compelling.

All too soon, he disappeared into the black shadows, leaving her wondering if him making an appointment for tomorrow morning signaled a capitulation—or whether he was planning something else.

Her bet was on "something else."

Drawing in a bolstering breath, she got down from the carriage, bade Dave a good night—then, on impulse, told him to call for her tomorrow morning. "At ten. Sharp."

"Aye, miss." Dave touched his cap. "I'll see you then."

Aileen smiled to herself as she turned and walked smartly through the gate and up the path to Mrs. Hoyt's front door.

★ ★ ★

After a refreshing night's sleep, Aileen awoke to the conviction that Captain Robert Frobisher was the sort of gentleman who would do all he could to curtail her endeavors.

He might be handsome; he might be compelling.

He might be an excellent kisser.

But he was also a man, more, one of a sort she knew all too well.

With a dismissive humph, she threw back the covers, rose, washed, and donned one of her skirt-and-jacket ensembles in a very pale shade of green. A crisp white blouse completed the outfit. After winding her locks into plaits she then fashioned into a coronet about her head, she felt ready to face her day.

She went down to take breakfast in the small dining parlor to the rear of the house. Eschewing the hearty porridge, she opted for fruit and cheese to accompany her tea and toast. Her excursion last night had left her distinctly peckish.

After completing her repast, she exchanged greetings with Mrs. Hoyt, then returned upstairs.

As she climbed the stairs, she considered what next she might do to track Will. If Frobisher was correct and Will had been taken by those slavers, then perhaps she should see if she could identify in which direction the slavers went when they took people out of the settlement.

She didn't immediately know how she might accomplish that, but she could spend the morning in the gardens working out her approach.

After checking her hair, she settled her straw bonnet over her coronet and pinned it in place, then picked up her reticule.

The sounds of a carriage drawing up on the street had her glancing out of her window just in time to see Dave draw his horse to a halt before the gate.

The gate Frobisher was opening.

She watched him step through the gate, then stride up the path.

After their encounter in the dark last night…

Sternly, she quelled an appreciative shiver. Sadly, there was no denying he looked even more impressive by day. The width of his shoulders, the way he walked, plus the air of command he projected all combined to make a significant impact on any woman with eyes.

Indeed, he was a great deal too sure of himself.

She scowled and flicked a glance at the small clock on the mantelpiece. Barely ten o'clock.

Not eleven as he'd said.

She gritted her teeth, then swung around and went quickly to the door. If she hurried, she might be able to slip out of the back door unobserved.

About to quit the room, she realized she'd forgotten her gloves.

With a muttered curse, she returned to her dressing table, swept up the offending articles, then quickly and silently left the room.

Pausing at the head of the stairs, she listened and heard Frobisher's deep voice asking for her. Mrs. Hoyt all but fell over her toes showing him into the parlor and garrulously assuring him that—indeed!—Miss Hopkins had yet to leave the house, and that she was sure Miss Hopkins would be very pleased to meet with him.

Aileen grimaced. In the circumstances, trying to avoid Frobisher might land her in even more difficulties. Such as explaining to Mrs. Hoyt why she didn't want to meet with him—a man Mrs. Hoyt's well-tuned antennae had already identified as a distinctly eligible gentleman.

And did she really want to give Frobisher the impression she was actively avoiding him?

On several counts, the answer was no.

A Hopkins did not run from an obstacle, no matter how irritating.

More, a wise lady did not run from a man of Frobisher's ilk, especially not after an impromptu kiss of the type they'd shared the previous night. That would be akin to waving a red flag before a bull—or running from a predator naturally inclined to give chase.

She could see no benefit in having Frobisher dogging her every step, trying to catch her.

The notion of what he might do if he succeeded…

As she heard Mrs. Hoyt back out of the parlor and the door click shut, then her landlady's rushing footsteps coming up the first flight, Aileen reached the conclusion that meeting with Frobisher and deflecting whatever barrage he sent her way was the safer, more certain, more sane and acceptable course.

She drew in a fortifying breath, then looked down and pulled on her gloves.

"There you are, Miss Hopkins!" Mrs. Hoyt, rosy cheeked and beaming, halted on the landing. "I was just coming to let you know you have a caller. A *gentleman* caller—a Captain Frobisher." Mrs. Hoyt's eyes grew wide. She lowered her voice. "*Ever so* handsome, he is."

Aileen summoned a smile. "Thank you. I was just on my way down."

Mrs. Hoyt turned and preceded her down the stairs. "I'll just be in the kitchen should you need anything, Miss Hopkins." Stepping off the stairs, Mrs. Hoyt abruptly halted and shot a questioning look Aileen's way. "That is"—she lowered her voice to the merest whisper—"unless you feel the need for a chaperon? I would be happy to oblige, if you wish."

Aileen's smile grew more genuine. "Thank you, but that won't be necessary. Captain Frobisher is a friend of my family."

"Ah. I see." Mrs. Hoyt nodded. "I'll take myself off, then. Just ring if you wish for any refreshments."

Aileen watched Mrs. Hoyt bustle into the nether regions, then she turned to face the parlor door.

After a second's hesitation, she drew herself up, reached for the doorknob, sent the door swinging wide, and with her head high—in what her mother would have termed her galleon mode—she swept into the parlor.

With a practiced movement, she swung around and shut the door, then, her head rising again to a distinctly challenging angle, she continued toward Frobisher. "Good morning, Mr. Frobisher. I trust I see you well?"

He had been standing before the fireplace examining an old map mounted above it; he'd turned and watched her entrance. As she approached, he shifted to face her and gravely inclined his head. "Miss Hopkins."

For most of their previous exchanges, he'd been sitting. She hadn't truly appreciated just how tall, how commanding, his physical presence was. Her brothers were tall; she was used to tall men. She just wasn't used to men like Frobisher, who seemed to possess some uncanny knack of fixing her senses and abrading her nerves.

That that abrasion was not unpleasurable only unsettled her all the more.

His hair was dark brown, a touch lighter than sable, and fell in wavy locks about his head. He was clean shaven, the sharply delineated angles of his cheekbones and squared chin displayed with a certain arrogant air, a clear signal to all with eyes that he was not a man to be trifled with.

He was dressed more conservatively than he had been last

night, with a pale lightweight coat over a conventional shirt, and with a brown silk cravat knotted about his neck.

He still looked dangerous.

To her leaping senses, he *felt* dangerous.

After last night, something primitive in her saw him as eminently desirable…

She slammed a mental door on her intrigued impetuosity.

She had to tilt her head still higher to keep her eyes locked with his. She halted with a safe six feet between them and opened her lips to tartly point out that he'd called an hour early.

He took the wind from her sails with the words "My men found the slavers' lair."

She stared at him. That was quite the last thing she'd expected him to say. Not that she didn't have confidence in his men's abilities. She simply hadn't expected him to admit as much to her, to include her…

He was watching her rather closely.

Last night, she hadn't been able to make out the color of his eyes. They were a strong, solid mid blue—rather like the man himself in their unwavering focus.

If she read him correctly, his utterance was an olive branch of sorts.

She could guess what he hoped to gain in return.

As to that, she would see, but in the meantime… "Where is this lair?" She waved him to one of the well-worn armchairs facing the sofa and moved to claim the sofa herself. After gathering her skirts, she sat and looked up at him. "Is it in the slum, as you thought? The one at the end of Undoto's street?"

With apparently unconscious grace, he sank into the armchair and nodded. "Right in the middle of a labyrinth of tiny lanes and alleys. Unless you know exactly where it is—or are following someone who does—it would be impossible to locate."

Robert captured her gaze—her eyes were a bright hazel, vibrant and alive—and calmly continued, "My men have found a hide of sorts from which to keep watch. Not so close as the house directly opposite, but in the house behind that. That house possesses a ramshackle tower, and we've rented the room at the top. It affords us an unrestricted view of the slavers' front door while being sufficiently distant that our observation won't alert them, and we're also free to come and go without risking attracting their notice."

She didn't bother pretending disinterest; she leaned forward and eagerly asked, "Are there any captives there at present? Have your men seen enough to determine that?"

"The slavers don't appear to be holding anyone in their lair at this time." He paused, then decided he may as well be hung for a wolf as a lamb. "My men have already been asking around—not directly, of course. But via the women the slavers rely on for cleaning and cooking, my men have established that at this moment, there are no extra captive mouths to be fed."

She frowned.

Before she could make a bid to take charge of the conversation, he rolled on, "Last night, you asked what my stage—my mission's goal—was." Her gaze lifted to his face; its intensity assured him that his new tack of including her was precisely the right one to take. Imperturbably, he continued, "My goal is not to find the slavers' lair. That's merely a step along the way toward fulfilling the mission I was asked to undertake—ascertaining the location of the slavers' camp."

"Their camp? In the jungle?"

He nodded. "From what we've determined, the modus operandi of this group is to seize people in the settlement and take them to the lair, either to gather them together or simply to report to their base. Regardless, they wait for night before they move their captives out through the slums and into the jungle. To an established camp. From what we've learned, there always is such a camp—the slavers don't deliver their captives directly from the settlement, or from wherever else they seize them, to the captives' eventual destination, but always congregate, slavers and captives, at their camp. Subsequently, they move their captives on in larger groups to whatever enterprise—whatever owner—the captives are destined for."

Her frown had turned puzzled. "Why bother with a lair here as well as a camp in the jungle?"

"My understanding is that while the locals—the inhabitants of the slums and also the local tribesmen living about the settlement—are wary of crossing the slavers and generally avoid doing so, they don't approve of the slavers' activities. Especially in this case, with the slavers taking Europeans from within the settlement. The locals fear the slavers, but they also fear the reactions of the British authorities if and when the slavers' actions come to light. The locals fear that any repercussions will impact on them, too." He lightly grimaced. "That's probably not an unreasonable fear. Consequently, the slavers keep to themselves in the slums and only move through the settlement at night—when the authorities are essentially asleep—and in turn, the locals tolerate them, or at least don't directly oppose them."

Her frown had deepened; he was visited by a ridiculous urge to reach out and, with his thumb, smooth it away.

Her next words refocused him on his current ploy.

"You've mentioned several times that numerous people—all European—have gone missing from the settlement, not just the officers whose disappearance triggered the investigation." Her eyes refocused on his. "How many people have vanished?"

He grimaced and admitted, "We don't know the full extent of it—not yet. We know of the four officers, but it's certain there will be more men who've gone missing and who no one's reported, and we believe that at least four young women and seventeen children of various ages have also been taken."

"Good *Lord*!" She sat back and regarded him in horrified astonishment. "How on earth could that happen?"

In a few succinct phrases, he explained. He concluded with,

"So our guess is that Lady Holbrook was instrumental—possibly via Undoto—in pointing the slavers at people she knew could be taken without causing sufficient alarm for the authorities to be alerted. She may also have played a key role in convincing her husband that there was no crime, as such, involved and therefore no need to take any action."

After a moment, his thorn shook her head. "This was bad enough when I thought it was only Will who had fallen foul of someone." She studied his face, his eyes, then her own narrowed fractionally. "Why are you telling me this?"

Because he'd realized that the only viable way to keep her safe was to keep her close. Then, when he—or more likely his men if he was dancing guard on her—located the slavers' camp, and they were ready to leave the settlement, he had every intention of hauling her back to London with him.

He wasn't past kidnapping her, not in such a case.

And it might well come to that, Hopkins that she was and with her brother among the missing.

But of that decision, he said nothing; he wasn't about to give her any advance notice. She was going to be difficult enough to manage as it was.

Quite a challenge, in fact.

In the small hours of the morning, he'd decided to view her as that—a challenge to his skills in manipulation and maneuvering. A touch of spice added to a mission that was otherwise shaping up to be rather boringly straightforward.

He looked into her eyes and confirmed her understanding, her reading of him. He had wondered if she would have the wit to realize his present behavior didn't fit his character. The incipient suspicion that had run beneath her simple question suggested she was well aware of the contradiction. Luckily, he had a distraction up his sleeve.

Still holding her gaze, he baldly stated, "Because I need your help."

She blinked. Twice. Then, still faintly suspicious, she asked, "How so?"

He crossed one knee over the other, set his laced fingers on his uppermost thigh, and did his best to appear relaxed but grave, and also faintly—but not too overtly—supplicatory. "As I've learned more about the situation here, it's become increasingly apparent that even with my men as support, there are areas of...expertise that I and my crew lack. For instance, having the ability to further investigate the kidnapping of the children. We know that the children's disappearances don't connect with Undoto's church, so how and from where are the children being preyed upon? Are they even being taken for the same reason—the same ultimate destination?" He looked directly at her. "If I or my men start asking around, we're unlikely to get far—not on our own."

He'd banked on the children being an angle that would appeal to her; from the expression on her face and the militant light that sparked in her eyes, he'd guessed correctly. Smoothly, he continued, "My men and I expect to have to watch and wait for several days at least, until the slavers leave their lair and return to their camp. We'll follow when they do, and then we'll have the information we were sent for. With that in hand, we're required to return to London and report. All well and good, but meanwhile, I'm anticipating several days of inaction, and rather than waste them, I would like to use the time to get some idea of how the slavers are stealing away children—how they have in the past, and if they still are. That's something extra to add to our knowledge of what's going on here that I would like to take back to place before those in London."

Her nod was decisive and, as he'd hoped, supportive. "I applaud such a stance. Seizing children?" Where another lady might have shuddered, she looked pugnaciously belligerent. "That cannot be allowed to continue."

"In addition"—he tracked the emotions flitting over her face—"I have a letter I would like to see on its way via the general post to the Admiralty." With his customary nonchalance, he drew the letter from his pocket, then met her gaze. "To the First Lord." He held the missive up. "I've written of what I've learned regarding Holbrook—who appears to be innocent and oblivious of his wife's involvement. Melville and those assisting him need to know that, so that they know they can and should leave Holbrook in place and uninformed."

He glanced at the letter. "I've also included various additions to what my brother reported—small matters in themselves, but they add to the wider picture and might prove crucial to those who come later." He returned his gaze to her face and met her eyes. "I have to allow for the possibility that, for one reason or another, I and my crew will be taken by the slavers, too. It's unlikely, but not impossible, and it's therefore important that this letter gets away."

A faint frown played about her eyes. "Why can't you just post it?"

He told her.

"Ah. I see." Her eyes were riveted on the letter.

"So I wondered if you would be willing to go with me to the docks and see this letter on its way."

Her brows rose as her gaze shifted to meet his. "Of course."

Her haughty agreement was music to his manipulative soul.

Aileen studied the faint smile that seemed to lurk about his eyes and at the corners of his well-shaped lips. She tried not to notice those lips themselves or, indeed, to allow herself to fall into the depths of his eyes. For some idiotic reason, she found them quite mesmerizing, but she knew better than to let him guess that.

However, she had a sneaking suspicion that she was being managed. Very artfully managed, but managed nevertheless. As someone who frequently managed others, she knew the signs—no man of his ilk was that guileless.

Still, as long as he continued to answer her questions and tell her all she wanted to know…

If it became necessary, she could always tip the scales and reverse the condition.

She blinked, refocused on his eyes—on the far-too-perceptive blue of them—then, deliberately imperious, she held out a hand, palm up. "If you wish me to assist you, you can trust me with that."

His eyes widened fractionally, but he smoothly sat up, reached out, and placed the missive in her outstretched hand.

She grasped the letter and nodded. "And you can also promise me that you will inform me of what you and your men learn as to the location of the slavers' camp."

He hesitated at that, but after a second of regarding her with an expression she couldn't quite fathom, he inclined his head. "You have my word I will share with you whatever we learn."

She took a second to replay his words, then permitted herself a small smile. She looked at the letter in her hand. "Right, then." She rose. "Let's be off to the post office."

He'd risen as she did. He smiled and fell in by her side as she made for the door.

He reached out and opened it. She sailed through, paused for him to join her, then walked out of the house with him by her side.

She was, she decided, as she allowed him to hand her up into the carriage, quite enjoying this.

Why not?

Playing to his expectations caused her no harm, and at least he'd come to his senses sufficiently to see the value in sharing what he knew and including her in his plans.

What his true motives were she didn't yet know, but she would learn of them eventually, of that she had no doubt.

He sat on the seat opposite. He'd given Dave directions to drive to Water Street and halt at a certain spot for them to walk down to the post office on the quay. Having seen him walk out with her, Dave had accepted his directions with a grunt. The instant Frobisher shut the door, the carriage jerked into motion.

As the carriage rattled down the hill, Aileen struggled to keep her gaze trained forward and to the side, denying the nearly overwhelming urge to study Frobisher. He, too, did the polite thing and didn't stare at her; she glanced at him once and found him looking out of the window.

Distractingly compelling he might be, but she'd already seen enough to judge him effective—the sort of man who could and would get things done. In his own way perhaps, but done nonetheless.

If she had to work alongside someone to learn what had happened to Will—to lay the groundwork for his rescue—then she would far rather it be with a man like Frobisher.

She might not entirely trust him, but he was a sort of man she understood—the sort of man she had an affinity with, a man like her brothers. He would respond to much the same goads, would react in what to her were predictable ways.

Until she had reason to decide otherwise, her best way forward was to play by his rules. He'd been sent by the paramount authority to search for information to pave the way for all those taken, including Will, to be rescued. That was her ultimate goal as well. Working with Frobisher rather than against or despite him made singular sense.

And she had to admit that the notion of children—and young women, too—being seized by the slavers to serve some blackguard's nefarious ends had fired her ire.

She'd lived her entire life in safety, in the sure knowledge of being surrounded by those who cared.

What it would be like to live without that net of unstated security she couldn't imagine, but she knew many young women—and children—did.

In the wider scheme of things—in the larger cosmos—surely she owed those who hadn't had her privileged life something?

She could give them her championship, if nothing else.

She could work beside Frobisher and see what she could do, even while she assisted him as required and supported him in furthering Will's cause.

There was, indeed, a lot to recommend Frobisher's way forward—regardless of whatever his true motives were.

If she'd learned anything in a life filled with loving parents and three managing brothers, it was that in achieving one's goals, one took whatever path offered.

She glanced again at Frobisher; he now seemed sunk in thought.

She shifted her gaze away and set her mind to the challenge of how to learn more about the missing children.

As the carriage turned into Water Street, she flicked a glance at Frobisher. "Mrs. Hardwicke is the minister's wife." When he met her gaze, she continued, "She might well have information about the missing children, especially as you said that they, too, are European, by which I assume you mean primarily English."

He nodded, then said, "Mrs. Hardwicke was the source of our information on the seventeen children that have gone missing."

"Indeed?" She smiled intently. "In that case, she is undoubtedly the best person for us to question."

He shifted. "I already have a list of the names and ages of those taken that she provided to my brother."

Aileen inclined her head. "That's a start, but there are several other facts to which Mrs. Hardwicke is very likely privy, and those might give us a more definite idea as to how the children were taken, and specifically from where."

The carriage was slowing; the intersection they wanted was coming up on the right.

Across the carriage, she met Frobisher's blue eyes. "I suggest, sir, that I should post your letter, and then, as it is still midmorning, we should adjourn to the rectory and see what more we can learn."

He held her gaze; she sensed he wasn't accustomed to following someone else's directives. But then the carriage rocked to a halt—and he bowed his head in agreement. He stepped down and gave her his hand.

As she descended to the pavement, she fought to suppress a no doubt unwise, stupidly triumphant grin.

Eight

From the shadows of the alley that ran alongside the post office, Robert watched Miss Hopkins—how was it he didn't yet know her first name?—march along the quay and sweep in through the door, exchanging a polite nod with a gentleman who promptly held the door for her and raised his hat.

Robert inwardly humphed. The woman moved with the aplomb of a force of nature, the effect augmented by those snapping hazel eyes and the crowning glory of her brilliantly glossy hair. Her bonnet hid most of her distinctive locks, but tendrils hung in ringlets on either side of her face and about her nape. Those tendrils tended to bob and tremble in a thoroughly distracting way.

He found it disturbing that he even noticed such things, but with her...he couldn't seem to rein his senses in.

The urge to step out of concealment and sidle up to the window and check that she'd met with no difficulty bloomed. He clenched his jaw against the impulse; there was no reason to imagine anyone would think her sending a letter to the Admiralty was odd—and if anyone was insane enough to question her, she was more than capable of putting them in their place.

Even if someone noticed the plainly male script of the address, he felt confident she'd concoct some glib story and deliver it with a haughty air.

She had a very good line in haughty airs.

He slouched against the building's siding and kept his head down. An uneventful minute ticked past. The impulse to just take one quick look through the window pricked at him. But he really couldn't afford to be recognized—and stepping free of the shadows onto the open quay in the middle of the morning would definitely risk that. If just one person recognized him, the news that another Frobisher had appeared in the settlement would spread, and speculation would swell—and the villains might take fright.

He shifted, restless—then he hit on the one thought that effectively doused the urge to peek through the window and check on his new co-conspirator.

What if she spotted him?

He was still debating the likely outcome when she sailed out of the post office, came marching along the quay, then turned down the alley and swept past him and on.

As he'd directed, she didn't spare a glance for him; as she walked on, he fell in behind her. Only after she'd rounded the first corner did he lengthen his stride and catch up to her.

He glanced at her face. Her expression was...just a touch triumphant.

Something inside him eased, relaxed. "No difficulty?"

"None." After a moment, she glanced at him and met his eyes. "I told you everything would go smoothly." She looked ahead and tugged up her gloves. "Now let's get to the carriage and drive to the rectory."

His lips twitched; the idea of what his crew—let alone his brothers—would think at seeing him following her directions...

He sobered as he realized he wasn't sure if they would laugh—or feel sorry for him.

How the mighty had fallen and all that.

But he was only acceding to her command to placate her. And while her direction matched his own. If she diverted from his predetermined course, then he would seize the wheel and haul her back, but until she did, there was no reason he could see to rock this boat.

Dave was waiting where they'd left him, at a spot where an overhang screened those climbing into and out of the carriage. As soon as they were seated and the door closed, the old cockney set his horse in motion.

Neither Robert nor Miss Hopkins spoke as they traveled back up Tower Hill, past Mrs. Hoyt's boardinghouse, and on to the rectory.

As he handed Miss Hopkins down, he murmured, "My brother and sister-in-law became acquainted with Mrs. Hardwicke—they spoke with her on several occasions. If you need to use a name for me, introduce me as Mr. Aiken, a friend of your family."

She met his eyes, her gloved fingers gripping his, then nodded.

He offered his arm, and she took it. As they walked up the short path, she dipped her head his way and murmured back, "Is there any chance Mrs. Hardwicke will recognize you?"

He hid a grimace. "Declan and I look similar, so she might. If she does, I'll claim he and I are distant cousins. But I'm counting on her not being able to place me—and I intend to fade into the background and leave the questioning to you."

She grinned and patted his arm in a soothing manner.

He cast her a speaking look as they halted before the door, then he smoothed his expression, reached out, and knocked commandingly.

A little maid saw them into a small but comfortable parlor, then went to fetch her mistress. Robert saw Miss Hopkins to the sofa, then moved to an armchair beyond its end, out of the light falling through the windows.

Mrs. Hardwicke walked in briskly a minute later. "Good morning." A stern-faced matron, she looked at them keenly as they rose, her gaze traveling from Aileen to Robert—and there Mrs. Hardwicke's gaze halted.

Aileen plastered on a smile and stepped forward. She held out her hand. "Good morning, ma'am. I hope you remember me—

Miss Hopkins. I called several weeks ago during one of your afternoon teas."

Mrs. Hardwicke's expression cleared and she grasped Aileen's fingers. "Of course, my dear. We didn't have much chance to speak, I fear."

"No, indeed." When the minister's wife's gaze strayed again toward Frobisher, Aileen waved airily, rather dismissively, his way. "This is Mr. Aiken." She gave Mrs. Hardwicke barely a second to exchange a polite nod before barreling on, "I'm visiting the settlement for a short time, and I've heard some rather disturbing rumors. We thought you might be the best person to ask for the truth."

"Rumors?" Mrs. Hardwicke frowned. "I'm not sure a minister's wife is really the best source—"

"Oh, it's not *that* sort of rumor." Aileen glanced at the sofa.

"Please." Mrs. Hardwicke gestured. "Pray be seated."

Aileen sat, pleased when Mrs. Hardwicke chose to sit in the armchair facing her.

Frobisher waited until both she and Mrs. Hardwicke had settled their skirts, then resumed his seat, sinking as far into the shadows as he could.

"You see"—Aileen leaned forward, capturing Mrs. Hardwicke's gaze—"we've been walking around the shops in Water Street, and we heard from several shop girls about children going missing." She straightened. "It's something of an interest of mine—I'm aware of the work done by the Foundling House in London—and...well, I did wonder if there was some problem here and, if so, what help I might be able to provide, even if only to take news back to the right people in London."

She now had Mrs. Hardwicke's complete attention; the woman had all but forgotten Frobisher's existence.

After several seconds, Mrs. Hardwicke moistened her lips. "My dear, if you can get anything done, I, for one, will pray for you every night."

Aileen widened her eyes. "So the rumors are true?"

"Well, I don't know what you've heard, but what I can tell you is that through my husband's mission here among the poor, I'm aware of at least seventeen children who have vanished over recent months. And there may very well be more." Mrs. Hardwicke's expression hardened. "And no matter what those in higher office may claim, these children have not run away. They've been kidnapped, although by whom and for what I cannot begin to guess."

"Good gracious!" Aileen sat back. She paused as if considering, then asked, "Tell me—the children who've vanished. Do they have anything in common? Do they attend the same school or orphanage, or...?"

"Oh, my dear! There's no orphanage in this settlement—as you most likely can guess, that's one of the last things any town gives a thought to. And as for schools, they've only just started talking of establishing a grammar school for the children of the Tower Hill families. Those in the slums will be waiting a long time for any sort of schooling."

"In the slums? So all the children who've vanished have come from there?"

"Sadly, yes. If that weren't so, perhaps their disappearances would have attracted more attention, but..."

Aileen frowned. "Those who have vanished—did they hail from the same area of the settlement?"

Mrs. Hardwicke sat back. From her expression, no one had previously asked her that question, and she was re-examining what she knew. After several moments, she slowly said, "You know, I believe you may be right." She met Aileen's eyes, then glanced to her left. "Let's have a look at the map."

She rose and led Aileen to a framed map that hung on the wall to one side of the door. "This was given to my husband earlier this year, so it's reasonably up to date."

She raised a hand and trailed her fingers over the various streets of the settlement. Aileen looked closer; the harbor was easy enough to locate, as was the fort and Tower Hill. The slums were equally easy to pinpoint due to the density of the streets and alleys.

Mrs. Hardwicke's finger descended, and her lips firmed. "Here." Slowly, she traced a circle around the slum to the southeast of the eastern end of Water Street. "All the children who've vanished lived in this area. In the warren between the shore and the eastern end of the commercial district."

"I see." Aileen glanced over her shoulder. Frobisher looked tense, as if wishing that he could see, too, but although he'd stood when she and Mrs. Hardwicke had risen, he'd remained in the shadows.

Mrs. Hardwicke's hand lowered. She continued to stare at the map. "You know, I never thought to look at the disappearances that way. The adults who've gone hail from all over the settlement, but the children...they all come from that area."

"Do you have any idea whether the children there go to some special place or gather anywhere in particular?" When Mrs. Hardwicke glanced at her, patently puzzled, Aileen explained, "If they don't go to school, and presumably they're too young to work, then what do they do all day?"

Mrs. Hardwicke gave the matter some thought, then offered, "I really don't know, my dear, but I assume they play."

A moment later, Mrs. Hardwicke shook herself from her thoughts. "My dear—I've been dreadfully remiss. Would you and... Mr. Aiken, is it?—care for some refreshment?"

Aileen smiled, thanked Mrs. Hardwicke, but declined her offer, and immediately excused them on the grounds of having learned what they'd come to find out and having taken up quite enough of Mrs. Hardwicke's time.

"I plan to return to London in the not overly distant future," she told Mrs. Hardwicke as that lady showed them to the front door, "and I promise to bring up the matter of the missing children with those I know will have an interest in the case."

Mrs. Hardwicke smiled resignedly. "Thank you, my dear. I pray every day that, whether it be through your agency or someone else's, this matter will be investigated and no more children will vanish."

Aileen nodded and clasped Mrs. Hardwicke's proffered fingers.

Robert nodded to Mrs. Hardwicke, then took the resourceful Miss Hopkins's arm and escorted her down the path.

She waited until they were in the carriage and rolling down the hill before stating with evident satisfaction, "So now we have a definite place to start."

Robert wondered precisely what she meant, but rather than inquire, he complimented her on her performance and her insightfulness.

In any shared endeavor, it was always good policy to give a junior partner their due, and he was, in truth, distinctly impressed.

He hid his smile when she all but preened.

* * *

As he'd assumed he would, he all too soon learned exactly what his newly recruited partner had meant by "having a definite place to start."

She initially suggested they quarter and search the entire slum, from the rim of warehouses at the border of the commercial district all the way to the shore of the cove east of Kroo Bay.

Luckily, he'd foreseen her likely start. As they'd left Mrs. Hardwicke's parlor, he'd trailed behind long enough to note the name of the maker of the map she'd been studying. Dave knew the mapmaker's shop, tucked away on a side street not far from the docks. He drove them there, and Robert escorted Miss Hopkins inside.

Fifteen minutes later, they climbed back into the carriage with a map of the settlement finalized in the previous month and including the slums in helpful detail.

Detail enough to engross Miss Hopkins. *What the devil is her first name?*

Robert folded the other map he'd bought, one of the coast and interior extending well beyond the bounds of the settlement. That map was far less definite, but contained more information than any map of the area he'd yet seen. He slipped it into an inner pocket of his coat.

"Perhaps you might ask Dave to drive us to the end of this street." She angled the map, pointing with a gloved fingertip. "From there, we can walk into the slum to the areas in which children most likely gather."

He saw where she was pointing, then rose, lifted the trapdoor in the ceiling, and did as she'd asked. He sat again; the carriage started rolling, and he trained his gaze on her.

She continued to frown at the map she'd taken charge of and didn't seem to notice.

He wasn't accustomed to working with anyone other than his crew; working with Miss Hopkins as a partner was going to demand several degrees of adjustment. He decided he might as well make a start. "As it seems we're destined to work together in this business, I can't continue to think of you as Miss Hopkins. I've already given you my first name—what's yours?"

She stared at him for a moment, then simply stated, "Aileen," and went back to studying the map.

Aileen. He looked at what he could see of her face beneath the rim of her bonnet—at her bright hair and determined expression—and decided the name suited her.

"Very well, Aileen. Why do you believe the slum children will gather in any particular area?"

She looked up at him. Faint surprise showed in her eyes. Then she straightened and folded her hands on the map. "You have siblings, as do I. When you were children, if you'd been left for any time unsupervised and with nothing to do, what would you have done?"

"We would have gone out looking for...well, adventure. Our version of adventure back then."

"Exactly. And if you knew of a place where other like-minded children gathered, you would have gone there, would you not?"

He grinned faintly as memories rolled over him. "There were four of us, so we didn't always need others, but at times, yes. We joined the local packs."

She nodded briskly. "From what Mrs. Hardwicke told us, the children of the families who live in the slums, those who are as yet too young to find work, have no school or any other formal daytime occupation. So in the way of children everywhere, they'll congregate in groups to play. But"—she lifted the map, tipping it so he could see the close-drawn lines—"the alleys of the slums aren't wide enough to even toss a ball. So they'll gravitate to the areas that are."

She smoothed the map over her lap. "That's why I was so pleased the cartographer had a very recent edition." With a fingertip, she pointed. "He's marked the places where fires, or buildings simply falling down, have created spaces between the houses. In lieu of any real playground or common, that's where the children will play."

He leaned forward, forearms on his thighs, and studied the map, drawn in by her rationale and infected by her enthusiasm. He saw the areas she meant, considered, then nodded and sat back. "We'll start by sweeping across the slum, working steadily from the warehouses to the shore, checking all those areas and any others we find."

He sensed her approval. When she raised her head, he met her eyes. "We'll check all the likely areas within the slum itself, but for my money, we'll find the places we want along the shore. More possible adventures, more features likely to catch a boy's interest, at least."

She considered, then inclined her head regally. "You may well be right."

The carriage slowed, then rocked to a halt. Dave's voice came from above. "Far as I can take you, miss, sir. D'you want me to wait here?"

Aileen reached for the door handle, but Frobisher beat her to it. She was forced to wait while he descended first, blocking the doorway while he cast an apparently idle yet alert glance around. Finally, presumably satisfied that no danger lurked, he stepped aside and offered her his hand.

She stifled a humph—*he* was the one people might recognize, not her—but she had little choice beyond mentally gritting her teeth, placing her fingers in his, and letting him assist her to the ground. Immediately after he released her, she looked down and shook out her skirts. As she straightened, she glanced at him from the corner of her eye. He was surveying their surroundings; she could only hope that he hadn't noticed any sign of the leaping of her pulse, the catch in her breath, or the tension that gripped her every time they touched.

Every time he drew near.

Mercifully oblivious, he turned and looked up at Dave. "Yes. Wait here." He paused to glance at her, then looked back at Dave. "Or rather, meet us here later. We're likely to be several hours."

Dave nodded. "I'll go and get me lunch, then. I'll come back in two hours and wait for you just here."

With a crisp nod, Frobisher closed his hand about her elbow. Aileen paused to send an approving nod of dismissal to Dave before allowing Frobisher to steer her across the street and into what, according to the map, was the main alley running across the slum.

As the dimness of the alley engulfed them, he released her, and she realized she'd been holding her breath. She had to conquer her reactions to him, but she couldn't think of that now, not with him pacing by her side.

"Where to first?" he asked.

With her reticule dangling from her wrist, she flicked the map out and held it between her hands.

She blinked at it for several seconds, looking at the streets…

Frobisher reached across, tugged the map from her grip, rotated it through one hundred and eighty degrees, then returned it to her fingers. She managed to force out a "Thank you."

Then she concentrated. A second later, she pointed to their right. "Turn at the next lane—it should lead us to the first of the cleared spaces."

He nodded and strolled on, his pace one she could easily match.

Head high, she reminded herself that when she kept her mind focused on what they were doing—on the details and execution of the segment of his mission she'd decided to take on—she managed well enough. As long as her wits were fully engaged, her senses remained, if not unaware of him, then at least sufficiently quiescent to conceal what was, in reality, an avid, not to say rabid, interest in him.

She'd never had to deal with such a disruptive, distracting, and potently impulsive compulsion before. While one part of her definitely did not approve, far too much of her found him—and even more the reaction he evoked in her—intriguing and utterly fascinating.

But as long as she kept her mind under control, her wits focused on what was at hand, and did not under any circumstances allow her senses to slip sideways and wallow in memories of that kiss in the night...

A piece of flapping washing lightly slapped her on the cheek.

She jumped, realized what had happened, and felt color rise in her cheeks—not from the slap but from realization of how far from reality her senses had led her.

"Are you all right?" He dipped his head to look under the rim of her bonnet.

"Yes. Quite." She looked ahead and marched on. "I was absorbed and didn't see it."

She forced herself to make the comment true and turned her attention to the houses—dwellings that passed for such—that they were passing. More specifically, she noted the people.

She'd traveled to India when David had been stationed there and had also visited cities along the Mediterranean and European coasts. Her previous experiences had given her the knowledge of how to book passage from London to Freetown; where other ladies would have stumbled, she'd known what to do.

Her exposure to cities in many countries had left her aware that it wasn't only London or Edinburgh that had slums. Every city had them. More, as in London, while some slum areas might be inhabited by natives, other slums—like those of the East End and around the London docks—were home to a predominately immigrant population.

That was the case in this particular slum. Virtually all those she saw were of European origin. The English were most plentiful, but the French, Spanish, Italians, Greeks, Dutch, even Russians and those of the Scandinavian countries were also represented. In terms of occupation, among the men, she noted sailors, fishermen, navvies, carpenters, and land-based laborers moving through the narrow alleys; among the women, she saw tavern wenches and housewives, washerwomen and fishwives, craft workers of several types, and, of course, the painted ladies.

Several of the latter, lounging in doorways like cats in a spot of sun, cast sleepy yet distinctly come-hither looks at Frobisher as he and she walked past. Surreptitiously, she checked, but as far as she could tell, he didn't even register the women's interest; his attention was directed farther out, beyond the immediate space through which they moved, as if he was constantly scanning for any hint of approaching danger.

As if he was intent on detecting it long before it had any chance of reaching them.

That was confirmed when they reached the first open space on their map. When she would have marched out of the alley into the area, he put a hand on her arm and halted her in the alley mouth.

Surprised, she glanced at him.

"Careful." His gaze was focused into the open area—and up.

Up wasn't a direction in which she often glanced. She followed his gaze—and saw a pendulum-like contraption dangling from the rough framework of a new construction already being put up in the soon-to-be not-empty space. A makeshift crane of sorts, it swung a load of wood, more or less at head height, across the path along which they'd been walking.

She lowered her arm away from his touch and frowned. "That's hardly safe."

The glance he cast her was faintly amused. "There's little that's safe in a slum."

She swallowed a humph and consulted the map. "There might be danger, but there are no children lurking. We may as well make for our next potential spot."

They did—and discovered the locals had turned the area into a fire pit, apparently for burning refuse.

Aileen tried not to breathe as they hurriedly walked on.

Two stops later—at an open space that was empty for the simple reason that it was filled with a large extrusion of jagged rock—she looked around in mounting exasperation. "I've seen plenty of babies and very young children, but none beyond the age of toddlers still clinging to their mother's skirts."

Surveying the area, he nodded curtly. "The others have to be somewhere." He met her gaze. "That only vindicates your thesis—all the older children must be gathering to play somewhere. We just haven't yet come across the spot."

She met his gaze, then narrowed her eyes at him. "By which you mean to say I'm being impatient."

He shrugged. "I'm impatient, too, but"—he flicked the map she still held in her hands—"we still have several spots to check, and my money was always on the areas by the shore."

She hesitated, then said, "Do you want to skip the other spots within the slum and go straight to the shoreline?"

He shook his head. "Our current strategy means we're being thorough, and who knows what attraction—meaning ruin or potential game—one of the other spots might hold?" He glanced at the map. "So where to next?"

They checked three more areas shown as open spaces on the map. Two had been turned into impromptu marketplaces full of sharp-eyed adults, and the third was a dank and rather fetid hole even a rat might have thought twice about entering.

Finally, more than an hour after they'd commenced their hunt, they turned toward the shore of the cove. A smaller indentation in the coastline immediately to the east of the wide-mouthed Kroo Bay, the cove lacked the busy wharves and the large commercial ships. Instead, its rough sands played host to a range of fishing vessels. Some were anchored out from the shore, bobbing on the waves, while others had been hauled up on the sands and lay tilted on their sides like beached whales.

A ragtag group of children ranging in age from about six to perhaps twelve years old, girls as well as boys, were swarming over two upended fishing boats; they were playing some game that involved much clashing of sticks that were clearly meant to be swords.

Robert only had to halt ten yards away and fix his gaze on the children for them instantly to become aware of him.

To his surprise, instead of their faces lighting with innocent expectation and curiosity, instead of the boys, at least, racing up to swarm around him and badger him with questions—as always happened when he appeared among children at home—these children fell silent, shifting to face him and eying him warily.

From the corner of his eye, he saw Aileen taking note. She had come to stand beside him; she glanced from the children to him, then she looked back at the children, smiled in an easy, reassuring fashion, and walked forward.

The children's gazes shifted to her. Their expressions eased; curiosity lit their eyes.

Interesting. Men are dangerous. Women are not.

Perhaps understandable, given where these children were growing up.

Resigning himself to guard duty—distant at that—Robert turned and pretended to survey the beach so that he wasn't looking directly at Aileen and the children as she crouched before them.

"Hello."

He was close enough to hear the children shyly chorus a greeting back.

Then one small poppet said, "You have very pretty hair."

"Thank you." Aileen looked at the older boys and girls. "What game are you playing?"

It was apparently their version of pirates versus the navy. Robert felt his lips twitch. While he could have given them chapter and verse on that particular story, Aileen made a surprisingly good show by asking several of the right questions. By the time the children had described the play-world they'd created in sufficient detail to satisfy themselves that they'd done their creativity justice, the group had drawn close around Aileen.

She'd gained their trust in a little more than ten minutes; Robert silently owned to being impressed.

Then she said, "We've heard that some children about your age have gone missing from their homes near here." She looked around the group. "Have any of your friends gone missing?"

The children studied her for a second, then one of the older boys shook his head. "Nah. *We're* too smart to want to go off looking for our fortunes—that's something we do in our games, and we can still go home to our mams at night."

"But you've heard of children going off to seek their fortunes?" Aileen asked.

Many heads bobbed.

"Not our lot, though," the tallest girl said. "The ones that go off with the men from the jungle are all from the group as plays at the Far End."

The way she said "Far End" made it clear the words designated a place.

Aileen tipped her head. "The Far End—where's that?"

"Way over there." The boy who'd spoken pointed along the beach to the east. "There's another group as plays in the middle, 'bout the old beached buoy, but far as we've heard, none of them have gone. But the Far End is the biggest lot of children about here, and lots of them have gorn off."

"I see." Aileen rose. "So right at the end of this stretch of beach?"

Many children nodded.

"You can't miss it," the tall girl said. "There's a pile o' rocks reach into the water there—the Far End children play on and about them."

"Thank you." Aileen took a step back. "I'll let you get back to your game."

The children grinned. Within seconds, even before Aileen, trudging back over the sands to Robert's side, reached him, an argument had broken out over who had held the advantage before the interruption in hostilities.

Aileen halted beside him and arched a brow. She looked down the length of the beach. "I can see the beached buoy, but I can't see any rocks. Can you?"

He was nearly a foot taller than she. "Just. They're nearly as far past the buoy as the buoy is from here."

She sighed and started walking.

He directed her down to the ribbon of washed and more firmly packed sand edging the waves. "The going will be easier down there."

At first, they walked in silence.

Aileen paced by his side, her skirts shifting with each step. Her gaze remained trained on the sand before her feet. Eventually, she said, "They really have nothing beyond their own imaginations—not even wooden swords."

"And," he replied, in much the same reflective tone, "very likely those sticks will soon be claimed for some fire."

In the sand above the beached buoy, they saw another group of children, these a trifle more bedraggled in appearance than the group playing about the boats, building what appeared to be a small village of sand castles. Their implements were their hands and several bits of broken crockery.

The group noticed them—suspicious glances were directed their way—but when they didn't stop, the children paid them no further heed.

Aileen frowned. "It seems odd that these children"—she glanced at those they'd just passed and waved back toward the boats—"have instinct enough to be suspicious of any men trying to lure them away." She looked ahead to where, several hundred yards farther along the sands, a dark gray jumble of rocks marked their destination. "Yet apparently, the children playing about the rocks are susceptible to whatever story the slavers are spinning."

After a moment, he said, "Children usually have good instincts when it comes to evil. But I suspect we'll discover that the children who play about the rocks are, in general, older, and that they'll also be feeling more desperate. Desperate for themselves and also for their families. Desperation can overcome instinct—that's what the slavers or any like them count on."

Puzzled, she glanced at him; his expression, usually deceptively mild, looked faintly grim. "Why do you say that? That these children will be more desperate."

He met her gaze, then tipped his head toward the ramshackle houses bordering the sands. "Because I suspect each group of children hails from one section of the slum, and we've been heading east—away from the settlement's center. The families who wind up on the edges of the slum—farthest from the amenities of the settlement and its protections—are almost certainly the most destitute, the most downtrodden."

"Ah." She nodded and faced forward. "The most desperate."

"Indeed."

There was an edge to the word that told her that he didn't approve of the situation any more than she did, but they were both too old to imagine they could help everyone.

Today, they were looking for a way to help a group of children—those missing as well as those at risk of being taken. One did what one could when the opportunity offered; in cases like this, that was all they could do.

The rocks proved to be something of a natural breakwater. They jutted up through the sands, reaching almost to where the line of dwellings edged the beach.

With a touch on her arm, Frobisher directed her up the beach and around the spine. They stepped clear and immediately spotted a group of children playing in and about a conglomeration of flat rocks that held tidal pools cluttered with flotsam and jetsam.

Aileen halted beside Frobisher in the shadows thrown by the rocky breakwater and studied the group.

It differed from the previous two in several respects. The children were more numerous—Aileen counted well over twenty heads—and their clothes were more ragged and their limbs more sticklike.

The instant she looked at the harshness in their faces—the gauntness deprivation had already etched in their features—she knew this group would require a different approach. There were no games in these children's world.

She pulled up her reticule and wriggled the drawstring open. "How many pennies do you have on you?"

Frobisher didn't question her, just reached into his pocket and pulled out his coin purse.

Between them, they had over thirty pennies—enough for her purpose.

She handed him her coins. "You hold them. Follow me, but as you did with the others, stand back and don't frighten them."

After pulling the strings of her reticule tight and letting it fall to dangle from her wrist, she picked up her skirts and started down the beach.

As before, the children saw them coming. And as before, they noted that she was in the lead. That left them unsure of whether the approach constituted a threat.

She smiled and halted some yards away—enough to make it clear that she wasn't about to try to corner them. This time, she didn't open with any hello. She let her skirts fall, clasped her hands at her waist, and calmly stated, "I have a proposition for you all."

Immediately, they gathered before her, still wary enough to keep their distance, but their expressions made it clear they were entirely willing to hear her out.

"I"—she glanced over her shoulder to where Frobisher had halted several paces up the beach; he was scanning the beach and not—overtly, at least—looking their way, very much a man on guard and, by implication, no threat to her or the children—"*we* would like some information." She returned her gaze to the children and let her eyes roam over them as if assessing their ability to deliver.

One of the older boys shuffled forward half a step. "'Bout what?"

She studied him for a second, then said, "We've heard that some children have gone missing from around here." Awareness rippled through the group; glances were exchanged. "We're not after the children themselves," she hurriedly added. "We wish no harm to them or any other children whatsoever. However, we would like to know where the children went—how, with whom, and why they left."

That they'd come to the right people—those who had answers—was apparent in the considering, assessing looks the children gave both her and Frobisher, and also each other.

Eventually, the boy who'd spoken rubbed his hand over his mouth, then said, "If'n we tell you, what's in it fer us?"

She let her gaze sweep the grubby, still faintly suspicious, yet oddly innocent faces. "One penny. Each. A penny given to each of you, for your own."

The boy frowned. "But I can tell you everythin'—you can just pay me."

"No!" Another boy pushed forward. "I'll tell yer."

"Me—pick me!" came from multiple throats as several of the older children jostled to stand before her.

Aileen held up her hands, palms out—and waited with unshakeable patience for the pushing to stop and the shouting to cease…

The children got the message.

When they were once more lined up and quiet, listening, she stated in a tone that brooked no argument, much less disobedience, "One penny to each and every one of you. Those are our terms. We don't care who answers our questions, only that we get the answers—all of the answers we want." She glanced over her shoulder; Frobisher had edged a touch closer, but remained a good three paces away. "I will ask the questions, and when we're satisfied we've heard all we need to learn"—*all you can tell us*—"you will line up, youngest to oldest, and this gentleman will give you each a penny."

That way, the younger ones would have a chance to run home and hide their penny before any of the older ones could take it from them.

Satisfied she'd arranged the situation to the best of her ability, she returned her gaze to the group. "So—first question. The children who've gone missing—how many came from your group?" She waved to the rocks around them. "From the children who play around here?"

The children traded looks, then one girl started rattling off names, counting on her fingers. The others called additions. When the roll call finally ended, they'd recited nineteen names—two more than Mrs. Hardwicke had known of.

Aileen nodded. "Very well—nineteen. Now, were any of you about when these children left?"

Lots of nods. Virtually every head bobbed.

"Did the children leave with some men?"

Another round of nods.

"Not all at once," one of the girls said. "Those that went with the men went off three or four or five at a time."

"Aye." One of the boys loitering at the rear of the group caught Aileen's eye. "The men come and tell us about how they have work for us, and ask how many of us would like to go with them and make some money." There was more than a hint of cynicism in his tone.

"What they *say*," another of the older boys put in, "is if we go with them into the jungle, we'll make our fortunes, just like explorers an' all do." His gaunt face lit with nascent hope. "When next they come, I might just go." He threw a challenging glance at the boy at the back of the group. "Better'n just hanging around here getting nothin' but older."

Aileen swallowed the impulse to insist he do no such thing; she needed to be careful. "These men—who are they?"

Several children shrugged. "Don't know, do we?" the first boy said. "It's all a big secret—this...project of theirs. They don't want others learnin' of it and trying to fight them for it, do they?"

"What do these men look like?"

Bits and pieces of description tumbled forth.

"*Big*—big bruisers, some o' them."

"Mostly like us, English or mix, not natives."

"They carry knives—big knives and cutlasses on their hips."

"One had a pistol."

"There's one as comes and talks to us—s'plains things to us. It's usually him as talks."

The picture the children painted was of a group of four or five men, usually English, who came to visit the children by walking along the beach as Aileen and Frobisher had. Sometimes the men approached from the west, sometimes the east, and sometimes through the slum itself. They departed with the children they'd recruited by walking either east or back through the slum. The man in charge was the one who spoke with them, making promises of gainful employment; it was transparently clear that, somehow, that man had succeeded in winning the trust of most of the children.

"Do you know—have you heard—any of the men's names?" Aileen asked.

But that was too much to hope for.

She thought rapidly, then asked, "Do the men take any of you who want to go?"

Heads were shaken. "They pick and choose," one of the girls said. "They want strong ones. When Robbie wanted to go"—she nodded at one of the boys—"they wouldn't take him 'cause he had a broken arm."

"I'm waiting for them to come back." Robbie held out his skinny arm and flexed the elbow. "Right as rain now."

His eager expression had Aileen biting her tongue while she rapidly thought of how to ask the most vital question. "I would have thought," she said, "that your beds here, no matter how shabby, would be better than slaving away in the jungle, who knows how far away from your families."

"Aye, well." The older boy who'd first spoken shrugged. "It comes down to what they're offering, don't it?"

An older girl with wispy pale hair shot him a look, then faced Aileen. "We've families, see? Our mams are working as hard and as long as can be, but there's not much work to be had, even for them, and there ain't no jobs nor nothin' for us to do to help, but the little ones have to be fed, and the landlady has to be paid. And all we can do is hang about and wish we could do something useful, but we can't." She fixed her gaze on Aileen's face. "So when the men come...some of us take the chance they're offering and go. It might be hard work, but if we can make some coin to help our mams and the little ones…well, why wouldn't we?"

Aileen understood—all of it. That the men who were taking the children were trafficking in hope, preying on these children's innocent and wholly laudable wish to help their struggling families.

She drew in a deep breath and inwardly lectured herself that she couldn't simply issue orders and make these children's world right. She exhaled. "I see. Very well—one last question. Have any of the children who've gone come back?"

She was certain she knew what the answer would be, but hoped that through articulating it, some, at least, of the older children tempted to go with the men might *think*—might use their innate wariness to consider what the answer might mean.

The boy at the rear of the pack, the one with world-weary cynicism far too deep for his years etched into his face, snorted and looked away.

"Nah," Robbie answered. "None who've gone have yet come back, but then the project's still going, ain't it?" His grin suggested he was glad it was, because that meant he still had a chance to join those who had gone, and "make some coin."

Aileen felt anger burn, but ruthlessly tamped it down. Railing at the children, trying to make them recognize the danger and stay away from the men…

She wouldn't succeed—arguing against hope was always a losing proposition—and worse, she would put the children's backs up by attacking something they equated with helping their families.

She drew in another breath, then turned her head and glanced at Frobisher.

He looked as grim as she felt, but from the watchful—warning—look in his eyes, she gathered he read the situation in the same way and saw the same danger she did. "Anything more?" she asked him.

"Do the men come at regular times?" His deep, resonant voice rumbled over her and the children. "Or do they come after a certain number of days?"

She turned back and looked at the children, and arched her brows.

"They usually come in the afternoons."

"But if you mean which days, they're not regular-like at all."

"Can't even remember when last they came—must be weeks ago now."

"They've only come about four times."

"Maybe once a month?"

"Always in the afternoons." Several nodded.

When nothing more was forthcoming, either from the children or Frobisher, Aileen nodded. She stepped back and waved toward him. "Form up in a line, then—youngest first. And *no* arguing—I won't believe that you don't know who is younger than whom."

The children gave her a careful look, but did as she bid them.

Having apparently divined the purpose behind her organizational strategy, Frobisher handed out the pennies literally one by one, pausing between each to give the most recent recipient time to depart.

Which they all did, clutching their penny and racing over the sand to disappear into the slum.

Aileen followed the last lad—the one who had shown his suspicions of the men most clearly—as he approached Frobisher.

The lad took his penny and ducked his head.

As he started to step away, Aileen said, "You don't think going with the men is a good idea."

The lad cast her a glance from dark eyes. "No, mum. Plain as a pikestaff they're up to no good—why else would men come 'specially to seek out the likes of us? If they was offering honest work, there're hundreds in the settlement would line up to do it. Don't make no sense." The lad's gaze hardened. "But you was right to say nuffin of what you think—I saw you holding it in."

He darted a glance at Frobisher, but immediately looked back at Aileen. "It don't do no good to try to make 'em see. I got the bruises to prove it. They think I'm a coward for not going—the men asked me once't, and I said no."

His expression close to a sneer, the lad stepped back, then turned away. "No point trying to 'elp those as is determined to be blind."

Aileen watched him go. After a moment, she murmured, "No point trying to convince those blinded by hope to see."

"Indeed." Frobisher glanced down at her.

She felt his gaze traveling over her face.

When she finally gave in and glanced up, he met her eyes. "It's past noon. There was a cafe just outside the slum, near where we told Dave to meet us later. Why don't we go there and discuss our next move?"

She realized she was hungry. She nodded and turned to walk back along the beach.

Frobisher fell in beside her. After a moment, as if reading her mind, he murmured, "In circumstances such as these, replacing blind hope with a more healthy fear isn't something that can be readily achieved—certainly not in a few days. Trying to convince those children that the men who come for them are evil and should be avoided will simply cast *us* as people to be disbelieved, avoided, and possibly even feared."

Reluctantly, she nodded. "Whoever they are, the men have gained the children's trust. Us walking up and telling them that those particular men are untrustworthy isn't going to help."

A few paces later, she put the feeling circling through her brain into words. "Kidnapping—simply seizing the children and carting them off—would have been bad enough. This—this preying on their innocent dreams, using those dreams against them—is worse."

Robert didn't disagree. He looked ahead, then touched her arm and steered her up the sand toward the end of the main alley.

"As far as I can see, the only way we can help those children and keep them out of the slavers' clutches—and if God smiles, get the others back, too—is to finish this mission with all speed and take the information back to London so that the next stage can be launched."

He glanced down and met her eyes—saw and recognized the fierce light shining in them. "We'll do what we can, as fast as we can."

Her lips firmed. She nodded and lengthened her stride. "Let's find that cafe and decide what to do next."

Nine

Robert was happily surprised to discover that Miss Hopkins—Aileen—wasn't wary over trying unusual foods. The little cafe they stepped into, close by the spot at which Dave was to meet them, served a local version of Mediterranean-style snacks, some of which were spicy, although everything smelled delicious.

Wrapped in the cool shadows enveloping the counter of the small eatery, they perched on high stools, and apparently relaxed and animated, Aileen chatted with the proprietress over which of her many dishes she would recommend.

Once the middle-aged woman had filled plates for them both and they settled to eat, between bites, Robert asked, "Have you traveled before?"

His thorn—not so much of an irritant today—looked at him as if that was a foolish question. "Of course." After swallowing another mouthful, she added, "I seized the opportunity to travel whenever David or Henry were posted to faraway places—India, Gibraltar, Malta, and Egypt."

"So you enjoyed the different cultures?"

"I enjoyed the experiences, yes. But I have to admit that at the end of each journey, I was always happy to return to the green fields of England." She directed a sharply inquisitive glance at him. "What about you? You must spend most of your days out of England. Or is it Scotland?"

She wouldn't be able to guess from any accent; he didn't have any.

"Scotland—Frobisher Shipping operates out of Aberdeen."

When he didn't expand on that, she tipped her head and asked, "Do you spend most of your year on the waves?"

He waggled his head while he thought of the reality of his life. "I spend most of my time—roughly three quarters of the year, I suppose—on trips of one sort or another. But for most of those trips, the traveling itself takes only about half of the time. The rest…goes in waiting for those I've ferried to complete their business and be ready to return—and that generally is to England."

She studied him for several seconds, then stated, "You don't strike me as the sort to be a glorified ferryman."

He couldn't stop his smile. He tipped his head in a fencer's acknowledgment. "I usually take care of other business while I'm waiting."

The overt diplomatic purposes of his voyages were often a screen for activities rather more secretive and sensitive.

She pushed away her empty plate and sighed. "Enough of us." She caught his gaze as he looked up. "We need to decide what to do."

He edged aside his plate. "We need to decide what we can *effectively* do."

"First—what do we know about the children going missing?" She balanced on the high stool, held up her hand, and ticked each point off on her fingers. "The men—whoever they are—come roughly once a month, in the afternoon, and take four or so children, all hale and sufficiently strong to be able to work. Said men have managed to gain the children's trust to the extent that simply warning the children away isn't going to work." She'd run out of fingers. She stared at her hand, then met his gaze. "So what can we do?"

He felt his features harden as his earlier thoughts coalesced. "As far as I can see, we can do nothing directly—we could try, but both you and I know we'd be wasting our time." He looked down at the scarred counter and traced a scratch with one finger. "The best we can do is to see if we can further our mission via the children. If we can learn anything pertinent that might lead us to the slavers' camp. And that"—he looked at her—"depends on facts we don't yet know. Such as"—he tapped his finger on the table—"whether these are the same men—the same slavers—who have been taking adult Europeans."

She frowned. "How likely would it be to have two entirely unconnected gangs seizing Europeans from the settlement, one taking adults, the other children?"

He grimaced. "Not likely, but it's possible there are two separate gangs supplying the same mine, especially as the men come for the children during the afternoon, while the slavers move adults at night."

He paused, then went on, "Assuming that, regardless of whether it's children or adults they've seized, the slavers will take their captives to a jungle camp prior to moving them on, at this point, we don't know if the camp the children will be taken to is the same camp through which the adults are transported."

She blinked. "But it doesn't matter, does it? As you said, the children are most likely being taken for the same mine, so regardless of which camp we find—the one the children are taken to or the one the adults are taken to—then the trail they take out of that camp will lead to the same mine."

The mists in his mind cleared. He nodded. "You're right. The children's camp might not be the one I was sent to locate, but it will work just as well for our ongoing purpose."

"So!" She straightened on her stool. "How do we go about finding the camp the children are taken to? I assume the obvious way—by following the men who take the children the next time they come? And as they come in the afternoon—which they must as the children will go home at dusk—that shouldn't be as difficult as following them at night."

He swiveled on the stool and leaned back against the counter. Looking outside, he saw Dave arrive and draw the carriage up to the rough curb. "It might be weeks before the men return."

"I don't think so. The children said it's been weeks since they last came—it sounds as if they're due for a visit."

She was right, and it was definitely worth considering. His men were watching the slavers' lair in the settlement, but if there was another—possibly more direct—route to a jungle camp supplying their putative mine…it never hurt to have a fallback plan.

After a moment, he said, "One thing that continues to puzzle me is why they're taking only Europeans."

From the corner of his eye, he saw her brows arch.

"Perhaps," she said, "they are taking natives as well, but we simply haven't heard of it. We've only heard about the Europeans—that doesn't mean they're not seizing natives, just that they're not seizing natives out of the settlement."

He had to admit that was possible. "Something to ponder."

She looked at him; he could feel her gaze, searching and acute. "So what are we going to do about the children?"

He turned his head and met her gaze. Managed to keep his lips straight. "I take it you have a suggestion."

"Indeed. Why not ask that last lad, the one who doesn't trust the men and who has apparently tried to warn the others, to come and tell us when the men come back? We could offer him a reward to come and alert us."

It was a viable idea. Most importantly, if he agreed, she wouldn't insist on prowling the slum but instead wait for word… He narrowed his eyes, then shifted his gaze to stare absentmindedly outside. "We could tell him to bring the news to the inn where I'm staying—it's not far from here." He glanced at her, then away. "No point in him trying to report to you—even if a slum brat like him could get up Tower Hill to your lodgings without being challenged and chased home, Mrs. Hoyt's is too far away. Even if the men leave before I reach the shore, I should be in time to pick up their trail whichever way they go."

He looked at her and met a pair of hard hazel eyes.

"We," she stated. "When *we* reach the shore, *we* should be able

to pick up their trail." She lifted her reticule from the counter. "And I agree. So let's go and find that lad and put our proposition to him."

She slid from her stool and, head high, swept toward the open doorway.

Robert enjoyed the view for several seconds, then rose and followed her, exceedingly careful to keep his smile off his face.

★★★

They returned to the shore, saw the lad in the distance, and managed to attract his attention and beckon without alerting any of the other children.

But when the boy joined them in the lane in which they were lurking, he was reluctant and skittish; he showed every inclination of shying away, and only Aileen's presence and her quick, reassuring words held him.

She had her work cut out convincing the lad to aid them; Robert held his tongue and did nothing more than gravely nod every time the boy's sharp gaze darted to him. The lad was quick to understand what they were asking, and eventually, he succumbed to Aileen's persuasion and agreed to help them.

Robert offered the lad half a crown, with the promise of a whole crown if he delivered a useful warning. A crown was riches to such a waif; Robert had little doubt the boy would do his best to earn it.

When the boy reached out and took the coin, Aileen stepped aside; with her back to them, she took up position as lookout in similar fashion to Robert's role that morning, with her gaze fixed on the children playing in the distance.

Even though the lad was still nervous about dealing directly with Robert, he seemed grateful to Aileen for watching his back.

His manner straightforward, Robert gave the boy directions to the inn. The boy dutifully recited the directions back, hesitated, then asked what to do if Robert wasn't there.

Robert glanced at Aileen; her attention remained fixed on the distant children. He looked back at the lad and quietly recited the directions to the hide his men had established in the slum farther up the hill. The boy appeared to know his way around that area, too; again, he recited the directions back without faltering.

Satisfied, Robert lightly clapped the boy on the shoulder; he ignored the way the lad jerked and nearly leapt away. "You're doing the right thing. Possibly the only thing you can do to help your friends—those too blind to see."

The boy met his eyes, searched them for a second as if to confirm he was sincere, then he ducked his head and sidled back.

Robert let him go and lowered his arm.

The boy looked at Aileen—rather curiously. The lad waited. When she glanced around, met his gaze, and smiled, he bobbed his head. "Missus." Then he thrust his hands into the pockets of his ragged too-short trousers, put his head down, and slouched off. Not to rejoin his playmates but deeper into the slum.

When Aileen looked questioningly at him, Robert kept his expression impassive. "Are you ready to return to your lodgings?"

She nodded. "Yes. We may as well go back and sit in comfort while we plan our next move."

As to that, he had his own plans, but rather than invite an argument, he stepped back, let her walk past him, then fell in beside her.

Side by side, they walked out of the slum and back to Dave and his carriage.

* * *

Robert fully intended to part from Aileen once they reached Mrs. Hoyt's boardinghouse; he needed to go into the slums and check in with his men. Given he'd devoted the better part of his day to squiring Aileen about and letting her involve herself on the periphery of his mission, he assumed she would be weary and content to rest and recuperate.

Or whatever gently bred ladies did after spending all day striding about a settlement in the tropical heat.

When Dave drew the carriage up outside Mrs. Hoyt's, Robert climbed down. He handed Aileen down—but before he could take his leave of her, she slipped her hand from his and swanned up the garden path.

Accepting that he probably should see her to the front door, he followed; rather than speak from a distance, he climbed the porch steps in her wake. But instead of pausing there, she opened the door and sailed straight through—and finally halted in the front hall. She was looking to her right. She frowned. "Damn."

He'd halted just over the threshold; he heard the muttered curse clearly. Following her gaze, he saw a closed door.

"There's someone in the parlor," she whispered. She reached back and tugged his sleeve. "Come upstairs, but for God's sake, be quiet."

She released him, raised her skirts, and went swiftly up.

Leaving him standing in the front hall, staring after her.

He spent a bare second debating whether to follow or turn around, stride outside, and go on his way… That would lose him all the points he hoped he'd gained through their morning's excursions.

Silently—he could be more silent than she might imagine when he wished—he closed the front door and climbed the stairs. He found her waiting before a door in the upper corridor, the one to the corner room overlooking the front garden.

Before he reached her—before he could speak—she opened the door and went into the room.

Frowning, he was forced to follow, but halted just over the threshold. He glanced around—and she pushed him to the side as she quietly shut the door.

Then she looked at him. "As long as we keep our voices down, we can talk freely here."

All he wished to say to her he could have said on the front porch. Indeed, in the street.

"Miss Hopkins—"

"Given we're now working together and we're in private, it's acceptable to use my first name."

What precisely did she mean by *working together*? While he was digesting the implications of that, she walked to the writing desk, placed her black reticule upon it, sat on the stool before it—the only stool in the room—and looked up at him. "As it's already afternoon, it seems unlikely we'll receive any summons from that lad today. So what's next on our list to tackle?"

Our list? He studied her, his gaze taking in the brilliantly brassy shade of her hair and the direct, confident gaze she leveled at him. He reminded himself that he was a diplomat; he could talk his way out of almost anything. "Miss—" He inclined his head. "Aileen."

He paused.

Sitting upright on the stool, she widened her eyes at him, transparently encouraging him to continue.

Looking into her bright, browny-hazel eyes, he accepted that, regardless of his inclinations, with her, direct opposition would in no way be wise. He gripped his hands behind his back and settled into a familiar captain's stance. "As I mentioned this morning, my men are watching over the slavers' lair. They'll be expecting me to look in, to learn what they've observed."

"I take it that should the slavers leave to lead captives back to their camp, you intend to follow."

He nodded. "With my men."

"I see." She looked down and frowned. "Obviously, it will be impossible for me to accompany you on such an action given it will occur in the dead of night."

And will involve stealthily negotiating dangerous slums and who knows how much jungle. He contented himself with a curt nod. "Indeed." Relief flowed down his spine, and he released his hands and straightened. "However, as promised, I will keep you informed of what we learn."

"Excellent." She raised her head and smiled at him. Then she rose and picked up her reticule. "And as there's nothing more I can do in the matter of the missing children at this time, and as I am now a partner in your mission, I believe I will accompany you to your men's hideaway and view the slavers' lair."

No. He bit back the bald refusal, but couldn't quash the instinct that had him stepping across to block her path to the door. "I don't think that would be wise."

She halted and looked up, into his face. "Oh? Why not?"

He held her gaze and felt his jaw tighten. "The hideaway is buried deep in a slum—definitely no place for a lady."

She blinked those brandy-colored eyes at him. "My dear Frobisher, we've just spent the last several hours going back and forth through a slum. While I would prefer never to walk such streets alone, there's obviously no reason I cannot do so in broad daylight with you by my side."

"That was *there*—the lower east slum." A feeling awfully like panic tickled his nape. "The slavers' lair is in the slum over the hill from Undoto's church. It's a much rougher, meaner area and, as I said, unarguably unsuitable for you to enter."

She made a dismissive sound and shifted as if to get around him. He countered the move, remaining directly between her and the door.

She stiffened. Her head rose; her eyes narrowed. "If you will, Mr. Frobisher, please answer me this. By what right do you think to order me about? I am not one of your midshipmen."

"Obviously not. My midshipmen don't argue."

"I daresay. But as we've now established that I am not yours to command, then"—the damned woman stepped close, her face tipping up so it was inches below his, her bodice all but brushing his chest—"I suggest you turn around, give me your arm, and we can pretend this little contretemps didn't occur, and like the partners we have agreed to be, we can go down to the carriage and drive to the slum. And while you are consulting with your men, I will study the slavers' lair."

He couldn't see anything beyond the stubborn and oh-so-feminine determination in her face. "No."

Her eyes blazed. *"No?"* She raised her hands as if to push him back—as if she could.

He never quite understood what happened next. Her hands flattened against his chest, and a raging storm of impulses crashed through him, blinding him to anything beyond the compulsive need to keep the damned woman safe.

However he could.

Entirely without thought—governed wholly by impulses he didn't understand but that she effortlessly goaded and provoked—he reached for her, hauled her up against him, and slanted his mouth over hers.

He kissed her with force, with deliberation, with an intent he fully comprehended.

So he could leave her wrung out, limp, and compliant—and safe in her room.

To that end, he tightened his hold on her, and when she gasped—in surprise or in shock or in simple reaction, he had no clue—he took immediate advantage, sending his tongue past her lips to claim, then plunder—

Sensation slammed into him. Hunger erupted and clawed.

He drew her yet closer, angled his head over hers, and with deliberate intent pushed them both into deeper, darker waters and set himself to devour.

The feel of her—warm, supple, and curvaceous—in his arms, the heady, intoxicating taste of her, all topped by the giddy realization that, far from wilting, the damned woman had clenched her small fists in his coat and was kissing him back, her lips against his, her tongue dueling with his, her ardor the very equal of his, fractured some wall inside him.

The diplomat—his façade—shattered, fragmented, and fell away, and his wilder side—the part of him he habitually held back, suppressed, leashed, muzzled—gleefully leapt free and seized his reins.

Hell. This would land him in deep trouble, and he knew it; trouble always followed when his wilder self led.

But he couldn't draw back—did not have the strength, mental or otherwise, to retreat from an exchange that had taken on a will of its own.

Aileen's wits reeled—and some part of her rejoiced. Which seemed strange, wrong, and yet…

Never had she indulged in a kiss like this. A kiss with a man like this, one more than capable of meeting her, matching her—*challenging* her.

And oh, Lord, he drove her *wild.* To desperation and madness.

To a level of feminine awareness she'd never previously attained.

His heat and hardness surrounded and cushioned her and locked her in a world where only he and she existed. Where the unforgiving pressure of his lips, the seductive caress of his tongue, and the flagrant temptation of his kiss became her consuming reality.

Giddy, driven, she clung to him and returned his fire with her own. She couldn't—wouldn't—allow herself to do anything else. Anything less. Sufficient remnants of rational thought lingered, enough to understand what this kiss was about.

To comprehend what he—instinctively perhaps—sought to gain by it.

She wasn't going to let him succeed, but…for a few moments at least, she could indulge. Could indulge him, and herself.

Could explore and experience this new level of fascination.

She'd never been tempted by sensation like this—never *craved* more, not like this. With an abandon she felt to her soul.

Throwing one's cap over a windmill had always seemed such a silly concept; she'd never understood how any intelligent woman could be so…well, unthinking.

Now she knew. With his firm, demanding, commanding lips on hers, she finally understood.

One didn't think when in the throes of *this*—one felt, one thrilled, one desired.

Coming up on her toes, she slid her hands up his chest, thrust her fingers into the silk of his hair, gripped, and pressed her lips and her body even more fully, even more flagrantly, to his.

Robert gasped, at least in his mind. His mouth, his arms, his body were all too engrossed in seizing and savoring her, in taking and wallowing in all she was offering...

And she was offering. The realization mentally rocked him back on his heels.

This wasn't how he'd expected this kiss to progress.

In some dim, heated recess of his brain, he knew he should end it—that it had been a mistake, a tactical error, that he should have remembered just how their earlier kiss had affected him.

His wilder side didn't care.

Not in the least.

His wilder side was immersed in the kiss, hungry and greedy and well-nigh insatiable. Being seduced by a sharp-tongued termagant was, apparently, entirely to his taste.

Then into that dim, heated recess—his remaining kernel of rational thought—another realization slid. One more potent, more insidious—more compelling.

He wasn't a novice when it came to women, far from it. Why, then, was he not in control here? How had this engagement transformed into something he'd never intended it to be?

Into a true exchange. A connection more personal and far more fundamental and direct than any he'd been a party to before.

Where was this tack—unexpected, unprecedented, and certainly unplanned—leading him?

His inner diplomat informed him he really did not want to know—that he should pull back immediately, before he was lost.

But his wilder side—the buccaneer inside him—wanted to find out.

This way lies danger should have been tattooed on her forehead. Lord knew, for him, that was the naked truth—and the ultimate lure.

Aileen reveled in a growing sense of certainty, of confidence—of knowing she could meet this man on this ground on equal terms.

She rejoiced in that discovery, yet an ever-growing sense of no longer being in control tugged at her awareness and sent welling wariness edged with concern to dim her delight.

On a gasp, she drew back—broke from the kiss, tipped back her head, and hauled in a much-needed breath.

She felt the unyielding pressure of his chest against her swollen breasts, the steel cage of his arms around her—became aware of the *moltenness* that had suffused her body. She dragged in more air, and her whirling wits steadied. Some semblance of strength reinfused her limbs.

She eased her grip on his hair, let her hands slide down to rest once more against the rock-hard planes of his chest as she brought her head upright and met his gaze.

Could blue eyes smolder?

That was definitely a question for later. Right now, she needed to take charge—to get her, and him, too, back on the path they should be treading.

But she found it difficult to drag her eyes from his, to haul her senses from the thudding, compelling beat of nascent passion.

Like an entity that was neither him nor her, it thrummed in the air around them.

She couldn't pretend it wasn't there—and from the growing wariness in his eyes, neither could he.

He didn't know what to do—with her, with what had erupted between them.

She read that truth in the hard planes of his face, in the set of his mobile lips.

Lips she could still feel on hers.

She dragged in another breath, pushed against his chest, and he let her step back, out of his arms. They fell from her. She quelled an urge to reverse her direction and feel them close about her again.

She'd felt safe—utterly and completely safe—while locked in his arms.

Given the hunger she'd sensed in him, that seemed a sure sign her wits had deserted her.

Enough. Get back on track.

She'd taken only one step away; she wasn't going to retreat any farther.

She raised her head and, deliberately challengingly, looked him in the eye. "I know why you kissed me. Quite aside from being—patently—unwise, I have absolutely no intention of allowing you to use such…tactics to manage me."

His lips tightened, and his eyes narrowed slightly, but he didn't try to deny her insight.

She was far too experienced to attempt to deny her part in their recent exchange, but neither was she about to mention it; she tipped her head up a fraction more and haughtily stated, "I believe it's time we were off. As I recall, you mentioned that your men will be expecting you."

He considered her for a long moment, then, once again, simply said, "No."

With that, he turned on his heel and stalked to the door.

"To get to the hideaway, I should follow the second alley to the left off the central way through the slum, which is the extension of the street that runs over the crest of the hill. Then—"

He growled and swung to face her. "You *were* listening when I gave the lad directions."

She looked at him pityingly. "Of course."

Plainly goaded, he ran a hand through his hair—hair she'd already thoroughly rumpled. Then he pinned her with an openly aggravated, very blue gaze. "Is there any way within the realms of possibility that I can convince you to stay here—in safety?"

She gave the question due consideration. "No."

He tipped back his head; jaw clenched, he gave vent to a sound eloquent of male frustration.

Calmly, she confirmed, "If you don't take me with you, I'll simply follow you, which will be a great deal *less* safe, so I really don't see why you won't simply surrender with good grace."

He straightened and looked at her.

She met his gaze and succinctly stated, "Where I go is not a decision that lies within your bailiwick."

Several seconds ticked by, then a muscle in his jaw tightened.

"Very well." The words sounded as if they'd been dragged from him.

All but grinding his teeth, Robert swung around and reached for the door. "Surrender" was not a word normally in his lexicon, but in this, it seemed, he was to have no choice.

He opened the door, waited while the thorn apparently now embedded in his flesh walked past, then he followed her from the room.

Ten

Aileen found it remarkably easy to abstain from displaying any smugness as she walked beside her scowling escort into the teeming slum.

He'd been correct in stating that there was a difference between the slum they had visited that morning and this one. This slum was significantly farther from the settlement's center, and its denizens were commensurately a great deal more desperate. Said denizens were also in the main not European, but mostly of mixed race.

The dwellings were smaller, more ramshackle, and more crowded. The sheer density of people was nearly overwhelming, the associated cacophony and the medley of smells well-nigh stifling.

She would never have set foot in such a place without an escort—preferably one similar to the one she presently had. A single glance at him was enough to have even the pickpockets giving them a wide berth. His ability to discourage all approaches, let alone any attack, lay not just in the way he loomed by her shoulder with his eyes constantly scanning their surrounds, nor simply in the way he scowled so ferociously at anyone who hove too close. More than anything else, his ability to deter lay in the dangerous way he moved—the menace he, apparently without effort, projected.

That said something of him—of the man he was inside.

On the outside, he appeared smoothly sophisticated, even debonair, but inside...she sensed that something far less civilized lurked beneath his polished exterior.

Five paces on, she hauled her mind from its fascination—fast becoming an obsession—and reminded herself that, in such a place, she, too, should be on guard.

They'd been walking down the narrow lanes and alleys for nearly fifteen minutes when he halted before a sagging wooden door. He glanced back along the street, then lifted the latch and put his shoulder to the panel—forcing it wide enough for her, at his wave, to slip past.

He followed her into a dimly lit, rather malodorous hallway. He pushed the door shut, cutting off the sunlight and leaving them in gloom.

Before her eyes had adjusted, she felt his fingers close around her elbow.

He steered her toward the rear of the hallway. "The stairs are this way. Step carefully."

A set of stairs appeared on her left. At his urging, she raised her skirts and started climbing. With him reassuringly close behind, she went up two rickety flights, then stepped onto a landing only fractionally less rickety. A single door lay ahead.

Robert stepped past Aileen and tapped on the door. "It's Frobisher."

As he reached for the doorknob, he cast a searching glance at his companion's face. He lived in hope that her sense of self-preservation was sufficient for a single exposure to the slum to be enough to convince her she didn't need to visit again. Although he'd seen signs enough that she was aware of the lurking dangers of the place, he could detect no hint of alarm, much less fear.

He set the door swinging inward and waved her inside, then followed at her heels.

His men had vacated the room on Undoto's street and transferred their pallets and bags here and made themselves comfortable. Benson, Coleman, and Fuller were sitting on stools about the small round table, while Harris was propped on a stool before the window, keeping watch. All four tensed as Aileen and he entered, but then they relaxed, rose, and nodded deferentially—first to him, then more formally to her; it always took the four several days to get out of the habit of leaping to attention and saluting him, as they normally would.

"This is Miss Hopkins." Robert waited while his men mumbled greetings and bowed. "Her brother Lieutenant Hopkins is one of those who've gone missing."

"Good afternoon." Aileen returned their nods.

Benson offered her his stool. "Here you are, miss. Sorry it's not a chair."

She smiled. "That's quite all right." She glanced at the window. "Actually, I'm interested in taking a look at the slavers' lair."

Robert trailed her as she crossed to the window. Harris stepped back and waved her to his stool, and with a gracious smile, she accepted and sank down. With her seated, the sill rose as high as her collarbone, but she could still see out well enough for her purpose. Robert halted by her shoulder. "It's the door you can see directly ahead—the house across the lane from the one whose roof we're looking over."

She nodded. "The man sitting on the stoop—is he one of the slavers?"

Robert glanced at Benson, who had come to join them; he arched his brows in question.

Benson nodded a touch grimly. "We believe so, miss. He's one of those who called on Undoto last night."

"He's not the leader, however," she remarked.

"No, miss. That one's a heavier man. Older, too."

After a moment, Aileen glanced up—at Benson, Harris, and the others, all of whom had joined them about the window. "Am I right in thinking that the slavers are, by and large, mostly European? Primarily English?"

His men had started to nod, but at the latter qualification, they paused. Coleman said, "I wouldn't say necessarily English, miss. Bit of a melting pot, countries like this. Easier to say that, generally speaking, we wouldn't expect to see any purebred natives running with any slave gang."

Aileen looked back at the house, at the thug lounging on watch on the step. "I have to admit that I've never understood the impulse to slaving, but in such a case as this, in a foreign country so far from home, to be preying on those who are essentially your own people seems peculiarly wrong."

There was nothing Robert could think of to add to that; she was correct—in this particular case, the sense of a more fundamental betrayal ran strong.

After a moment, he shifted and looked at his men. "So what have you seen? Anything of note?"

They described the few comings and goings from the house, all of which sounded entirely mundane. Robert grimaced. "That suggests that they're waiting, but have nothing definite on their plate as yet."

"I reckon," Coleman said, leaning against the wall, "that the first sign we'll see will be a messenger of some sort. These blokes"—with a tip of his head, he indicated the slavers' lair—"don't seem to go out during the day if they can help it. We asked around. The locals know what they are and don't like them. The bruisers pay for their meals to be brought in, and an old woman sweeps for them, but that's the extent of any fraternization."

Robert nodded. "They're outcasts even among the outcasts. So as we'd thought, this is a staging post and nothing more."

"Assuming a messenger does come," Benson said, "and fetches the slavers away, do you want us to follow them? Or should we keep our watch going here?"

His gaze on the door to the slavers' lair, Robert considered, then replied, "If all of the slavers leave, then yes, follow. If they leave the settlement, three of you stay on their trail, and one of you come and fetch me. However, if not all of them leave, then three of you remain on watch here, and one of you come and report." He paused, running through the scenarios in his mind. "If what we've been told is correct—and there's no reason to believe it isn't—then if they do leave to seize someone, they'll return here with their captive before they head off for their jungle camp. We need to remain focused on picking up the trail between here"—with his head, he indicated the slavers' lair—"and that camp."

Murmurs of "Aye, sir" came from his men.

His envisioning of what might occur, however, highlighted another, potentially difficult point. One that they needed to face, that he needed to specifically address.

He glanced at Aileen, seated before him with her gaze trained on the doorway to the slavers' lair. She might not appreciate what he had to say, but it had to be said.

"One thing." His men looked his way, and he continued, "If the slavers seize someone—or even several people—and bring them back here, we can do nothing other than watch and follow." He met his men's gazes one by one. He heard the *shush* of Aileen's skirts as she turned and stared up at him; he felt her gaze, but didn't meet it. He continued to look at his men. "We cannot risk our mission—and we absolutely must not risk the safety of those already taken." He paused, then put it as bluntly as he could. "We cannot rescue whoever the slavers kidnap next. We have to let them go. Allowing them to be taken is a sacrifice we must make for the greater good—so that in taking them to their jungle camp, the slavers can lead us to that location."

He thought further, then added, "Even when we find the camp, we will not be able to rescue those held captive there. If we're spotted, we run—we must do nothing to paint ourselves as any sort of true threat to the slavers, much less to the enterprise they're supplying." He shook his head decisively. "We have no other option. That's what we must do."

His men pulled faces and shifted, uneasy with the order, but they understood.

Finally, he looked down and met Aileen's bright gaze. For a moment, it remained distant, as if her thoughts were a long way away, then she refocused.

She looked into his eyes.

Then she nodded.

And turned back to looking out at the slavers' lair.

He and she left the observation post not long afterward. There was nothing happening. Nothing to see beyond the single man lounging in the doorway.

They made their way through the alleys and lanes without speaking. Robert noted that she was every bit as tense and on edge as he. Good. He was enjoying this leg of their daylong excursion as much as he'd expected—which was to say, not at all. His only hope was that she would feel sufficiently uncomfortable to be disinclined to venture to the hide again.

Despite the danger lurking around every corner, they reached the edge of the slum without incident. Dave was waiting with his carriage where they'd left him; Robert assisted Aileen inside, then followed and shut the door.

As the carriage lurched into motion, Aileen studied her escort's face. The late-afternoon light illuminated the brooding expression that seemed to reach far deeper than his features.

While they rocked along the rutted track, then at last turned west toward Tower Hill and smoother-surfaced streets, she reviewed what she'd seen, what she'd heard, what she'd learned.

Finally, she fixed her gaze on his face. "Thank you for taking me there. I know you didn't want to, but..." She drew a breath that was a touch tighter than she'd expected. "For me, seeing the slavers' lair, knowing that Will almost certainly passed through there..." She forced herself to meet his eyes. "It made all that's happened much more real. Together with our endeavors this morning, the information you've shared with me today has allowed me to grasp, and to understand, just how much larger than just Will this scheme is—and therefore how much broader your mission is. I know you've told me, but that sort of knowing is more hypothetical, while seeing makes things real."

She paused to marshal her thoughts. His gaze remained trained on her face. He didn't move, just continued to watch her—and to listen.

With a dip of her head, she went on, "I now comprehend the full extent of this mission, and that it can't possibly end with me or you, or even us working together. I now understand that what we might achieve here can only be a stage—a step closer to the end, but nothing more than that. That to keep those taken safe, what we do cannot and *must not be* more than that."

He didn't immediately respond, but his gaze never left her face.

Eventually, he shifted, resettling his long legs. Finally, he said, "If this afternoon, and the rest of the day, accomplished that, then"—he inclined his head in a gesture of acknowledgment—"I can only be glad."

And immeasurably relieved. Robert felt some of the coiled tension that had had him in its grip since he'd followed her out of her lodgings ease. At some level buried beneath everything else, his mind had already been grappling with the difficulties of getting her to accept precisely that—and, subsequently, to leave the settlement with him. If escorting her into and out of the slum had removed that hurdle, it had been well worth the pain.

They reached Mrs. Hoyt's establishment. He descended from the carriage, handed her down, then followed her up the path to the front door. She led the way in, and he followed. He was determined to go no farther than the front hall, but this time, she diverted through the door to the parlor.

Deeming that safe enough—anyone could walk in on them at any time—he followed her in and shut the door.

She halted in the middle of the room and faced him. "So what's next?"

He stopped with a decent yard between them. He studied her face and realized that his hope that the day's events had satisfied her desire to help had been misplaced. He thought quickly. "As far as I can see, there's little more we can do—not until the slavers kidnap another victim." And she wouldn't be involved in what followed after that.

She frowned. "What about the children? Surely there's something more we can do there."

"Not that I can think of." He could feel the tenseness that had earlier ebbed returning.

Openly dissatisfied and restless, she swanned closer. Eventually, she fetched up directly before him and looked up into his face. Her expression was determined. Her eyes held a militant gleam. "There must be something."

The words drew his gaze to her lips.

And focused his senses on her.

Opened his mind to the gamut of emotions that simply having her so close sent surging through him.

It was increasingly difficult for him not to acknowledge, to himself at least, that what he felt for her—termagant, thorn in his side, and utter distraction that she was—was no longer simple protectiveness of the sort he would have felt for any lady in similar circumstances, especially the sister of men he knew. If it ever had been only that.

What he felt for her…

Yes, he wanted to protect her, but the feeling—the passion—driving that impulse was so much stronger, more potent, and ran so much deeper than anything he'd felt before. Not for any woman. Not for any thing.

Only for her.

Given the intensity of all she evoked and provoked in him… no matter what his preference might be, he really wasn't blind enough not to see what that had to mean.

He'd embarked on this mission determined to complete it and return to England to find himself a wife.

It seemed he'd got the order of events wrong.

She'd been searching his face. Her eyes—those brilliant eyes the color of well-aged brandy—narrowed. "Tell me what I can do to help."

It was an order—a demand.

Her gaze lowered to his lips. She was transparently waiting for him to reply.

He knew he should take a step back, that danger of a sort he'd never before faced lay ahead. But he thought of Babington—of how he, Robert, would feel if he didn't seize the moment, if he didn't take the risk.

And he'd never backed away from a challenge in his life.

He caught her face between his hands, tipped it up, bent his head, and kissed her—hard, passionately, demandingly.

He kissed her just long enough to feel her respond—to feel the fire between them flare, to sense her body sway toward his and feel the light caress of her palm over the back of his hand.

Then he raised his head, hauled in a breath, and looked into her passion-hazed eyes. "If you want to contribute further to this mission, *stay here.* Stay safe."

He held her gaze for a second more, then he released her, turned, and walked to the door. He opened it and left without looking back.

If he'd left her reeling, that seemed only fair; a part of him was reeling, too.

Aileen blinked, straightened, and stared after him.

What the devil…?

She heard the front door open, then quietly shut. She dragged in a breath, then hurried to the window and peered through the lace curtains.

She watched him stride down the path. He halted by the carriage and spoke to Dave, then he strode off, and Dave turned the carriage and rattled away down the hill.

Aileen blinked again. She stood by the window, staring out,

seeing nothing, while she attempted to sort through the tangle of emotions in which he'd left her mired.

Damn him. What had he meant by that?

Stay here. Stay safe.

She snorted. His high-handedness knew no bounds.

But that kiss…intrigued her.

Put it together with the one before, and the one before that…

There was a pattern, wasn't there?

Earlier, she'd challenged him to state by what right he sought to corral her…had that kiss been his answer?

And the kiss moments ago confirmation?

Especially when pressed, men were inclined to resort to actions rather than words.

Was this one of those instances when words might not have been uttered, but he'd intended his actions to stand in lieu?

"How am *I* supposed to know?" She felt like throwing her hands in the air, but refrained.

She was, when it came to it, just as puzzled by herself—by her reactions to his actions—as she was by him. She felt she should be at least a tad outraged by such cavalier methods of persuasion. Instead, fascination and intrigued interest tugged at her mind, potent distractions.

It was unsettling all around, not least because she had no idea where he, she, or they together were headed.

She heard others moving about in the house. She didn't feel up to maintaining a rational conversation with anyone; she opened the parlor door, slipped out, and climbed the stairs.

Once safe in her room, she plonked down on the stool and stared unseeing out of the window. This—whatever it was between them—was so very different to any interaction she'd had before, she felt as if she was barely treading water, literally out of her depth.

The only thing that made the situation in any way acceptable was that she'd received the strong impression that he felt similarly afflicted.

If that was the case, then given his undoubted experience and her lack of it, she shouldn't be surprised at her uncertain state.

Eventually, her circling thoughts returned to her earlier—and still unanswered—question. "What can I do to help?"

If she applied the question to what was occurring between them, then she had no clue, but that wasn't what she'd been referring to. "Will—and Frobisher's mission." Her brother, and her commitment to rescuing him.

As she'd informed Frobisher, given all she now understood, she accepted that rescuing Will was not something she would be able to accomplish herself, either on her own or with Frobisher's help. But by doing what she could to assist with Frobisher's mission, at least she was contributing in a genuine way toward the efforts to rescue the missing.

She sat and looked out at the dying day, at the sunset that wreathed the sky with ribbons of bright pink and purple. Doggedly, step by step, she evaluated all they'd learned—and all they'd yet to find out.

Slowly, her eyes narrowed. "There has to be something I can do to learn more about the slavers."

★ ★ ★

"If we want to keep our backers happy, we need to increase production in keeping with the projections we showed them. And in order to do *that*, we need the second tunnel open and more men to work it. There's no way around that equation." The second man of the three who'd met previously in that particular little tavern took a long pull of his ale.

"That's all very well," the first of the trio to arrive at their watering hole rather peevishly countered, "but with Lady Holbrook doing a bunk and depriving us of her expertise, we need to find some other way to select more men *safely*."

After a moment of staring into his beer, the second man raised his head and looked across the table at the first man. "Why?"

The first man sighed. "Because we still need to ensure that Holbrook and Macauley don't get exercised over any disappearances. Trust me, we can't afford that." The first man sipped, then said, "However, as long as those two remain unconcerned, no insurmountable hurdles are likely to spring up along our path." The man shifted to face the table squarely. He laced his fingers around his glass and lowered his voice. "I've heard back about the five sailors and navvies we sent last week. They reached Dubois hale and whole, and he's happy to have them, but according to Kale, Dubois said he needs not just a few but more like thirty or so to meet our targets."

The third man nearly choked on his ale. "Thirty?"

"Not all at once," the second man stated. He met the first man's gaze. "At least, I take it Dubois means he'll need that number to get the second tunnel up to full production once that's possible."

The first man nodded. "That's my understanding. Dubois has enough men for now, but will soon need a lot more."

"We can't risk taking more from the docks," the third man, the youngest, opined.

"Definitely not," the first man agreed. He looked at the second man, who grimaced and downed his ale.

The second man set down his empty mug. "The squadron's expected back, most likely within a week or so, and as soon as the crews are released to shore, any rumors of disappearances are likely to reach the officers, and with Decker back in port, that's the last thing we need."

After a moment, the second man continued, "We've succeeded thus far because we've been careful. I suggest we don't change our stripes just because Dubois expects us to immediately fulfill his every request."

"Agreed," said the first man.

The third simply nodded.

Several seconds passed, then the second man asked, "Can we think of any alternative means of getting Dubois the hands he needs?"

"What about taking more older boys—the lads who are almost at the point of getting jobs?" the third man suggested. "Some of them are nearly as hefty as their fathers and more than strong enough to wield a pick or shovel."

The first man pursed his lips.

The second man stared at the third, plainly in thought.

Then the second man shrugged and looked at the first. "That might work as a stopgap, if nothing else. At least until we can find some acceptable way of selecting those men it's safe to take."

Slowly, the first man nodded. "All right—let's try that, at least for the moment." He looked at the other two. "Meanwhile, all of us can put our minds to finding a safe source to supply Dubois with more adult males."

Eleven

Frobisher's words on the inadvisability of trusting anyone in the settlement's officialdom remained in the forefront of Aileen's mind when, the following morning, she swept into the Office of the Naval Attaché.

Little had changed since she'd last been there. The three clerks still worked at desks along the wall; the same lanky individual with whom she'd previously spoken rose and, recognizing her, rather warily came to the counter.

Although Frobisher had advanced no definite evidence that anyone in the navy was involved in whatever heinous scheme was afoot, she had, nevertheless, determined to say nothing that might in any way alert anyone to his mission.

That was too important to jeopardize.

"Good morning." She'd dressed for the occasion—her mission for today—in another of her jacket-and-skirt outfits, this one a delicate pale lemon yellow with a crisp white blouse. She smiled at the clerk as sincerely as she could.

He didn't smile back. "How can we help you this time, miss?"

Clearly, she wasn't going to get any further with these dolts than she had the last time, but who knew? Pigs might fly. She parted her lips on her rehearsed speech—and saw a shadow move behind the frosted glass in the door in the rear wall of the outer office.

The door with the words "Naval Attaché" blazoned on it.

She redirected her attention to the clerk. "I understand that the naval attaché is in the office today. Please inform him that I,

Miss Hopkins, wish to speak with him." The clerk opened his mouth—no doubt to tell her his master was too busy to oblige her. Before he could, she rolled on, her tone increasingly pointed, "And perhaps you might tell him—" *That I've recently posted a letter to the Admiralty?* That was too close to Frobisher's mission. She substituted, "That I expect to be back in London soon and will be calling at the Admiralty."

She clasped her hands about the top of her reticule and, no longer smiling, arched an imperious brow at the clerk.

He debated for a second, then waved her to a chair by the side of the room. "If you'll take a seat, Miss Hopkins, I'll let Mr. Muldoon know you're here."

Buoyed by mild triumph—and a surge of anticipation over perhaps getting some worthwhile answers—she consented to sit on one of the three straight-backed chairs lined up against the wall. She placed her reticule in her lap and watched the clerk go to the door, tap, and enter.

The clerk shut the door behind him. She wondered how long she might have to wait.

A minute ticked past, then the door opened, and the clerk came out—followed by a rather handsome man in a plain suit.

The man's gaze found her. While the clerk returned to his desk, the man came forward and opened the gate to the side of the counter. "Miss Hopkins?"

Aileen rose and went forward. "Indeed, sir. I take it you are the naval attaché?"

The man bowed. "Muldoon, Miss Hopkins." He straightened and, with a wave, invited her to precede him into his office.

She passed through the gate, walked through the door, and halted in the space just beyond. The office wasn't large; directly in front of her sat a plain desk with two padded chairs angled before it. There were cabinets against three walls, a map of the settlement and its surrounds on the wall behind the desk, and to her right, a small window that gave onto some alley.

Muldoon followed her in. He shut the door, then moved past her to place one of the padded chairs directly facing the desk. "Please have a seat, Miss Hopkins. Then perhaps you might tell me how I and my office might assist you."

Aileen went forward, drew her skirts in, and sat. She watched as Muldoon rounded the desk and sat in the chair behind it. He was only a little taller than she was, so relatively short for a man, but he was built in proportion, and his features were striking—coal-black hair and intense blue eyes set in a face of sharp angles and planes. Irish or Cornish was Aileen's guess; he was a rivetingly handsome man…and she realized she was regarding him with supreme dispassion. The sight of him left her totally unmoved.

Apparently, *rivetingly handsome* wasn't enough to entice her senses anymore.

An image of Frobisher swam across her mind…

Hurriedly, she banished it. She had work to do. "Thank you for seeing me, Mr. Muldoon. As your clerks might have mentioned, I arrived in the settlement in search of information about my brother Lieutenant William Hopkins."

"Ah, yes." Muldoon rested his forearms on the desk and clasped his hands on the blotter. "Sadly, Hopkins vanished from the settlement some months ago."

"So I have heard. What I fail to understand is what Will was doing in the settlement at all, rather than being at sea with his ship. However, I have already been informed that your office has no knowledge of Will's movements. That is not why I have called today."

She paused, swiftly reviewing her rehearsed questions. She needed to be careful how she phrased her queries. "While attempting to learn more about my brother's disappearance, I discovered that, apparently entirely unconnected with Will's case, more than a dozen children—admittedly of the lower orders, but British children nonetheless—have also vanished."

Muldoon's attention was fixed on her. She couldn't complain that he wasn't listening.

She continued, "While I might not be able to further my brother's case in any meaningful way, I would like to inquire what the authorities have learned about the disappearances of these children. I understand it's an ongoing problem."

Muldoon frowned, then looked down. A second passed, then he drew a fresh sheet of paper onto the blotter and picked up a pencil. He wrote rapidly—several lines of script Aileen couldn't see well enough to read—then Muldoon looked up at her. "Matters such as this are handled by the governor's office. I'll ask his staff and see what I can learn."

She smiled. "Thank you."

His gaze on her face, Muldoon asked, "Is there anything else you've heard with regard to the missing children?"

Caution raised its head; she searched for the right words. "Well… I did hear a rumor about slave traders operating inside the settlement—that perhaps it was they who had taken the children."

Muldoon was scribbling again. "Rumors." Without looking up, he asked, "From whom?"

When she didn't immediately reply, Muldoon glanced up, his gaze rather sharper than it had been before.

Aileen wished she could color on command; it would have added a helpful touch of verisimilitude just then. "I…ah—I went into the slums. Just the edges, so to speak." She waved to the east, toward the slum from which the children had been taken. "I was asking after my brother, but instead I heard about the children and the rumors about the slave traders."

Muldoon had glanced in the direction of her wave. His frown grew more definite. "That is…worrying." He looked down at what he'd written and added another line. He glanced briefly up at her. "I'm glad you brought this issue to me, Miss Hopkins. I will certainly follow it up. Might I ask how long you plan to remain in the settlement and where we can find you?" He waved at his notes. "Once I have an answer to your questions, I will endeavor to inform you."

Her smile was entirely genuine. "Indeed, sir—I would appreciate that. I am uncertain as to how much longer I will remain here, but certainly for the next several days. You can find me at Mrs. Hoyt's Boarding House—it's not far from the rectory."

Muldoon jotted down the information. With that done, he briefly reviewed what he'd written, then he set down his pencil and pushed back from the desk. "Again, thank you for bringing this to my attention, Miss Hopkins. Rest assured I will set matters in train as soon as I possibly can."

He rose and rounded the desk.

Aileen came to her feet. Pleased beyond her expectations, she held out her hand. As Muldoon lightly gripped it and respectfully bowed, she said, "Thank you for your help, sir. If you should learn anything, please do send word. If I can at least get something done about these poor children, my trip to the colony will not have been in vain."

She was perfectly content to have Muldoon and his lackeys view her as a member of that tribe of well-to-do ladies who busied themselves with good works. And if, via Muldoon and his queries, she gained any insight into how nineteen children could be kidnapped from within the settlement, and slave traders walk its alleys with impunity, all with no reaction from the local authorities, she would count her morning's excursion a signal success.

Buoyed by a pleasant sense of accomplishment, she allowed Muldoon to bow her out of his office and escort her along the bustling quay and up the steps into the street.

With a nod, she parted from him at the top of the steps. Despite his quite remarkable handsomeness, his grip on her elbow hadn't affected her pulse in the slightest. Smiling, she raised her skirts and walked up the incline; she'd left Dave and his carriage waiting in the main street.

It had occurred to her that Frobisher's mission was to follow the path of the missing adults. At this juncture, they had no firm evidence that the children were being taken by the same band of slavers, let alone for the same end purpose. There was a distinct possibility that the disappearance of the children was completely unconnected with the missing adults. And if that proved to be so, then as she understood things, once Frobisher discovered the location of the slavers' camp to which the adults were taken, he was under orders to depart forthwith—leaving no one concerned over, much less looking for, the kidnapped children.

She'd told Muldoon the unvarnished truth. She couldn't in all conscience sail away from the settlement without doing whatever she could to ensure that *something* was being done about the children—those already taken and those who might yet be lured into the slavers' clutches.

Thoroughly satisfied with her morning's work thus far, she reached Water Street, released her skirts, saw Dave waiting, and headed his way.

★ ★ ★

The rest of her morning did not go quite so well.

Aileen reached the inn at which Frobisher was staying only to discover him absent. She'd remembered the directions he'd given the lad by the shore, and she confirmed with the landlady that a man of Frobisher's description was, indeed, in residence at the inn, but that he'd left after breakfast—to where, the landlady had no idea.

Aileen wasn't at all sure she trusted Frobisher to send to inform her if the lad arrived with word of the slavers appearing on the shore. He'd promised to inform her of anything he and his men learned; he hadn't promised *when* such information would be communicated—before or after any action had taken place.

Then again, several of the children had stated that the slavers came in the afternoon, so presumably, she wasn't missing any action at that moment.

She returned to Dave's carriage and debated her options. Most likely, Frobisher would be with his men in their hide, watching the slavers' lair.

Or perhaps some adult had been kidnapped last night, and Frobisher and his men were already following…but no. The landlady had said he'd been at the inn for breakfast, and the slavers carried their captives out of the settlement during the night. Aileen couldn't see Frobisher returning to his bed and calmly breakfasting at the inn while his men slipped through the jungle on the slavers' heels.

No. If she was any judge of character—and with men like him, she was—then he would be leading his men.

So they—he, his men, and she—were all still waiting. She for news from the shore, he and his men for the slavers to kidnap another adult.

She felt her lips set. Patience had never come easily. She rose from the seat and pushed up the trapdoor. "Back to Mrs. Hoyt's, please, Dave."

"Aye, miss."

She stared unseeing out of the carriage window as Dave drove her back up the slope of Tower Hill. She was sorely tempted to redirect him to drive out along the street that led to the crest above Undoto's house, but… Even if she persuaded Dave to accompany her—and she wasn't at all sure that leaving his carriage unattended in such an area would be wise—walking through that slum without a man like Frobisher by her side would be not just foolish but foolhardy.

If she wanted Frobisher—and others—to view her as a sensible and reliable partner, she couldn't behave like a reckless twit.

They reached Mrs. Hoyt's Boarding House for Genteel Ladies. Aileen left Dave with his carriage drawn up beside the curb; she'd paid for his exclusive services for a full week. Still trying, somewhat despondently, to think of something sensible to do, she walked up the path and into the boardinghouse.

It wasn't until she was in her room unpinning her bonnet that a potentially useful endeavor occurred to her. She laid the bonnet aside, considered the prospect, then turned on her heel and went downstairs.

She'd discovered that although Mrs. Hoyt wasn't a fan of Undoto's services—*"I have better ways to pass my time, miss"*—as a shrewd woman looking to make her way, Mrs. Hoyt posted advance warning of the priest's services on a little noticeboard by the dining room door. An aunt of one of the maids was a devotee, and so the postings were usually up to date.

Aileen reached the dining room door, searched the various notices—of recitals, church services, and the like—pinned to the board, and saw that—*yes*—Undoto was holding a service today.

She returned to her room, pinned her bonnet back on, and went out to the carriage.

Dave accepted her order with a grunt and duly sent the carriage rattling down the hill, then turned his horse to the east, toward Undoto's church.

She hadn't forgotten that the men she now knew were slavers called at Undoto's house to speak to the priest on the evening after he gave a service. "There *has* to be some connection—something that happens at the services." Something they hadn't yet identified.

Dave drew up outside the church a good twenty minutes before noon. Judging from the dearth of carriages outside, the bulk of the congregation had yet to arrive, but the church doors stood open, and a few people were strolling inside.

Alighting from the carriage, Aileen shook out her skirts, then tipped her head back and looked at Dave. "Why don't you go off and get something to eat? I expect to be here for about two hours." She pointed at the benches set under a row of trees along one edge of the forecourt. "I'll wait for you there."

Dave glanced at the spot, then nodded and touched his cap.

Aileen watched him drive off, then she walked toward the church.

She chose a position at the end of a bench a third of the way down the aisle. The spot gave her a decent view over most of the European congregation and also a clear view of the pulpit and the area before the altar. She sat and watched as the congregation streamed in. She saw Sampson, but of course, Frobisher wasn't with him. Another old sailor came up, and the two old tars settled in the back corner; if Aileen was any judge, they were entertaining themselves with comments on the ladies and gentlemen who had chosen to attend.

Despite watching everyone who entered, noting every interaction, she saw nothing even remotely suspicious. Once the service commenced, she concentrated unwaveringly on Undoto. She noted his every inflection, considered his every gesture. Searched for anything that might be a signal—although to whom and about what she had no clue.

At the end of the service, she concluded that Undoto most likely derived the information about those to be kidnapped—the information that he subsequently passed on to the slavers—from his exchanges with his congregation as they filed out of the church. That might explain why the slavers called at his house only on the nights following a service.

As he stood beside the door and shook hands and chatted, Undoto appeared genial, engaged, and in no hurry whatsoever. He spent at least half a minute with everyone who lined up to take his hand; with some—all of them Europeans, Aileen noticed—he spent significantly more time, and he clearly knew quite a bit about their lives.

She was careful to slip out of the church at a moment when, amid a crush of ladies, she could avoid Undoto. She spent the next half hour moving through the crowd of parishioners, Europeans and natives alike, who dallied in the forecourt, chatting with each other and also with Undoto after he quit his post by the door.

Smiling, the priest spoke with this one and that; Aileen watched closely and on several occasions saw Undoto ask what were clearly questions of certain European ladies—questions the ladies readily answered.

So easy. How long would it take a priest to ask a question here, one there, and build up a working knowledge of the Europeans in the settlement—where they lived, who was among each household, where the men worked, where the ladies shopped? It wasn't hard to understand why Undoto's position made him useful to the slavers.

She'd seen enough. She retreated to one of the benches, choosing the one most heavily shaded; with her complexion, she needed to take whatever steps she could to avoid freckling. She sat to wait for Dave to return.

She looked out at the stragglers still chatting in the forecourt and thought of how much the minister of the village church near her parents' house knew of his parishioners. A lot. Priests, ministers, vicars, and the like were trusted with all sorts of information—and the information Undoto would want, the sort of information the slavers would need, would, in the wider scheme of things, be considered relatively innocuous.

If that was Undoto's role—to provide the insights into people's lives that would give the slavers the requisite knowledge to seize particular individuals without being caught—then what had Lady Holbrook done? From what Frobisher had told her…

She sat in the humid warmth under the trees and, bit by bit, assembled a mental diagram of the slavers' scheme. Lady Holbrook had known who every European adult in the colony was—apparently even those who lived in the slums. She had also known her husband's prejudices and therefore had been able to guide the slavers—most likely in conjunction with Undoto—to seize people whose disappearance would either not be noticed or, alternatively, could be attributed to some other cause—such as going into the jungle in pursuit of their fortune, or in the wake of a particular man.

Aileen wracked her memory for the details of those taken. Perhaps in some cases there had been some other criterion involved in Lady Holbrook's calculations—for instance, something that would explain why those particular young women had been taken.

She mulled over the possibilities while the afternoon haze thickened and the shadows thrown by the leaves danced over and around her.

A nearby birdcall jerked her out of her near somnolence. She refocused on the forecourt and realized that all the other carriages had left, along with all the people. The church doors and windows had been shut, and even Undoto had gone.

Dave had yet to return, but no doubt he soon would.

Aileen lifted her reticule from her lap, rose, and shook out her skirts—

Black sacking fell over her head.

Her lungs seized. Then she hauled in a breath and opened her mouth to scream.

A hand clapped over the material across her mouth. She all but choked.

Her head was pulled back, the crown of her bonnet squashing against a meaty chest.

She tried to turn her head, tried to pull away, but then some other binding wrapped about her head and pulled tight over her mouth, gagging her completely. Then a brawny arm clamped around her waist, and she was lifted off her feet.

Desperate, she let her reticule fall to swing by its cord and reached for the shroud—for the gag.

Other hands snatched hers. In seconds, her wrists were bound.

Before she could even think of kicking, cords wound over and around her walking boots, and her ankles were lashed tightly together.

The man holding her was huge. He grunted and hefted her up and around. He settled her over his shoulder like a sack of potatoes, then started walking.

Panic reared. She tried to twist, to wriggle—to force the man to lose his grip—but his arm tightened about her legs, and her efforts did nothing, just made her gasp for breath.

She quieted and tried desperately to hear over her thudding heart. She found the lack of sight utterly disorientating. She struggled to re-establish her sense of direction. She thought the man was walking along the line of trees, using them for concealment. At least one other man was keeping pace alongside.

A chill ran through her as she realized that she was about to become one of the missing.

She dragged in a deeper breath and held it. She closed her eyes—she could see nothing through the hood anyway—and forced herself to assess using her other senses. She could still hear; she could still feel. If she concentrated, she might be able to work out where they were taking her.

Focusing on where they were going muted her panic; the more she forced herself to try to make sense of things and determine their direction as they carried her farther helped stave off her fear. Of course, the fear remained, blind and unthinking, but increasingly, the emotion dominating her mind was one driven by the most basic instinct—survival. Spurred by incipient desperation, her mind turned from witless gibbering to learning enough about what was happening around her so that she could find some way to free herself. Or to raise the alarm.

Unfortunately, her captors didn't carry her through any streets. Instead, they carted her to the end of the row of trees, then turned to their right and picked up their pace. The shushing of the trees' leaves fell behind, and she felt the sun strike unimpeded on her thinly clad back—but after what must have been ten or so yards, the men stopped in shadow again.

Eyes still closed, she tried to envision where they were. The rear of the church? Had to be; no other building was close enough. She heard the sound of a key being put into a lock and turned, then hinges creaked softly, and the man carrying her lugged her into deeper—cooler—shadow.

They didn't go far. As the thug carrying her lowered her to what felt like a straight-backed wooden chair, she opened her eyes behind the black material—in time to see light fade and vanish as the door through which they'd come was closed.

"Stay put," the man who had carried her growled in a rough, gruff, uncultured voice.

Trussed as she was, she could see no point in attempting anything else. Ten seconds of surreptitiously testing the bonds about her hands was enough to convince her that trying to wriggle them free would be wasted effort.

At least the rim of her bonnet kept the black material away from the upper half of her face, so she didn't feel entirely smothered.

She forced herself to relax in the chair, to conserve her strength. She continued to listen, to track the men as they moved about her. There were only two of them. Eventually, they settled on chairs or perhaps on the floor to either side of her. Then silence fell.

As far as she could make out, they'd come through the door she had days earlier seen Undoto use to enter the church.

She and her two captors remained where they were—as they were—for what felt like hours.

It was hot and close. The men didn't speak, either to her or between themselves, leaving her plenty of time to consider her predicament.

She had no doubt whatsoever that she'd been seized by the same slavers who'd been working with Undoto all along.

The same slave traders who had, almost certainly, also kidnapped Will.

For several minutes, she dwelled on the thought that if the slavers delivered her to the same place to which they'd taken Will, if London's assumptions were correct, she might well see her brother again. But she knew beyond question that Will would not welcome her with open arms. He'd be furious with her for coming after him and getting taken, too.

Not for the coming after but for getting taken, too. And she wouldn't blame him. If she had any say in matters, being made a captive herself would be her least-favored method for finding and rescuing Will.

That brought her back to plotting her escape.

She assumed—hoped—that her captors would take her back to their lair before they carted her into the jungle. She evaluated every option, but she couldn't imagine any way in which she might get free—not without help.

Not without someone rescuing her.

That led to thoughts of Frobisher and his men.

She felt sure his men, at least, would be watching the slavers' lair. They expected the slave traders to take any captive they seized back to that dwelling deep in the slum not all that far away.

If her captors did, indeed, carry her there…would Frobisher be watching? Would he realize the captive was she?

Frowning beneath the black hood, she thought of what he might recognize. He wouldn't be able to see her face or hair, not unless her captors removed the hood, and she didn't think that at all likely.

He hadn't seen her lemon-yellow outfit before. She seriously doubted he would recognize her half boots.

What else? There had to be something.

Uncomfortable, she shifted on the wooden chair and felt the weight of her reticule resting against her thigh. She was faintly amazed the thugs hadn't taken it from her. Then again, they no doubt assumed it contained nothing more than the usual bits and bobs ladies carried. Not that her pistol was currently much use to her; with her wrists bound, she didn't have enough play in her fingers to open the tight neck of the reticule sufficiently wide, and she wasn't so foolish as to draw a pistol when she couldn't see where she was aiming.

But the reticule itself was something Frobisher might recognize—ugly, dull black lump that it was. She'd chosen it for practicality, not beauty.

And if it provided the means for Frobisher or his men to recognize her, it would have served her well.

But recognition was all she could hope for. Rescue was out of the question, at least not from that quarter.

She could still hear Frobisher declaring—in his authoritative captain's voice—that under no circumstances could they rescue the next person or persons the slavers seized. That, instead, they had to let the slavers have their captive so they could follow the trail to the slavers' camp.

And she'd agreed with him; if she viewed his mission dispassionately, she still did.

She just hadn't expected to be the next person seized.

Regardless, she had been, and she did not—could not—expect him to put her welfare above his duty, her safety above that of all those already missing, no matter how assiduously protective he'd been.

No matter those kisses.

Although she had no idea why she'd been taken—what had caused the slavers to target her?—it didn't truly matter. She'd made her bed, and now…

Thinking of Frobisher in conjunction with a bed wasn't a wise idea.

Under the hood, beneath the gag, she grumbled a *Damn!* She had a feeling that in moments of weakness, she'd be thinking of Frobisher in relation to a bed—any bed—for a very long time.

How unfair that the only man to have ever sent her mind down that path was the one sworn by his duty to let her slide into the hands of slave traders.

If she'd been able to speak, she would have made several pithy remarks.

Instead…

Although restricted by the hood and the gag, she drew in a deeper breath and tried to focus on what she could sense, what she could deduce.

Tried again to think of any possible way to remove herself from the slavers' clutches.

Because, realistically, there wasn't anyone likely to step in and save her.

She reached that depressing conclusion just as the men stirred. They exchanged comments; as far as she could understand, they were debating whether it was time to move her.

Apparently, it was. They both approached her. One hauled her to her feet, then a covering made of some strong but not rough material—canvas?—was wrapped around her.

She was helpless to prevent them trussing her up like a parcel; they wound cords about the wrapping to keep it in place. One large flap came over the top of the hood, blocking out even the faintest suggestion of light and plunging her into Stygian darkness. Then the huge man, the larger of the two, hoisted her up over his shoulder again and started off. She heard hinges creak, and then they were out in the simmering heat once more.

The men trudged along. She jounced slightly on the thug's shoulder, but soon she sensed they were climbing—presumably ascending the hill above the church. But from the sound of their footsteps, they weren't walking along the street itself but through laneways and alleys. She could no longer detect light or dark at all, but she sensed a difference in temperature. The sun had set; she felt sure of that.

Surreptitiously, she eased her bound hands this way and that. Bit by bit, she guided her wrists and her reticule between the folds of her cocoon. Finally, her wrists slid clear of the covering. A few yards farther, and her reticule fell and swung from the cord about her left wrist; she prayed and did her best to keep it from hitting the thug carrying her. Luckily, he seemed oblivious to any swaying tap; he didn't so much as pause in his pacing.

Then she sensed the closer atmosphere of the slum close around them.

They were nearly to the lair. She'd done everything she could, yet any chance of escape—of winning free—remained as far away as ever.

★ ★ ★

The day had waned, evening was nigh, and black night hovered not far distant. Robert stared over the ramshackle roofs of the slum, his gaze locked—as it had been for the past hour—on the doorway of the slavers' lair.

He'd spent most of the day with his men in their tower-room hide, taking turns keeping watch.

He'd walked into the slum shortly after breakfast. He and Aileen had made no plans for further investigative forays that day, and he hoped his parting words had sunk into her brain and taken hold.

He could hope.

But short of her managing to intercept the lad from the shore if the boy came to tell him that the slavers had returned to take more children—and even if she did, Robert felt reasonably confident she would send the boy on to him—he couldn't see what else she might do.

How else she might insert herself into his mission.

But now that they had the slavers literally in their sights, he needed to concentrate on the job he'd been sent to do. He didn't have time for the distraction of brandy-colored eyes, looks that challenged him on multiple levels, and a tongue honed by a too-accurate understanding of what levers to tug to manage him.

He wasn't up for being managed, by her or anyone else.

After this was over, and he'd stopped by on his way out of the settlement and swept her up, they could address the powerful attraction between them. They would have plenty of time to explore that on the journey back to England.

For now, his mission had to come first. He had to put duty first.

Especially now that something was afoot.

A messenger had come running to the slavers' lair half an hour before midday. He'd delivered what had turned out to be a summons to the man lounging in the doorway. Both messenger and doorkeeper had gone inside.

Robert had sent Coleman and Fuller out to circle the lair and watch the rear exits; they'd already determined that there were two. As it transpired, after several minutes, two of the slavers plus the messenger had left via one of the rear doors and slipped away through the lanes, heading toward the settlement.

Coleman and Fuller had seen the three men go, but per Robert's orders, as all four slavers hadn't left the lair, Coleman and Fuller had noted the direction in which the three had gone, then had returned to the hide to report.

That had been nearly six hours ago.

In the intervening time, Robert had prayed that his decision to allow the slavers to go wherever they'd been summoned and not split his forces had been sound. That the hypothesis that the slavers would always return to their lair before taking their captives into the jungle would prove to be correct.

He hoped like hell that the slavers he'd let go would come back and not take any captive they'd seized straight out of the settlement.

It had been a tense six hours.

But now the shadows were deepening—the sun had set, and the usual blackness would soon envelop all—and judging by the way the two slavers remaining at the lair kept looking down the alley toward the settlement, they were, indeed, expecting their comrades to return, presumably with some victim.

The atmosphere in the hide grew more sharply expectant with each minute that ticked past. Robert sent Coleman and Fuller back to their posts at the rear of the lair, just in case the slavers returned from that direction.

Finally, the slaver sitting on the stoop staring down the alley stood up. His gaze remained locked farther down the alley; from the tower room, Robert couldn't see any part of the alley itself.

The slaver glanced into the house, saying something to his friend inside. The first man looked back down the alley, then grinned. His friend joined him at the door and beamed at whatever they could both now see.

His gaze trained on the lair's doorway, Robert waited for those coming up the alley to appear.

Then they did.

The two men who had gone down to the settlement trudged into view. The larger was carrying a trussed, canvas-wrapped bundle draped over his shoulder.

The bundle was clearly a person, but… Robert squinted. Surely the trussed figure was too slim and too short to be a man.

A youth?

"Oh, me God." The whisper came from Benson, hunkered by a corner of the sill and peering out, too. Benson glanced up; Robert looked down and met his eyes. Horror etched Benson's features. He pointed at the tableau playing out in the doorway of the slavers' lair. "Ain't that…?"

Robert snapped his gaze back to the doorway. The brute carrying the trussed figure angled his burden to pass through the door frame, giving Robert a glimpse of what Benson, viewing proceedings from a slightly different angle, had already seen.

Two delicate white wrists lashed together poked free of the confining shroud. Dangling from one wrist by a black cord was a familiar black reticule.

They'd all seen it before—Robert many times—perennially hanging from Aileen Hopkins's wrist.

A flap of canvas covered her head. There was nothing else of her to be seen.

The black reticule swung at the slaver's side as he carried his burden into the shadows of the house. Robert thought Aileen's curled fingers moved, but he couldn't be sure.

He stood frozen, staring at the now empty doorway—the gaping maw through which she'd been carried.

He felt as if he'd cracked his head on a spar.

His lungs weren't working properly, either. It took effort to haul in a breath—to fight to find some anchor for the thoughts whirling in his head.

For the emotions churning in his gut.

Benson and Harris said nothing, just watched him.

Robert swore. He raised both hands and raked them back through his hair. He laced his fingers, gripped the locks.

He still couldn't manage to drag his gaze from the doorway.

He'd laid down the law, declaring unequivocally that they had to accept that whoever the slavers seized next, they would have to let that person go—a sacrifice for the greater good.

His words taunted him.

Had the slavers taken anyone else, his way forward would have been unambiguously clear. He would have followed the course of duty come what may.

Now…the choice that faced him was duty—or her?

A brisk *tap-tap* on the door, and it opened. Robert and the others turned to look as Fuller and Coleman slipped into the room.

"What?" Robert demanded.

"Whoever they've got, they've set them down inside, in the middle room. But that's not all—six new slavers have arrived. They came up from the other side and slipped in through the rear door just now."

"Six more?" That put paid to any thought Robert might have entertained of simply barging into the lair and taking Aileen back.

He grimaced and looked back at the window. There was no point pretending he didn't know what he was going to do.

Duty was one thing.

Aileen Hopkins was something else entirely.

He glanced at Benson and Harris, then looked at Coleman and Fuller. "The person they've seized is Miss Hopkins. And our plans have changed. We're going to take her back."

Twelve

Aileen sat on the wooden floor on which she'd been placed, a plank wall at her back, her legs stretched out in front of her.

She remained loosely wrapped in whatever covering her captors had trussed her up in. Her reticule had landed on the floor beside her. Her hands remained bound, as were her feet, and the horrible black hood was still in place, along with the suffocating gag.

Despite the restriction of her senses, she was fairly certain she was inside the slavers' lair.

They'd definitely traveled well into the slum, and as they'd approached this place, she'd heard other men call rough greetings, and her two captors had responded. Then those others had gathered around, and the man carrying her had turned and climbed several steps.

He'd shifted her; they'd been passing through what she'd registered as a doorway before she'd truly realized.

Frantically, she'd tried to wriggle her fingers, but in a heartbeat, her moment for being recognized had been over.

The thug carrying her had walked deeper into the house, then had set her down where she presently sat.

She forced herself to listen to the slavers talk. There was nothing else to occupy her and keep her from giving in to burgeoning fear, so even though she couldn't imagine how she might escape—couldn't imagine not ending in the slavers' camp, and so couldn't imagine what good anything she heard might do anyone—nevertheless she listened for all she was worth.

Some of the men spoke English, but with varying and rather

thick accents; heard all together, they were difficult to decipher, and in some cases tell apart. Other men spoke with foreign accents, and most often, those men spoke some form of pidgin. She wasn't sure it was pidgin English and not pidgin something else. French, Dutch, German? She heard traces of all three languages.

The longer she listened, the more distinct the individual voices became. She set herself the challenge of distinguishing each speaker—a game to stop herself from dwelling on her fate. She soon realized there were significantly more men than the four she'd thought had been in the lair. She eventually identified ten, all garrulously talking.

She wished they would speak more clearly, but amid the babel, one man's voice stood out. It was…mellifluous. Mesmerizing in quality. Undoto had a compelling voice, but this man… Whoever he was, his voice was more a hypnotic weapon than a mere means of communication.

Deep and rolling, the cadences seemed more French than English. Several times, she had to blink and shake her head to overcome the effect and shift her focus to what one of the other men said.

After an extended round of exchanging what she considered the usual male greetings, the men settled to discuss their business. Apparently, one group had been sent into the settlement to fetch supplies of some specialized sort from a man named Winter. For the most part, however, the push to seize more healthy males for whoever their current customer was consumed the slavers; from their comments, she understood that they were forbidden to simply take random European males. The men to be seized had to be selected for them. And regardless of any temporary measures, the order they were supposed to fill called for men, not women or children.

Then the tone of the men's voices changed, and she realized they were talking about her.

She soon discovered it was possible to feel chilled while blushing. Crude jokes sounded crude regardless of any accent.

She sat unmoving, barely daring to breathe, feeling very like a blind rabbit in a room full of wolves. She tensed, expecting at any moment to feel grasping hands…

But none of the men came close enough even to touch her.

One name was repeated by several men, especially with respect to her. *Dubois.* Swallowing the fear that had risen in her throat, she started listening to the conversations again; as far as she could make out, she owed her unmolested state to Dubois or, more specifically, to the influence he wielded over the slavers.

That made her feel slightly better, relieving one source of her welling fear.

Was Dubois their customer? Or an agent acting for said customer?

Or was he the slavers' true leader?

From the way the men referred to him, she didn't think the latter was correct. She continued to listen, but the men's attention shifted to getting ready for something—whether that was leaving with her or seizing someone else, she couldn't discern before they moved into other rooms in the small house and the intervening walls muted their words below her ability to hear.

That left her with no effective distraction to keep her from dwelling on her fate. On her now likely, all-but-assured fate.

She attempted to reconcile herself to it; she tried to manage and rein in her fear by going over what she believed would soon happen, yet no matter how rational she tried to be, she could not bring herself to acquiesce to being taken as a captive into the jungle. Some stubborn, determined part of her continued to rebel—to insist that there *had to be* some way to win free, regardless of what logic suggested.

The one thing she did accept was that whatever occurred over the next few hours—between now and when the slavers carried her beyond the settlement's boundaries—had the potential to fundamentally alter the course of her life, and it was entirely possible that the change would be irrevocable.

Being faced with that prospect opened doors in her mind she would rather have left closed.

She couldn't stop herself from imagining the worst, that the irrevocable change threatening to engulf her would cut short her life, certainly her life as she'd imagined it would be.

Regrets fountained and washed through her.

Her parents, her brothers…but the one who stood out most clearly in her mind…

She hadn't realized Robert Frobisher had etched himself into her consciousness to that extent.

Yet her biggest regret was, indeed, that she hadn't had a chance to explore the unexpected, unprecedented attraction that had flared between them. Even though she hadn't allowed herself to properly examine it, she'd recognized the potential as a once-in-a-lifetime chance—a chance no sane woman should or would turn her back on.

Connecting like that, with a man like him—for a woman like her, that was the ultimate challenge. Missing that chance…she couldn't not see it as a failure of sorts, even if she wasn't to blame.

Anger rose, a fire in her belly, one that countered the chill of fear.

Because of the slavers, because of whatever scheme some faceless men had put in place—undoubtedly for their own gain—she was going to miss out on the greatest and most important challenge of her life.

She would fail through never having had a chance to seize it.

The emotional wound stung; she brooded and let simmering fury ferment—so much better, so much more welcome, than fear.

Abruptly, the men's voices changed, their comments coming quick and sharp. More like commands barked by a few of them. Not the one with the wonderful voice but others she'd heard several times.

Then heavy footsteps neared. One man crouched beside her; she could smell him even through the hood and wrapping. Hands seized her reticule and she tensed, but he only stuffed it back under the wrap. Then another man—she thought it was the same brute who had carried her throughout—grabbed her shoulders and effortlessly lifted her. Again, he hoisted her trussed body over his shoulder.

She didn't try to fight but let her body lie limply. No sense courting unnecessary bruises.

As she swayed with the man's gait, she tried to track their route. Not out of the same door through which they'd brought her into the house but through a rear entrance.

The man went down several steps, then he lengthened his stride and went tramping down some very narrow alley; she could sense the closeness of the walls to either side.

They were taking her out of the settlement.

She hoped that, at the very least, Frobisher and his men would see and follow and would continue until they reached the slavers' camp. At least his mission would be fulfilled.

Anger rose again, a hot wave that had the tips of her ears burning.

If fate or the deity or whatever god was listening would deign to give her another chance at living her life as she would—as she should—she swore she would seize that chance with both hands and not let go.

* * *

Nearly four hours had passed since the slavers had carried Aileen into their lair.

Lurking in the oppressive shadows cast by an overhang along the lane behind the lair, Robert fought to keep his mind from what might have happened inside the ramshackle building.

Coleman—the lightest on his feet and the least threatening in appearance—had ghosted close to the lair's side door and had slouched beside it for some time. He'd reported that the men inside were talking and, he thought, playing cards, and there'd been no sounds of struggle or ruckus.

Robert prayed that meant that Aileen was all right. Just the thought of what might have occurred…

He mentally swore and hauled his mind from that tack; it pushed him to the brink of madness and fractured his concentration—and he would need every ounce of that to rescue her and ensure she came to no further harm.

The past hours had been filled with plans and preparations. With ten slavers in the lair, storming it was out of the question. Regardless of whether he and his men could prevail in a fight of five against ten, the risk to Aileen, hooded and bound, was too great. With her effectively surrounded by the slavers, his hands were also tied.

It would be a different matter when the blackguards carried her out. The alleys and lanes were too narrow to allow even two men to walk abreast. With the slavers strung out in a line, picking off the guards and seizing Aileen was a plan with a decent chance of success.

His men were scattered all around. Benson, Fuller, and Coleman were, like him, watching the rear exits from the lair. Harris was keeping an eye on the front door, but as the alley at the front of the building led back to the settlement or farther up the hill, assuming the blackguards did as expected and carried Aileen into the jungle that night, they expected the slavers to leave via one of the two rear exits.

One exit gave onto the rear lane in which Robert stood. The other was the side door that opened onto a runnel that later intersected with the same lane, but also gave access to two other alleyways.

His men knew the plan; they'd helped flesh out the details. He and Harris had gone back to the inn, intending to fetch everyone's gear, take it down to the tender, and send it out to *The Trident*. Once they seized Aileen, they wouldn't be able to remain anywhere on shore. They could worry about fetching her baggage later.

Dave had been waiting—fretting and pacing—at the inn. He'd all but pounced on Robert, telling him how Aileen hadn't been waiting when Dave had gone to fetch her from Undoto's church that afternoon. Dave's information had filled in several gaps. Robert had calmed the old cockney and assured him they intended to get Aileen back. Thinking ahead, he'd arranged to meet Dave at the inn the following morning—to reassure him of Aileen's health and, possibly, to avail themselves of his services again.

Relieved and reassured, Dave had helped them load all their bags into his carriage and had driven them down to the side wharf from where they'd signaled *The Trident*'s tender.

When he and his men had first come ashore, Robert had ordered the tender to wait out in the harbor throughout the days and nights—ready to row in if and when needed. His quartermaster, Miller, had taken tender duty that night. A few words were all that had been required to alert the experienced Miller to the seriousness of the situation. Robert had ordered the tender back to the ship to unload the bags and alert the rest of his crew, then to return and, under cover of darkness, tie up close by the steps to Government Wharf.

Now everything was in place, and they were ready and waiting for the slavers to make a move. He was normally very good at waiting—or, at least, at feigning patience. Tonight, however, a species of fear he'd never felt before scraped along his nerves.

All around them, the slum was quietening, but with so many people crammed into such a small space, areas like this were never truly silent.

A soft cooing—like a dove's call—floated over the roofs. Robert stiffened. That was Fuller, who was hidden close to where the runnel from the lair's side door joined the lane.

From where he stood, Robert couldn't see the intersection itself, just the stretch of lane leading from it.

A second later, a slouching figure came ambling down the lane. Coleman mumbled as he passed Robert, "They're coming—three of them—and the middle one is carrying her."

Robert pushed out of the shadows, slung an arm around Coleman, and let his shoulders sag. As they lurched along like drunkards, he whispered a few last-minute instructions. Coleman nodded. At the next intersection, they drifted apart, Coleman going left, Robert right, into a tiny cross-alley.

He waited in the concealing shadows of someone's forgotten washing and watched the slavers march past. As Coleman had said, there were only three, marching in a somewhat strung-out line. The middle one, the same hulking brute who had carried Aileen into the lair, had her once more over his shoulder. Eyes narrowed, Robert swiftly took in everything of her he could; as far as he could tell, she was trussed *exactly* as she had been before, wrapped in an old sail with ropes about her knees, hips, and chest.

While at one level, he was conscious of abject relief, overall, the tension of the moment was too high, its demands too fraught, to allow any part of him to relax. Nevertheless, the more analytical part of his brain found it noteworthy that she—an attractive woman despite her temper and temperament—hadn't been molested, not to any degree. He hadn't thought slavers so…nice in their habits.

But now wasn't the time to ponder that oddity. With his senses focused on the little cavalcade, he slid through the shadows in its wake.

Soft coos, caws, and cheeps of doves, gulls, and sparrows—birds too common to catch anyone's notice—tracked the slavers as they wended their way down through the slum. Robert constantly gauged their position relative to the rest of the settlement and specifically to Government Wharf.

They'd agreed that the sensible course was to allow the slavers to carry Aileen as long as they followed a tack that didn't veer away from the wharf. Unfortunately, the path the slavers took shifted increasingly to the east, farther and farther from the settlement's center.

When the trio of slavers swung into a lane that led directly eastward, out of the settlement, Robert signaled for his men to close in. He'd recalled Declan's description of how he and his men had retaken Edwina in much the same circumstances; he saw no reason not to use the same maneuver, albeit with a few additions of his own.

Coleman loomed out of the shadows several yards ahead of the first slaver. The slaver slowed, as did the two at his back. As if merely ambling up the same lane, as he approached the first slaver, Coleman asked the way back to the wharf.

The slaver visibly relaxed, his hand falling from the hilt of his cutlass. He swung and pointed to the west.

And Coleman coshed him.

Before the first man hit the ground, Harris had materialized from the shadows and coshed the third.

And Fuller and Benson, who had been crouched like sacks among barrels lining the lane, leapt up and flung themselves at the man carrying Aileen.

Startled, he backpedaled. He shifted his hold on Aileen as he prepared to turn and flee.

The instant the slaver glanced back up the lane, Robert, who had silently come up behind the man, plowed his fist into the slaver's jaw.

The huge man swayed, blinked. His hold on the canvas loosened.

Robert grabbed the bundle that was Aileen and hauled her to him.

Immediately, she started struggling.

"Be still!" He swung around, interposing his body between her and the big slaver.

She sagged in his hold.

He heard a thud as he hoisted her up against him and quickly looked around.

Benson and Fuller had dealt with the man who had carried Aileen. He now lay sprawled in the dust.

Robert's men were trained to incapacitate rather than kill; when they were on diplomatic missions in regions not under British control, killing could lead to unhelpful complications. Although that didn't apply here, long-standing habits were hard to break.

But all three slavers were down and out, and Aileen was in Robert's hands. Their rescue had been an unqualified success.

He propped Aileen against him and was reaching for a knife to cut the ropes wound about her when the sound of rapid footsteps reached them.

Someone—some man—was pounding down the lane.

Harris, the farthest up the lane, swung to block the newcomer.

Another of the slavers rounded the last bend. He saw their shadowy figures ahead. "Hey, Joe. Wait—"

The newcomer skidded to a halt. His gaze flicked over them. Even with Harris in the way, he saw—

The slaver's eyes widened. He turned and fled.

On the balls of his feet, Harris glanced at Robert.

His expression grim, Robert shook his head. He pulled out his knife and sawed at Aileen's bonds. "Our best bet is to get moving as quickly as we can."

A laudable ambition; there was just one problem. Aileen had been bound and restrained for so long she had trouble making her legs work. When Benson and he succeeded in pulling the canvas away from her, she sagged and caught his arm.

He swore and swiftly dispensed with the gag, then the black hood, while Benson cut the ropes about her ankles and Coleman freed her wrists.

Her face, finally revealed as she pushed her bedraggled bonnet back, was an unbelievably welcome sight.

She gasped, coughed, but then valiantly gathered herself, straightened, and nodded. "Thank you." Her voice was hoarse. She glanced at his men, then looked back at him and met his eyes. "I didn't expect… I thought—"

He grasped her hand. "Never mind that now. We need to go."

They started toward the harbor, but she could barely stumble along.

She didn't complain, but whispered an apology even as she hobbled as fast as she could.

He squeezed her hand reassuringly. Carrying her would only delay her recovery, and if they had to run… Clasping her hand firmly, he urged her on. "It'll get better the farther we go." He sincerely hoped so, because they weren't out of the woods—in this case, the slum—yet.

They hurried along a curving alley that cut through the lower reaches of the slum. It would eventually land them on the edge of the commercial district somewhere near the inn, but that outer bastion of civilization was still a considerable way ahead.

Aileen struggled to get her bearings as she shuffled and skipped along, but in the end, gave up. Robert Frobisher had come and rescued her. At the moment, that was more than enough for the part of her brain still able to reason to grapple with. The rest of her had to make do with impulse and instinct, both of which pushed her to simply pin her future to Robert's mast and follow him wherever he led.

Now was not the time to question, much less quibble.

He'd been right about her limbs remembering how to function the farther they went—the more she used them. Gradually, full responsiveness returned, restoring her confidence.

She was almost back to normal, almost moving freely, when the first sounds of pursuit rose behind them.

Robert swore and glanced back, but the close-packed dwellings denied him any sight of their pursuers.

Benson fell in behind him. Without breaking their stride, they rapidly conferred. They were still in the slum, still had perhaps as much as half a mile to go before they could expect to find wider streets.

He and his men were accustomed to fighting in close quarters, but such circumstances usually meant one could find a useful wall to put at one's back. In contrast, a slum was the sort of place where attack could come from any direction at any time. He couldn't play a defensive hand. And they had to keep moving.

He sent Harris into the lead, with him and Aileen behind, and set Benson, Coleman, and Fuller in a staggered array at their backs.

Predictably, the first wave of pursuers fell on them from the rear. Benson, Coleman, and Fuller accounted for most; Harris took out one who'd thought to flank them, and Robert dealt with another.

They took no injuries beyond a scrape or two.

But the men they'd defeated hadn't been the slavers they'd seen at the lair.

And that was by no means the end of it.

Robert had thought—had been led to believe—that the people of the slum wouldn't rise to the slavers' call. They hadn't in Declan's case, although that had been a different slum.

Whether the slavers had simply learned a thing or two and called in favors, or if the locals here did not share the general anathema for the breed, Robert didn't know, but suddenly they found themselves facing wave after wave of attackers.

The only point in their favor was that the attackers—when pushed—would prefer not to die. They weren't that committed to the slavers' cause.

He and his men changed tactics—they no longer pulled their blows—and succeeded in beating those attacking back.

Despite the restrictive spaces, they were now shifting constantly in a fluid, protective constellation around Aileen. She'd kept up well. One glance at her face showed her usual stubborn determination in evidence. Robert caught a wink of light on steel and realized she was carrying a small dagger. He was surprised at his lack of surprise. He realized it hadn't even occurred to him that she might cower rather than fight.

He'd barely had time to register that when a man rushed out of a side lane to engage him—and another man lunged at her from out of a window.

But she'd sensed the second man; quick as a flash, she slashed with her knife, and the man howled and drew back.

Robert's men had seen; he hoped others had, too. That she would strike at them would make men like these hesitate, and that was all the opening he and his men needed.

The attackers had slowed them. They were still a hundred yards or more from the edge of the slum, and still the attackers came on, trying to pen them in, to hold them back from any chance of safety.

Where are the slavers?

Increasingly, Robert worried about that.

Dealing with the attackers had taken a toll on him and his men; luckily, they were accustomed to battles that raged for hours, if not days. Even doing this much running and regrouping wasn't anything new to them.

But the slavers didn't know that. This sort of prolonged fighting would have worn down most others to a far greater degree.

Finally, the end of the alley loomed ahead. Beyond lay a well-graded street, the space bathed in faint moonlight.

And—surprise!—the slavers suddenly appeared, filing in from the end of the alley and forming up in a solid wall of muscle bristling with steel.

A wall their rushing race forward was hurling them toward.

Their local assailants howled and fell in on their heels—a rag-tag army pushing them forward into the slavers' arms.

Twenty yards.

Robert realized he was grinning as he hadn't in years. He reached for Aileen's hand, gripped it hard.

Ten yards.

And he spied the opening he needed. "To me!"

He darted to the right into a tiny lane and towed Aileen behind him.

Harris, Benson, Fuller, and Coleman raced after them.

What followed... If the situation hadn't been so fraught, it would have been hilarious. He hadn't played a game like this in years—and the very real and immediate danger added an edge to the thrill.

The trick was to react unpredictably. To do what your opponent or pursuer least expected—or, better yet, didn't expect at all.

They had nothing to lose and everything to gain.

Robert dropped all restraint and just...played.

To the top of his bent.

They raced in and out of alleys, up and down lanes, apparently randomly.

When they came upon three slavers hunting for them through a narrow alley, they fell on them and trounced them. His men were also now grinning from ear to ear.

As for Aileen, somewhere along the way, she'd acquired a long-handled cast-iron skillet. Her style with it was quite impressive.

They encountered group after group of searchers, but as their pursuers had dispersed to look for them, the numbers were now on their side, and they dealt with the opposition with alacrity.

Ultimately, the opposition thinned.

They raced right, left, up, and down—and eventually, entirely by design, they raced unimpeded into the wider street bordering the slum via the alley they'd originally been on.

The slavers were now scattered, hunting for them through the narrow alleys.

Nevertheless, a call rang out. The slavers had left someone on watch.

Robert didn't waste breath swearing, nor did he pause to let his men and Aileen catch their breaths; instead, he rushed straight on—into the maze of narrow streets between Water Street and the quay.

He'd wondered if the slavers would follow.

One group did, and he cursed. "Another group will try to outflank us via the quay." He immediately changed direction, dragging Aileen, still manfully—*womanfully?*—keeping up, down a street that led directly to the relatively open expanse of the quay.

Dark water glimmered invitingly beyond.

They spilled onto the worn planking of the quay barely ahead of another group of slavers—as Robert had suspected, sent to cut them off.

The slavers were too close to simply run for it.

Robert swung Aileen behind him as he faced the latest threat. His men lined up alongside him, swords and knives in their hands.

The slavers—four of them—raised their cutlasses and charged.

"Miller!" Robert roared.

"Here, sir!"

Robert glanced swiftly to his left and saw Miller standing in the stern of the tender, steering it closer. He spared a glance for Aileen. "Go! Get into the boat."

The tide was in, the tender riding high enough for an easy descent.

He swung back to face the slavers just in time to get his sword up to counter a swinging blow.

Nevertheless, he knew when Aileen was no longer behind him.

The fighting wasn't elegant. No one wasted time with any rules.

The slavers were grimly determined. They pressed hard, but Robert and his men had decades' worth of desperate fighting beneath their belts; they used their hilts, their fists, their boots. They had the four slavers bloodied and down in good order—but then the five who had tracked them through the warren attacked.

Robert head-butted one slaver. He seized a split second to confirm that Aileen had been helped down to the tender before swinging his full attention back to the fray and the next slaver trying to slice him open.

They would have won in the end, but Robert caught a glimpse of more men coming pounding along the quay. Where the devil were they all coming from?

"Break!" It was a signal his men understood. It didn't mean fall back but push forward hard—and then run.

Coleman, Fuller, and Harris threw their opponents back, then ran and scrambled over the edge of the quay, dropping down to the tender Miller had brought close.

Robert would have followed, but Benson got trapped between two opponents—

Instead of backing away, Robert cut down his own opponent and threw himself against the second slaver pressing Benson.

Benson made the most of his help, tripped the slaver still facing him, then turned and ran for the tender.

Robert swung his long sword—longer than any cutlass—in a sweeping arc, forcing the onrushing slavers to jump back.

He whirled to follow Benson—and had to leap back himself from the shiny blade a leering slaver brandished far too close to his face. The man had crept around in the shadows and come up behind him.

The slaver grinned viciously. "Not so fast, me good sir."

Crack!

The explosive percussion of a pistol shot—close, utterly unexpected—shocked everyone.

The leering slaver jerked and lost his grin. His blade tipped, then fell from suddenly nerveless fingers.

Everyone had frozen.

Robert's pounding heart kicked, and he shoved the crumpling slaver toward the man's fellows and dove for the edge of the quay.

He slapped his hand on the stone edging, vaulted over the side, and dropped into the tender. "Go!"

Miller, with help from Harris, was already swinging the tender away, out from the stone side of the quay.

Several slavers lined up along the edge, looking to join them, but a forest of blades made them think again.

The gap between the boat and the quay widened. Weighed down with so many on board, the tender moved sluggishly, but then Coleman and Fuller got two more oars into the locks and added their strength to that of the pair of midshipmen who had come out with Miller and were already rowing for all they were worth.

The slavers brandished their weapons—but then a shout from back along the quay drew their attention.

As the slavers cheered and ran off, Robert, still standing, searched the night… "Damn! They've found a boat. A smaller one." He quickly scanned the harbor, then sat on the bench in front of Miller, next to Aileen, and pointed to where a flotilla of merchant vessels were anchored in what to an outsider would have appeared a haphazard and crowded conglomeration. "In among the hulls. And break out all the oars. It seems we're not finished with tonight's game of Catch Me Who Can."

Grunts and snorted laughs greeted that, but the oars were quickly passed around, and soon there were three pairs of oars pulling them through the dark water.

Robert took the last set of oars passed back to him and Aileen. He bent to set them down.

"I can row."

He glanced at her—and realized she was struggling to shove a small pistol into her reticule. The same black reticule that had bumped and swung from her wrist all the damned way.

He raised his gaze to her face. "It was you who shot that slaver."

She succeeded in forcing the pistol inside, pulled the ties tight, then scowled at him. "Who else?"

He glanced back at Miller, who met his gaze and shrugged. He'd assumed his quartermaster had, for some reason, brought a pistol with him.

"Now." She resettled her bonnet, then waved at the oars Robert still clutched in his hand. "Give one here."

He blinked, considered arguing—dismissed the notion. She might not be able to pull as strongly as he could, but he could adjust, and they would get just that bit more speed…and that might prove crucial.

And she had shot a man for him.

She took the oar he handed her and quickly and efficiently set it into the oarlock. Once he'd done the same with the oar he still held, she nodded at him; she let him set the beat, then she bent and matched her stroke to his, as far as she was able.

Once the tender was steadily arrowing through the waves, and the mammoth black shapes of the merchant hulls loomed ahead of them, Robert glanced back at their pursuers.

"They're gaining, but they won't be fast enough." Facing forward, he nodded toward a dark passage between two of the large ships. "Through there, Miller, and keep tacking. I want to lose them in the maze. But let's make them think we're doubling back toward some ship in the pack, and meanwhile, we'll slip out of the harbor to *The Trident*."

"Aye, aye, sir."

They rowed steadily on.

The repetitive action soothed Aileen—quietened the sudden panic that had flared and let her heart slow to a more normal rhythm.

She'd never been so frantically fearful in her life.

Not while they'd been ducking in and out of slum alleys being chased by slavers and, it had seemed, a good portion of the denizens of the slum besides. Her blood had been up, and although danger had plainly lurked, fear hadn't claimed her…

Until she'd seen the slaver wave his sword in Robert's face.

She'd already had her pistol in her hand. She'd aimed and fired without a thought—no conscious decision had been required.

He'd come for her. He'd forsaken his mission—or at least his best chance of completing it—in order to rescue her.

He'd broken his own orders.

She didn't need anyone to tell her he wasn't the sort of commander who did that, not without some compelling reason.

He'd been willing to act in a way that didn't just show but proclaimed—to himself, to her, to his men—that she meant enough to him to be a compelling reason.

That was both a humbling and a somewhat scarifying thought.

She hadn't allowed herself to think too much about him—not in relation to her—because...

Because...

Because she was something of a coward. Because she hadn't been sure if he felt anything for her, and they'd known each other for only two days—forty-eight hours, that was all. How on earth could they possibly feel like this? As if they'd known each other for half their lives and had simply been waiting for the other to appear...

The rational, sensible part of her scoffed that it was nonsense—that it had to be. But most of her—the true her—knew it was real. That those three kisses they'd shared—those hadn't been any accident.

Not on his part, and not on hers, either.

Well, possibly the first, but certainly not the second or the third.

It wasn't that something was happening between them—something *had happened*, and both of them knew that. Recognized and understood that.

That they were still coming to terms with that, each in their own way, was hardly surprising.

Circumstances hadn't given them much time to think.

She glanced along her shoulder at him. His gaze was fixed

ahead; he'd murmured directions to Miller several times, but otherwise he and his men seemed to be concentrating on navigating swiftly in between the looming vessels.

There was very little light on the water between the ships. She could barely make out his face as, sensing her gaze, he glanced her way.

After a second of looking at her, he murmured, "Are you all right?"

She nodded, then whispered, "Thank you for coming after me."

He held her gaze for a moment, then despite the dimness, she saw the ends of his lips lift in a smile both cynical and self-deprecatory before he faced forward. "I'll always come after you."

The words hovered between them.

Because you're mine was the bit he left unsaid.

But the implication was unmistakable. Unmissable.

Aileen wasn't sure whether to frown or shiver.

Behind them, the slavers were a great deal less quiet than they were, allowing them to know which way to go to put more distance between them and their pursuers.

Eventually, the curses faded altogether, and the tender nosed quietly out of the harbor and into the estuary.

Aileen scanned the waters ahead of them. Miller seemed to know where he was going; she presumed Robert's ship, *The Trident*, lay more or less directly ahead, somewhere in the dark.

Ships in harbor or even on the sea normally had small lamps burning along the rails.

The Trident was a black mass that suddenly loomed up out of the night beside them, no lamp in sight.

Quiet words were exchanged, then a rope ladder came tumbling down. Robert sent his men up, until only she, he, and Miller remained. The other man was lashing lifting ropes to the tender's heavy rings fore and aft.

Robert turned to her. "Can you manage the ladder? Or you can sit and be winched up with the tender."

She knew from her brothers that the latter was considered weak—the province of helpless females. "I can manage the ladder."

A quirk of a smile played about his lips—as if he could read her mind—but he nodded. He sent Miller up, then he held the ladder for her. Once she was on it and climbing, he came up after her, keeping only a rung or so below her—no doubt so he could catch her if she fell.

She didn't fall. She didn't even slip.

On reaching the gap in the ship's side, she took the hand of a gentleman, almost as debonair as Robert himself, and allowed him to help her up over the lip of the deck.

Finally on her feet, she shook out her skirts and felt the weight of her reticule bump against her thigh.

Robert appeared beside her. As his men rattled the panel back into place, he took her hand and bowed with formal grace. "Welcome aboard *The Trident*, Miss Hopkins."

"Thank you, Captain Frobisher." She left her hand in his and looked up—and up. And yet farther up... Her lips formed a soundless O. "*This* is the ship I saw sailing in...it must be a week ago." She lowered her gaze to his. "I thought it the most graceful vessel I'd ever seen. She's one of the new clipper ships out of Aberdeen, isn't she?"

He smiled. "Indeed."

Robert beckoned his senior crew forward and introduced them to Aileen. He felt weary, yet happy. Oddly content. He'd thrown away his best chance to quickly and effectively bring his mission to a close, yet he couldn't have proceeded in any other way.

Now he and his men were back, safe on *The Trident*'s deck, and Aileen was, too.

And if he'd needed any sign that this was where she belonged, the look on her face as she'd taken in *The Trident*'s sails…that look had held all the fascination and passion with which he might hope his wife would view his ship.

Thirteen

Once the men's various wounds had been tended—something Aileen insisted on assisting with, helping to bind cuts, clean scrapes, and salve bruises—Robert gathered his officers—as well as Benson, Harris, Coleman, Fuller, and Aileen—in his cabin.

He steered Aileen to the chair anchored before his desk. He ruthlessly suppressed the tumult of impulses that insisted he wrap her up in cotton batting; despite her ordeal, despite the shock, urgency, and frantic action of her rescue and their escape from the slavers—despite having shot a man—she appeared composed, determined, and, as always to his senses, vibrantly alive.

Alive and apparently intent on remaining so, which soothed his abraded instincts a tad.

But dealing with what lay between them—the surging emotions that seemed startlingly complementary—would have to wait.

Along with everyone else, she was focused on his mission. His officers were waiting to hear what had happened, and he needed to work out what should be done next.

What could be done next.

Sinking into the chair behind his desk, he hid a grimace. He'd thrown his carefully ordered plan overboard; now he needed to determine what could be salvaged.

"First things first." He focused on his bosun, Wilcox, who was lounging against the wall closest to the door. "As Miss Hopkins reminded us, we've been anchored here, in the same position and running the same name, for a week. Let's change the name and take her a little farther down the estuary. Don't bother to put into any cove—just anchor in the main channel." He glanced at his second-in-command, Jordan Latimer, who had taken the second chair before the desk. "The better to make a quick run to deeper waters should Decker return before we leave."

Jordan dipped his head. "It never hurts to be prepared."

Robert looked at Wilcox. "Convey the orders, then return here."

"Aye, aye, sir." Wilcox opened the door and slipped out.

Robert looked at the other officers—Hurley, his master and navigator, Miller, and Foxby, the steward—all propped in various poses against cabinets or the walls, then at Benson, Harris, Coleman, and Fuller, standing at their ease beyond the chairs and facing the desk. "For the benefit of those who weren't with us in the settlement, let's review what we'd learned prior to the most recent action."

Concisely, he outlined what he and his men had gleaned from Sampson and had subsequently learned about Lashoria and Undoto, and how that had led them to watch Undoto's house—and how in turn that had led them to connect with Aileen.

At his invitation, she detailed what had brought her to the settlement and what she'd done in the preceding days that had ultimately led to her being in a carriage, watching Undoto's house at the same time.

"While I was with Miss Hopkins"—Robert reclaimed the reins—"attempting to learn her purpose in being there, four slavers arrived." He described how Undoto had welcomed the men, and also the atmosphere when they'd departed, and the insistence by the leader, possibly the man known as Kale, that some unspecified "he" needed more men, but they had to be the right men, and Undoto was supposed to find said victims. "Subsequently, while I saw Miss Hopkins to her lodgings, the others"—he nodded at Benson, Coleman, Fuller, and Harris—"followed the slavers into the slum on the other side of the ridge above Undoto's church." He went on to describe the slavers' lair and the hide they'd set up to keep watch. He also sketched in broad-brush fashion what he and Aileen had learned about the missing children.

His plan to follow the slavers into the jungle to determine the location of their camp had been known to all his men. "That brings us to this morning."

"So what happened?" Foxby asked. "Did they kidnap someone?"

"As we're not heading straight back to London," Jordan said, "I assume something in your so-simple plan went awry?"

Robert met Jordan's cynical gaze; his best friend had often warned him that he didn't make sufficient allowance for the unexpected. In this case, Jordan had been more correct than Robert had any intention of letting him know; if he did, he would never hear the end of it. He transferred his gaze to Aileen. "After breakfast this morning, I went to the hide to keep watch. But what's probably more to the point is what you did. I can't see any reason why the slavers would suddenly have been ordered to kidnap you, yet they were. That suggests that you triggered an alarm. Nothing we did yesterday would account for it, so"—he leaned forward, resting his forearms on the desk as he fixed his gaze more intently on her face—"what did you do this morning?"

Aileen studied his blue eyes, studied his expression. Although she saw an intensity of focus, she detected no animosity, no shred of blame. She drew in a breath that was tighter than she would have liked. "First, let me say that while I didn't expect to be kidnapped, I am exceedingly glad that you"—she glanced at the four men lined up on her right, then looked back at Robert—"saw fit to rescue me. I hadn't expected that—I know how important it was to you and your mission that you took the first chance that offered to follow the slavers back to their jungle camp. So…" She hauled in another breath and inclined her head to him. "Thank you. Now." She straightened. "As to what I did this morning." She frowned. "I visited the Office of the Naval Attaché."

Mr. Hurley, the navigator, said, "I thought you'd visited there before. Before we reached here."

She nodded. "I had. But the first time, I spoke only with the three clerks. They were officious and unhelpful. But this morning, the naval attaché was in his office—he hadn't been there the first time I called." She paused, remembering. "I didn't actually say anything to the clerks themselves, beyond asking one of them to tell the attaché I wished to speak with him…and that I expected to be back in London shortly and would be calling at the Admiralty."

She raised her gaze to Robert's face. "I thought that would at least get me in to see him—and it did."

His expression grew grimmer. "It might also be what got you kidnapped. What else did you say?"

"Muldoon—the attaché—asked me into his office. The clerks heard nothing more of what I said—only him. I asked…" Again, she paused to make sure she had it right. "I'd rehearsed what I would ask to ensure that I said nothing that would direct attention toward you or your mission. I made it plain that while I failed to understand why no one there knew anything about Will, that wasn't the purpose of my visit." As the conversation came back to her, she locked her gaze on Robert's face. "I said I'd heard of children going missing, and that I wished to know what the authorities were doing about it. He said the governor's office dealt with such things, but that he would ask." As her memories rolled on, a chill slithered down her spine. "*He* then asked *me* if I'd heard anything else in relation to the missing children…and I told him I'd heard rumors that slave traders might be involved." The chill intensified. "He asked me where I was staying so he could send word…"

She stared at Robert, her eyes widening as full realization

dawned. "Good Lord! It's not just someone in the Office of the Naval Attaché but the attaché himself who's involved."

His expression unrelentingly grim, Robert nodded. "It has to be Muldoon. Either directly or indirectly, he had to have sent the message to the slavers at the lair. The messenger arrived about half an hour before noon." He paused, then asked, "What time did you reach Undoto's church?"

Puzzled, she frowned at him, wondering how he'd known.

He read her question in her face. "When I went back to the inn later, I found Dave waiting to tell me he'd left you at Undoto's church, but that when he returned to fetch you, you'd disappeared. By then, I'd seen you carried into the slavers' lair."

"Oh. Poor Dave." She grimaced. "He left me at the church at about twenty minutes before midday."

"By then, the messenger had already arrived at the lair, so said messenger had to have been sent by Muldoon or by someone he contacted immediately after you'd left him. Undoto hadn't seen you yet, and there wasn't time for any innocent official query passed on by Muldoon to have inadvertently alerted someone in the governor's office—not unless Muldoon sent an urgent query, and why would he have done that?" When she reluctantly nodded, Robert asked, "So what happened next?"

She described sitting through the boring service, then waiting outside and evaluating Undoto's and Lady Holbrook's likely contributions to the slavers' scheme—and then being seized, hooded, gagged, and carried off. "I'm sure they held me in one of the back rooms of the church—the vestry, so to speak. That was the only building it could have been—all the others were too far away."

"We know Undoto is involved with the slavers, so it's unsurprising that the slavers use the church from time to time." Robert's gaze traveled over her face. "And then?"

She related how they'd waited with her in the vestry for several hours, more or less in silence, then had carried her out and into the slum to what had been the slavers' lair.

Latimer leaned forward, his forearms on his thighs, and with a solicitous expression said, "I realize it must have been quite distressing for you, Miss Hopkins, but did you hear anything the slavers said while you were in their lair?"

Aileen thought she heard a soft snort from Robert. She struggled not to glare at Latimer. "Of course. I listened to everything I could. Sadly, only five of the men in the lair were English, and they had various accents, and the hood and wrapping didn't help. The others used various pidgin dialects. Several, I'm sure, were foreign—French, German, perhaps Dutch. Of the ten men in the house, there seemed to be three leaders of sorts, but the one name I heard mentioned in relation to the missing people was Dubois. Several of the men spoke of him, and I gather I was destined to be taken to him."

Robert caught her eye. "Is Dubois their customer, or might he be the ultimate leader of the slavers?"

"I can't be sure, but I would wager on the former. That was the implication. And there was one other name mentioned," Aileen went on. "Several of the slavers had, I gathered, arrived in the lair that evening, and at least three were there to fetch some sort of supplies from someone named Winter."

"Supplies?" Robert's eyes narrowed in speculation. "It seems odd they'd need to fetch ordinary supplies from a specific person."

"Indeed. I gathered that these supplies were special. The way the men used the word 'supplies,' they could have been referring to equipment or parts of sorts." She met Robert's gaze. "Something that is supplies, but not food or clothing or anything like that."

"Mining supplies." Robert nodded. "That would fit. So we now have two names—Dubois and Winter. I haven't heard of either before, and nor, to my knowledge, has London."

"Dubois in relation to the people," Latimer said. "And Winter in terms of necessary supplies for a mining operation."

Robert looked at Aileen. "Did you hear anything else of use?"

"Possibly not of use, but of note. One man's voice was exceptional." She met Robert's gaze. "You've heard Undoto. This man's voice was significantly more compelling—a mesmerist's voice." She looked at Latimer. "The other men were indistinguishable from hordes of others, but that one voice was distinct."

Robert sat back in his chair; the movement drew everyone's attention to him. "It seems that despite the apparent reverse, we've actually learned quite a lot. To continue our tale, after we'd seen Miss Hopkins carried into the slavers' lair, we reworked our plan." He saw consternation pass over Aileen's features and rolled on before she could apologize again. Briefly, he outlined their preparations and then, in minimal detail, described the rescue up to the point of them losing the slavers amid the commercial hulls in the harbor.

"So the slavers now know we're watching them?" Hurley asked.

Before he could reply, Aileen stated, "Again, I can't express how very sorry I am to have disrupted your plans."

Robert caught her gaze and shook his head. "You shouldn't be. Via you being kidnapped and us rescuing you, we now have three pieces of vital information London didn't ask for, but which they'll be exceedingly happy to have—namely, that Muldoon is one of those involved in the scheme, that Dubois is the man the missing people are destined for, and that someone named Winter is supplying the operation with essential supplies, most likely specialist mining supplies. There really was no viable way to approach the investigation from that angle, but you being kidnapped has allowed us to make significant inroads on that front."

The stubborn woman didn't look convinced.

Robert swiveled to look at Hurley. "And to answer your question, I don't believe so. We took care to do nothing to alert the slavers to our true interest in them. All they saw will lead them to believe that in taking Miss Hopkins, they somehow brought us down on their heads. We found them carrying her out of the slum, seized her back, and ran. We didn't try to pursue them, and as far as they know, we've escaped onto some ship and will vanish on the next tide."

He looked back at Aileen. "We still have our hide—the slavers know nothing of that. We can continue to watch them. And you were the only one taken today—there was no other opportunity that we missed while rescuing you."

He glanced around at the others. "As far as I can see, we've secured three potentially crucial pieces of information without having lost anything we might otherwise have gained. We can continue with our plan as was, maintain our watch on the hide, and when the slavers seize their next victim or victims, we can—"

"Actually"—Jordan grimaced—"you might not have that much time."

Robert arched a brow Jordan's way.

"Decker." Jordan sat straighter. "According to the scuttlebutt, he's due back any day—certainly by the end of the week."

"I've heard the same," Aileen said.

Regarding Robert, Jordan arched his brows. "Then again, you do have that letter from the First Lord giving you authority to call on Decker's assistance...?"

"No." Lips setting, Robert shook his head. "Decker and I do not get on, but more than that, although it appears that Muldoon is able to act of his own volition in this business, we cannot as yet rule out Decker himself being involved. And I don't know who will be sent down next to follow up on this mission. If it's Royd...heaven help us all—and Decker, too. But we don't need to give Decker advance warning of such a possibility."

Jordan pulled a face. "True." After a moment, he asked, "So then what?"

Robert straightened in his chair. "We do what we can do in the time we have. Tomorrow, we'll resume our watch from the hide. Meanwhile, Mr. Hurley, take *The Trident* as far east from Kroo Bay as is reasonable. We'll take the tender into the easternmost cove of the settlement and walk in. If Decker appears, we'll operate for as long as we feel we can. He'll most likely be swamped with business for the first few days—he won't immediately have time to look at what other ships are nearby. We'll have to choose our moment before he does and slip past the squadron in the dead of night."

There were nods all around. Aileen studied the faces and saw nothing that looked remotely like downheartedness. This group was accustomed to dealing with reverses, remaining on course, and steadily charting their way forward.

As if to underscore that, Robert said, "So our mission remains—we have to learn the location of the slavers' jungle camp." He glanced around. "I really don't want to have to return to London without that information. Aside from all else, that will mean a five-week minimum delay while London sends down some other operative to learn that fact—and that's another five weeks those missing might not have."

The slightly ominous ring to those words pushed Aileen into speech. "What about the children? If they are being taken by the same band of slavers to the same camp, then if the slavers arrive to take another group of children… That lad said he would come and warn us. If that happens and we follow the children…"

Robert regarded her steadily, then inclined his head. "You're right. That is still a possibility."

"Do you think," the man called Benson asked, "that once we escaped, those slavers chasing us would go back to their camp? Perhaps to report?"

Robert considered, then shook his head. "I doubt it. Their orders about who to seize are coming from inside the settlement—from Undoto, from Muldoon, previously from Lady Holbrook, and we don't know from who else." He paused, then said, "Thinking back to what Miss Hopkins and I heard the senior slaver who called on Undoto say to the priest, it sounds as if the slavers are sent in with…for want of a better word, an order to fulfill—so many adult men, young women, or children. It's up to those in the settlement to point them at suitable people to take. If that's how it works, then the slavers currently in the settlement were sent to seize more men, not women. I can't see that those who lost Miss Hopkins to us are going to feel it necessary to return to their leader back at the camp to report that."

"True enough," Coleman said. "If you're sent from home to fetch a rooster, you don't go back just to report you found a loaf of bread but lost it."

Aileen wasn't sure she appreciated being equated with a loaf of bread, but she agreed with the logic. "So the slavers who gathered in the lair will still be there—still waiting for a summons to snatch selected people."

Most nodded, including Robert. "And," he said, "four were already there, and six more arrived this evening. Even allowing that three or even four have come to fetch supplies, that still suggests that the slavers are expecting to take more captives, and most likely soon." He glanced at the other men. "From what I gathered from Lashoria's servant, the slavers are not really welcome, even in the slums, so six or seven men seems a lot to have sitting in the settlement for no reason."

A sense of quiet optimism had infected them all—a positive sense that they still had a chance of completing their mission. Aileen looked at Robert; he seemed to be juggling scenarios in his mind.

As if sensing her regard, he met her eyes. After a second, he nodded as if having made some decision. Then he glanced at his men. "Right, then. We have a few days at least, and with any luck, that may be enough. We'll resume our watch on the lair. You four"—he looked at the four men who had accompanied him into the settlement—"will need to exercise caution in returning to the hide, but you know what you're doing. Pull back if you get any hint that anyone there realizes you were part of the group the slavers chased tonight."

Benson nodded. "We'll go back in during the day. Mostly only women out and about at that time—those locals as helped the slavers tonight were all men."

Latimer nodded. "Good point."

"Indeed," Robert said. "And for my money, even the men who supported the slavers tonight weren't all that eager. Ten to one, they'd been coerced. So we'll resume our watch on the lair, and meanwhile, we'll wait to see if the slavers who've been taking children return for more." He glanced around and met his men's eyes. "We have two potential avenues, either of which could lead us to the jungle camp. With luck, one will turn up trumps, and we'll be able to set sail for London before Decker hoves on our horizon."

"Amen to that," Latimer said.

Robert stood. "Thank you, gentlemen—to your usual stations for tonight, and our shore party will leave at first light."

★ ★ ★

It was several hours after midnight before Aileen finally found herself alone with Robert.

The steward, Foxby, having ascertained that neither his captain nor she had eaten since breakfast, had insisted that he should be allowed to serve them a meal while Latimer and Hurley made their reports. She'd been impressed by the scope and quality of the fare assembled so rapidly; the clam soup had been excellent, the fish stew nicely spiced, and the goat and mutton remarkably succulent. The trifle Foxby had laid before them to complete the repast had made her smile. She'd thanked the steward sincerely and had smiled at the cabin boys.

Both had seemed rather round-eyed to have a lady—any female, she supposed—on board.

She'd listened with half an ear to Latimer's and Hurley's reports; she'd sailed often enough to have a sound grasp of the day-to-day business of captaining a ship. While she would normally have been more interested in the details, tonight—or rather this very early morning—she'd had other matters on her mind.

As had Robert. Although he'd appeared to give his officers his full attention, his gaze had flicked more than once to her face. He'd eaten steadily and did not encourage his men to linger. When the final dishes had been cleared, he refused Foxby's suggestion of brandy. He rose and walked with Latimer and Hurley to the door, along the way crisply confirming his orders for the morning.

She listened and noted that he made no mention of her accompanying him when he returned to the inn to await a possible summons should the slavers return for more children.

He saw Latimer and Hurley out and shut the door.

Then he paused, facing the panel.

Aileen rose. She smoothed down her skirts, then tipped up her chin. "I will, of course, go with you tomorrow—I will need to fetch my belongings from Mrs. Hoyt's, and I will need to be there to ensure the lad doesn't grow wary and refuse to work with you."

Several seconds passed. He continued to stare at the door. Then he simply said, "No."

"Yes." She made the statement evenly. "This is just as much my plan as yours."

He didn't move for several heartbeats, then he reached out.

She heard the lock snick home.

Robert swung around and looked across the cabin at the one woman in the world who seemed able to set his blood pounding with nothing more than a challenging, upward tilt of her stubborn chin.

In that moment, he felt…untethered. Lacking his customary leash.

A gentleman of the sort suggested by the diplomatic veneer he habitually affected would have declined to argue with her and offered her his bed while he sought a pallet with one of his officers or a hammock among his crew.

He wasn't that sort of gentleman.

And she—of the bright eyes, brilliantly brassy hair, and unrelentingly direct personality—effortlessly connected with the real him, the buccaneer at his core.

He stalked toward her.

She didn't back away, didn't glance away—she didn't give an inch, not her—although she did put her hand to the desk beside her as if seeking the reassurance of some solid support.

Their gazes locked and held. He halted before her, with a mere foot between her hems and his boots. His expression felt set, unyielding and grim. He searched her eyes, looking for…he knew not what. "Do you have *any* idea what I felt when I saw that slaver carry you into their lair?"

His tone was harsh, rough, the words wrenched from deep inside him.

As if the question re-evoked them, the emotions rose up—and poured through him and *engulfed* him again.

They rocked him to his foundation and threatened to sweep him away.

When they'd first struck, in that moment of sheer horror in the hide, by main force he'd held the feelings and the impulses in, reined them back.

But this time she was there, with her head tipped back to meet his gaze and her brandy-colored eyes spitting bronze-green fire. "I imagine you felt as I did when I saw that slaver brandish his sword an inch from your throat."

Their gazes remained locked as they each drew breath; resistance and defiance burned in them both. There was no give in her, and none whatsoever in him.

Emotions rose in a tumult between them—his, hers—clashing, merging, transmuting. Then the amorphous storm seemed to coalesce, overtaken by hunger and need, crystalizing into raw desire, a near-violent hunger, and a yearning that reached to his soul.

He felt stripped bare by the force of his own emotions.

Only to be scorched by the heat of hers.

He felt the inexorable tug, the escalating magnetism forcing them together. The undeniable compulsion to take that last step, haul her into his arms, and plunge into the beckoning maelstrom.

Before he moved, she did.

Unwaveringly certain, Aileen took the last step to close the distance between them—knowingly, with the full force of her considerable will. Hadn't she prayed to all the gods to be given this chance to live her life—to seize him and explore this uncharted territory? Now fate and the gods had granted her wish, and she was determined to grasp the moment with both hands and let it take her where it would.

To surrender to this path and follow where it led.

To set aside all reservations and live life to the fullest.

With her gaze locked on his eyes, on the passion she could see darkening the blue, she drew her hand from the desk and stepped to him. Stretched up, slid her hands over his shoulders, locked her fingers in his hair, drew his head down, and kissed him.

And felt the shudder that wracked him.

Sensed him holding on—to his control, to his responses. Still holding against the whirlwind of wanting despite the aching need she could all but feel in him.

She traced the seam of his lips, then parted hers and invited him in.

He groaned.

And gave in.

He plunged into the kiss and surrendered, as she had, not to her but to the living entity that beat at them with burning wings.

Passion.

She'd never felt it before, but she knew what it was.

He angled his head and took control of the kiss, and their hunger ignited.

She pressed closer and felt his arms close around her and lock tight, holding her against him.

Emboldened and oh, so very sure, she curled her fingers in the dark silk of his hair and followed his lead, fed their fire with her own hunger, her own escalating need.

Robert felt more grounded, more anchored—more himself—than he'd felt for years. As if he'd shed some outer casing, some restrictive armor, and was, for the first time in a very long while, free to simply be.

Himself.

The man he truly was with the woman who made him so. Who demanded he be himself and who would accept no less.

Who seemed to see straight through his veneer and deal directly with his true self.

She confounded him and delighted him.

Countered him, provoked him, and somehow balanced him.

Their lips and mouths fused, hot and urgent. She tasted of honey and trifle, and beneath that, of an elixir that was uniquely, quintessentially, her.

Their hands shifted and gripped—tight, tighter; their tongues dueled and incited, laced with a heady blend of hunger and need, of passion and wanting. He felt as if they were careening in a carriage with no reins, plunging headlong with no thought for direction.

He struggled to summon wit enough to think. Through the fogging haze of burgeoning desire, he wondered if he shouldn't slow them down—at least a fraction. With that goal in mind, he shifted, intending to press her back against the desk long enough to make some attempt to seize their reins.

But she shifted, too, backing, swiveling. His feet followed instinctively. Locked in their embrace, in a searing kiss that was rapidly turning incendiary, they waltzed…

To the bed.

Their thighs bumped against the raised side. She flung her arms around his neck, locked her lips on his, and pressed herself to him in flagrant invitation—and he forgot about slowing down.

Forgot about everything beyond her and the need to have her. A need that had been born in the instant he'd first seen her, that had grown with each hour spent under the threat of danger, and finally forged by the cataclysmic shock of their near brushes with death.

In some rational corner of his mind, he understood the sudden escalation of their needs.

Hers, and his.

But that didn't help. His need had grown steel-tipped claws; it shredded the remnants of his control and sent them flying on the winds of passion.

Desire burned.

He shrugged out of his light jacket and let it fall to the floor. They were too greedy, too hungry, to allow their lips to part. As her fingers found the knot in the neckerchief at his throat, he set his palms and fingers to sculpting her curves. To caressing, fondling, tracing, then claiming.

Aileen shuddered. Her senses fractured. Compelled, she clung to the kiss, to the heated exchange of desire and hunger, while she grappled with the sensations his knowing hands wrought. With the way her breasts swelled and firmed beneath his hand, with the sharp, delicious spike of sensation that streaked down her nerves when his fingers found one well-sheathed nipple and artfully tweaked.

If he'd been detached, she wouldn't have responded, but he was so patently caught by the same needs, swept up by the same swelling, welling tide of sensual compulsion, that every touch made her quiver, every firm caress sent her senses flying.

Yes, yes, *yes*! She flattened one of her hands over one of his, holding his palm to her breast. How long she'd waited to feel this.

This wanting, this hunger, this connection.

This elemental need of another—male and female—of what that other could evoke.

Could provoke.

Of what they could share.

Their lips parted; eyes half glazed with passion met from beneath heavy lids. She couldn't bear to lose the taste, the touch of his lips on hers, and it seemed he felt the same; their lips continued to brush, to seek and touch, to sup as she felt his fingers deftly unbuttoning her tightly fitting jacket.

She fell on the laces at his throat, flicked them loose, undone. Sent her hands to grab fistfuls of his loose shirt and tug the material free of his breeches and up.

Robert broke from the tantalizing, teasing, temptation-laced kiss and stepped back. His eyes met hers—bright and burning—as he seized his shirt and whipped it off over his head.

He tossed it aside, and her gaze shifted, locking on the bared planes of his chest.

For an instant, the look on her face held him spellbound.

They'd left the lamps burning. Neither needed the dark, each too intent on exploring all they were. Instinctively, they'd wanted the light—so their eyes and all their senses could feast.

Over the years, many women had looked on him, many with open appreciation. Yet never had he had a woman look at him as she did—with a species of wonder and openly covetous joy.

And more. There was assurance in her gaze, a bold confidence combined with brazen determination—for him, to him, she was the epitome of challenge, even in this.

He seized her arms, hauled her to him, and slanted his lips over hers.

Sensed the gurgle of appreciative delight the kiss trapped in her throat, then she seized him back, returned the kiss with fervor, and fed back to him every iota of passion he lavished on her.

They were evenly matched. He'd never thought he would

think so, not of any woman, not in this arena, but with her, it was true. There was no hesitation in her touch, no drawing back. Just the same drive that drove him, focused on the same inevitable and openly desired objective.

Her jacket hit the floor; she helped him with the tiny buttons closing her blouse, and it soon followed.

Her hands skimmed his chest, fingers testing, claiming, even as he wrestled with the laces of her skirt.

Her fingertips grazed his nipple, and he paused, caught, trapped by the sensation, suddenly teetering on a sensual edge he hadn't known was there. Not so close. He hauled in a tight breath, found her lips with his, and dove back into the kiss, seeking an anchor through the swirling haze in his mind.

She pulled back from the kiss on a gasp. "Let me." She pushed his fumbling fingers aside and swiftly undid the laces, then pushed her skirts and petticoats down. One hand splayed against his abdomen, she balanced and stepped free of the froth. Clad only in a chemise so fine it was translucent even in the poor light, she raised her head, met his eyes, and boldly closed the few inches between them.

His lids fell, and he groaned at the feel of her as she pressed herself to him.

Beyond his control, his hands smoothed over her curves, over the indentation of her waist and down, around. He filled his hands with the globes of her derriere, then he gripped and lifted her to him, held her against him, molding her hips to his.

Aileen exulted in his unalloyed desire, in the heat as his lips again found hers. She rejoiced as her nerves sizzled, sparked by the giddy sensation of his hard, muscled torso impacting her softer curves. In the heady delight of seeing how much the sensation affected him, too.

Desire was a steady beat in her blood, passion a resonating thrum. She'd toed off her half boots and left them buried beneath her skirts, but she wasn't inclined to waste further time removing her stockings—not when the evidence of his reciprocating desire was so blatantly declared to her senses, his erection a rigid rod pressed to the cradling softness of her belly.

She wanted him, and he wanted her, and she saw no reason to dither—to even pause.

A heartbeat later, she had the buttons at his waist undone.

He broke the kiss, clapped a hand over hers at his waist. His eyes, burning blue beneath weighted lids, met hers. "Are you sure?"

She couldn't manage the frown that deserved. "No. I'm *certain*!"

She slipped her hands free from his restraining grasp, curled her fingers into the material of his breeches, then tugged, simultaneously sinking down.

His breeches and thin linen underdrawers slid over his hips. Determined, she wrestled them down to his calves.

Heard him curse, but her attention had fixed, transfixed, on the proud jut of his erection.

Oh, my!

Robert stared down at her—at the expression on her face. Then the damned woman licked her lips.

And he was lost.

He caught her arms and hauled her up before she could think of any next move. He heard a throaty laugh before he captured her lips, her mouth—and devoured and claimed in an effort to corral her every thought.

The kiss set the final spark to a conflagration they'd both knowingly built, one so tinder-dry—so passion-soaked—it erupted into all-consuming flame.

Her hands, his, reached, tugged, grabbed, and seized. They broke for a gasp as he hauled her chemise off over her head.

Then they fell on each other again.

She refused to let him free of the kiss. He had to sit on the edge of the bed and blindly shed his breeches, small clothes, boots, and stockings. She still had her stockings on, fine woven cotton held up by improbably lacy garters. He rather liked the thought, and they wouldn't get in their way. But he wanted her hair loose—wanted that burnished glory sliding over his skin.

She wanted to rush on, but when he refused to budge while tugging at her braids, she made a desperate sound in her throat and helped. Between them, pins rained on the floor, then her braids unraveled—and he had her as he wished.

Their lips locked, their mouths fused, he crushed her to him, then tipped backward, twisting and tumbling them onto the bed.

She landed half beneath him, and every last rein snapped.

He couldn't control anything—not himself, and certainly not her.

Not them.

They came together in a blaze of heat and passion, whipped on by impulses too powerful to resist.

This interlude was nothing like his customary sophisticated, experienced interactions; this was different.

It was so much more.

This was him with no shield, stripped bare by passion as he'd never been before. He could barely find breath in the maelstrom of need.

In the grip of a hunger like no other.

For her.

Aileen could barely cope with the onrush of sensations—with the glorious feeling of his weight upon her, of his hands upon her bare skin. The incredible feel of his skin—rougher than her own, yet stretched tight over hard muscle—pressing her down, of the crisp hair adorning his chest rasping her tightly furled nipples, of the coarse hairs on his thighs and groin abrading her delicate, so sensitive skin.

Then his lips found her breast. He lipped her nipple, and she thought she'd died.

Then he suckled, and she bit back a scream.

A dark sound rewarded her.

He proceeded to play her body like an instrument. She'd heard of the analogy, but she hadn't ever imagined any man might manage to so overwhelm her…

He did. Despite the passion that gripped them both, that whipped them on with a near-violent fury, he fought and seized the time to open her eyes to the manifold pleasures, to open her senses to wonder.

When with a final, devastating lick he sent her senses soaring and she came apart on a sobbing scream, she saw stars—and felt the elemental implosion of ecstasy for the very first time.

And at last, he rose over her. With care, with a restraint so fraught it made his muscles quake and quiver, he sheathed himself, inch by inch, in her softness.

The impact…was so much more intimate than she'd ever dreamed. The sensation of him there, stretching her body, forging in and claiming, eventually filling her to the hilt, was shattering.

It shattered a dam she'd built inside herself so many years ago she'd forgotten it was there.

He withdrew a little way, then forged in again, and she arched beneath him.

And opened her heart to him.

Gloried and cleaved to him, held him and rode with him as with her open encouragement the last vestige of his restraint fell away.

Robert was lost—lost on a plane of glory and passion he'd never before breached. She was so much more than any woman he'd had before; she met him, matched him—and challenged him to the end.

The sheer power of their joining swept him—them—away.

Driven. Owned. By their passion.

No—by what powered it, what lay behind it.

He could not—would not yet presume to—put a name to it, but he sensed it there, within them both, nascent and yet so potent.

So far beyond desirable that mere mortal minds could not encompass its glory.

They raced to the end, to the ultimate peak. They reached the pinnacle and soared.

Into the cataclysm of ecstasy, into the soul-searing brightness of that ineffable, internal sun.

They clung to each other, minds overwhelmed by the glory, bodies overcome by the scintillating pleasure that stretched for miles and minutes uncounted...

Eventually, the brightness faded.

Finally, they spiraled down to the here and now, to the covers of his bed. To the pleasure that spread beneath their skins, the peace that flowed through their veins.

To the synchronous thudding of their slowing hearts and the warmth of each other's arms.

★ ★ ★

Later, when he'd disengaged and lifted from her, and they'd shifted and rearranged themselves beneath the covers of his bed, he lay on his back with her a warm weight against his left side, her head pillowed on his chest, in the hollow below his shoulder.

He stared up at the canopy. And wondered what came next.

She didn't leave him wondering for long. "Incidentally"—her words were muffled, her breath wafting over his chest—"this changes nothing. I'm still coming with you tomorrow morning."

His protectiveness stirred. Even in the few days he'd known her, he'd grown accustomed to the instinctive reaction she provoked, but to his surprise, the compelling impulse to keep her locked away in his cabin, safe from all possible danger, was tempered by a recognition, an evolving understanding.

Of her.

Of what being with her—of her being his and, possibly, him being hers—actually meant.

What consolidating that state might, and most likely would, require.

Trust, obviously. But also accommodation.

He'd seen how both worked between Declan and Edwina.

With Aileen…in order to hold her, as he most definitely intended to do, could he offer any less?

He knew that for him, the time was not yet right to speak of the future; it was almost certainly not the right time for her, either. He needed to push hard to complete his mission, and she needed to satisfy herself that she'd done all she could to find and rescue her brother.

They needed to get both missions squared away before they would feel free to focus on their personal lives.

So discussing the future was for later. But as for tomorrow morning…

"To remind you"—she smothered a yawn with one hand—"we can't be sure that if I'm not with you, that the boy from the shore will approach you, even for the princely sum of a crown. Even if he does, he won't lead you back to wherever the slavers appear—you know that as well as I do. He was too skittish of you, and that didn't really change."

He couldn't argue; he didn't try. Even while talking to him, the boy had constantly shot glances at her, and her presence had reassured the lad.

"On top of that," she went on, her voice growing heavy with sleep, "should the slavers come to fetch more children, we—all of us involved in this mission of yours, all whom it touches—cannot afford to let the opportunity slip. Not with the prospect of Decker arriving…and you'll have to explain the significance of that sometime."

His lips twisted. He dropped a kiss on her glossy head. "I will. Sometime when we have more time." And they were both fully awake.

"Anyway." She snuggled down, curling against him. "What it boils down to is that we have to make the best possible effort to find the trail to the slavers' camp and follow it. And me going with you to the inn tomorrow in case the lad comes to summon us is therefore necessary and desirable."

He wasn't at all sure about desirable, but necessary… "All right." He had to respect her commitment, that was all there was to it. He hugged her tighter. "I'll agree to you going with me to the inn on one condition."

She shifted her head to squint up at him, suspicion overlaying her features. "What condition?"

"That from the time your feet leave *The Trident*'s deck, you remain with me, literally by my side, until we return to the ship."

She looked into his eyes, then she smiled and nodded. "Very well."

Fleetingly, he tightened his arms about her. "So you promise?"

Her smile deepened. "Yes, I promise." She settled her head on his chest again; he only just caught her final murmur, "As long as I'm with you, I'll be content."

The words sank into him, carrying the warmth of the sentiment deep. He felt his lips curve, and he closed his eyes.

And surrendered to sleep.

Aileen felt him relax, felt him slide into slumber. She was sleepy, yet her senses still thrummed. Pleasure remained, sunk to a deeper level now.

Contentment buoyed her.

She closed her eyes, and a fleeting memory drifted across her mind. Her conviction, when she'd been hooded, gagged, and bound in the slavers' lair, that whatever happened over the next few hours would fundamentally alter the course of her life.

She hadn't been wrong. But she'd got her deepest, dearest wish—the one that had surfaced when she'd been most desperate.

She'd found her way into Robert Frobisher's arms, into his bed.

And as she'd promised whatever deity had granted her the chance, she would hold tight and not let go.

Fourteen

They landed in the second cove to the east of the harbor a little after sunrise and walked for an hour before they reached the inn. By that time, the settlement was waking, the usual bustle of a day just commencing spilling into the streets.

The six of them went into the inn and settled about their previous table.

Aileen sat beside Robert; while the others pulled up chairs, she glanced his way. "The children did say the slavers have thus far appeared in the afternoon."

He nodded, but said nothing further as the innkeeper's wife hurried to their table.

The woman bobbed a curtsy to Aileen and was patently pleased to have the men back. She quickly took their orders, then supplied them with a hearty breakfast.

Benson, Coleman, Fuller, and Harris ate their fill, then took their leave to head into the slum.

"I'll leave a message with the innkeeper if we get word that the slavers have come for more children." Robert considered the four, then said, "If by midnight tonight you've seen no action at the lair, gather any gear from the hide, check back here for Miss Hopkins's bags as well—we'll leave them with the innkeeper or his wife—and take everything out to *The Trident*. I would rather you spend the night there—you can return to the settlement tomorrow morning and set up watch again."

Benson nodded. "And if you don't get word about the children?"

Robert glanced at Aileen. "We'll go back to *The Trident*, too."

To his relief, she smiled in agreement.

He dismissed the four men with a nod. On their way out of the door, they passed Dave, coming inside.

Cap in his hands, Dave saw Robert and Aileen, grinned, and made his way to their table. "There you are, miss! Right glad I am to see you again. No harm taken?"

Aileen smiled at the driver. "As you can see, I'm perfectly well, thanks to Captain Frobisher and his men."

Dave nodded to Robert. "Right, then. Anything I can do fer you today?"

They had Dave drive them to Mrs. Hoyt's Boarding House for Genteel Ladies.

Mrs. Hoyt was sorry to see Aileen go, but was also intrigued. "So you're heading home, then?"

Busy folding her nightgown on the bed, Aileen nodded. They'd decided that was the wisest story; it was also true, although they didn't expect to set sail that day. "As soon as we can."

Robert was standing by the window, pretending to look out. Mrs. Hoyt cast her bright gaze over him, from the top of his head to his heels, then she leaned across the bed and patted Aileen's arm. "Good catch, dear."

With a nod and a wink, Mrs. Hoyt departed, leaving Aileen smiling as she packed the last of her belongings into her second bag.

When the door closed, Robert turned from the window. She glanced up, and he caught her eye. "She made me sound like a marlin."

Aileen laughed. She closed the bag and did up the strap. "There. Done."

"Good." He picked up that bag and the larger one waiting at the foot of the bed. "I have to commend you on managing to travel without a bandbox. Let's get going."

Still smiling, she opened the door, then together they walked to the stairs.

Dave drove them back to the inn. Aileen insisted on paying him; Robert insisted on adding a sizeable tip. They parted from the old cockney with sincere wishes for his continuing health—and he rather pointedly returned the sentiment.

After Dave and his horse had rattled away, Robert carried Aileen's bags into the inn and left them in the care of the innkeeper's wife, explaining that someone, most likely his men, would fetch them later.

Aileen was standing by the inn's main window, looking out into the dusty street. He walked through the taproom to join her.

As he drew near, she stiffened, then she whirled. She saw him and grabbed his arm. "The boy's here. He's come!"

She hurried toward the door; Robert followed at her heels. As they neared the open doorway, the boy warily peeked in. He saw them and jerked back.

Aileen beamed at the boy as she stepped through the doorway onto the narrow strip of paving stones before the inn's door. "Do you have news?"

The boy ducked his head. "Aye. They've come." From the way he darted glances all around, he expected to be upbraided and chased off at any second.

"I thought the slavers usually came in the afternoon." Robert's tone held a soupçon of suspicion.

Instead of taking offence, the boy merely nodded. "Aye. They've come early. Earlier than they usually do." Concern showed in his face. He looked at Aileen, then shot a glance at Robert. "Me crown?"

Robert closed his hand about Aileen's elbow. "When you show us—there's no other way for us to know if you're telling the truth."

Aileen shot a chiding look his way.

But although the boy frowned, he tipped his head toward

the shore. "Best hurry, then. They usually take half an hour or so, talking the silly beggars into it and then selecting the ones they want, but given they've come early, who knows how long they'll stay?"

Robert nodded. "Lead on. We'll follow. Stop when you have them in sight."

"Wait!' Aileen looked at Robert. "You have to leave a message, remember?"

Robert softly swore. He looked at the boy. "A moment." He ducked into the inn. It took him a bare minute to scribble a note and leave it with the innkeeper's wife, along with a good-sized tip.

He returned to the door and stepped outside. Instinctively, his hand brushed the hilt of his sword, belted at his hip, as he took Aileen's elbow—whether to steady her over the rutted streets or make sure she didn't outpace him, he wasn't entirely sure. He nodded to the boy. "Let's go."

The boy ducked his head. Thrusting his hands into his pockets, he walked rapidly down the street. A little way along, he slipped into an alley that led into the slum.

Robert and Aileen strode after him, keeping several paces behind. As they crossed an intersection, Aileen twisted her elbow from Robert's grip, but immediately reached for his hand.

Appeased—pleased—Robert closed his hand around her fingers, and together they hurried on.

The lad led them deep into the slum, eventually halting in the mouth of an alley that opened onto the sand a hundred yards farther to the east of the rocky outcrop.

The boy looked out, then drew back into the deeper shadows. He pointed out and to the right. "They're still there."

Keeping to the shadows, Robert edged to the alley mouth; her hand still in his, Aileen followed at his shoulder.

Out on the sand just above the line of the waves, three men—all armed, but not as heavily as those they'd previously seen—

were talking to a gaggle of children. Robert scanned the men's faces. He didn't recognize any of the three.

He dipped his head and murmured to Aileen, "Have you seen any of those men before?"

She shook her head. Then she frowned. "Can we get closer? Close enough to hear what they're saying?"

Robert looked at the boy.

The lad stared back. "Me crown?"

Without another word, Robert handed the coin over. "Can we get closer?"

"Aye." The boy tipped his head back up the alley. "I'll show you."

He led them through a series of ever-narrowing lanes to the mouth of a runnel that gave access to the shore. Robert glanced down it; the group of men and children lay directly beyond the runnel's other end.

The lad stepped back. "I done all I can." He met Aileen's eyes. "I'm off."

She smiled at the boy. "Thank you. You did the right thing. We'll do our best to stop this and bring the others back."

The boy studied her for several seconds as if trying to gauge her sincerity, then he bobbed his head, shot a wary look at Robert, and slipped away.

Robert turned back to the scene on the shore.

Aileen walked quickly to the runnel's end; using his hold on her hand, he stopped her before she stepped out of the shadows. Her head tipping, she frowned in concentration.

Robert tuned his own ears to the men's deeper voices.

Then Aileen gave a small gasp; her eyes widened, and she looked at him. "I can't make out the words, but that voice..."

He listened—and heard what she had. "The man with the wonderful voice."

"*Yes.* The one in the slaver's lair—that's him. I'm certain of it." She peeked out again, then drew back and met his eyes. "That means this is the same group of slavers—and *that* means that if they take any children, they'll most likely take them to the same place, the same camp, doesn't it?"

Lips setting, he nodded. After a moment more of fruitless listening—they were just too far away to make out words—he leaned out and peered along the line of increasingly ramshackle dwellings straggling away to the east, hugging the shoreline until the sand ended and the jungle closed in. Quickly registering the direction of the breeze, he ducked back.

Aileen looked questioningly at him.

He turned back up the runnel, tugging her with him. "We can't get physically closer, but the breeze is blowing from the northwest—if we move farther east, we might be able to hear more clearly."

They tacked eastward through the tiny lanes and chose the second runnel along to test his theory. They fetched up at the end. Keeping to the shadows, they strained their ears…

"…so if you come with me and work hard, you'll be able to make enough to move up the hill."

It was the man with the mesmerizing voice who was speaking. Robert adjusted his sword and shifted position so that he could peer past the end of a sagging porch. The man had hunkered down so that his head was level with, or even lower than, those of the children gathered around him.

The man continued, "I don't say as it'll be easy, mind, but we've told you what we're offering, and all you have to do is tote baskets back and forth, and you'll be taken care of while you earn. Your friends who joined us earlier are all there, busily working and earning. And because things are going so well, we're expanding the business, and we've space to put on five more of you older ones." The man slowly rose to his full height. He surveyed the children with what outwardly seemed a genial smile. "Five only, mind—we don't want to take too many. That would reduce the rate of pay to the others, you see?"

One tallish girl raised her hand and called out, “Will we be able to send our coin back to our mas, then?”

The man smiled, the picture of benevolence. “You’ll be able to bring it back yourselves on one of your break days.”

Another girl frowned. “None o’ the others have come back yet—ain’t they had break days?”

“Ah, well—we don’t force our workers to take break days, only if they want. Of course, you get paid for the days you work, so…” The man shrugged, but he was grinning, as if he was privy to some special secret. “Guess they’ve decided it’s better to work more and gain more to put aside before they come back.

“So!” He clapped once, then he looked over the heads again and spread his hands. “Who’s up for joining us, heh?”

Dozens of hands shot into the air.

“Me!”

“Me!”

“Pick me!”

“I’m stronger!”

Jostling started among the children. The man held his hands out, waving at the group to calm. “Now, now. That won’t help. You know the drill. Line up, and let’s take a look at you.”

Aileen was shocked to see how many children pushed and nudged themselves into a long line. “Good Lord! He’s like a pied piper.”

Grimly, Robert nodded. “Good analogy. But this one uses his voice instead of a pipe.”

“Just look at the other two.” Aileen glared at the other two slavers who were standing a step back from the chief procurer with huge grins wreathing their faces. “Pleased as punch, they are.”

“Hmm.” Robert was studying the same sight. “That makes me suspect that the mine is rather hungry for workers—or at least the slavers are keen to snare some captives for it.”

She glanced at him. “So you think they’re recruiting them to work in the illicit mine?”

He nodded. "I think much of what he told them was the literal truth. That's why he can be so convincing. And the truth disguises the lies—like the fact they'll never receive any wage—and also the bits he leaves out, such as the fact the children who go will never be allowed to come back."

Aileen looked out at the children—at those lined up, all vying to prove their worth to the slavers. From this angle, she could see the naked hope in their faces—the desperation to seize an opportunity for betterment, for themselves and also their families.

The pied piper made his first four selections rapidly—taller, stronger, older lads, perhaps twelve years old or more—but the final berth fell to a choice between a rather weedy boy or the tall girl who'd spoken.

The girl was twelve at least, and sturdy and strong as well as tall for her age. But another younger mite with the same dishwater-blond hair clung to her hand.

"Can I take her, too?" the tall girl pleaded. "She won't be no trouble, I swear."

The pied piper pulled a regretful face and shook his head. "Sorry, luv, but it's not worth me hide to allow her into the camp." He glanced at the weedy boy, then looked back at her. "If you'll leave her behind, you can come with us." He shrugged. "Up to you."

The tall girl looked down at the little one. As if sensing what was coming, the younger one started shaking her head—at first slowly, but then faster as she clung to her older sister's hand and started to wail, "No, no no, *noooo*!"

The look on the older girl's face as she looked down at her sister made Aileen's heart constrict.

Then the older girl looked at her friend, beside her. "Can you take her to Ma?"

"You're going?" the other girl asked. But she was already reaching for the mite.

Her chin firming, the tall girl nodded. "Aye. Ma needs whatever I can bring home."

There was a world of weary, downtrodden despair in both the older girls' faces.

Aileen felt so sad for them. So sorry.

She looked at the little mite, weeping and flailing as the second girl pulled her away.

Aileen turned her attention to the slavers, and her anger flared and burned.

Wisely, the pied piper and his cohorts had stood back and let the little drama play out without interfering.

But as the tall girl turned away from her wailing sister and straightened her shoulders, the pied piper beamed again and waved her to the end of his line of soon-to-be captives.

"Right, then!" He rubbed his palms together, then looked at the small crowd of children remaining. "Shall we have a bit of a cheer, then, for those lucky enough to be selected?"

The children duly cheered as the pied piper turned and led his small troop of five off along the sand. The other two slavers fell in at the rear, turning back only to smile and wave at the children left behind.

Aileen felt faintly nauseated. Robert gestured at her to draw back. Sliding deeper into the runnel, she mimicked his movements on the opposite side of the narrow space and put her back to the wall as, ten yards away, the pied piper led his smiling, yet already faintly nervous band along. Several of the children glanced back—at the life they were leaving.

Unwittingly, possibly forever.

Aileen held her position and waited while the other two slavers passed the end of the runnel and trudged farther along the sand.

Robert's gaze locked with hers. His blue eyes searched her face, her eyes.

Before she could say anything, he murmured, "No. We cannot rescue those children."

"But they're *children*! They're innocents."

His features hardened. "I agree. If there was any other way..." He glanced toward the beach, then looked back at her and met her gaze. "But this is likely to be our only chance to locate the slavers' camp—certainly in the next few days. Think—why take more children? And specifically older ones. According to our list, before, they took those aged six to ten years old. Why the change?"

She blinked. Frowned.

"Because they haven't been able to take adults—not recently." He reached out and took her hand. "Not easily and safely. Not since Lady Holbrook fled." He moved back to the end of the runnel and peered around the corner. Then he glanced back at her. "We need to see where they go."

She wasn't going to argue about that. She raised her skirts and kept up as they stepped out from the cover of the runnel and skirted the dilapidated buildings lining the shore at that point.

Ahead, the pied piper led the children off the beach and back into the straggling outskirts of the slum.

They kept well back; being so tall, Robert could see ahead well enough to allow them to keep a decent distance.

After nearly ten minutes, he murmured, "They're very sure of themselves. They haven't glanced back once."

Just as well. As they continued into poorer and poorer areas, Aileen was starting to feel distinctly visible. At least she'd elected to wear her dark navy skirt and jacket, along with her darker blouse. The quality still stood out, but a pale green or lemon yellow would have stood out even more.

The heat was already oppressive. Although she'd grown somewhat accustomed to it, the air still felt as if it weighed on her shoulders. Despite the threat to her complexion, she'd left her bonnet, somewhat the worse for yesterday's wear, in Robert's cabin, and she was glad she'd decided to leave off her petticoats. Her skirt might hang rather limply about her legs, but the sartorial gaffe was hardly relevant around here.

They trudged on. As far as she could tell, they were heading steadily east. She slipped her fingers into Robert's hand, gripped, and tugged. "Do you think they're heading out of the settlement?"

He frowned; his hand closed around hers. "I assumed they would take them to the lair, but we passed the turnoff in that direction a while back—they're definitely not heading that way."

They paced steadily along. Her eyes on the ground, her hand in his, she thought, then offered, "The children said that these slavers—and they must have been talking about the same ones—used to come in the afternoon. But those times, they took only younger children." She glanced up and met Robert's gaze. "Young children can't walk all that far. Perhaps, on those occasions, they did use the lair, or at least some other place to pass the night before walking farther."

He shrugged and looked forward. "Perhaps they just walked through the night."

She humphed dismissively. "Have you ever tried to walk far with young children in the dark?"

He smiled faintly. "No, but I take your point." After a moment, he went on, "However, following that reasoning, it would suggest that today, the slavers came in the morning because they knew they would be leaving with older children—children able to walk the distance to their camp before nightfall."

Aileen glanced around. "I thought you said the slavers generally didn't walk the settlement openly during the day, or at least not with their captives in tow. They held me in the church rather than carry me through the streets."

"Adult captives, yes. Through the better areas, including the better slums, yes. But the areas we've been passing through are inhabited by the dregs of the settlement's population. And on top of that, these captives are children who are not restrained but marching along quite willingly, and the slavers were careful to leave the shore well away from the neighborhoods where the children might be known."

After a moment, she said, "So they might not stop but continue walking all the way to their camp."

Robert softly swore. He should have done it earlier, but... He stopped and drew Aileen to a halt, facing him. "I have to keep following them. This looks like our best chance—possibly will be our only chance—to learn the location of the slavers' camp before Decker arrives and starts asking awkward questions." He met her eyes. "I want you to go back to the inn and wait for the others there. Tell them what I'm doing"—he glanced to where the small band trudged along, then looked back at her—"and in which direction I'm heading. And then go back to *The Trident* with them."

She stared at him for several heartbeats, then, slowly, shook her head.

He hissed out a breath. "This is not the time to argue—"

"I agree." She held up a staying hand. "But it seems you've forgotten." Her brandy-bright eyes locked with his. "You asked me for a promise that, once I left *The Trident*'s deck, I would not under any circumstances leave your side—and I gave it."

He stared at her.

Her lips lifted faintly, as if acknowledging that she knew perfectly well this wasn't what he'd meant. "I'll have you know, I keep my promises."

He looked at her—took in the unwavering light in her eyes and her determined expression. He dropped his chin to his chest and not so softly cursed.

"We're in this together. We'll go on together." She shook his hand and tried to tow him around. "Come on. We have to keep up. Because I do agree with you—this might well be our last viable chance to learn the location of that damned slavers' camp."

Robert swallowed his growl, gave in to her urging, and fell in at her heels.

Hand in hand, they dropped back onto the trail of the pied piper's little band.

★ ★ ★

Aileen had been happy to give Robert the promise he'd asked for because, even while in the assured safety of his cabin and wrapped in his arms, she'd foreseen that the same promise would ensure that, if danger lurked when they were ashore, she would be by his side, as per his request, to help him—to guard his back.

With three brothers of her own, she knew very well that men like them—like Robert—rarely considered that the women they felt protective over might feel the same way about them.

Very possibly for the very same reason.

But she was used to male obtuseness, so Robert's grumbling and his two further attempts to persuade her to leave him and retreat to safety—safety as he saw it—didn't fray her temper. Rather, they bounced off her inner armor.

If anything, his attempts made her want to smile.

Not that she did. No sense baiting the bear.

They continued to walk farther and farther east. Eventually, they left the outlying hovels of the settlement behind and walked into the darkness of the jungle.

And the simple act of following the little band became rather more fraught.

The jungle was dense, the path more like a corridor cut through the greenery. Formed by the tramp of many feet over many years, and evidently well enough used to ensure that the way remained clear, the path constantly twisted this way and that, skirting around the boles of larger trees and palms. On such a winding path, they had to creep closer to the little band to ensure they didn't lose them down one of the intersecting paths. But being close enough to hear the slavers meant the slavers could hear them. Luckily, the earth of the path was soft, kept damp by the humidity and a layer of decaying leaves; their boots made little sound.

They tracked the slavers more by the occasional comment or cough, or the clink of weapons.

At one point, Robert paused and drew out the map of the settlement and surrounds he'd bought from the mapmaker. Aileen peered around his shoulder as he aligned the map, then pointed to a winding line leading out of the settlement.

He put his lips to her ear. "This is the path we're on." He traced the squiggly line from the settlement; she tracked the direction with her eyes until his finger tapped a wedge of blue at which the line ended. "It leads to one of the inlets that run inland off the estuary." He refolded the map, tucked it away, then retook her hand. He bent close to say, "I'm hoping they'll turn aside before we reach the inlet, but chances are they won't. A camp this side of the inlet would be too close to the settlement—and would probably encroach on the lands of one of the nearby village chiefs."

She nodded and fell in behind him as he led the way on.

Occasionally, well-trod paths led off the one they were on, presumably leading to those nearby villages. Robert kept his eyes peeled, but they saw—and were seen by—no one. The jungle lay somnolent under a blanket of equatorial heat. Every now and then, they crossed or walked beside tiny rivulets; it was easy enough to find potable water, and he encouraged Aileen to drink.

She seemed to be managing well enough in her cotton skirt and jacket, and her half boots appeared sturdy and well soled. He wouldn't have minded removing his lightweight jacket, but the dun color helped camouflage the white of his linen shirt.

Midges buzzed, especially when they drew near water, but as long as they kept moving, the insects seemed too sleepy to follow.

His mind ranged ahead, gauging how far they'd come and how much farther it might be to the inlet's shore. How much farther the slavers' camp might be if it was, as he suspected, hidden in the jungle on the other side of the inlet.

He didn't realize he'd muttered his last question aloud until Aileen, now using both hands to manage her skirts as she followed behind him, murmured, "I've been thinking about that. Children can only walk so far in a day, and I seriously doubt even children this old will walk far in the dark. Also, the slavers aren't carrying any supplies."

"You're right." The observation gave him heart. He stopped and took her hand to help her over a fallen palm. "Unless they intend to stop at some village—and from all we've heard, that shouldn't be on the cards—then it appears they expect to make it to their camp by the end of the day."

They continued on. After several moments, her voice a bare whisper in deference to the little band still trudging thirty to forty yards ahead, she asked, "What if the place they stop at tonight isn't their permanent camp but just… I don't know—a staging post of some kind?"

He considered the prospect; it gave his mind something to do while they mindlessly put one foot in front of the other. "If I've understood the relations between the slavers and the local chieftains—and I'm not at all certain I have, not correctly—then maintaining even temporary camps within a chieftain's territory is unlikely." He grimaced. "Sadly, it's not impossible."

"Will we be able to tell if the camp we reach is the permanent one?"

"Yes." He was confident of that. He glanced back at her. "The buildings will be more solid, on some sort of foundations. A temporary camp will be something they can pack up and move at a moment's notice."

She nodded and continued slogging doggedly along in his wake.

He faced forward. "Regardless, whatever camp we find tonight, we'll have to return to the ship."

From the corner of his eye, he saw her nod. "Your orders are to go no farther than the first camp and to return to London and report." When he glanced at her, she caught his eye. "That's correct, isn't it?"

He couldn't hide a grimace. "Yes, but…my orders didn't take into account a temporary camp." He weighed his options, then said, "If the camp we reach tonight is merely a temporary staging post rather than the permanent jungle camp of this group of slavers, then we'll still return to the ship tonight, but if Decker hasn't yet sailed in, I'll bring some of my men with me tomorrow, and we'll follow the trail on. Hopefully, to the permanent camp."

He felt the sharp glance she threw him, but didn't react, didn't look back.

As they walked on, slowing now and then, and halting when the group ahead of them halted, he recalled her comment that the slavers were carrying no supplies. In his estimation, that suggested they were expecting everything they needed to be at their camp—which increased the odds that it was the permanent camp the group was making for.

The camp he'd been sent to locate.

They crested a shallow rise in the path—and twenty yards ahead saw blue water glimmering in the sunshine. The jungle came to an abrupt end about fifteen yards ahead, leaving a short stretch of river sand running down to the water's edge.

They could see the slavers and the children milling in a group on the packed sand a little way to the right.

Another smaller path angled away to their left, leading diagonally to the jungle's edge. Robert reached back, grasped Aileen's sleeve, and drew her in that direction. He didn't take his eyes off the slavers until they were once more screened by trees and palms, but the three men didn't seem at all alert, even to the chance that someone might have followed them.

Then again, in this part of the world, few people would be fool enough to follow slave traders into the jungle.

Exercising extreme caution, they crept to the edge of the trees and undergrowth, eventually crouching in a bed of smaller palms above the strip of muddy sand edging the tidal river.

Aileen dismissed an errant thought that the palms were remarkably like those to be found gracing fashionable London ballrooms. Hunkered beside Robert, her shoulder against his, she peered out. Down on the sand, the three slavers were standing loosely around the five children while they waited for two other men to row a largish boat to shore.

Also on the sand between their hiding place and the slavers' group stood three natives. All carried spears. They wore loose trousers with the legs rolled up, but their chests were bare. The natives watched the slavers; without word or gesture, their animosity was apparent.

The slavers knew the natives were there. Although they appeared to ignore them, all three slavers watched the trio from the corners of their eyes.

With a crunch, the rowboat beached. It was a sturdy craft, big enough to hold perhaps ten adults. It was painted a blue-gray with green trim, and a crude depiction of the sun glowed brightly on either side of the prow.

The pied piper immediately led the children to the boat and helped them, one after the other, to clamber in.

The children were edgy, openly nervous, but when directed to sit on the benches, they obeyed.

The three slavers pushed the boat off the beach, then scrambled in. The two men on the oars bent their backs and stroked, and the boat moved away from the shore. The pied piper grasped the tiller and turned the boat up the inlet. Two more oars were put in place, and the other two slavers sat and added their strength to the effort, and in short order, the boat glided smoothly away upstream.

Aileen watched it go. She tensed to rise—Robert's hand on her arm held her back. She glanced at him, a question in her eyes. He shook his head at her and mouthed, "Wait."

He looked at the three natives. She followed his gaze.

The three men had started a low-voiced conversation in what sounded like one of the local tongues. After a moment, they seemed to come to some decision. Hefting their spears, they continued along the river's edge in the direction the rowboat had gone.

Only when the men had disappeared from sight did the weight of Robert's hand ease from her arm. She straightened and shook out her skirt, then stepped back onto the path and walked the last yard down onto the sand.

She peered up the inlet. "So do we walk along the sand?" She looked at Robert, who had halted beside her.

He was consulting his map. "No." After a moment, he looked up—along the sandy bank in the opposite direction to that in which the slavers had gone. "There's supposed to be a small village on the shore of the inlet just downriver from here. Those three men must have come from there." Refolding the map, he tucked it away, then reached for her hand. "With any luck, they'll have a canoe we can hire."

She glanced up the inlet. "But won't they get away?"

"We couldn't have followed over open water anyway—they would have spotted us, and there isn't any feasible reason for us being here other than we're following them."

She looked at him and frowned. "Then why the canoe?"

He glanced at her, a faint smile playing about his lips. "You saw their boat. They'll pull into shore somewhere." He raised his head and, with his free hand, waved all around them. "How hard will it be to spot that boat? It's not as if there are dozens of others we might confuse it with."

"Ah. I see." After a moment, she added, "I've only paddled a canoe once. On a lake. I wasn't especially good at steering it."

This time, his grin surfaced fully. He squeezed the hand he held. "Don't worry. The knack will come back to you. And anyway, I'll steer."

Robert started them walking along the inlet's shore. He wasn't at all sure how accurate his map was with respect to distances, so he was relieved to see huts lining a clearing above the shore roughly a quarter of a mile farther on.

As he'd hoped, a small flotilla of lightweight canoes were upended in a regimented row along the bank. The natives along the coasts in these parts used canoes for river, estuarine, and sometimes even near-shore ocean fishing.

Several natives approached as, with Aileen beside him, he halted beside the canoes. Most, he noted, were two-man canoes; he pointed at one, then, by way of sign language and a smattering of general-use pidgin, proceeded to hire a canoe for the rest of the day. He intimated that he expected to be out on the water until very late. The man with whom he'd been haggling waved the point aside and conveyed that as long as he had the canoe back by sunrise, all would be well. In return for several shillings, the men handed over a full water skin as well as one of the better canoes; they'd noted Aileen's black reticule and seemed to find it exceedingly amusing.

She'd done the right thing and remained slightly behind him, her eyes downcast, but he'd sensed she'd been following the exchange, alert for any hint of danger.

After thanking the men who had set the canoe into the water in the shallows before the village, Robert held the prow and, grasping Aileen's hand, steadied her as, with her other hand, she swept up her skirts, then stepped into the bobbing craft.

He held it steady while she settled on the forward bench. When she nodded, he shoved off and scrambled aboard. Swinging around, he adjusted his scabbard, then sat on the aft bench, seized his paddle, and stroked them back from the bank.

With a sailor's sixth sense, he took note of the currents—at that hour helpfully flowing strongly up the inlet—then started paddling.

They were out in the center of the river when Aileen added her strokes to his. Gradually, her confidence grew, and then they were skimming swiftly up the river; it was more than a hundred yards wide at that point.

They passed the spot where the slavers had boarded their rowboat. Soon after, the inlet narrowed. A little while later, after they'd rounded the next bend, Robert called softly, "You search the left bank. I'll search the right."

"Given they got into a boat, won't they have crossed the river?"

"Not necessarily. If they're heading much farther upstream, then going via the river would be faster, even if they could have reached the same place through the jungle."

He held to a course following the center of the gradually narrowing river, giving the eddies created by underwater snags closer to the banks a wide berth.

They'd traveled perhaps a mile farther when Aileen shifted and sent the canoe wobbling. "There!"

She was pointing to the left bank, just a little way ahead. Quickly, he slowed the canoe, then turned the prow toward the bank.

"You have sharp eyes." He could only just detect small patches of blue-gray through the branches the slavers had draped over the hull. They'd hauled the rowboat up the bank and upended it, concealing it above the high-water mark of the tidal river.

As Aileen and he glided closer, they saw the gouge left by the hull as it had been dragged out—and just beyond, the opening to a shadowed path leading deeper into the jungle.

Rather than beach at the same spot, Robert turned the canoe parallel to the bank and paddled some thirty yards back downstream. He slowed and nosed in to the bank where a tree jutted over the water. "This should do."

He caught the branches and pulled himself out and up onto the almost horizontal trunk. Once on the bank proper, he bent and pulled the canoe in, then helped Aileen use the same tree trunk to disembark.

Together, they hauled the canoe out of the water and stowed it amid a thicket of palms. Robert slung the water skin over one shoulder, then they backtracked along the bank, ducking under palm fronds and dodging around trunks.

They reached the rowboat. Via the sunburst on the prow, they confirmed it was definitely the slavers' craft.

They left the rowboat as it was and walked to where the path led onward. A large number of fresh footprints had recently churned the damp, dark earth at the opening to the path.

Side by side, they stood and surveyed the dense conglomeration of fronds, trunks, and large pendant leaves to either side of the narrow path. The thickness of the jungle, the sense of impenetrability, was far greater on this side of the inlet than the other.

Robert drew in a breath, then pulled out his fob watch. They'd left Mrs. Hoyt's house at just after nine o'clock. They'd parted from Dave shortly after. Robert estimated they must have set eyes on the slavers with the children at about ten o'clock. He opened the watch and tilted the face to catch the heavily filtered light.

"What time is it?" Aileen asked.

"Just after two o'clock." He closed the watch and returned it to his pocket. He met her eyes. "I thought it would be later."

She arched her brows. "So did I." She looked back at the path leading onward. "How far do you think we'll have to go?"

"I have no idea." He stared into the gloom. "But if those children can walk there, then we can."

He glanced at her in time to see her chin firm. "Indeed." She met his gaze, held it for a second, then she tipped her head toward the path. "Shall we?"

He couldn't hold back the smile that lifted the ends of his lips. He reached out, closed his hand around hers, raised it and pressed a kiss to her gloved knuckles, then he lowered his arm, settled her hand in his, and walked forward.

Together, they headed deeper into the dark of the jungle.

Fifteen

If the morning had been humid and muggy, experienced from beneath the thicker canopy of the undisturbed jungle, the afternoon turned oppressively sultry. The heat seemed to hang like a leaden miasma, slowing them—forcing them to stop often and drink from the skin the villagers had so helpfully provided.

They hadn't caught up to the slavers and the children, but then, they hadn't tried. Evidence of the group's passing was easy enough to see in the footprints pressed into the soft earth of the path.

At one point, Robert crouched and studied the traffic crossing one clearing. He rose and met Aileen's eyes. "Lots of people, back and forth. And some of those imprints are old. I doubt this leads to any temporary camp."

She nodded.

He retook her hand, and they continued on.

Courtesy, no doubt, of that frequent traffic, the path remained clear. It was also relatively flat. Only the heat and the oppressive way the jungle seemed to weigh on their senses made the trek wearying.

But it was definitely that.

Although it had been years—nearly a decade—since he'd ventured into areas such as this, Robert recalled sufficient jungle craft to find several large, succulent fruit and numerous handfuls of berries. It was enough to keep them going, steadily forging on.

Moving along the floor of the jungle was reminiscent of swimming underwater; the breeze stirring the canopies high above caused beams of light, highly filtered and muted, to shift almost dizzyingly around them—much as if they were drifting on errant currents.

Occasionally, the harsh caw of a bird sounded. Several times they heard monkeys screeching. But for the most part, their journey was wrapped in a silence that felt thick—as if their senses were muted by invisible padding.

He'd just checked his watch again, finding it to be nearly four o'clock, when they heard a boy's voice.

Robert and Aileen froze.

From not far ahead came "It's just a little farther—we're almost there."

The pied piper. They listened as he continued to talk, cajoling the children into continuing walking. Judging from the sound of his voice and the occasional whine from the children, the band was still moving, but more slowly now.

The commentary the pied piper instituted, no doubt to distract the flagging children, served to warn Robert and Aileen when they, along with the company ahead, neared the camp.

Robert tightened his grip on Aileen's hand. Still following the trail, but ever more cautiously, they reached a widening in the path. Robert halted; holding Aileen beside him, he cocked his head and listened.

Then from ahead, they heard "Here we are! Welcome to Kale's Homestead!"

Robert widened his eyes, then he dipped his head and whispered to Aileen, "Kale is the leader of our particular gang of slave traders. Definitely not a nice man."

Aileen met his eyes. "But that means we've found the right camp, doesn't it?"

Struggling to mute a surge of triumph, he nodded. "So tramping all the way here has been entirely worthwhile."

"Now remember," the pied piper went on, his distinctive voice floating through the jungle's stillness, "this isn't your new workplace. We'll only be staying here a night or two—just to see if any others will be joining us. Then we'll escort you on to your new jobs."

Robert scanned their surroundings, then tugged Aileen off the main trail onto a narrow, even more twisting route in and out among the palms and trees. They moved slowly and silently, angling forward.

Through the intervening leaves and shrubs, they caught glimpses of a large clearing ahead—presumably Kale's Homestead. Then the troop of children came into view—still strung out in a line with the pied piper in the lead. They were marching into the large open area at the center of the camp; eyes wide, the children were looking around curiously, drinking in all they could see.

Robert crouched behind a stand of finger-leaved palms.

Her hand still in his, Aileen settled beside him. A narrow gap between various bushes and leaves afforded them a decent view of the camp.

"Kale's Homestead" was, indeed, a permanent jungle camp. Five solidly built huts were placed in a horseshoe arrangement, with two huts on one long side, two on the other long side, and a larger, longer hut—presumably the slave traders' headquarters—across the head of the horseshoe. The open expanse between the huts played host to a large fire pit with logs serving as benches circling it.

The path the children had been brought in on led into the open end of the horseshoe. Robert noted two other paths leading out of the camp—to the right and to the left of the main hut. By his estimation, the path to the right led more or less due east, deeper into the interior, while the path to the left of the hut angled north.

"There are men in at least one of those huts."

Aileen's whisper drew his attention back to the huts. And he saw what she'd noticed—at least two man-sized shadows moving inside the open door of the hut to the right of the main barracks.

His mind had applied the word "barracks" instinctively. He

looked back at the main hut, confirming that it was large enough to serve as both meeting place and dormitory for eight or even ten men, then he narrowed his eyes and studied the hut in which the shadowy men seemed to be congregating just inside the door.

"There's a barred gate blocking that doorway," he murmured. "That's not a hut—it's a cell."

He glanced at the main hut. "The larger hut is where the slavers stay."

"Both the inner huts," Aileen whispered, "the ones closer to the main hut, have barred gates as doors, but the huts closer to us, farther from the main one, don't."

He nodded. "Some of the slavers will use those." Swiftly, he surveyed the layout of the camp. "If I was designing a camp of this sort, I'd do something similar. It's easy enough for just a handful of slavers to watch over quite a few captives. Unless the captives could lay hands on some weapons, escaping wouldn't be easy."

While Robert and Aileen had been studying the camp, the children had been led to the log benches before the main hut and told to sit facing the fire pit. The pied piper had left his two helpers to watch over their increasingly uneasy victims and had gone into the main hut.

Now the door of the main hut opened, and a man they hadn't seen before walked out onto the narrow porch. He wasn't large—neither tall nor broad. Compared to the other slavers, he was of medium height and build, more wiry than heavily muscled. But what he lacked in inches and weight, he made up for in menace; that quality emanated from him in a palpable aura.

Robert shifted. "Kale." It had to be. Not even the large slaver in the settlement had been anywhere near as commanding.

As evil.

The man was fair skinned, of European extraction, mostly English if his features were any guide. His hair was a dirty blond, unkempt and rather fine. He looked to be somewhere in his late thirties. A long slash marred his face, running from his right temple, nearly touching his eye and scoring deep into his cheek, just missing his prominent nose and ending at his lip. The puckering of the scar dragged his right eye down and left his upper lip distorted in a permanent sneer.

Kale halted on the porch and surveyed the scene before him. He wore baggy trousers tucked into knee-high boots and a loose, wide-sleeved shirt—the costume most slavers favored—with a grubby blood-red sash tied about his waist, along with a leather belt from which a cutlass hung.

He braced his boots, planted his hands on his hips, and as the pied piper came to stand at his shoulder, Kale focused on the children sitting on the logs with their backs to him.

Even from thirty yards away, the utter dispassion—the complete absence of feeling—in Kale's expression was evident.

Robert heard Aileen draw in a slow breath.

"This the best you could get?" Kale glanced at the pied piper. "A girl?"

So deep in the jungle, the silence, the stillness, allowed his words to carry clearly.

The pied piper shrugged. "Next best was a weakling, and she was stronger."

The children had twisted around at Kale's comment, but the men watching them called their attention forward again. Reluctantly, the children turned back to face the fire pit, but their instincts were clearly leaping—not one of them was comfortable having Kale behind them.

Slowly, his eyes on the girl, Kale nodded. "You're right. Dubois won't care as long as they're strong enough. She'll do."

Kale glanced back into the main hut. "So let's make them comfortable."

Several other slavers had already come out, slipped past Kale, and gone to the hut where the men were being held. Sudden shouts from the men inside were drowned out by the slavers shouting back.

The children started. Wide-eyed, they stared toward the ruckus.

"Oh no," Aileen whispered.

Robert followed her gaze to the main hut. More slavers were coming out. These carried shackles in their hands.

Before the children realized what was happening, they were surrounded by slavers.

"No! Wait!"

"What are you doing?"

The boys tried to struggle, to resist, but were ruthlessly—and all too easily—held in place.

In shock, in desperation, the children looked at the pied piper. He'd followed the other men and stood over the group as the other slavers swiftly and efficiently snapped the shackles about the children's ankles.

Still smiling benevolently, the pied piper gestured for them to calm down—just as he had before. "This is just a precaution so none of you wander off." He waved at the jungle all around. "It's dangerous out there. Lots of wild animals lurking."

His smile remained in place—but the children, finally, saw through his mask.

Their faces fell.

Aileen, watching the girl, saw the light in her eyes—her hope—fade, then snuff out. In that instant, the girl stopped believing and became nothing more than an empty husk, a shell.

Someone who expected to exist, but not live. And even that only for a limited time.

Aileen realized that in reaction, she'd pressed her fingers over her own lips. She lowered her hand and compressed her lips, firmed her chin.

Then she looked at Robert.

He was waiting to meet her eyes. Swiftly, he studied them, studied her expression. "No." Although the word was a mere whisper, it still held the overtones of command. "We *cannot* rescue them."

She looked back at the camp, at the children now standing and being herded toward the other holding hut; they shuffled awkwardly, having to learn how to manage in the shackles. Her voice shook as she said, "No child should ever have to learn how to walk like that."

"You'll get no argument from me."

After a moment, she dragged in a breath. "I've never wanted anyone dead before, but those men—all of the slavers, but especially Kale and his pied piper…" She drew in another tight breath and flatly stated, "I want them dead."

Robert's hand squeezed hers. "You're not alone in that." Seconds later, he added, "So come and help me get the information we need to ensure you get your wish."

She stared until the children vanished into the hut, then she turned her head and met his gaze. It was steadfast and unwavering; he was as committed as she. She drew in another long breath and nodded. "Yes. All right." She glanced around. "So this is where the camp is—what more do we need to know?"

"Not we, but whoever comes after." Robert shifted and carefully rose from their hiding place. He tipped his head, indicating that they should continue circling the camp. As Aileen rose, too, and they moved quietly back from the clearing's perimeter, he explained, "As we have the time and the opportunity, we should reconnoiter and learn as much as we can, so that whoever comes next—and I expect they'll be sent to deal with Kale—will have as much useful knowledge as we can give them with which to plan."

Slowly, they tacked through the jungle, taking their time and exercising all due caution as they circled clockwise around the camp. They counted the slavers—three had walked the children in, plus Kale and five others made nine in total.

They crouched again and watched as, with the children secured in one of the barred huts, the slavers brought out the men who had been locked in the opposite hut. There were only two, both young, perhaps twenty years old; their clothes suggested they might be navvies. The pair looked angry, but also somewhat stunned to find themselves shackled in a jungle camp; from the comments that drifted to Robert's and Aileen's ears, it seemed the pair had drunk themselves into a stupor one evening and then woken as shackled captives.

"They weren't taken to the lair," Aileen whispered.

"It doesn't seem so," Robert whispered back. "Unlike most of those who we know have been taken, it sounds as if these two weren't specifically chosen but opportunistically snatched from a slum tavern."

She frowned. "Could there be a reason for that?" She glanced at him. "For the slavers changing their ways?"

"Perhaps. With Lady Holbrook gone and possibly no one else being able to fill that role… From what Kale said, it sounds like this Dubois might be growing less choosy about who owns the hands he gets to put to work." He tugged her up. "Come on."

They continued their careful reconnoitering. Eventually, they reached the first of the paths leading out of the camp and farther into the jungle. They'd moved well back from the camp's boundary; several bends in the path hid them from anyone in the clearing. Robert crouched and examined the surface of the track, shifting leaf mold so he could study the earth beneath.

Aileen stood silently beside him, her gaze locked on the path leading from the camp. But nothing stirred, and no one came.

Robert rose and brushed his fingers on his breeches. "Lots of use over the last months." He looked through the trees toward the second path. "Let's take a look at the other one."

The light was fading by the time they reached it; Robert had insisted on drawing back even deeper into the jungle as they'd circled behind the main hut. But the instant they stepped onto the other path, the one leading directly east, it was obvious it hadn't been used in a very long time. Jungle vines looped across it, many at head and body height, and the leaf litter lay thick and undisturbed. The occasional sapling poking up in the middle of the track put the matter beyond question.

Robert met Aileen's eyes. "Dubois's operation lies to the north—or wherever that other path leads."

She nodded and glanced around. With the light dimming, the area felt more…unwelcoming. Eerie and unsettling.

"We've learned all we can." Robert retook her hand. "Let's make our way back to the track to the inlet."

She hid her relief and fell in behind him. Although it was only late afternoon, under the jungle canopy, the dipping of the sun toward the horizon created something akin to an extended twilight.

They could see the path to the inlet through the palms when Robert halted. They'd reached a spot where a dip at the base of a massive tree would allow them to sit and watch the path, out of sight of the camp should anyone look their way, but also close enough to hear anyone coming from that direction.

When Aileen glanced questioningly at him, he met her eyes. "I don't think we should venture down that path just yet. They may have other men bringing in supplies—either food and water or those mining supplies from Winter. The last thing we want to risk at this point is walking into the arms of any slavers."

She nodded. "Now we have the information you were sent for, and indeed, more, we just need to get safely back to your ship."

"Exactly." He drew her to sit on a moss-covered log. "It took us more than two hours of steady walking to get from the edge of the settlement to the inlet. Although we walked more slowly still, we managed the distance from the inlet to here in just over an hour and a half. That means that if we leave here as soon as it grows dark, then even if the slavers in the settlement set out to bring more captives to the camp tonight, we should have reached the inlet, retrieved our canoe, have returned it to the village on the shore, and set out from there before the slavers and their captives reach the inlet." He met her gaze. "If we walk back to the settlement along the same path we took to the inlet, we'll risk running into any slavers heading for their camp. Instead, I think we should stick to the shoreline and walk downriver along the inlet's bank and onto the shore of the estuary. Once there, we should be able to signal *The Trident*, and they'll send a boat to fetch us."

She nodded and leaned her shoulder against his, shifting her hand to twine her fingers with his. Looking out into the twilight, feeling his fingers grip hers, she smiled. "Anyone would think you were used to such planning."

He snorted, but said nothing more. They sat quietly waiting as the dusk deepened and the jungle night coalesced around them.

The sounds of the camp—of cooking and eating, of the slavers feeding their captives and then herding them back to the huts—were filtered by the intervening trees and thick foliage. Aileen listened, but heard no sounds of protest from the children. She had to own to a certain relief that the girl had been shackled along with the boys, fourth in the line, and not singled out. If there was any good aspect to the man Dubois's apparent need of strong children to put to work, it was that it held out some hope that the girl was worth more to the slavers unmolested.

Gradually, twilight gave way to night. They sat in companionable silence, yet it wasn't the silence of the merely acquainted, or even of good friends. She could feel the warmth of Robert's shoulder against hers, of his thigh like warm steel alongside hers. She could hardly be surprised that them being intimate had changed things, yet she hadn't expected that change in intrinsic awareness to be so…effortless. As if being intimate had opened some door in her soul and connected her to him—and presumably him to her—in a wholly unforeseen and amazing way. She would have thought being so intensely aware of him, of the physical reality of him, would scrape her nerves raw. Instead, his nearness soothed, as if in finding him and taking him as her lover, she'd found and integrated into herself an essential piece of her life that had until then been missing.

Missing from the life she needed to live, the life that was her rightful destiny.

If any had tried to tell her that such a fundamental change could happen so quickly—in a few days and a few short hours—she would have laughed, yet it had. She had from the first felt that he was someone she'd been waiting her whole life to meet.

Now, she supposed, she knew why—because he was the critical piece of her heart she'd been missing.

As she sat in the gathering darkness with him warm and vital beside her, she dwelled on that, on him and her, and found the prospect entirely to her liking.

Night finally fell, a blackness that was almost impenetrable. She was relieved to find that, having sat through the gradual fading of the light, her eyes had adjusted well enough for her to have sufficient vision to at least be able to avoid trees and walk a path. The camp had quietened, although they could still hear talk and conversation enough to suggest that the slavers were sitting around their fire pit and talking.

Robert tapped her arm, then slipped his hand free of hers and stood. He stretched, settled his sword belt about his hips, then reached a hand down to her. "Time to go."

She nodded. Placing her fingers in his, she got to her feet.

A clawing beast fell on her head.

She screamed.

So did the monkey—an ear-splitting screech.

Panicked, she batted at the thing as it gripped and clung to her left shoulder while its hands plucked and tugged at her hair.

At her hair comb.

Dragging the tortoiseshell comb from her hair, the monkey bared its teeth at Robert as he reached for it, screeched again, then leapt to the branch from where it had come and raced away.

Aileen staggered. She clutched Robert's arm. Her heart was racing. She felt giddy and dizzy and could barely breathe.

Robert caught her, steadied her. Abruptly, he raised his head. Then he swore beneath his breath.

He clapped a hand over her parted lips, dipped his head so he was looking her in the eyes. He mouthed more than said, "They heard. They're coming. We can't outrun them." He flicked his eyes upward, then met her gaze again. "I'm praying you were tomboy enough to have learned how to climb. I'm going to lift you up. As quietly as you can, climb into the canopy."

Eyes wide, she managed a nod. Then his hand fell away, he turned her to face the tree, gripped her about the waist, and hoisted her up.

She grabbed onto a branch, set her jaw, and swung her legs up and over. Then she pushed to her feet, reached for the next branch, and climbed. Her skirts weren't ideal, but at least the material stopped twigs and bark from tearing her skin. Her gloves protected her hands. She paused, looked down, and saw Robert leap for a branch on the other side of the trunk. As soon as she saw that he was up, too, she turned her attention to obeying his orders; in absolute silence and as fast as she dared, she climbed.

Once she was above the lower canopy and cocooned in dense foliage, she halted and clung to the trunk. Her heart was pounding, her breath coming short and fast. She hugged the tree, then as silent as a wraith, Robert joined her. He stood on a branch opposite the one she was on and slung an arm about the bole above where her arms circled it. He leaned close and breathed, "They didn't see us."

Barely moving her head, she nodded. He didn't say they were safe, because they weren't.

He murmured, "I'm hoping they think it was just monkeys fighting."

It seemed strange to pray to be taken for a monkey; nevertheless, she did.

Robert prayed, too. Opting to climb a tree and strand himself—let alone her as well—with violently inclined slave traders hunting beneath their feet had gone against nearly every instinct he possessed. Every one save the one that had kept him alive for all his seafaring years.

Being a captain had honed it; he often had to make split-second decisions on which his life and the lives of all his crew hung. The ability to assess a situation in the blink of an eye had saved his skin more times than he could count.

If they had tried to flee, they would have been caught. There was no possibility that Aileen could run fast enough to escape the slavers. And just as he had put her ahead of his mission in rescuing her the day before, he would have been unable to leave her—he would have been captured or, more accurately, would have allowed himself to be taken, too.

And his mission would have failed utterly.

But that blasted monkey and her scream had been both disaster and possible salvation combined.

Given they'd managed to get into the canopy without being spotted, if they could remain undetected for long enough, the slavers would conclude that all they'd heard had been monkeys and give up their search.

Or so he hoped.

His nerves remained stretched taut, waiting for any sign that the slavers had discovered their position. Their precarious position. Various scenarios ran through his head—ways he could react if they were found. None held out any real hope of escape. It was wait, or surrender.

They waited. In silence, barely daring to breathe.

After a while, he shifted his head, trying to find some paler slice of darkness through the enfolding leaves, but the thickness of the canopy combined with the night to defeat him.

Eventually, they heard heavy footsteps trudging toward them along the path. They held their breaths, but the footsteps continued on and past, heading toward the camp. The slavers who had rushed out to search were returning. Several deep grumbles reached them; Robert strained his ears and made out a curse directed at all monkeys.

The footsteps faded as the slavers straggled into the camp.

When silence—or what passed for it in the jungle night—once more engulfed them, Aileen shifted and looked at him. He couldn't see her face well enough to make out her expression, but assumed she was waiting for some sign.

He leaned closer to her and whispered, "We need to wait to make sure no slaver has hung back, waiting to see if anyone emerges—if there was anyone here."

She nodded.

He wished he could monitor the time, but there was insufficient light to read his watch face. They shouldn't leave the safety of their leafy hideaway too precipitously, but neither could they remain overlong. If they did, that would increase the chances of them running into a group of the slavers coming from the settlement.

Finally, he decided they had to risk descending. Through the darkness, he tried to catch Aileen's eyes. "Stay here," he murmured. "I'm going to drop down and assess the situation. If all's clear, I'll tap on the bole twice." He demonstrated. "Don't move until I do." He saw her head nod, but before he could move, she reached for and caught his neckerchief, tugged his face to hers, and pressed her lips to his in an almost desperate kiss.

She released him and whispered fiercely, "Take care."

Despite all, his lips were curved in a smile as he lowered himself, branch to branch. He paused on the last, reaching with all his senses, but he detected no one close. Lightly, he dropped to the ground.

Every faculty on high alert, he moved silently around the tree, then scouted the way to the path.

He saw no one, sensed no one. The spot where they would

rejoin the path was at least two bends away from the camp, out of sight of any likely sentry.

Satisfied, he returned to the tree and tapped twice on the sturdy trunk.

A minute later, Aileen sat on the lowest branch. He reached up, and she let herself fall; he caught her and smoothly swung her to the ground.

He looked around as she shook down her skirts, then he grasped her hand.

She met his gaze through the dimness and nodded.

He set off through the bushes, leading her back to the path.

Once on it, they traveled as swiftly as they could. She held up her skirts and hurried along, keeping pace with his longer strides.

They were most of the way to the inlet before he accepted that the chances of pursuit had diminished to miniscule and relaxed his vigilance—or rather, switched the focus of his attention from behind them to in front of them.

Yet even while his senses scanned the jungle all around, a part of him remained intensely aware of the woman by his side. He was quietly amazed by how resilient and determined she'd proved to be. How capable, how committed, and...well, determined again. Perhaps stubbornness fed into that trait, but most females he knew would have crumpled long before now.

Would have become a burden of one sort or another.

She hadn't. She'd matched him more or less every step of the way.

That he found that attractive had to be some monumental trick of fate.

They reached the inlet in what he thought was good time. They made their way straight to where they'd stowed their canoe. It was something of a relief to find it still there, hidden as they'd left it. While Aileen leaned against a trunk, catching her breath, he pulled out his fob watch, opened it, and angled the face to catch the glimmer of moonlight off the water.

"What time is it?" Aileen asked.

"Nearly eight." He shut the watch and straightened, tucking the timepiece back into his pocket. Then he bent and started brushing branches and leaves off the canoe. "We need to be past the point where the path from the settlement reaches the inlet before half past eight to be sure of escaping the notice of any incoming slavers."

A heartbeat later, Aileen was helping him clear the canoe. He launched it, then handed her in. She scrambled to the front bench. Once she was settled, he got in, picked up his paddle, and pushed away from the bank.

They didn't speak, simply paddled as hard as they could.

He kept them in the center of the river; along such an open stretch, there was no point in hugging the shore in the hope of escaping detection. The ripples created by their craft would give them away as surely as a direct sighting.

At least the tide had turned and was flowing downstream; although not strong enough yet to be of much help, at least there wasn't any resistance.

"There it is."

Aileen's quiet words floated back to him. He glanced to his left and ahead and saw the opening in the jungle—a darker splotch against the interminable foliage that lined the edge of the thin strip of sand.

He faced forward and put his back into his strokes; they shot past the spot. Fifty yards on, he angled the craft into the shore, ultimately realigning the hull so that they were traveling parallel to the bank, about twenty yards out.

The new course would make them harder to spot from the slavers' departure point, now well to their rear, but he prayed they wouldn't encounter any snags.

They didn't. Finally, they spotted the village on the shore. He brought the canoe around and allowed it to run up onto the narrow strip of beach.

He clambered out, then helped Aileen to climb out.

She immediately turned and, grasping the canoe's side, helped him drag it up out of the water.

He considered, then, with a sigh, accepted that it would be wiser to line it up with all the others, leaving nothing to suggest that anyone but the villagers had been using it.

Between them, they wrestled the craft up onto the coarse grass and turned it over.

He shrugged off the water skin and tucked it underneath the overturned hull. They'd drained the skin during their rush to the canoe.

He straightened and turned.

Aileen was there. She stepped up to him, caught his lapels, and dragged his face down to hers. She kissed him—hard.

When she drew back, he blinked. "What was that for?"

Still holding his lapels, she looked into his face. Washed by moonlight, her expression looked both triumphant and fierce—his very own Boadicea. "That's for getting us this far." She released him and turned to look along the inlet's bank. "Now let's get back to *The Trident* and head for home."

He found he was grinning. He caught her hand. "It's amazing how often we think alike."

She laughed, soft and low.

Hand in hand, they walked out of the village and onto the path that would ultimately take them to the estuary's shores.

* * *

There was just one problem with their plan. They were exhausted.

They'd started their day before dawn—and the night before hadn't been uneventful. Since breakfasting, they'd been on the move, and most of their hours of walking had been under fraught circumstances, under the ever-present threat of discovery and imminent danger.

Then had come the past hours of near panic and flight.

It was hardly any wonder they were both drooping.

After Aileen had stumbled for the third time—and nearly taken him to the ground, too—Robert drew her to a halt and pointed up the beach to where another village slumbered in a clearing back from the shore. "Let's see if they have a place we can rest. There's no reason we can't. No slavers are going to search for us there, and *The Trident* will still be waiting in the morning."

Aileen managed to make her head move up and down in a nod. Finding the strength to move her feet through the sand was increasingly difficult, even with Robert's help. She'd never known what it felt like to be at one's last gasp, but she knew now.

Luckily, he was in better condition. He half carried her up the gentle slope onto the grassy bank, then let her prop against him while he spoke with the local headman who came out in response to Robert's hail. Fortunately, the old man understood English, although he only spoke a form of pidgin.

She could barely keep her eyes open as they followed the old man to a hut at the edge of the village. Perched on stilts two steps above the ground, the hut was a simple affair with walls of the same woven panels as so many buildings in the area, a thatched roof, and a swath of heavy woven fabric for a door.

Coins changed hands, clinking in the night. Then the old man folded the fabric aside, showed them inside, then left them.

In the sliver of light the moon cast across the floor, she made out a crude pallet. She staggered to it and tried to let herself down. Robert caught her arm, then eased her to the rough sheet.

She remained awake long enough to see him walk to the doorway. For a moment, he stood outlined against the black velvet sky, then the fabric fell and darkness reigned. Her lids closed even as she heard his soft footsteps draw nearer.

She hung on to consciousness only long enough to hear the soft clatter as he set his sword belt on the floor and to feel the sag of the pallet as he lay down beside her. Then she surrendered and let sleep have her.

Robert heard her breathing slow. After a moment, he reached out and gently eased her closer, settling her within one arm.

The heat was well-nigh stifling, although a faint draft of cooler air found its way past the edges of the door covering, bringing slight—very slight—relief. Yet regardless of the warmth, he needed to have her close, near enough for him to sense if she moved.

For some reason, his instincts found that incredibly important, and he was not up to arguing with them.

Easier to give in—to them and to everything he felt for her.

He closed his eyes.

A second later, evidently dead to the world, she muttered, "We *have to* get the children back."

He was glad she was asleep, because he wasn't up to arguing that with her, either. But he knew beyond question that the best route to securing the safe rescue of all those taken was via completing his mission.

And he knew without asking that she wanted to rescue her brother and see him safe again.

Regardless…he couldn't stop his mind from evaluating the possibilities. From considering whether it might be possible to raise a force sufficient to the task and go after the slavers, and through them, to strike directly at the operation behind…but no.

In his heart, he could argue such a course. In his head, he knew there were simply too many ways such an action could go wrong—and the price of failure would be the deaths of all those already taken. All they would find when they reached wherever the northerly track from Kale's Homestead led would be a pile of dead bodies.

He was perfectly certain Aileen would rather next see her brother alive than dead.

But they'd succeeded in their goal—they'd learned the location of Kale's camp. Beyond that, they needed to cling to what was increasingly sounding like a realistic hope that all those missing were still alive.

Still alive and working for a man named Dubois.

For Robert, certainly, that knowledge, combined with the unexpected bonus of having found the one woman he could imagine taking to wife—the one woman he was *going to* take to wife—was enough.

For now.

Enough, at least, to be going on with.

Exhaustion reared in a wave, then crashed through him and dragged him under. He sighed, and all thought faded, and he tumbled headlong into sleep.

Sixteen

He woke to pitch darkness and the feel of soft fingers and an equally soft palm pressed against his lips.

The sensation of firm curves that were already familiar pressing down on his chest stopped him from overreacting.

Then he remembered where they were.

He blinked his eyes wider and made out the oval of Aileen's face. He raised his head slightly, and she removed her hand and leaned close to breathe, *"Outside. Listen!"*

He sent his senses questing farther—and detected the low-voiced conversation that must have woken her. It was coming from a distance—several huts farther down and closer to the shore.

The headman from whom they'd hired the hut spoke rapidly—as if in answer to a question, and also in protest.

"See, that makes no sense, old man." Kale's deep, slightly raspy voice was too distinctive to mistake.

Aileen rolled away and off the pallet and quietly stood. Robert silently rose to his feet as the headman protested angrily again.

"No, no." The pied piper's tones were, as always, placating and soothing. "It's like this, see."

Robert put out a hand, located his sword belt, silently lifted and untangled it, and swiftly buckled it about his hips. By the time he had, Aileen had circled the pallet and was standing by his side, her black reticule clutched in one hand, her gaze fixed on the hanging covering the doorway.

A stiff breeze was blowing off the water; it carried the pied piper's dulcet tones to them.

"We know some gent and a lady are out here somewhere. One of our scouts was walking out with a woman from a village upstream, and he saw the pair in a canoe heading upriver our way."

Robert turned, walked to the rear wall, and started carefully feeling his way across it. He was sure he'd glimpsed the frame of a woven-panel window close to the corner before he'd lowered the hanging and plunged them into darkness.

"Our scout asked about and learned that the gent and lady had hired the canoe from the village back a-ways, near the path from the settlement."

The headman said something; as no sound of immediate approach followed, presumably the headman was, for whatever reasons of his own, continuing to deny all knowledge of them.

Panic—mostly due to Aileen being with him—tapped at the back of his mind, but Robert held it at bay and methodically felt along the wall. Then his fingertips caught on the barely raised edging of the window flap.

"We don't tolerate people pushing their noses into our territory, any more than you chiefs do." That was Kale. He sounded impatient.

Praying that the hinges would make no sound, Robert eased the flap from its frame, pushing it out and up. He peered out—and saw the jungle a mere yard away.

"Our man rightly went to get help from our men in the settlement," the pied piper continued. "He reasoned that the gent and lady would return the canoe and then head back to the settlement."

"But they didn't," Kale growled.

Robert leaned out and looked down. Through the dimness, he could just make out that the ground outside was higher than the floor. Aileen appeared beside him and peered out, too.

Again, the headman spoke, this time at some length.

Robert put his lips to Aileen's ear. "You first."

To his surprise, she nodded—then she held up a hand, and he saw she was gripping her pistol. She breathed back. "I can cover you from outside."

They didn't have time for him even to work out what he felt about that. He gripped her waist and hoisted her up.

"But these people have to be somewhere, chief, and seems like your empty huts would be a good place to hide." The pied piper's voice grew fractionally clearer—fractionally nearer—yet still he didn't seem in any hurry. "No fault of yours if they've slipped inside to hide, now is it?"

The headman continued to talk, but it was clear he'd bought them as much time as he could; from the sound of their voices, the pied piper and he, and presumably Kale, too, were now walking toward the huts.

Robert's nerves leapt. Aileen's skirts took a degree of frantic manhandling to get over the sill. Then he climbed out after her.

The instant his feet hit the ground, they both reached for the flap and excruciatingly carefully eased it down. The flap fitted snugly back into its framing.

They didn't wait for more. His heart thumping, he grasped her hand and, ruthlessly quashing the impulse to run blindly, called on discipline honed over the years and moved slowly, steadily, and stealthily forward. Silently, they melted into the denser darkness of the jungle.

He struck directly away from the shore. When more than a hundred yards of jungle darkness lay between them and the village, he halted. They both turned to look back and listen. The telltale sounds of heavy-footed men searching through the empty huts filtered through the dense vegetation.

He bent his head close to Aileen's ear and murmured, "They won't be able to track us, not at night, not in this terrain. But they'll have the path to the settlement covered—we won't be able to escape that way."

"What about our original plan?" she whispered. "Go along the inlet to the estuary and then around to where we can signal *The Trident*."

He nodded. "That's still our best bet. But..." He grimaced. "If I was them—if I was Kale and as determined to seize us as he seems to be—as well as blocking the way back to the settlement, I would also get some canoes or rowboats on the water, string them out along the river, and keep watch from there."

There was, obviously, only one good option for them. He turned toward the estuary. "We need to find another canoe as quickly as we can and get on the river ahead of them."

Gripping her hand more tightly, he started off on a course roughly parallel to the inlet's shore.

Aileen trooped more or less blindly behind Robert, placing her feet where his had been. Her vision was adjusting, yet he seemed able to see better than she could. She placed her trust in his experience, in his instincts and abilities, and followed.

She wondered what would happen back at the village—whether they'd left anything to suggest they'd been there. She didn't think they had. She hoped Kale and his men simply searched and went on, and left the headman and his people unharmed.

They were a decent way north of the village and had started angling back toward the inlet's shore when distant crashes and curses suggested that their sometime presence in the village had been discovered, and someone was attempting to follow their trail.

Robert said nothing, just increased his pace.

She kept up, raising her skirts so they wouldn't tangle her feet.

It soon became apparent that the searchers had picked up their initial direction from the rear of the hut. The sounds of pursuit faded deeper into the jungle along that tack, in the general direction of the settlement.

Robert glanced back; he listened, then his teeth flashed in a swift grin. "That's bought us a little time. Just pray the next village along has canoes."

He faced forward, and they forged on, through a darkness that, to her at least, was only one step away from impenetrable.

Despite that, it was she who glimpsed the line of thatched huts through the forest of jungle palms. She tugged Robert's hand; when he glanced at her, she pointed. He saw and changed course.

They entered the slumbering village from the rear. Silent as shadows, they picked their way between two huts and saw—*thank God*—a line of canoes overturned on a strip of grass above the sand.

They ran lightly across the open area before the huts, straight to one of the small craft. He picked up one end. She gripped the other. They lifted and carried the light craft down to the night-dark water, then flipped it and let it down into the gentle wavelets. Her boots in the water, her skirt hems soaking it up, she anchored the canoe as Robert raced back and grabbed two long-handled paddles.

He returned in an instant. He held the canoe as she hiked up her wet skirts and clambered in. He pushed off and jumped in, handed her a paddle, then settled and started to stroke.

They quickly found their rhythm and were soon smoothly slicing downriver toward the distant estuary.

Robert knew they had some way to go before they hit the estuary's deeper waters and more definite waves. His instincts roared at him to go faster—to pour his all into spiriting Aileen as far away from Kale and his men as he could get her—but he had to balance speed with endurance. They had to last long enough to reach a location somewhere along the estuary where they could be sufficiently sure of being free of the slavers to put into shore and build a signal fire. If they couldn't do that, they would have to make direct for *The Trident.*

Both options would require strength, stamina, and luck. Both held unforeseeable dangers—dangers he couldn't plan for.

As he bent to the task of sending the canoe skimming over the waves, he was aware of the more coolly detached side of him pointing out that facing ridiculous, high-risk, no-sure-option tests like this was why he'd so long ago turned his back on such escapades.

But the wilder side of him, the part that simply being with Aileen brought so much closer to his surface—the part that exulted in a thudding heart and the exhilaration that fighting and the threat of imminent danger sent singing through his veins—gloried in the challenge.

In reality, the only blight on his current state of being was that she was with him—that she was facing the same dangers, the same trials.

His gaze touched the back of her brazenly brassy, stubborn, and beautiful head. He knew without asking that she wouldn't have scripted her part in this adventure in any other way. His protectiveness was his burden to bear, and all in all, she'd accommodated him where she'd felt she could.

He knew that, acknowledged that.

In some deep inner place, he accepted that—that he had to allow her to be herself, just as she'd hauled him along, step by step deeper into this careening adventure, and shown him—revealed to him—the buccaneer that still lived inside him. And reminded him of the joys of embracing that side of himself and living life with his whole being.

She'd encouraged him to be the man he truly was, the man he was meant to be.

A shout echoed eerily over the water, coming from somewhere behind them.

He inwardly swore and picked up the pace.

Aileen glanced back, but only to match her pace to his.

They pushed on—but it was soon apparent that Kale had, indeed, thought as Robert had, and had sent men in canoes to patrol the inlet.

The only advantage they presently had was that Kale's men were behind them and had yet to spot them. They were coming on quickly, but no alarm had yet been raised.

That wouldn't last. The final stretch of the inlet was open water—and just as they arrowed into it, the moon sailed free.

Robert held to a course that would take them straight out of the river mouth into the gently rolling breakers of the estuary. The shoreline along that stretch was likely to harbor many submerged snags, and trying to hug its shadows and slip around the coast wouldn't aid them now—now their pursuers were coming on.

Sure enough, a shout went up from behind. They still had perhaps three hundred yards to go to the line of breakers.

He upped his stroke rate, calling out to Aileen, "Stroke. Stroke."

She quickly adjusted, and they forged ahead.

Two hundred yards.

One fifty.

He risked a swift glance behind.

Three canoes were bearing down on them, each powered by two heavily muscled slavers.

Looking farther back, he glimpsed a larger canoe carrying three men—two men paddling with Kale in the middle, barking orders, his cutlass in his hand.

Robert faced forward. He clenched his jaw and plowed his paddle through the water with as much efficient force as he could.

Efficiency was going to be the key.

Kale had clearly worked out what his quarry would do; Robert felt a moment of respect for the man's intelligence—not least because Kale had respected his.

But there was one thing Kale hadn't judged correctly—and she was sitting directly in front of Robert, paddling for all she was worth.

Two well-muscled men in a canoe should have been able to

overhaul a gentleman and a lady in short order, no matter the expertise of the gentleman. But Aileen was a good deal lighter than any man, and she was paddling well enough to account for her weight and a bit more besides.

Kale's men were still gaining, but they weren't gaining fast enough.

Of course, Robert's hope might yet be dashed—that once they hit the estuary with its currents and much choppier conditions more reminiscent of the open sea than the relative calm of the river, Kale's slavers wouldn't know how to handle the flimsy river craft and the advantage would tip Robert and Aileen's way.

But they had hope.

"Keep going," he yelled to Aileen. "We're almost there!"

She tipped her head up and back to call, "There, where?"

"Trust me!" He couldn't help but grin. "We're going straight through that line of waves ahead."

She might have muttered something, but the strengthening wind whipped her words away.

Twenty yards. Ten.

Robert yelled, "Stow your paddle and hang on!"

Aileen reacted immediately. She stuffed the paddle down by her feet and clutched the sides of the canoe with both hands.

The prow hit the first frothing wave and reared upward. She shrieked and turned her face away.

Spray drenched her, then the prow thudded back down and she felt Robert change his rhythm, then they were suddenly shooting along parallel to the line of the waves.

She didn't wait to be told but hauled her paddle out and started stroking desperately again.

As Robert steered them over another wave, she cast a swift glance behind and saw no one.

But she could hear Kale swearing and cursing, verbally whipping his men on. She gripped her paddle tighter and pulled for all she was worth.

The visibility over the wide waters of the estuary was better than on the river. The moon had risen and cast a silver light over the scene, etching edges in brightness and turning every shadow darker in contrast.

They crested another wave—and this time she looked ahead. She desperately scanned the waters of the estuary, but saw no tall ship looming.

"It's to the right," Robert called as the canoe wallowed. Together, they bent and sent the craft skimming forward, taking advantage of the patch of smoother water that followed the crest.

When they topped the next crest, she swung her gaze further to the right—and saw the ship—the graceful, elegant ship she'd first sighted days ago—standing well out in the estuary, its stern angled their way.

"Pray they see us soon," Robert yelled.

At least he'd had *The Trident* moved farther down the estuary; it was now anchored closer to the inlet's mouth than it had been.

It was still, he suspected, too many yards away.

He put his back into forging ahead before the next wave lifted them high. He glanced back. As he'd expected, the rougher waters of the estuary had slowed the slavers. But none of the canoes had capsized—he buried that faint hope. And Kale wasn't anywhere near giving up the chase.

Robert swallowed his curses; he didn't have breath to spare to utter them. His back, arms, and legs burned, and they still had a significant distance to go.

He could read the currents, the wind, and the waves better than most experienced sailors, and certainly far better than any slave trader. He used every scrap of advantage he could wring from that knowledge and kept their craft in the lead as they forged closer and closer to *The Trident.*

Then a flare shot up from the stern—a signal that they'd been seen and identified.

Help would be scrambling to get under way, but would his men be in time?

The tender would be out on the estuary or even in the harbor; he doubted they could make it back in time to be of much help. The secondary tender would need to be launched, and that would take time…

He put aside all calculations and paddled.

Despite his focus, he couldn't stop his mind from juggling the probabilities. He'd felt sure, earlier, that Kale would do his damnedest to capture them, to take them alive.

But faced with the prospect of them escaping… Kale would want them dead.

Dead men—and dead women—told no tales.

His grip on the paddle kept slipping, the handle wet, his palms sweating. The need to hold tighter made the muscles in his forearms scream; he gritted his teeth and, his gaze locked on Aileen's brassy head, plowed on.

The tide had started to ebb. It drew them toward *The Trident*, adding just a touch of speed, but it added just as much to the canoes pursuing theirs, and to their disadvantage, with the turning of the tide, the waves started to abate, stripping away whatever small advantage they'd been able to seize from the rougher water.

He didn't need to look to know that two of the canoes Kale's men were driving forward were closing.

Boldly, Kale bellowed, "I don't care how you do it, boys—just stop the buggers!"

Robert looked up. *The Trident* was still over a hundred yards away. He glanced back and knew they weren't going to make it.

Even as he looked, a flight of arrows arced over his and Aileen's heads and rained down, peppering the closest pursuing canoes.

Curses flew. Robert grinned grimly. He faced forward and picked up the rhythm. "Keep going!" he yelled to Aileen, who had belatedly glanced back; she hadn't seen the arrows fly, just heard the commotion when they'd struck.

Like a well-drilled sailor, she fell to, but she was tiring, as was he. Every stroke, every yard, was hard won, increasingly painful, increasingly exhausting.

But neither he nor she eased back, much less were of a mind to surrender, to give up. In unwavering accord, they kept on, driving as hard as they could for the safety of *The Trident*'s steep side.

He reached to his hip and loosened his sword in its scabbard—just in time.

His fingers were still on the hilt when one of the slavers' canoes—pushing hard—hove up on his left.

The slaver in the prow raised a club and brought it down.

Instinct took over. Robert twisted sharply, and the club barely grazed his left shoulder.

The slaver overbalanced, tipping toward Robert.

His sword already out, up, and swinging, Robert struck where the man's tipping, bowing motion exposed the spot where shoulder met neck—a killing blow.

But the sudden shifting of his weight sent their own canoe pivoting, swinging the prow and Aileen toward the middle of the action—away from *The Trident* and toward Kale's canoe as the slavers' leader, his face contorted in a vicious snarl, drove hard toward them.

His heart thudding in his ears, Robert saw the two other slavers' canoes, although now each with only a single injured man paddling—*The Trident*'s archers had hit their marks—angling to flank and ultimately surround them.

And there were *more* slavers in canoes coming up hard in support of Kale.

They were fifty yards from *The Trident* and were being hit by backwash from the ship; all the canoes and players in this drama were bobbing up and down to such an extent that *The Trident*'s archers couldn't risk another salvo.

Pistols and rifles would be even more dangerous.

They were within sight of his crew, but his men could only watch.

To complicate everything, sea fog, which often hung about the mouth of the estuary and sometimes reached some way down it, chose that moment to send insubstantial ghostly fingers creeping stealthily over them.

Dimming the moon's light.

The fog was not there one moment; in the next, it swirled and engulfed them.

Swearing, Robert seized the momentary distraction and battled to swing their craft around—to head toward *The Trident* again, but even more importantly to put his own back between Aileen and Kale. But the wallowing canoe with the dead slaver hanging over the side impeded even that much maneuvering; he had to grasp the other canoe's prow and push it away—nearly overbalancing in the process.

Everyone in the increasingly constricting knot of canoes was still close enough to see each other through the enfolding fog. Kale's gaze locked on Robert and Aileen; his lips curled in a ferocious snarl, then he thrust his cutlass in their direction, roared, and his canoe speared toward them.

The Trident's tender shot out of the sea fog. Its prow rammed into one of the half-crippled canoes and overturned it.

Whoever was at the tender's tiller adjusted course.

On a surge of power supplied by six trained oarsmen, the tender plowed toward Kale's canoe.

Kale saw; he and the pair of slavers in his canoe switched their attention to the impending threat.

The tender and canoe both swung to come alongside each other.

The slaver in the front of Kale's canoe suddenly reared and swung a machete toward the figure in the tender's bow—Benson.

Stout, burly, and with his legs braced, Benson staved off the blow with his sword and countered with a thrust from his dagger. The slaver crumpled, toppling overboard—but his sudden lurch tipped Benson forward, half over the tender's side.

The shift of weight rocked Coleman, angled beside Benson in support, back on his heels, flailing and off balance.

Kale's lips peeled back from his teeth, and he raised his cutlass high.

Robert caught his breath; he was already reaching for the throwing blade in his boot even though he knew he would be too late to save his long-time man.

Kale's blade started its descent, angled to come down with force on the back of Benson's exposed neck—

A shot rang out. The sound was hideously, ear-ringingly loud in the fog.

Kale screamed and dropped the cutlass.

He clutched his shoulder and half spun, half fell back into the canoe.

Coleman regained his balance and leapt forward; his cutlass in his hand, he dragged Benson back into the tender.

As had happened before, the shot had stunned everyone.

This time, Robert didn't need to look to know who had fired it.

The second slaver in Kale's canoe took one look at the armed and determined men crowding in the prow of the tender and frantically employed his paddle to turn and pull away.

The remaining slaver in the canoe closest to Robert and Aileen's made haste to follow.

Benson, upright again and with Coleman at his shoulder, looked at Robert. "Should we give chase?"

Benson, Coleman, and the other men in the tender were all but straining at the leash discipline placed upon them, waiting expectantly for Robert's order to pursue.

But he recalled the other canoes he'd spotted. He shook his head. "There are more of them out there."

And if Kale had a blind bit of sense, he would mass his craft on the edge of the fog and wait to fall on the tender as she emerged from the disorientating murk.

As the men reluctantly stood down, and the tender got under way again, angling toward them, Robert leaned forward and closed a hand on Aileen's shoulder. "Are you all right?"

She was looking down, stuffing her pistol back into her reticule. She'd carried the heavy lump of black fabric throughout their adventure, clinging to it or having it dangling from her wrist through every moment, however fraught. He was intensely grateful that she had, but he still thought it the ugliest reticule he'd ever seen.

Finally cinching the reticule's neck tight, she looked around and met his eyes. Hers burned with shades of anger. "I was aiming for his head."

He knew better than to grin. He pressed his lips together and nodded. He squeezed her shoulder in wordless support. "I doubt Benson will care. You still saved his life."

Aileen humphed, let the reticule dangle, and reached for her paddle. She met Robert's eyes. "To the ship?"

"Yes, thank God."

The sea fog was lifting, and the first rays of dawn were painting the sky in shades of soft pink when, under close escort from the tender, they finally reached *The Trident*'s side.

A rope ladder had already been lowered, but she discovered that getting onto it from a bobbing canoe was far harder than from the tender. In the end, Robert shifted to the middle of the canoe, then lifted her onto the lowest rung.

Once on the ladder, she accomplished the climb with relative ease.

Hurley and Wilcox were waiting at the top to help her onto the deck.

She felt like falling to her knees and kissing the planking—or at least giving thanks to the heavens. Over the past twenty-four hours, there had been too many moments when she really hadn't known what their future held.

"We heard a shot," Hurley said. He glanced at Robert as he stepped up onto the deck. Hurley was clearly perplexed, presumably knowing Robert hadn't been carrying a pistol.

Robert nodded at Aileen. "That was Miss Hopkins. Thanks to her..."

There was pride in his eyes as he filled in what had happened on the water for his officers. Because of the fog, they hadn't seen any of the latter stages of the engagement.

Aileen basked in the glow of Robert's praise as she stood by the railing and watched the tender's crew come aboard and the tender itself made ready for winching onto the deck. When Robert paused in his recitation, she turned to the gathered officers. "And indeed, we're very grateful to whoever thought of shooting those arrows. That made a critical difference, too."

Robert nodded and thanked Latimer, whose quick thinking had been behind the archers' efforts.

"I'm just sorry we couldn't do more." Latimer looked at Aileen with a hint of a rueful smile. "Trust me when I say that was a few tense minutes for all of us here. We thought that pistol shot had to have been you, but we didn't know whether it was a good sign or a bad one."

"Captain."

They all swung around as a crewman came lumbering from the stern.

He drew up before the officers, paused to nod to Aileen, then looked at Robert and reported, "You won't believe it, but those beggars are coming for us." He pointed astern.

Along with Robert and the officers, Aileen hurried up to the poop deck, to the stern rail, and looked out.

A flotilla of armed slavers in a motley collection of canoes and rowboats were determinedly hauling nearer through the remnants of the fog. Aileen narrowed her gaze on the figure in the middle of one of the canoes. “Damn,” she muttered. More loudly she said, disgust lacing her tone, “Kale survived.”

The slavers’ leader had a bandage wrapped about his upper right arm, but the wound seemed only to have fired his fury.

“Actually,” Robert said, “I’m glad he did.” He caught her gaze as she shot a scowl his way. “If Kale had died, we have no way of knowing what might happen to his operation—his camp. At present, he and that camp are our only connection to this elusive Dubois, his enterprise, and all our missing people.”

Latimer, standing on Aileen’s other side, his gaze assessing the on-coming threat, snorted derisively. “What do they think we are? Some helpless merchantman?”

“As it happens,” Robert replied, his tone taking on the crispness of command, “that’s exactly what I hope Kale does assume we are.” Turning from the railing, he met Latimer’s eyes, then Aileen’s. “Just think. At present, all Kale or Muldoon knows is that you”—Robert tipped his head at Aileen—“started to poke your nose into the children’s disappearances. Then when they kidnapped you, you were rescued by some sailors.” He gestured to himself and the tender’s crew, hovering nearby and listening—waiting for their next orders. “Us. Subsequently, you and I—presumably with me acting as guard to you—saw the slavers gathering children on the beach and followed them all the way to their camp. And subsequently, we’ve scurried back to this ship.”

He glanced at Latimer. “If that’s what they think—including that we’re some lily-livered merchantman—then we’ve accomplished our mission without endangering the missing people.” He looked at Aileen, then raised his head and looked around at all the others—officers and crew—waiting to learn what came next.

Robert grinned. “So we are, indeed, going to play the part of a lily-livered merchantman. One that happens to have rather a lot of sail to call on.”

His grin widening, Robert looked at Hurley. “Mr. Hurley.

Do you have that course I asked for—our fastest route home—plotted?"

Hurley's smile split his face as he snapped off a salute. "Aye, sir."

"Then all hands to the ropes, boys!" Robert's voice rang down the ship. "Let's find ourselves some wind—we're heading home!"

A cheer went up from the crew. Even before it faded, Aileen heard the clanking rattle as a team of sailors flung themselves on the main capstans and winched the heavy anchors aboard.

Others swarmed into the rigging. Still others raced along the decks, shutting this, swinging that into place, making all ship-shape and ready to sail.

Robert clapped Latimer on the shoulder. "The wheel's yours. Take her out of the estuary, keeping as far north as you can—the last thing we need is to run into Decker on his way in. If you see him, pretend you don't. He might huff and puff, but he won't fire."

Latimer grinned and cockily saluted. "My pleasure."

Robert turned to Benson, Coleman, Harris, and Fuller. All four stood waiting, either to be dismissed to their usual ship-board duties or to whatever other tasks Robert had for them. He smiled. "I'm very glad to see you all here." He bent a wry look at Benson. "Hale and whole."

The big man shifted. "Aye, well. I've the lady to thank for that." Awkwardly, he bowed to Aileen. "It's thanks to you, miss, that I've still got me head. I won't be forgetting that."

The other men murmured in agreement.

Aileen blushed and disclaimed, "Anyone would have done the same."

"Anyone who happened to carry a loaded pistol everywhere they went." Robert shook his head at her, but kept his opinions on that to himself. He didn't want to think of what might have gone wrong with firing a pistol that had been left loaded for so long; he didn't need more gray hairs.

Instead, he returned his gaze to his loyal men. "From me, from

Miss Hopkins, from the First Lord himself, thank you for your help today and throughout our time in the settlement. You all did well." He gave them a moment to soak in the praise, then in a more normal commander's voice asked, "I take it you fetched everything from the inn?"

"Aye, sir." Coleman went on, "We found your note when we came down to the inn. We left our bags there and searched on the beach for you, but found no trace—you must have been long gone by then. So we went back to the inn, picked up all the gear, and brought it out to the ship like you'd ordered."

"But then," Harris took up the tale, "we didn't know what to do, so we joined the tender's crew and set up a continuous watch."

"We figured," the laconic Fuller said, "that if you came back to the settlement, you'd hail the tender from the same cove we came in at. So we kept the tender at the mouth of that cove, but out far enough that we could keep an eye trained on the ship, just in case you signaled direct to her for a pickup."

"We saw the flare and came running," Benson said. Rather ruefully, he shrugged. "Might not have been my finest moment, but at least we got to you in time to deny those beggars what they wanted."

"Indeed." Robert surveyed the four men. They'd put in as many hours as he and Aileen had, and had probably got little to no sleep over the past night. "You're free of all duties until the start of the dogwatch. Eat. Get some sleep. You've earned it."

The men came to attention and snapped off salutes. "Aye, aye, sir!" they chorused.

Robert watched the four head down to the main deck. He felt Aileen's fingers slip into his; he closed his hand about them, then stepped back to the stern rail and looked out at the dwindling figures of Kale and his men, left impotently shaking their cutlasses at them as *The Trident* gained speed and smoothly drew away.

Then Latimer found the wind. He called for topsails and topgallants in short order.

Robert draped an arm around Aileen's shoulders; with the warmth of her tucked against his side, he looked across at Freetown as they swept past—at the distant conglomeration of roofs huddled around the harbor and dotting the flanks of the hill above. They were too far out to see anything distinctly; they could barely make out Government Wharf.

Elation poured through him. He'd done what he'd been sent to do.

And he'd discovered so much more.

Even as the deck rolled beneath his feet and Latimer called for the royals to be unfurled and, minutes later, *The Trident* lifted and surged anew, cleaving through the waves arrow-fast, and the last glimpses of Freetown faded into the haze of morning, Robert sensed this leaving was not yet complete.

He tightened his hold on Aileen. He looked down, and when she glanced up and met his eyes, he murmured, "We'll be back. I can sense it."

She searched his eyes, then nodded. One of those definite nods of hers that left no room for argument. She looked back at the fast-disappearing shore. "This isn't finished. You, me—we have more to do." After a moment, she went on, "We saw too much. And after seeing, we won't be able to simply go home and leave this to someone else to deal with—not completely."

He felt heartened that she understood. He, too, looked out over their frothing wake. "We'll have to hand the mission over to whoever is sent in next. But that doesn't mean we have to walk away entirely."

She caught his gaze. "That we have to wash our hands of it."

"To leave the missing—the men, women, children, and your brother—to an unassisted fate." He found her hand, raised it to his lips, and brushed a kiss over her knuckles. "We'll be back."

Together.

The word hovered between them; it didn't need to be said.

But of course, that sent his thoughts winging ahead.

He slipped his fingers from hers and wound both arms around her; he tucked her more firmly against him, her back to his chest, and leaned against the stern rail. Together, they watched the morning's glory break over the sea and sky. The wind whipped past them, and the waves *shushed* along the hull as *The Trident* carried them forward and on.

His heart swelled, and he gave thanks they were there, together and alive—more vibrantly alive than he'd ever felt before—with the knowledge he'd been sent to find in their keeping.

The knowledge necessary to mount a viable rescue of her brother, and the children, and all the others.

Triumph filled him. A sense of joy, of elemental self-discovery, swamped him, held him, buoyed him.

This was who he was meant to be.

As *The Trident* speared out of the estuary and heeled into the open sea, he drew his arms from about Aileen, claimed her hand, tugged her from the rail, and headed for the ladder to the main deck and the stairs to his cabin below.

Seventeen

Robert strode faster and faster toward his cabin. Her hand locked in his, Aileen had to all but run to keep up. Rather than complain, she gave a soft, sultry laugh. The sound flowed through him in a rush of giddy warmth.

They encountered none of his crew, which was just as well; the emotions he'd held at bay through the past twenty-four hours—that the pressure and demands and outright danger had forced him to keep suppressed—had broken free, snapped their leash, and now geysered through him. Demanding release.

Demanding acknowledgment.

Demanding appeasement.

They reached the door of his cabin. He opened it and towed her through. He spun her as he shut the door, pressed her back against it, stepped into her, dipped his head, and slanted his lips over hers.

Her lips, those luscious lips, curved, then parted. Her hands caught his head, fingers sliding into his hair to hold him there, close, as she welcomed him in, welcomed him home.

With joy, he plunged into her mouth, tasted, claimed and incited, delighted and reassured by her wordless understanding. By her blatant encouragement.

By her glorious acceptance.

Aileen clung to the kiss, to him, and rejoiced.

They had so much to celebrate, so much to savor. But this...*this* came first. This restatement of their commitments—to each other and to life. This declaration of intent—of their determination to have this and all it meant. All it presaged, all it would lead to.

They had accepted this path—they'd made that decision the last time, the first time they'd come together, here, in his cabin.

But then, there'd been hurdles before them, immediate and vital matters to be addressed. So they'd gone and done their duty—they'd achieved their goals and fulfilled their commitments to others.

Now…these moments were for them.

These heated, giddy, hungry, increasingly desperate, and needy seconds.

His lips demanded, commanded, and she gave. She surrendered all she was, gave him all she was—all her passion, all the fullness of her desire, all the love she held within her—without reservation. With her lips and tongue, through the ensuing duel of their senses, she laid herself before him and invited him to take.

Gloried when he did. When he eased his grip about her waist and sent his hands skating upward to close about her breasts.

He kneaded, the pleasure just this side of painful, then his long fingers found the buds of her nipples through the thin fabric of her jacket and blouse, and tweaked. Sensation lanced through her, sharp and sweet, and she gasped through the kiss.

Then she kissed him back, as hungry as he, every bit as ravenous, and sent her own hands skating down over his shoulders, over his chest. In his immediate response—through the hardening of muscles already taut, through the hitch in his breathing—she sensed his reaction. And lurking behind that, she sensed his control—and beyond that, she glimpsed the full measure of all he held back.

Seething, powerful—undeniable.

Just that glimpse was enough. Her own hunger, her need of him—of *this*—soared.

Desire welled, then overflowed. Passion erupted and rushed in its wake.

She poured all of it—all she felt, all she wanted—into the kiss, and felt him, and that potent emotion that surged between them, ignite.

He pressed closer, the rock-hard planes of his body impressing themselves on her curves in a flagrantly primitive fashion.

She ignored his neckerchief, his jacket, his shirt; sliding her hands between them, with her lips and mouth hotly engaged with his, she searched and found the buttons at his waist. Slipped them free.

Robert groaned as she closed her small hands about his aching shaft.

While some tiny and increasingly distant part of his mind was faintly shocked—by her boldness, by his own driven intention—a far larger part gloried in the openness of her desire, in the uncompromising directness of her passion.

Thank God.

Because he felt the same. Because he, too, could not stand against the compulsive beat of need that hammered so very heavily in his veins, deafening him to all reason.

He needed her. Now. Here.

Nothing was powerful enough to deflect that driving want.

His hands were already hauling up her skirts, even while her clever hands and fingers—inventive more than experienced, but no less effective for that—reduced any control he might have managed to gather to shreds.

Then he found her bare hips beneath her bunched skirts. Closed his hands about the smooth curves.

She released his member, slapped her hands to either side of his face, and held him steady while she fused their lips and poured fire and lust down his veins.

Driven, whipped, and goaded far beyond rational thought, he hoisted her against the door and nudged his erection between her thighs, and she wrapped her long legs about his hips and wriggled…

They both broke from the kiss, gasping, heads lifting, their lids weighted and heavy as they both drew in huge, frantic breaths.

As they both seized one finite split second to savor the sensation as the head of his erection eased into her slick, heated channel.

Then he tightened his grip on her hips and slammed home.

Her lids fell; on a soft moan, she arched into him. One shoulder pressed to hers, he watched her face as he withdrew and thrust again, then he settled to a rapid, pounding beat and watched the beauty of her passions flow across her face as she accepted and held him, as her body surrendered and her sheath clamped about him, and they raced up the precipitous slope of imminent ecstasy.

Then he dipped his head, captured her lips, and drank in her cry as she climaxed in his arms in a maelstrom of passion.

It still wasn't enough, not for him. Not for the him that so needed to claim her—the him whose protective instincts had been abraded to near madness by the events of the past days.

He felt the contractions of her sheath fade. She'd locked her legs about his hips; holding her against him, he stepped back from the door and carried her to his desk.

The surface was clear. Halting before it, he set her hips on the edge, then laid her down.

Aileen felt the cool wood of the desk against her back. She wrestled her lids up enough to look at him as he pushed her skirts to her waist. He glanced up and met her eyes.

She studied his features. There was nothing of softness in his face, no give, no quarter. Only a stark need, a ruthless hunger.

A sense of quiet wonder bloomed inside her as she realized she was looking at the real Robert Frobisher without any veneer at all.

He shifted against her, and she felt him like corded steel within her, large and intrusive, but oh, so very welcome.

He made her feel needed; an elemental want burned in his eyes.

He made her feel desired—as if she was as essential to his well-being as he now was for hers.

Most importantly, he made her feel whole. Whole in a physical sense, complete in a way she'd never imagined. But most wonderful of all, he made her feel whole emotionally, as if in him—with him—she'd found her true place.

Her true reason for being.

She felt him brace his feet on the floor, pressing his hips deeper between her widespread thighs. His gaze drifted from hers, lowering to gaze at what he could see... The air played across her naked belly, and she fought a silly blush. As if he somehow sensed her reaction, his gaze flicked up to her face again, then he reached out and closed his hands about her already swollen breasts.

He squeezed as he withdrew, then he plunged deep again.

Her lids fell on a soft moan as sensation flowed through her, from where his hands claimed her breasts to where they joined, from where he repeatedly filled her to a steady, relentless beat, and pleasure burgeoned and rose in a long, rearing wave within her.

It felt earthy and delightful and wondrous.

Addictively delicious.

Robert watched her face as he claimed her. As he made her his in this most fundamental way.

He felt the moment—its significance and importance—in his bones. Felt all the façades, all the other shades of his personality—those he employed with everyone else—fade and fall away.

Leaving only him—the true him—exposed. The him that needed to bury himself so deeply inside her that she would never be free of him again.

Or he free of her.

He'd known that having her as his wife was his destiny for days, had sealed that fate as his future twenty-four hours before. But he hadn't foreseen the enormity of this thing—the sheer ungovernable force of his own need, of his own commitment to their shared path.

But all of that—all he truly felt—came together in him now and flowed through his veins like the headiest elixir.

He let that incomparable feeling have free rein and rejoiced as he drank in her responses, as she closed her hands about his wrists and writhed on his desk, soft moans and sobs falling from her kiss-swollen lips as he plundered her body and she took him in.

And held him. As she claimed him as he claimed her.

She gasped and came apart again, clung and clasped him tight as his own storm broke, as the tension imploded and streaked down every nerve and he climaxed in a paroxysm of pleasure so intense he literally saw stars.

And he finally understood what it was to love—to make love with no barriers, with nothing held back—with no safety net at all.

In that last moment of lucidity, as, propped on his braced arms, he hung over her, spent and wrung out, yet still floating on that distant plane that could only be reached, it seemed, this way, he finally comprehended the totality of what he'd invited into his life.

And realized he wanted it—that he would fight to the death for it—to keep her, and it, and all it meant.

Forevermore.

★ ★ ★

Later, moving like ones drugged and with nothing of their customary decisiveness, they disengaged, bathed, and fell into his bed.

Bliss still coursed through their veins. Wrapped in each other's arms, naked limbs entwined, they surrendered to the moment.

They slept, for how long neither knew. They woke and made love again, lazily, this time, spending long moments in mutual exploration, in furthering their understanding of the delights of shared pleasure.

Later still, cocooned in a warmth that had nothing to do with physical sensation, a glow that reached past his bones to his soul, Robert lay on his back, his arms crossed behind his head, and stared at the canopy.

Aileen lay sprawled half over him, her head on his chest, her hips angled over his, her legs tangled with his; her fingers idly plucked at the wiry hair that decorated his chest.

Carefully, he drew in a breath, feeling his chest expand against her cushioning curves. His eyes still on the canopy, he stated, "Just so we understand each other fully, I intend asking for your hand. However..." He frowned; he pressed his lips together as he searched for the right words to explain his nebulous yet insistent compulsion. "I'm captain of this ship. Asking you to marry me while we're on board—especially while we're at sea—is tantamount to asking you to tie your life to mine while you're completely and utterly in my power."

She shifted over him, raised her head, and studied his face.

He felt her gaze, debated, told himself he was a coward, and met it.

She searched his eyes. For a long moment, she considered him, then she murmured, "I am going to accept, you know."

He grimaced and looked up—away—again. "It's not that. And Lord knows, I don't want you to say no, but... I need you to say yes when you could, if you wished to, say no." He glanced at her again. "Does that make any sense at all?"

Her features eased. Her lips curved gently, and she patted his chest. "Yes. It does make sense." She held his gaze, far more fearless—more fierce, truth be told—than he. "You're a considerate man, Robert Frobisher, and you have a deep mind. I'm looking forward to unraveling all its intricacies."

He wasn't sure if that was a promise to look forward to or a threat likely to lead to damnation. But she'd agreed... "I thought," he said, somewhat diffidently, "that we could use the voyage to learn more about each other." He focused on her eyes again. "I know your family, but I don't know you." When one brassy-brown brow arched, he smiled wryly and amended, "I know a lot about the sort of woman you are, enough and more to know I want you as my wife, but I know next to nothing of what made you as you are, virtually nothing of your personal background."

"And I know next to nothing of yours." She studied him for a moment, then her brows quirked. "Does it strike you as odd that we've known each other for only a handful of days, yet we're both envisaging spending the rest of our lives together?"

He hesitated, but her eyes—the openness, the lack of screens or distance—encouraged him to say, "From the moment I laid eyes on you, I knew you were the woman I'd been waiting all my life to meet. And I'll remind you, you had a loaded pistol leveled at my heart at the time."

She smiled—a preening, delighted, very feminine smile.

He jiggled her. "Well? You're supposed to say something similar back."

She laughed. "That's the diplomat in you speaking, but..." Her eyes twinkled. "I will admit that, when I first set eyes on you, albeit from afar—when you attended Undoto's church with Sampson—I definitely noticed you in a way I have never noticed any other man. Almost as if a deeper part of me, some primitive instinct, knew you were the man I would want for my own."

He felt ridiculously satisfied. He tightened his arm about her. "So I'm to be yours?"

She snuggled her head down again. "If you will be, I'll return the favor."

He smiled and felt contentment slide through him; it wasn't an emotion he had a great deal of experience with, but he recognized it and gloried. "That's good enough for now." He couldn't resist adding, "Although I suppose I should warn you that Frobishers have never been considered...easy mates."

She snorted trying to suppress a laugh. "You've just made me reconsider allowing my brothers to speak to you prior to us marrying."

He chuckled—then he heard a rattle and a thump outside the door. He raised his head and heard footsteps retreating down the corridor. Almost immediately, the ship's bell started to clang. He counted four strokes, then glanced up at the window across the stern. "Four bells, and it must be the afternoon watch." He pushed back the covers and got up. "And I suspect that rattle and thump was Foxby delivering a tray."

Aileen pushed up in the bed, her brow wrinkling. "Four bells…that's what? Two o'clock?"

Robert nodded. After pulling on his breeches, he headed for the door. "Come on." He paused with his hand on the door latch. "It's time we got started."

She arched her brows and swung a bare leg out from under the covers. "Started on what? Our journey home is already under way."

His attention had deflected to her long, slender limb. He raised his gaze to her eyes and smiled. "Not that journey—the other one. The one that leads into our future."

Her eyes rounded, but she immediately rose.

He drank in the sight, then—perfectly certain there was no crew member lurking—he opened the door, bent, and picked up the tray Foxby had left. He stepped back, kicked the door shut, and carried the tray to his desk.

Wrapped in his sheet, Aileen joined him there—ready and eager and perfectly willing to make a start on their next shared adventure.

★ ★ ★

Through the rest of that afternoon and into the evening, Robert settled back into his long-established position as captain of *The Trident.* Yet Aileen only had to appear—not even by his side but simply within his or his men's sight—to underscore how much even that aspect of his life had changed. And would change still further.

To a man, his crew respected and valued her. Shooting to save him had won their respect, but shooting to save Benson had won their hearts. Not one of them accorded her anything but smiles and the offer of ready hands should she need assistance.

They watched over her, too, as she walked his decks; although he would trust every one of his men with his life, it still took him a few hours to convince his primitively protective side that he could, indeed, trust them with her, too.

That, and also that she was by no means a weak woman unable to protect herself.

Once he'd achieved that acceptance, his crew's support gave him a modicum of mental space, enough to allow him to resume his duties and effectively reassert control of his vessel.

By evening, when after the meal—one he and she had taken with his officers in his cabin—he emerged onto the deck for the later dogwatch, he felt unexpectedly settled. More deeply at peace than he'd felt possibly ever before, and certainly looking forward with an enthusiasm for life that, over the past years, he now accepted he'd been lacking.

That he'd lost, but found again, now that Aileen had come to stand by his side.

He was amused to discover that she appeared to take that definition of her position somewhat literally. He'd left her in the cabin unpacking her bags and stowing her belongings in the space he'd cleared for her, but he'd been at the wheel for barely five minutes when, a warm shawl wrapped about her head and shoulders, she emerged from the companionway. She stood surveying the deck—much as he often did—then she turned and climbed the ladder to take—resume—her position beside him.

The ship was heeling quite strongly, not yet dangerously so but enough to have waves breaking over one side. He glanced at her. "You'll get damp if not drenched standing out here."

She shrugged. "I won't melt."

He faced forward and hid his grin.

That was all they said to each other for a considerable time. But he sensed she was taking in everything about the ship, noting how his watch scurried about the decks in response to his commands, and what changes those commands resulted in. The sails, the ropes, the shifts in the wind, and how he managed them.

Aileen drew her shawl tighter about her shoulders. She found herself fascinated all over again by this until-now-unseen side of him—the captain in action commanding his ship. It was all she could do to quell an appreciative shiver. There was something about the sight of him standing with legs braced, his hands riding lightly on the huge oak wheel, his gaze trained on his sails and yards as he guided his ship onward at what, to her, felt like reckless speed, but which, she'd been informed by the crew, was nothing unusual for this vessel, that did rather more than tickle her fancy. Even as she glanced at him, the wind ruffled his dark hair, flicking it away from the planes of his face, leaving the chiseled lines revealed.

She drew in a deep breath and looked out over the ship—at the crew who had been so welcoming, and also forthcoming; they'd answered all her inquisitive queries without reservation.

Fascination and curiosity for the moment appeased, she gave herself up to the quiet of the evening, to the wide expanse of blue-gray ocean stretching away in every direction, to the steady surging of the sea beneath the hull, to the music of the waves rhythmically *shushing* susurratingly over the railing, the melody occasionally punctuated by the crack of a sail, the creak of a spar, or the caw of a passing gull.

The skies were tending gray, clouds massing off the larboard side.

"A storm's coming." Robert's voice slid into her thoughts.

"Do you think it will catch us?"

He studied the horizon for several seconds before replying, "The northern edge of it will whip over us." She felt his gaze touch her face. "But we won't be slowing—better for us to race through and past."

She nodded. "I'd heard that ships like this usually run with all sails flying, day and night, and through all weather." She looked up at the sails—counted. "You have seven up on each mast, but that's not the most you can carry, is it?"

"There's one more set—the moonrakers—but in weather like this, I tend to keep them in reserve." After a moment, he said, "You clearly have your sea legs. Have you sailed often before, or is the ability an inherited one?"

She laughed. "A bit of both, I suspect." Without waiting to be asked, she filled him in on how much sailing she'd actually done while visiting far-flung ports in pursuit of her brothers.

Robert listened and learned. He wasn't surprised when, in return, she asked him about his family. This was, after all, what this next phase would entail, with each of them filling in the background of the other. He did surprise himself with the emotions he felt while describing his parents, his brothers, his cousins. The connections he didn't normally think of, that he took for granted, yet that made him the man he was.

In telling her about his parents, and admitting that for most of their married life, his mother had sailed with his father—no point trying to hide that, because his mother, Elaine, would certainly inform Aileen of it the very first chance she got—he recalled a long-buried conversation with his mother, one from a decade ago, when he'd been so much younger. When he'd just been setting out on this seafarer's life and had still been somewhat starry-eyed as to what his future would hold.

He'd asked his mother how he would know when he met the right woman for him; even now, he could hear her reply echoing down through the years. *When it happens, you'll know. When she looks at you, you'll feel ten feet tall, and at the same time, you'll feel so grateful that she sees you and accepts you as you truly are that you'll want to fall groveling at her feet.*

With those words ringing in his brain, he looked at Aileen.

She felt his gaze and looked up—her brandy-colored eyes fully open and wide, her gaze direct, honest, and unshielded—and he saw himself reflected in her eyes, knew that she saw him as he truly was.

And knew his mother had spoken true.

He smiled, and Aileen arched her brows.

With one arm, he reached out and tugged her to his side. His other hand on the wheel, he bent his head and found her lips with his—felt simple joy rise through him when she immediately responded, warm and soft and simply her.

When he raised his head and looked forward again, checking the waves ahead, from the corner of his eye, he saw her tip her head, regarding him shrewdly, then she asked, "What was that for?"

He grinned. "That was for being you."

Her laugh was all sunshine and happiness. When he glanced sidelong at her, she caught his eyes. Then she smiled and settled under his arm.

And together they looked forward as he steered *The Trident* on, to the end of this journey and into the one beyond.

★ ★ ★

They saw out the dogwatch, then retreated to his cabin.

They undressed and prepared for bed, all the while—apparently both of them—telling themselves they were too old to need to indulge again so soon.

That conviction lasted only until he slid beneath the covers and bare skin touched bare skin.

Had mere lust ever burned this strongly?

An hour later, when they both lay slumped on their backs, staring up at the ceiling as their hearts slowed and their skins cooled, he remembered his intention in setting out on this mission. And snorted in self-deprecation.

"What?"

Without looking her way, he murmured, "I left London with the firm intention of dealing with this mission quickly and cleanly—so I could return, report as required, and then set about rectifying the lack in my life by looking about me for a wife." He turned his head and met her curious gaze. "It never occurred to me that completing the mission might, itself, result in me finding said wife."

She smiled, then laughed—that throaty, sultry laugh that never failed to catch at something deep inside him. "Fate, my darling, has been playing with you."

He gathered her to him and dropped a kiss on her head. "Strangely, I find I don't really mind."

She settled with her head on his chest, one hand resting over his heart. After a moment, she said, "Fate's been playing with me, too. I left London determined to find and rescue Will, but…after learning of your mission, I had to give up my direct approach."

He murmured softly, "That must have hurt." Although the comment was light, faintly humorous, it was, he knew, also the truth. Until that moment, he hadn't fully realized what she'd given up in following and supporting him—for the greater good.

She didn't pretend otherwise. "It was a…wrench, but I know it was the right thing to do." Tipping her head back, she looked up at him. "I had to accept that the best way to secure Will's rescue, as well as that of all the others, was to do all I could to ensure your mission succeeded."

"And together we pulled it off." He picked up her hand, carried it to his lips, and pressed a warm kiss to her palm. Then he returned her hand to where it had been, a warm, soft weight over his heart.

She settled again. "So how long do we have before we reach London?"

"If the skies are clear tomorrow, we'll go to full sail. Another twelve days should see us home." He rubbed his chin against the silk of her hair. "We'll put into Southampton and take a coach from there."

They filled the next minutes with increasingly sleepy and idle comments, until the slumber of the sated claimed them.

* * *

Five days later, in the out-of-the-way tavern beyond the western end of Water Street, the three Englishmen met as they had before, in that hour between the end of the working day and any evening entertainment.

As usual, the first man arrived, paid for his ale, then took the mug and retreated to the table in the corner. A few minutes later, he was joined by the third man. Clutching his mug, the third man sank into his usual seat at the end of the table and nervously sipped his ale.

The first man cocked a brow the third man's way. "How are things up at the fort?"

The third man shrugged. "Nothing out of the ordinary, thank God." He glanced at the door, then looked at the first man. "Where's Muldoon?"

"No idea," the first man said. "But it's not like him to be late." A hint of tension showed in his voice.

The third man shifted on his chair.

The door opened; both men looked that way.

Both released silent sighs of relief when Muldoon sauntered in.

He didn't glance at the corner table but went straight to the bar counter. He paid for his ale, lifted the mug and drank, then he turned and came to join them.

Sliding onto the bench opposite the first man, Muldoon looked at the third man, then met the first man's eyes. "We've had a slight hiccup, but if we keep our heads, I doubt anything will come of it."

The first man didn't look convinced. "What happened?" His voice now held a steely note.

Muldoon sipped, then lowered his mug. "A Miss Hopkins came calling at the office."

"Hopkins?" The first man frowned. "Any relation of Lieutenant Hopkins?"

Muldoon nodded. "His sister. The first time she called, I was out. Apparently, she asked my clerks why her brother had been ashore when he disappeared, rather than with his ship—which, of course, they couldn't tell her, given they don't know." Muldoon looked at the first man. "You should have warned me she was sniffing about."

"And how could I do that?" the first man countered. "I had no idea the woman was in the settlement."

Muldoon frowned. "She didn't register with the governor's office?"

The first man shook his head. "Believe me, I would have noted that name. She never appeared on any of our lists. This is the first I knew she was here." The first man paused, then asked, "Where's she staying?"

Muldoon shook his head. "She was staying at Mrs. Hoyt's, but I've recently learned that she's left the settlement."

"Oh?" The third man was studying Muldoon. "And did we have anything to do with that?"

Muldoon grimaced. "Yes, and no."

When he didn't continue, the first man snorted derisively. "Just spit it out, man—we don't have all day."

Muldoon met the first man's eyes; some of his customary belligerent confidence returned. "She called again a week ago. I was in, and she demanded to speak with me. I assumed she would ask about her brother again, but no. She wanted to know what the authorities knew about children going missing, and whether we'd heard rumors of slave traders operating inside the settlement. She also happened to mention that she was leaving for London soon and planned to call at Admiralty House."

"Good God!" The third man's voice was weak.

Both Muldoon and the first man cast the third an impatient glance. "Don't panic," Muldoon told him. "I doubt she'll do any such thing, and even if she does"—he switched his gaze to the first man—"between us, we have any official inquiries covered. Anything she reports will simply be put down to the usual hysterical rumors female minds are wont to fix upon when visiting such uncivilized climes."

The first man grinned coldly and raised his mug. "Exactly." He sipped, then fixed his steady gaze on Muldoon's face. "Go on."

It was plain Muldoon would rather not, but… "Unsurprisingly, I sent word to Kale to kidnap her. As usual, he and his men were efficiency itself—they're getting restive, not having much to do these days. We really need to work out some way to keep them occupied—more adults, not just children."

The first man studied Muldoon's face. "So I take it Miss Hopkins is now with Dubois."

"No." Muldoon grimaced again. "She was rescued by some sailors. Who, exactly, we don't know, but whoever they were, they knew what they were doing. They knew how to fight, and they seemed to know the settlement well. They escaped through the slum, onto the wharf, and had a rowboat waiting. Kale's men gave chase, but lost them amid the hulls in the harbor."

"So you've no idea from which ship they came?" the third man asked.

Muldoon shook his head. "But that wasn't the end of it. If you recall, we'd told Kale to get more children to Dubois—older ones. The morning after Miss Hopkins's remarkable escape, Kale's men went down to the shore and selected a group of five older slum-rats. They walked them out of the settlement, on to the inlet, and ultimately to Kale's camp with no problem. But later that evening, the men in the camp heard screeching and screaming. They were convinced, all of them, that the scream came from a woman. They went out in force and searched, but found no one. So they put the episode down to monkeys fighting and left it at that.

"But in the small hours, Kale got word from his men in the settlement that one of their number—the one who patrols the nearer shore of the inlet—had seen a gent and a lady in a canoe heading upriver the previous evening toward Kale's camp. Kale's man recognized the canoe as one hired from one of the local villages. Bright boy that he is, he reasoned that the gent and lady would return the canoe and then head back to the settlement, and he realized he would get more immediate help from the group he knew were coming up from the settlement that night, so he'd gone and met with them, and they'd set up an ambush on the path from the inlet back to the settlement. Then they'd sent word to Kale."

"Kale caught the pair?" the third man asked, clearly in hope.

Muldoon met the first man's eyes and shook his head. "Kale came to see me last night. He wasn't happy. The gent and lady between them gave his men the slip—they returned the canoe, but rather than head back to the settlement, they walked north along the bank."

"Good God." The first man frowned. "Why?"

"That became clear later." Grimly, Muldoon continued, "Kale's no slouch—he nearly caught up with them again, but they grabbed another canoe and took off for the estuary. He and his men chased them down, but by then they were in the estuary itself—the eastern reaches—and there was a ship there, standing off. A bloody great full rigger, as near as I can make out." Muldoon paused to down a mouthful of his ale.

"So they—the gent and the lady—got away?" The first man pushed aside his mug and fixed his attention squarely on Muldoon.

Muldoon nodded and set down his mug. "Kale nearly had them, but the blasted woman—and it *had* to have been Miss Hopkins—shot him. Winged him." Muldoon snorted. "Turned out she'd shot one of his men the night before, too. That one wasn't so lucky." Muldoon sighed and pressed his fingertips to his forehead as if massaging an ache. "I had to pay Kale off. Enough to keep him happy. Well, happy enough. For now."

The first man sat back and stared at Muldoon. After a moment, he said, "First question—who the hell was the man with Miss Hopkins? And second, what ship took them up?"

Muldoon's lips compressed into a thin line. Then he shook his head. "Damned if I know who the man was. Kale wasn't much help with descriptions—the man could have been any Englishman. As for the ship..." Muldoon hesitated, then confessed, "I went through the harbormaster's register for that period, including those ships that were supposed to have already sailed. Whatever ship it was, the captain didn't register with the harbormaster's office."

"What does that mean?" the third man all but squeaked.

Muldoon shrugged. "It could mean a host of things, but most likely the vessel's captain didn't feel any need to make his presence in these waters known. He might have been a corsair or a buccaneer putting in for water or supplies. If he didn't need to come into the harbor and register and pay the fees, why would he?"

The first man tapped the table with one fingernail. "Let's assume Miss Hopkins and the fellow with her saw Kale's camp. Is she—or the man—likely to cause us trouble?" The first man focused on Muldoon. "Is Miss Hopkins likely to take her tale to the Admiralty, as she intimated?"

Muldoon stared back at him, then grimaced. "If I had to wager on it, I would say she will. She was that sort of pushy female—bossy and not about to back down."

The first man nodded. "All right. As you said, between you and me, we can deal with any official inquiries that get sent this way." He glanced at the third man. "Given we're alert to the possibilities, it's unlikely anything will slip through enough to rock our boat." He refocused on Muldoon. "Did Kale have anything to report from Dubois?"

"Yes." Muldoon paused to drain his mug. Lowering it, he wiped his lips with the back of his hand. "Apparently, Dubois was happy enough to have the older children—he said he could use them immediately. But he repeated that if we want the second pipe up and running to full capacity as soon as Dixon opens it, then he'll need more men. I gather he rather underscored *men.* He told Kale to say he didn't see any need for more women, or more children, but more men are essential if we want production to increase."

The first man pulled a face. "Given our recent communications from our esteemed backers, we're going to have to find Dubois those men."

The third man shifted. "In that letter you showed me—the last one—they sounded…impatient."

Muldoon snorted. "They don't know what it's like down here. They're all sitting safe and cozy in their London clubs." He paused, then, his gaze on the table, said, "If I had our time again, I don't know that I would invite them in as we did. We might have needed their cash, but we sure as hell don't need them breathing down our necks. If we misstep and get found out, it's *our* necks in the noose. They're so wealthy and well connected, they'll get no more than a slap on the wrist, but the three of us?" Muldoon pulled a bitter face. "We'll swing."

After a moment, the first man said, "The only thing I would do differently is ensure that they didn't know our names. Sadly, they do, which means we haven't any choice but to meet their demands, no matter how unreasonable said demands may be."

The third man turned his empty mug between his hands. "Or, at least, make it seem as if we are."

Muldoon and the first man both turned to stare at the third.

Sensing their attention, he looked up. "What?"

Slowly, Muldoon shook his head, then he wryly grinned. "You're coming along at last, Winton—in terms of this enterprise, that's the first truly canny contribution you've made."

Eighteen

Twelve mornings after their departure from Freetown, Robert sat at his desk and diligently wrote in his journal. During this voyage more than any before, the practice of documenting all daily occurrences, describing his findings and detailing his conclusions, had assisted immeasurably in plotting his course.

He glanced across the cabin. Aileen lazed on his bed, her gaze locked on one of his earlier volumes detailing some of his adventures in the Caribbean and southern American colonies. She was immersed in the tale. He watched her turn a page, then smiled and returned to putting the finishing touches to their current adventure. He was, more or less, up to date.

He had set down his pen and was blotting his last line when footsteps came pounding down the corridor. Aileen looked up. Robert shut the journal, opened the bottom drawer of his desk, and dropped the book in. As he shut the drawer, a sharp rap fell on the door. "Come," he called.

The door opened, and Wilcox looked in. His bosun smiled at Aileen, then snapped a salute Robert's way. "Lieutenant Latimer's compliments, Captain, but he thought you'd want to know that it looks like we're chasing *The Prince* up the Channel."

"Are we, indeed?" Robert looked at Aileen. In reply to her questioning look, he explained, "Caleb's ship." He rose. "Thank you, Mr. Wilcox—we'll come up."

"Aye, sir." Wilcox departed, shutting the door.

Aileen set a marker in the journal she was reading, shut it, and laid it aside, then she uncurled her legs and rose from the bed.

Robert watched, a silly, contented smile on his face as she shook out her skirts, then, with her usual brisk stride, came to join him. He opened the door. As she passed through it, she asked, "Why is it of such particular interest that your brother is sailing up the Channel ahead of us?"

"Because," he said, following her from the cabin and closing the door, "Caleb loves a race—and he loves to win. What he has yet to realize is that we—Declan, Royd, and I—humor him."

"Oh, really?" Aileen knew enough about brotherly competitiveness to accord that statement the skepticism it deserved.

But as she emerged onto the main deck, she was thrilled to see the cliffs of England forming a gently rippling white-and-green line across the horizon. "I hadn't realized we were already so close." She leaned into Robert's hold on her arm as the deck pitched.

They'd been chased up the Atlantic by a succession of storms, but under full sail, *The Trident* had raced before the winds. They'd beaten up the coast in what she'd been informed was near-record time, and overnight, the ship had swung into the mouth of the Channel.

Robert assisted her to the ladder and up to the poop deck. They exchanged nods with Jordan Latimer, who presently had charge of the wheel. Aileen halted by the front rail, looking out over the main deck. Robert stood behind her, his legs braced and his hands on her shoulders, screening her from the stiff breeze.

Now they were nearing the coast and the various ports, there were other vessels sharing the waves. Lumbering merchantmen, lighter passenger ferries and laden barges plying the cross-Channel routes, and even a few yachts dotted the steel-blue expanse, but the tall-masted ships drew the eye, their sails a medley of whites and pale golds in the morning sun.

"There." Robert extended his arm and pointed to the stern of a ship that must have been at least half a mile ahead of them. To Aileen, the ship looked much the same as *The Trident*, but

Robert explained, "*The Prince* has a somewhat wider beam—she's not so sleek—and she's yet to be modified to the level of *The Trident*." He paused.

Aileen glanced at his face and saw his eyes were narrowed, his expression assessing.

Then he glanced at Latimer. "We can't catch him this side of the Solent, not with the lead he already has. But"—Robert grinned—"we can certainly close the distance and give him a thrill."

Latimer laughed. "I thought you'd say that." He nodded at the sails. "Do you want to do the honors? He's your brother, after all."

Robert's grin turned to a full-blown smile. He nodded to Latimer and lightly squeezed Aileen's shoulders. "Stay here and hold on," he murmured. Then he released her and moved farther along the rail.

She watched as he gripped the rail and, spotting Wilcox on the main deck, called down to the bosun, "Mr. Wilcox. You'll have seen *The Prince* ahead of us. What say we give her a little nudge?"

Wilcox and every crew member within hearing beamed.

"Aye, Captain!" Wilcox replied.

Robert laughed. He glanced at his brother's ship, then looked to his own sails and started rattling off orders. The crew leapt into action. Some swarmed up into the rigging like monkeys. Others raced to man various winches or haul on ropes. Aileen tried to keep track of what was happening, but the changes were so numerous—and they kept coming.

And *The Trident* surged.

Aileen gripped the rail, understanding now why Robert had told her to hold on. She'd thought the ship had been traveling rapidly before, but now...now it felt as if the hull lifted out of the water and raced across the top of the waves.

Exhilaration gripped her.

Alerted by the sudden lift in speed, more crew members scrambled up from below. They recognized *The Prince*, immediately understood the game afoot, and waited eagerly for orders. Soon they, too, were scrambling into the rigging or set to one of the innumerable winches. As Aileen understood it, the aim was to glean every last ounce of power possible from the wind while maximizing support from the currents and simultaneously minimizing drag.

The Trident steadily gained on *The Prince*. Those on *The Prince* noticed the closing ship, recognized her, and then the race was truly on.

Caleb—Aileen had little doubt it would be he at the helm of his ship—tacked to block Robert's onward rush.

But Robert had already anticipated his brother's response, and even as *The Prince* veered, *The Trident* was already tacking to take up a new and unimpeded line.

It was a game, of course, but both brothers played to win, and their crews threw themselves wholeheartedly into the tussle.

There was plenty of laughter and good-natured scoffing and jeering, and not a few insults were hurled over the water as the ships drew close, then closer.

Nevertheless, as the Solent opened before them, Caleb's *The Prince* still held the lead—but *The Trident*'s prow lay just off her stern.

Caleb's crew laughed and whooped in triumph as Robert, still grinning hugely, conceded and, now at the helm himself, brought *The Trident* into line behind *The Prince*.

Both brothers and their crews then turned their attention to navigating the more crowded shipping lane leading to Southampton Water. Sails were progressively furled, and the ships both slowed.

They were among the larger vessels coming in, and the tide was running their way. Other craft moved aside to give them clear space to smoothly sail on.

Eventually, they glided into the glassy reaches of Southampton Water. Aileen looked up at the masts, at the sails, and with a surge of something akin to pride, imagined how both ships would appear if viewed from the cliffs—a pair of graceful beauties gliding effortlessly and majestically over the almost mirror-like water.

In the end, *The Trident* had to hold just inside the mouth of Southampton Harbor to allow *The Prince* to dock first at the company's wharf. The sun was well up, and the typical morning bustle filled the air by the time *The Trident* finally tied up and the end of the gangplank thumped down on the dock.

Ten minutes later, when Robert took Aileen's hand and assisted her onto the gangplank, he wasn't the least surprised to see Caleb waiting at the end of the plank, an insouciant smile on his handsome face.

His youngest brother was nothing if not insouciant.

He was also insatiably curious. Caleb's entire face had lit at the first sight of Aileen. As she reached the end of the gangplank, he reached for her hand to assist her down the last step. "Hello."

Aileen beamed. "Good morning. I'm Miss Hopkins."

"Caleb Frobisher." Caleb swept her a bow. As he straightened, his gaze shifted to Robert's face, and his grin returned. "How, now, brother mine?"

Robert answered with a cynically raised brow and a studiously uninformative nod. "Caleb."

Caleb searched his face, glanced at Aileen, then looked at him again and asked, "So—are you going to tell me what's going on?"

Robert gripped Aileen's elbow and started them walking along the dock. He and Caleb needed to report to the company's office to sign their ships back into harbor and authorize payments to their crews.

Caleb fell in on Aileen's other side, but kept his gaze trained on Robert's face.

Robert knew well enough that Caleb wouldn't let go but would keep badgering, and if Robert didn't give him something, his little brother was only too likely to start pestering Aileen—in his usual, thoroughly charming way. But how much was it wise to reveal? "What makes you think there's anything going on?"

"Oh, I don't know." Caleb thrust his hands into his breeches pockets and sauntered along. "Perhaps the fact that *The Trident* came into the Channel from the south, rather than the west and your usual hunting grounds."

Robert inwardly winced. He'd hoped Caleb hadn't seen *The Trident* early enough to notice that.

"Or," Caleb went on, "perhaps it was the sight I got of Declan running south under full sail a month or so ago, and now you return in much the same manner from the same direction. Or maybe it was Declan pretending he didn't see *The Prince* at all as he flew past—but of course he did." Over Aileen's head, Caleb met Robert's eyes. "It's obvious something's up—that some unusual operation is under way. So…what is it?"

Robert shrugged and looked ahead. "You'll learn soon enough."

"Yes, but I want to know now."

They'd reached the end of the wharf proper. Crossing the busy street gave Robert a moment to think. He caught the curious—intrigued—gaze Aileen threw him as they gained the opposite pavement and started toward the row of shipping company offices farther along the street. He glanced at Caleb, now rather moodily keeping pace. "I have to get Miss Hopkins to London with all speed. What's *The Prince*'s next voyage?"

Caleb shrugged. "I don't know." He waved back at the wharf. "I just ferried a bevy of merchants and diplomats—the usual trade mission—home from Lisbon." He looked ahead. "I'll have to see if there's anything waiting at the office."

They reached the office of Frobisher Shipping, and Caleb held the door for Aileen. Robert steered her through, then followed, leaving Caleb to bring up the rear.

The clerk behind the counter recognized them and immediately beamed. "Captain Frobisher. Both of you. It's good to see you both back." Higginson had been with the company since Robert and Caleb's grandfather's day and stood on no ceremony with any of the family. Higginson directed a circumspect bow Aileen's way. "Miss."

Then Higginson hauled first one heavy ledger, then a second one from beneath the counter and set them down. His eyes bright behind round spectacles, he looked from Robert to Caleb and back again. "So—who's first?"

Robert glanced at Caleb and arched a brow.

Caleb waved him to the counter. "I seriously doubt *I'm* in any hurry."

"Thank you." Robert leaned on the counter. To Higginson, he said, "He got in first by a whisker, but I need to get Miss Hopkins here to London as soon as possible."

"I see." Higginson hid a smile. "Right, then. So..."

Robert had to focus his attention on completing the usual paperwork and details. That left Aileen to Caleb and his wiles. At first, Robert listened with half an ear, but while Caleb was quick with his questions, Aileen had by then taken his measure—and Robert had already warned her of his youngest brother's daredevil streak. Trusting in her to continue to evade Caleb's inquisitive forays, Robert gave his full attention to signing off on his voyage.

Aileen had retreated to the front of the small office. She stood before a window on which was emblazoned a logo of a ship under full sail, along with the words "Frobisher Shipping."

Caleb, of course, had joined her. She had to give him credit for not even attempting to hide his intent to interrogate her. He simply smiled, a smile full of what she suspected was his hallmark cheery charm, then peppered her with questions.

She found herself battling a grin even while she was forced to think quickly to avoid letting slip anything about Robert's mission. In many ways, Caleb reminded her of Will; he was persistent like a tick, but so engaging one couldn't hold it against him, and the devil-may-care glint in his bright blue eyes was nothing short of an invitation to recklessness.

To join him in whatever harebrained scheme he might concoct.

She considered Robert a handsome man, but his style was more polished, more sophisticated and debonair. Caleb was equally attractive—almost the same height, with similar clean-cut, faintly austere features, and much the same broad-shouldered but lean and somewhat rangy build, plus that ineffable male strength both the Frobishers she'd encountered seemed to ooze—but in a more flamboyant, histrionic, basically younger way.

Robert was a mature version, shaped and polished by his experiences; Caleb had yet to face the same trials, the same level of challenges—had yet to be forged in that degree of fire.

That conclusion firmed as, denied any of the information he sought, Caleb heaved a huge, put-upon sigh. "You're not going to tell me, either."

His melodramatic despondency made her smile. She laid a hand on his arm. "Truly, it's too serious to be lightly or widely shared." She glanced at Robert as he bid the clerk goodbye, then straightened and turned from the counter. "I'm sure your brother—brothers—will share the tale with you eventually."

Just as Will would have done, Caleb replied with an entirely ungrateful grunt.

Robert shot Caleb a warning look as he joined them. He retook Aileen's arm and said to Caleb, "We're going to take a fast coach to London. *The Trident*'s remaining here for the nonce, so most likely, I'll be back. If you're still here, I'll tell you what I can then."

Entirely sober now, Caleb met Robert's gaze. Caleb held the contact—direct and just faintly accusing—long enough for Robert to start to wonder if perhaps it was time—

"Caleb?" Higginson called from the counter—very likely sensing that a confrontation was brewing and seeking to head it off.

Caleb held up a staying hand. He didn't shift his gaze from

Robert's eyes. "How," Caleb said, his voice low, the conversation clearly just between the two of them even though Aileen stood near enough to hear, "am I ever going to prove I can be trusted with more than ferrying merchants when Royd will never give me a chance?"

Robert held his brother's gaze. He pressed his lips together, knowing the question was honest and heartfelt. After a moment, he murmured, "You have to earn his trust."

And earning that was never going to be easy, not for the youngest—the most flippant and carefree—of their brood.

Not when it was Royd they were speaking of.

"And how," Caleb replied, his tone rough and laced with resentment, "am I supposed to do that when Royd will never trust me?"

And that, Robert had to admit, was a very good question. As he searched Caleb's face, his expression—the latent anger in his eyes—Robert wondered if, perhaps, Royd, Declan, and he had failed to pay sufficient attention to the fact their little brother was now twenty-eight years old with more than five years of captaining his own ship under his belt.

Robert felt the tug of wanting to take the time to explain more to Caleb then and there, but others had even more claim on him. He glanced at Aileen, then looked back at Caleb. "We have to get going, but I'll come back and answer your questions."

Caleb's lips twisted in a faintly disbelieving expression, but then he wiped it from his face and smiled at Aileen. He took her hand and bowed. "A pleasure to meet you, Miss Hopkins."

Aileen, bless her, smiled back, and with a teasing light in her eyes, replied, "I suspect we'll see more of each other in the future, sir."

Caleb's eyes widened. He looked from her to Robert. "Really?"

Robert clapped him on the shoulder. "Later."

He steered Aileen out of the office. On the pavement, he

wound her arm in his and started them walking toward the posting inn his family favored. "Thank you for distracting him."

"Will it work, do you think?"

"For about three minutes."

Fifteen minutes later, after sharing a pot of tea while the horses were put to and their bags, fetched from the ship, lashed on, Robert handed Aileen into their hired carriage. He followed her in, shut the door, then sat back and held her hand as they rattled out on the road to London.

★ ★ ★

Caleb finished with Higginson, then headed back to the wharf. His hands in his pockets, he strode along, his thoughts churning. So Robert had found his match in Miss Hopkins—who, in Caleb's view, possessed a certain martial gleam in her eye, the sort of gleam of which their mother would approve.

Good for Robert. Caleb found he had it in him to wish his brother and the intriguing Miss Hopkins well—even if Robert had refused to divulge what new mission he and Declan had been drawn into. That it was a secret suggested it was one of those endeavors the family undertook for the government or the Crown, and one thing Robert hadn't denied was that both Declan and he had been involved—it seemed consecutively.

And that was distinctly intriguing.

Caleb drew level with *The Prince*. He halted at the foot of the ship's gangplank. Hands still sunk in his pockets, his gaze fixed on the worn timbers before his feet, he stood and thought of what he'd sensed in Robert.

Had the mission ended completely?

Or had Robert merely successfully completed a part of it—as, presumably, Declan had before him?

After a moment, Caleb murmured, "It's the latter." The more he thought of Robert's attitude—his insistence on racing to London, no doubt to report—the more Caleb felt sure that there was yet more to be done. That the mission—a highly secret and therefore exciting one—was ongoing.

Slowly, Caleb raised his gaze to the ship docked behind his. Robert's. Caleb was well known to Robert's crew.

Caleb knew of Robert's habit of recording everything bar his sexual exploits in his journal.

Caleb also knew where Robert kept his current volume.

Caleb's lips curved. Then he smiled broadly, drew his hands from his pockets, and strode along to *The Trident*'s gangplank. He swung onto it and climbed. As he neared the deck, he saw Latimer and grinned. "Permission to come aboard, Mr. Latimer."

Latimer moved to meet him and gripped the hand Caleb offered. "How are you, you graceless scamp?"

"Excellent, thank you." Caleb turned his most guileless smile on Robert's lieutenant. "Robert's off on his way to London. Apparently, he forgot a book he wanted—he asked me to fetch it from his cabin and send it on to him."

Entirely unsuspecting, Latimer waved Caleb to the aft companionway. "You know your way around. Just let the watch know when you leave."

"I won't be long." Walking backward in the direction of the aft hatch, Caleb continued, "I have to get reprovisioned as soon as possible. I believe we'll be off again, more or less immediately."

Latimer laughed and waved him on. "No rest for the wicked."

Caleb swung to face the hatch, his grin growing darker. "Indeed."

Opening the hatch, he swung down the ladder and headed for Robert's cabin.

* * *

The carriage drew up outside a fashionable town house in Stanhope Street.

Aileen looked up at the pleasant façade and wondered whether she should renew her argument that she should put up at a hotel. But Robert had insisted that his brother and sister-in-law would never forgive him if he let her slip away, so here she was…allowing Robert to hand her down and escort her into the home of a duke's daughter.

She stood on the porch, looked at the door, then looked at Robert. "Are you sure—" She broke off as the door opened.

A supercilious butler regarded them both—then broke into a welcoming smile. "Captain Frobisher! We're delighted to see you back." The man's gaze touched Aileen, and his smile widened. He stepped back and held the door. "Please, come in—come in."

"Thank you, Humphrey." With a hand at the back of her waist, Robert steered her over the threshold. "Are my brother and Lady Edwina in?"

"Indeed, they are, sir." The butler looked down the front hall. "And here they are."

"Robert?" A fairylike lady in a blue gown, her pale blond hair piled on her head, came rushing forward. "Thank heavens you're back." The lady pulled Robert down to her and hugged him, but her inquisitive blue eyes had already fixed on Aileen.

As the lady released him and he straightened, Robert said, "This is Miss Hopkins."

"Please—just Aileen. I'm honored to meet you, Lady Edwina." Aileen started to curtsy, but her hostess caught her hands.

"No, no. No formalities here." Lady Edwina squeezed Aileen's hands, then held them for a moment as she looked at Aileen—met Aileen's gaze with one equally direct—then Lady Edwina beamed. "Oh, I believe we'll get on *famously*. Do call me Edwina."

Meanwhile, a tall gentleman Aileen had no difficulty placing as another Frobisher, presumably Declan, had followed Edwina into the hall. He'd grinned, and he and Robert had clapped each other on the back, then turned to watch Aileen and Edwina.

"And this"—Edwina waved negligently at the gentleman—"is Frobisher…no, that won't do, not when there's two of them. My husband, Declan, Aileen, but first, have you and Robert had luncheon?"

Edwina opened her big blue eyes wide, but before Aileen had a chance to reply, she rattled on, "No—I can see you haven't. You must be famished. Humphrey?"

"Indeed, ma'am." The butler turned from directing several footmen carrying Aileen's and Robert's bags up the stairs. "If you will go through to the dining room, I will have Cook assemble a cold collation."

"And if you will excuse me for a moment"—Declan shared a glance with Robert—"I'll send word to Wolverstone and Melville that you're back."

"Excellent!" Edwina looped an arm about Aileen's waist and drew her down the hall. "Come and sit, both of you. While we feed you, you can tell us all."

Aileen expected to feel overwhelmed, but by the time they reached the end of what proved to be a substantial and quite excellent meal, she felt thoroughly included, embraced by both Declan and Edwina without reservation.

Then again, very little conversation—very little of their telling of their tale—had been needed to demonstrate that she and Edwina shared quite a few traits, as did Robert and Declan. Edwina's assessment hadn't been wrong; they would get on famously.

They already did.

As Declan and Edwina knew the basis of the drama unfolding in Freetown, no preparatory explanations were required, and Robert and Aileen told their tale freely, with Edwina exclaiming and Declan looking grave at all the right points. It was clear that they grasped the ramifications of the events as clearly as Robert and Aileen.

"So your poor brother is, we presume, stuck with all the others in some compound—the one we think contains a mining operation that is, at least in part, run by a man named Dubois." Edwina looked from Robert to Declan. "So what's the next step?"

Declan exchanged a glance with Robert. "The mine itself, do you think?"

"Possibly." Robert pulled a face. "But there might yet be more to this." He paused, then went on, "The degree of organization bothers me—this is not just any old cobbled-together, spur-of-the-moment, make-it-up-as-we-go-along scheme."

He met Declan's eyes. "You know how most slavers operate—they just snatch people up and then sell them on to whoever wants them. This enterprise, for want of a better word, may use slavers as suppliers, but they're doing so by giving the slavers a specific list of people they want taken. On top of that, the enterprise itself is relatively local, or so it seems, and above all, it's remarkably tightly run. There's been a great deal of thought and effort put into concealing both the enterprise and those behind it, and I can't help asking myself why that is so."

Edwina stared at Robert, then grimaced, too. "You're right. It's tempting to think of this as the usual sort of blight where everything is obvious and a force can be sent in to clear it all up, but..." She leaned her elbow on the mahogany table, sank her chin into her palm, and frowned rather ferociously. "Aside from all else, how will you know how many men to send, and what sort of force, without knowing anything pertinent about this mine?"

"Or worse"—Declan slouched down in his chair—"without knowing whether this Dubois is yet another layer of concealment, so that even if we follow that trail you found and get to him, we'll still be too far from the mine—"

"And our going after Dubois triggers the one thing that we are at all costs determined to avoid." Robert glanced at Aileen. "We can't risk the perpetrators learning that we know of the mine prior to our attack—"

"Because the instant they do, the lives of all those missing will be forfeit." Aileen shook her head. "There's no way around it, is there? It will take at least one more..." She looked at Robert and Declan. "What do you call yourselves when on a mission?"

Robert smiled faintly. "Operatives. And you're correct—it will take one more operative, one more voyage to the settlement and back, to learn who Dubois is, and whether attacking him will be the same as attacking the mine itself, and if so, what force will be needed to take the entire operation in one fell swoop." He met Declan's gaze. "Because that's the only way we're going to be able to rescue the people who've been taken."

★ ★ ★

Later that evening, as she closed the door to the room the kindly housekeeper had shown her to earlier in the afternoon, Aileen could barely believe how comfortable she felt, embraced and included as if she was already a member of the family.

She walked to the window and looked out. Night shrouded the garden at the rear of the house. She leaned her shoulder against the window frame and let her mind wander—let it absorb the refreshing coolness of an English spring night and the corresponding reality that she was no longer in a country not her own, in a land full of exotic sights and dangers unimagined.

Having assimilated that, her mind moved on to the subject that dominated her thoughts.

Prior to dining, they'd received a reply from the Duke of Wolverstone; despite wishing most urgently to hear their news, His Grace, along with Lord Melville, was attending some vital meeting of a Lords' committee, and neither expected to be available for at least another day.

After dinner—a meal during which she and Robert had encouraged Declan and Edwina to fill them in on social news—with the others, Aileen had sat about the fireplace in the cozy drawing room and talked well into the evening. Declan and Edwina still clearly felt passionately involved in the ongoing mission, and that had bolstered Aileen's determination to remain abreast of developments, too. As with Declan and Edwina, she and Robert might have played their part, but they hadn't reached the end of the mission—the crime at the heart of it had yet to be resolved and the damage put right.

The four of them had spoken openly. They'd been unfailingly

in accord as they'd shared their views on the settlement, on the business opportunities, the social structure, and on the sad lack of attention paid to those in the slums, particularly the children.

The latter still weighed heavily on Aileen's mind. Every time she remembered the sight of the older girl's face when, in the slavers' camp, the girl had realized she and her fellows had been duped—that loss of innocence and the dying of hope—Aileen felt as helpless as the girl doubtless had.

Aileen hated and refused to feel helpless.

In such a context, anger was a much more useful emotion.

When she and Edwina had declared their intention to retire, Robert had elected to remain downstairs with Declan. They'd repaired to Declan's study to talk business and ships.

Aileen had no idea how long she'd stood staring into the dark, but now she heard movement in the room next door. The room Robert had been given.

She didn't stop to think. She walked to the door, opened it, stepped into the darkened corridor, shut her door, and walked to his.

Robert was standing in the middle of the room he'd been given, staring absentmindedly at nothing while in his mind, he juggled potential answers to the questions he and Declan had posed to each other in the study.

He looked up as the door opened. Blinked, then smiled—to himself as well as at her—as Aileen slipped inside. The lamp on the tallboy had been left burning; as she shut the door behind her, leaned back against it, and studied him for an instant, then came walking boldly to him, the lamplight set bronze flames dancing over her brassy-brown hair.

She halted directly before him. She opened her mouth—

He placed a finger across her lips. "Before you start, I have something more important than anything else to say to you."

She kissed his finger, then tilted her head, her brandy-bright gaze questioning.

He looked into her face, into her eyes. "I love you. You know that as well as I do. And you love me. So"—he caught her hands in his; without taking his eyes from hers, he raised first one hand, then the other, to his lips and brushed a kiss over her knuckles, then he held her fingers securely—"will you marry me, Aileen Hopkins, and join your life with mine?"

One tawny brow rose. "Will you let me sail with you as your mother sailed with your father throughout most of their married life?"

He'd expected it, yet he still had to bite back a groan. "Yes. As long as you accept that a ship has but one captain."

She laughed soft and low, and her smile lit her face. "Of course, my love." She raised her arms and twined them about his neck. "You can be the captain." She stretched up and brought her lips to his. "Just as long as I can be the captain's wife."

She kissed him—and a relief he hadn't known he'd been waiting for flowed through him. Slowly—almost reverently savoring the taste of her lips, the honeyed sweetness of the surrender she offered him—he closed his arms about her and drew her nearer as she stepped even closer and pressed her body to his.

The promise was there, explicit in every touch and caress that followed. That they had this already established between them, and neither had any intention of letting it go.

Of letting love slide through their fingers.

As night closed around them and the darkness swallowed their sighs, their soft moans of pleasure, and eventually, her scream of completion and his answering groan, they pledged their troth in far more than words.

Through body, through mind, soul-deep they reached for each other and twined, and claimed anew, forged anew, what they wanted from life.

This, together. Forevermore.

They seized it and clung—and silently vowed to never, ever let go.

* * *

Later, much later, when the storm had passed and they lay slumped and sated in his bed, inevitably their minds turned to plans, to the future.

To their wedding, of course, and their families and how to break the news, and also to exchanging thoughts of where they might live…later.

After…

There was too much hanging over them for them to easily put aside.

Aileen sighed and stated the obvious. "We aren't going to be able to settle and look forward and plan with our whole hearts until this wretched business is done." Through the shadows, she studied Robert's face. With one fingertip, she traced his stubbled chin.

He caught her hand, nipped her questing fingertip, then he echoed her sigh. "You're right. There's too much left undone. We succeeded and came home with the information I'd been sent to get, and you learned what happened to your brother and that he's most likely still alive, but along the way we learned too much to simply hand over the information, step back, and with a clear conscience go on with our lives."

She nodded, her hair shifting on his chest. "Declan and Edwina feel the same."

"They do." He started tracing her bare shoulder. "After you and Edwina came up, when Declan and I were talking, we tossed around the notion of waiting to see what came next." He caught her gaze. "We can elect to take our ships out of service—for a month or so at least. Declan has *The Cormorant* anchored in Southampton Water. I believe I'll send *The Trident* to wait alongside. Then, when we hear more, we can decide how to respond—if there's a need, we can be ready in a day or so to sail to Freetown again."

She studied him, as much as the shadows allowed her to see. "You think there's going to be a…large engagement, don't you?"

He nodded. "I think this is bigger than anything we've yet considered. Every inch we get closer, every new fact we learn, it seems to expand. Whatever action is required to put an end to whatever this is, it'll take men and ships to get down there and get it done."

She looked at him for a long moment, drinking in all she could sense as well as see. "I'll be sailing with you."

His chest rose and fell on a sigh. "So I supposed." His tone was resigned. "But we can save the arguments for later."

She smiled. "All right."

She settled her head in what seemed its rightful place—in the hollow below his shoulder. Let her body sink against his as he cradled her alongside him.

For now, they had each other. For now, they had *this.* It was infinitely more than either had started their recent journey with, and until tomorrow came and the clarion of duty sounded again, they could rest on their laurels, in each other's arms, and take joy in the moment.

In this most precious of blessings—a newfound love.

Nineteen

Another day passed before they received the anticipated summons to meet with Wolverstone and Melville at Wolverstone House.

It was late morning when Robert and Aileen, accompanied by Declan and Edwina, were admitted to the mansion in Grosvenor Square. By then, they were impatient to make their report; there was a growing sense among all four that at some point in the mission, time would become critical, and the lag in their ability to act as they traveled back and forth wasn't an impediment shared by the other side.

The villains could act and continue to act—could even bring an end to their scheme—while they, the agents for good, were trooping back and forth over the seas to London.

Wolverstone's butler showed them directly into the drawing room with a "His Grace, Her Grace, and the others are expecting you."

Robert shot Declan a sharp glance; his brother, too, had noted the oddity—why "others" plural?

They followed their ladies into the room and discovered the answer.

They were greeted first by Minerva, Duchess of Wolverstone. Her Grace was intrigued by Aileen's presence, but immediately grasped her connection to the matter. Minerva made the introductions—for Aileen to her husband, Royce, Duke of Wolverstone, and Viscount Melville, the First Lord, both of whom were known to the other three.

Then Minerva turned to the other gentlemen present, all three of whom had risen to their feet and stood waiting. "Lady Edwina Frobisher, Captain Robert Frobisher, Captain Declan Frobisher, and Miss Aileen Hopkins—permit me to introduce Major Rafe Carstairs, who, although retired from active duty, functions as something of a liaison for the army in those matters that require discretion."

Minerva paused to allow a tall, sandy-haired gentleman with pleasant features, openly curious blue eyes, and the telltale build and upright posture of a cavalry officer to exchange nods and shake their hands. Then she smoothly continued, "And Jack, Lord Hendon, who these days masquerades as the head of Hendon Shipping." Minerva shot a glance at Robert and Declan. "Something of a competitor for your family's business—as I understand it, on *all* levels."

"We're acquainted," Robert told Minerva rather dryly.

Minerva smiled serenely. "I suspected that would be the case."

Hendon was another tall man, another ex-army officer, but unlike Carstairs, Hendon had been ten years or so from that job—not that it had ever been his only occupation. Although older than the Frobisher brothers, Hendon was nevertheless of their generation.

After Hendon had finished attempting to charm their ladies, Robert and Declan shook hands.

Minerva turned to the last gentleman—a tall, well-built, dark-haired man with an air of benign reserve, of noble solidity, who had waited patiently to greet their party. "And this is the Marquess of Dearne, who is..." Minerva arched a brow at the marquess—for all the world as if inquiring just what he was. Then with a quirky smile and a flick of elegant fingers, she continued, "Well, simply Dearne."

With a laughing smile, Dearne offered his hand. "Just Christian, please."

"Indeed." Once everyone had finished shaking hands, Minerva waved Aileen and Edwina to the sofa opposite the one she had been sharing with Dearne. As the men found seats amid the armchairs and straight-backed chairs angled about the twin sofas, Minerva resumed her position and stated, "I suggest that, in this case, first names will make all our lives easier."

Everyone accepted that decree, which, Aileen noted, immediately resulted in a more relaxed ambiance, a much more accommodating atmosphere in which to make their report.

Wolverstone—Royce—invited Robert to do so, and between Robert and Aileen, with occasional additions from Declan and Edwina to weave together connections to their earlier findings, their story was told.

"So now we have the location of the slave traders' permanent camp in the jungle!" Melville—he was the only one who hadn't volunteered his first name—clapped his hands together. He glanced at the other men. "So—what's next?"

"First, congratulations on a challenging job well done." Royce inclined his head to Robert, and to Aileen. The other men echoed the sentiment, Melville somewhat perfunctorily, but the others with due gravity; Aileen sensed the others better understood the nature of the trials Robert, his crew, and she had faced.

Smoothly, Royce continued, "I think it pertinent to note that with each leg of this investigation, the central situation grows more fraught, not less."

Christian, now leaning forward, his forearms on his thighs and his hands clasped between his knees, nodded. "That's something we need to bear in mind as we plot our way forward—that every step we take closer to exposing the enemy also risks exposing us to them."

"Indeed." Rafe's voice held a hard edge. "We must never lose sight of the consequences of them learning of our pursuit too early."

"I concur." Jack glanced at Robert. "And I agree with Robert's assessment that the degree of planning—the number of layers with not many connections between—suggests that whoever is behind this has a lot to lose should their identities become known. And in this world, in this sort of situation, 'a lot to lose' means money, position, or power, or most likely all three."

"And," Royce added, "when threatened, villains of such ilk will react without mercy to protect themselves."

Melville was frowning. He looked from one face to the next. "But surely, now we know the location of the camp—and which track to follow from it, and that the man the slave traders deal with is called Dubois—our way forward is clear." The First Lord spread his hands. "We'll send a small force to the settlement, they can collect whatever they need there, then march on the slave traders' camp, take the slavers into custody, and march on and capture this Dubois and his enterprise, and that will be that." He brushed his hands together. "The problem will be wiped out and taken care of."

The others stared at Melville. Several seconds of silence ensued.

Then Christian said, his tone exceedingly even, "Our first consideration is, in fact, not the enterprise itself but the safety of those captured to work within it. After the recent matter of the Black Cobra, I'm sure the Prime Minister would be the first to stress that."

Aileen noted an approving gleam in Minerva's gray eyes as Her Grace, one of the greatest of the current crop of grandes dames, nodded. "Indeed." Minerva turned her acute gray gaze on Melville. "In this case, it must be people first, saving face for the government second."

The First Lord of the Admiralty looked as if he would like to protest—to push his case for immediate and decisive obliterating action—but in this company, he didn't dare.

"The problem," Royce said, sitting back in his armchair, "is that we have no evidence that Dubois isn't—as others have proved to be—yet another layer and not the final enterprise. Every layer uncovered risks triggering an alarm, and the closer we get to the enterprise itself, the more that risk increases. And once the alarm is triggered, the enterprise—if our assumptions are correct, the diamond mine—will immediately be shut down and the impressed workforce massacred." Royce's dark gaze rested on Melville. "The very last thing any of us would want is to reach the mine only to discover a pile of dead bodies and the villains long gone."

Melville blanched. After a moment, he firmed his jaw and curtly nodded. "Very well. So what do you propose?"

Robert quietly said, "We need to send someone to take over Kale's camp, and then wait for Dubois to come to him—or to at least make contact. The next thing we need to know is who Dubois is, and how he and his talents, whatever they might be, fit into the villains' scheme."

"Agreed," Jack and Rafe both said.

Declan nodded and looked at Royce.

He, too, nodded. "There's no other way forward—none that has a decent chance of keeping those taken alive." He looked around at the other men. "So that's the next stage of the mission defined. The only remaining question is who do we send?"

"Relevant to that," Declan put in, "is that we still don't know who of those in the settlement are involved. Lady Holbrook was, but it seems not her husband. However, it's unlikely there isn't someone else in the governor's office who is a part of this—there's been too much managing of Holbrook, and that is still going on. Thanks to Aileen, we now know Muldoon, the naval attaché, is involved. But we know nothing either way about Decker or others in the local naval command. Given Dixon was taken first—his talents being a key requirement in getting any mine under way—it seems highly likely that someone in the fort is a party to this, and there may be others elsewhere in the settlement's governing structures." Declan met Royce's gaze. "Whoever we send in must be able to operate without help from that quarter and also know the ways of stepping around the...apparatus of government as it applies down there."

Royce and the other men all nodded.

Rafe said, "While I can point to men in the corps who would in most situations be able to circumvent the bureaucracy if so ordered, none of them have any experience in jungle climes or, indeed, in settlements like Freetown." He met Christian's eyes, then looked at Royce. "I'd be hesitant to put forward any of their names—not for this mission."

Christian looked at Royce. "I'm faced with the same problem. I have men of the right caliber, but none with the relevant, and in this case essential, experience."

Jack was looking at Robert and Declan. "I'd say your men and mine are better placed to take this on. But of us all, you Frobishers have the most appropriate and useful experience. And the contacts, too. All of you know the African coast far better than most others. And while Declan went in openly, Robert appears to have slipped in and out with none the wiser—well, other than Babington, who's on our side—so even if another Frobisher ship is seen near Freetown, given the weeks that will have passed, there's no reason anyone would immediately grow suspicious. So who else of the Frobishers is available? What about your brothers—or that cousin of yours?"

Robert looked at Royce. "Royd would do it. He could accomplish all you need—"

"With one hand tied behind his back." Declan's lips twisted in a wryly affectionate grin. "Just to make it more interesting."

Royce gave a soft snort. He knew Royd well. "No doubt. However, I want to save Royd for the final leg of this mission." He met Robert's and Declan's gazes, then looked around at the other men. "That final leg is going to be the crucial one in all ways, and frankly, we need a man of Royd Frobisher's caliber and, shall we say, *commanding* personality to carry it off successfully. So I'm reluctant to send Royd in yet—not when this is almost certainly not the final leg."

After a moment, Royce added, "And as this is unlikely to be the final leg, that raises the issue that Royd—and his personality—are not small things, easy to conceal. I would hesitate to send him in for anything *other* than the final leg."

Jack grimaced. "I can see your difficulty all too well." He, too, knew Royd. Again, Jack looked at Robert and Declan. "So what about that cousin of yours? Lachlan, is it?"

Robert looked questioningly at Declan, but Declan grimaced.

"Lachlan would have been a good choice," Declan admitted, "but he sailed out of Bristol three days ago with a bevy of departmental secretaries and a small horde of engineers bound for Quebec. He won't be back for at least a few months."

"Not Lachlan, then." Christian frowned. "I know we have at least one other of your cousins on our books. A Kit Frobisher?"

Jack choked, then coughed.

Declan shot him a glance. "Our Kit is like Jack's Kit. While our Kit would leap at the chance—and possibly be able to carry it off—as I'm sure Jack will agree, even suggesting it would be a very bad idea."

"Ah." Understanding dawned in Christian's eyes. "I see."

Rafe's sudden smile said he understood, too.

Only Melville was left entirely at sea; he looked from one face to the other in mounting puzzlement.

Before he could open his mouth and ask, Jack held up a hand. "Don't ask. Trust me, you, of all people, don't want to know."

Melville looked taken aback, then he glanced at the others. When no one contradicted Jack, Melville humphed and looked down, busying himself with settling his coat sleeve. "Well, what are we to do, then?" He looked sharply at Royce. "Who are we to send?"

Royce turned his head to look rather quizzically at Robert and Declan. "You have another brother—Caleb. He's younger, but he can't be that young—he's been sailing for at least a decade. What about him?"

Robert and Declan shared a look.

Then Declan said, "Caleb's twenty-eight. But..." He trailed off, then glanced at Robert.

Robert's expression was severe, but Aileen sensed that his feelings about Caleb weren't straightforward, much less clear. After a second's hesitation, Robert said, "Caleb and his ship, *The Prince*, are, as far as I know, currently in Southampton Water. We followed him into port two days ago. But before you leap on that, you need to consider Caleb's record."

Robert paused as if gathering his thoughts, then went on, "Of us all, in certain ways, Caleb has taken the longest to grow up. He's the youngest of us all, including our cousins, and he has an...irrepressible and immutable belief in his own invincibility. That's partly our fault. Caleb has a long history of rushing into situations that any sane man would think twice over directly confronting, but when said situations turn sticky, he's been able to rely on us—usually Royd, but sometimes me, or Declan, or Lachlan—to turn up and rescue him. We've done that since Caleb was a boy."

"Even Kit," Declan mumbled, "has hauled his arse out of a wringer a few times."

"So what you're saying is that Caleb rushes in where angels fear to tread, with little to no regard for personal danger, in the sublime and usually correct belief that others of his family will rescue him if matters go awry." Minerva arched a brow at Declan. "Your Caleb's attributes sound like potential assets in these circumstances."

"He's a daredevil," Robert stated; whether he thought that was good or bad couldn't be discerned from his tone. "There's no hedging around that. He sees, reads, and assesses situations as well as any of us, but while we might consider caution, Caleb never will. He thrives on danger—on spitting in fate's eye and coming out the victor."

Declan said, "If there's any possible way he can take a situation and make it even more dangerous, for himself as well as everyone else—both those with him as well as those pitted against him—you can guarantee he'll choose that course."

"Caleb is predisposed to take risks," Robert went on, "rather than consider safer paths. Royd is most like him in temperament, but maturity and responsibility have muted Royd's spontaneity and taught him the paths of wisdom."

"Caleb, on the other hand, has a very hazy notion of the concept of responsibility—not to himself, not to his men, not to others around him." Declan frowned, then admitted, "Possibly to his mission. Despite the trouble he gets into, he always gets that done."

"What about his men—his crew?" Rafe asked.

"He has an excellent crew," Robert said. "Most have been with him for more than five years, some for all of his sailing life. They're of the same ilk as he is. They share his temperament, his liking for risk-taking, for the thrill of facing danger—the more unexpected, the better."

Declan softly snorted. "You can't rely on his crew to act in any restraining capacity—they'll follow him wherever he leads and cheer while they're doing it."

With his head tipped, Rafe considered the brothers. "You do realize that that is, in fact, a rather good reference for the mission we're discussing?"

Declan blinked; he looked rather struck. Robert, Aileen suspected, had already realized.

A soft tap fell on the door. Royce called, "Come."

The butler entered and advanced, carrying a salver. "An urgent message, Your Grace, ferried on from Stanhope Street." The butler halted beside Robert's chair and offered Robert the salver.

Robert looked at the missive lying upon the silver plate, then, rather slowly, raised a hand and took the letter. Sitting back in the chair, he studied the writing on the missive's face for an instant, then, as he turned the letter over and slid a thumb under the blob of sealing wax, he glanced at Aileen.

Just that brief glance, and she knew who the letter was from.

No one said anything. No one even stirred as Robert unfolded the missive and read it; a single sheet, it wasn't all that long.

As Robert took in the meaning of the words inscribed in a slashing black script over the white sheet, he heard Caleb's voice from two days before ringing in his mind, asking how Caleb was supposed to gain anyone's trust when no one ever gave him the chance.

His little brother had seen his chance and seized it.

And Robert discovered that he couldn't find it in him to disapprove.

Raising his head, he looked around the circle of expectant faces. "It appears our discussion is moot."

"Moot?" Melville said.

Catching Declan's frown, Robert handed him the letter. "As I said, when I left Southampton, Caleb and *The Prince* were in the harbor." He met Royce's gaze. "They no longer are." He tipped his head toward the letter Declan was perusing. "Caleb sent that to inform me that he and *The Prince* are on their way to Freetown. He intends to strike straight for Kale's camp and follow the trail from there."

Royce frowned. "How will he know..." He broke off and, still looking at Robert, amended, "How does he know about the camp?"

Robert inwardly sighed. "He's taken my sailing journal. It contains a complete record of the mission I was sent on—and therefore also contains all the pertinent details Declan and Edwina previously established. The journal also includes everything I, my men, and Aileen discovered—including a copy of the map showing the way to Kale's camp, descriptions of Kale and several of his men, and even diagrams of the camp itself." Robert grimaced. "I would have offered you a copy to give to the next man sent, but..." He shrugged and looked at Declan as his brother reached the end of Caleb's epistle...and said nothing. Caleb's feelings over never being trusted with critical missions had shone through.

And unless Robert missed his guess, Declan had recognized as well as he had that Caleb's assertions were true.

A short silence ensued as everyone assimilated the news, then thought further to what it might mean.

Melville frowned direfully. He looked at Royce, then at the Frobishers. "I am not at all happy about your brother taking matters into his own hands. He has acted outside all proper authority. You've both got fast ships—you must sail after him and stop him, and turn him back."

Robert blinked. He didn't need to glance at Declan to sense his brother's instinctive—and adverse—reaction to the suggestion. It would be the end of Caleb's captaincy—virtually the end of his life. "No." When Melville huffed and looked ready to bluster, Robert continued, his tone unyielding, "He has at least two, if not three, days' start. Our ships might be a fraction faster, but we won't catch up with him this side of Freetown, and two Frobisher ships sailing into the estuary stand no chance whatsoever of going unnoticed, especially as Decker is now almost certainly in port."

"And indeed," Jack put in, "why would you?" He cocked a brow at Melville. "The man's gone off to do what's needed, and by all accounts, he's well able to accomplish the task. Why interfere?"

Melville shifted and looked exceedingly unhappy, but no one else seemed inclined to rail against Caleb's preemptive action.

Finally, after studying the men's faces and exchanging glances with Edwina and Aileen, Minerva observed, "After all that's been said, I cannot help but note that, perhaps, this was meant to be, and your Caleb has merely…dispensed with the bureaucratic stage—the discussions, the dithering—and cut straight to the heart of the matter, as, indeed, it seems it's his nature to do."

Slowly, somewhat pensively, Royce nodded. "This might, indeed, be the best answer all around." He glanced at Christian, Rafe, and Jack, then at Robert and Declan. "We have no one else half as suitable to hand, and I share your concerns that, at some point, time will become critical. In acting as he has, your brother—as my wife has so sapiently remarked—may have changed nothing other than to save us several days."

Melville was still fussing, still frowning. "So what are *we* to do now?"

"Now?" The merest hint of a smile playing about his long lips, Royce relaxed in his armchair and shrugged. "As Caleb has metaphorically filched the baton from our hands, he's left us with no choice but to sit back—and wait to see what comes."

* * * * *

If you enjoyed Robert and Aileen's adventure,
don't miss the next installment in
Stephanie Laurens'
The Adventurers Quartet*,*
a set of sultry, sweeping adventure-romances
featuring four buccaneering brothers
and four adventurous ladies.

Read on for a sneak peek from Volume Three,
THE DAREDEVIL SNARED,
to find out who picks up the baton
and takes on the challenge in the next stage
of the on-going mission.

Available from MIRA Books
on June 28th, 2016.

Three

Caleb paused to pull the neckerchief from about his throat and wipe the sweat from his brow. This was the second day of their trek along the path leading—originally, at least—north from Kale's camp. They'd followed the well-trodden path more or less north for most of yesterday, but in the last hours before they'd halted for the night, the track had veered to the east.

Today, the path had started to climb while angling more definitely eastward. And they'd started to come upon crude traps. Phillipe had been in the lead when they'd approached the first; he'd spotted it—a simple pit—and they'd tramped around it without disturbing the concealing covering. From then on, they'd kept their eyes peeled and found three more traps, all of varying design, clearly intended to discourage the unwary, but it had been easy enough to avoid each one.

If they'd needed further confirmation that they were on the correct path, the traps had provided it. But there hadn't been another for several miles.

Caleb glanced around and saw nothing but more jungle. His internal clock informed him it was nearing noon. He couldn't see the sky; the damned canopy was too thick. Accustomed to the wide expanses of the open sea, he was getting distinctly tired of the closeness of the jungle and the dearth of light. And the lack of crisp fresh air.

Phillipe had been walking with Reynaud in the rear; he came forward to halt beside Caleb. "Time to take a break." Phillipe pointed through the trees. "There's a clearing over there."

Caleb fell in behind his friend, and their men fell in behind him. They trudged ten yards farther along; the track remained well marked by the tramp of many feet. The clearing Phillipe had noted opened to the left of the path. Their company shuffled into it. After divesting themselves of seabags, packs, and weapons, they sprawled on the leaves or sat on fallen logs, stretching out their legs before hauling out water skins and drinking.

Luckily, water was one necessity the jungle provided in abundance. They'd also found edible fruits and nuts and carried enough dried meat in their packs to last for more than a week. If not for the stifling atmosphere, the trek would have been pleasant enough.

Phillipe lowered himself to sit beside Caleb on a fallen log. With a tip of his head, he indicated the jungle on the other side of the path. "We've been angling along the side of these foothills for the last hour. The path's still climbing. I've been thinking that, following the inestimable Miss Hopkins's reasoning, the mine can't be much farther. The children who were taken—certainly the younger ones—would be dragging their feet by now."

Caleb swallowed a mouthful of water, then nodded. "I keep wondering if we've missed a concealed turn-off, but the traffic on the path is as heavy as ever, and it's still going in the same direction."

They'd been speaking quietly, and their men had, too, but Phillipe glanced around and murmured, "I think, perhaps, that when we go on, we should keep talking to a minimum."

Caleb restoppered his water skin. "At least until we've found the mine. The jungle's so much thicker here, we could turn a corner and find ourselves there. We don't want to advertise our presence, and we definitely don't want to engage."

Phillipe's long lips quirked wryly. "No matter how much we might wish otherwise."

Caleb grunted and pushed to his feet. Phillipe followed suit, and three minutes later, their party set off again, tramping rather more quietly through the increasingly dense jungle.

Fifteen minutes later, their caution proved critical. Caleb caught a fleeting glimpse of something pale flitting about a clearing ahead and off the path to their right. Phillipe was in the lead. His eyes glued to the shifting gleam, Caleb seized his friend's arm and halted. Their men noticed and froze.

Phillipe shifted to stand alongside Caleb, the better to follow his gaze. The intervening boles and large-leaved palms made following anyone's line of sight difficult.

Caleb couldn't work out what he was seeing—a gleam of gold, a flash of…what?

Then the object of his gaze moved, and Caleb finally had a clear view. "It's a boy," he breathed. "A golden-haired, fair-skinned boy in ragged clothes."

"He's picking those berries," Phillipe whispered. After a moment, he added, "What do you want to do?"

Caleb scanned the area. "As far as I can tell, he's alone. I can't see anyone else, can you?"

"No. And I can't hear anyone else, either."

"If we all appear, he'll take fright and run." Caleb considered, then shrugged off the pack he'd been carrying and handed it to Phillipe. "Keep everyone here until I signal."

Accepting the pack, Phillipe nodded.

Caleb made his way quietly toward the boy, dodging around trees and taking care not to alert his quarry. The lad looked to be about eight, but woefully thin—all knees and elbows. He was wearing a tattered pair of dun-colored shorts and a loose tunic of the same coarse material. It had been the bright cap of his fair hair, gleaming as the boy passed through the stray sunbeams that struck through the thick canopy, that had attracted Caleb's attention.

The boy was circling a vine that had grown into a clump, almost filling one of the small clearings created when a large tree had fallen. The bushy vine bore plump, dark red berries that Caleb and his company had already discovered were edible and sweet. His attention fixed on his task, the boy steadily plucked berries and dropped them into a woven basket.

Despite the boy's bare feet, the basket suggested he hailed from a group of some kind; from the features Caleb glimpsed as the boy moved about the bush, the lad was almost certainly English.

He had to be from the mine.

Caleb reached the edge of the clearing. He hesitated, then said, "Don't be afraid—please don't run away."

The boy jerked and whipped around. He grabbed up the basket, his knuckles turning white as he gripped the handle.

His blue eyes wide, the boy stared at Caleb.

Caleb didn't move other than to slowly display his hands, palms open and clearly empty, out to either side.

The boy was poised to flee.

If he did, Caleb doubted he could catch him, not in this terrain. "I've been sent to look for people—English people kidnapped from Freetown." He spoke slowly, clearly, evenly. "We think they're being used as labor for a mine. We're searching for the mine." He paused, then asked, "Do you know where the mine is?"

When the boy didn't respond, Caleb remembered that the mine was conjecture and rephrased, "Do you know where the people are?"

The boy moistened his lips. "Who are you?"

He wasn't going to run—at least, not yet. Caleb was usually relaxed with children, happy to play with them, to join in their games. When convincing children of anything, he knew the literal truth was usually advisable; they always seemed to sense prevarication. "I've come from London. People have been searching for those kidnapped, but we've had to do it bit by bit—carefully. To make sure the bad people who are behind the kidnapping don't get wind of us coming to help." *And kill all the kidnapees.* He stopped short of voicing that truth.

The boy was still staring at him, but now he was studying him, his gaze flitting from Caleb's face over his clothes, his sword, his boots.

"I'm going to crouch down." Moving slowly, Caleb did. If he'd stepped closer to the boy, he would have towered over him—too intimidating. And laying hands on the lad from a crouch would be that much harder.

Sure enough, as Caleb settled on his haunches, the boy noticeably relaxed. But his gaze remained sharp; although he constantly glanced back at Caleb, watching for any threat, he started scanning the shadows behind Caleb. "There are more of you, aren't there?"

"Yes. I asked them to stay back so we didn't frighten you." Caleb paused, then offered, "There are twenty-four more men back on the path."

The boy blinked at him. "So there's twenty-five of you all together. All armed?"

Caleb nodded.

The boy frowned; he seemed to have lost his fear of Caleb. After a long moment of calculation, the boy shook his head. "That's not going to be enough." He met Caleb's gaze. "There's more mercenaries than that at the mine, and they're all fearsome fighters."

So there is a mine. And it is nearby. Caleb tamped down his elation. "We're not the rescue party. We're the advance scouts. Our mission"—and he could almost hear his eldest brother, Royd, groaning over him telling a boy, a young boy he didn't know anything about, such details—"is to locate the mining camp and send word of it back to London. Then the rescue party will be dispatched, and they will have the numbers to put paid to the mercenaries."

The boy studied Caleb's face, searching his eyes as if to determine whether he spoke the truth—then the lad smiled gloriously. "Cor—they're *never* going to believe me when I tell 'em, but the others are going to be in alt! We've been waiting ever so long for anyone to come."

The excitement in his voice was infectious, but… Caleb waved both hands in a "keep it quiet" gesture. "Before you tell anyone, you need to remember that our mission must remain secret. The mercenaries at the mine must not learn that we're here." Caleb locked his gaze on the boy's eyes. "If the mercenaries realize rescue is coming, it could be very dangerous for all the people kidnapped."

The boy's delight faded, but after a second, he nodded. "All right." He looked at Caleb, then glanced out into the jungle again. "So what're you going to do now you've found us?"

"I'm hoping you can take us closer to the mine—to some place from where we can see it but not be seen ourselves. Can you do that?"

"'Course!"

"But before we get to that, I want to hear what you can tell me—us—about the mine and the encampment." Caleb swiveled and glanced behind him, then looked at the boy. "What's your name?"

"Diccon."

"I'm Caleb. And if it's all right with you, Diccon, I'd like to call my men closer, so we can all hear what you say."

Diccon nodded.

Caleb rose—slowly—and beckoned his men to join them. They tramped through the jungle following the route he'd taken, leaving as little evidence of their passing as possible. Each man nodded at Diccon as they reached the clearing. They all sidled in, trying not to crowd Diccon despite the limited space. Several hunkered down, including Phillipe.

Caleb did, too, again bringing his face more level with Diccon's. "Right, then. This mine—does it have a fence around it?"

That was all he had to ask to have Diccon launch into a remarkably clear and detailed description of the camp—more like a compound—that surrounded the entrance to the mine. Crude but effective outer walls, with huts for various purposes. Mention of a medical hut had Caleb and Phillipe exchanging surprised glances.

Diccon's description wound to a close; he'd mentally walked in via the gate, then taken them on a clockwise tour describing every building they would pass.

"That's extremely helpful," Caleb said, and meant it. "Now—how many mercenaries are there?"

"Hmm." Diccon's features scrunched up. He had set down his basket, and from the way his fingers moved, he was counting. Then his face cleared. "There be twenty-four there right now, plus Dubois, and six are off taking the latest batch of diamonds to the coast for pickup."

Caleb blinked. "So it's definitely diamonds they're mining."

"Aye," Diccon said. "Thought you knew that."

"We'd guessed it, but until now, we couldn't be certain." Caleb tilted his head. "You said the mercenaries take the diamonds to the *coast* for pickup—not Freetown?"

"Nuh-uh. At least, we—all of us in the compound—don't think so. Far as we've been able to make out, they take the strongbox toward the settlement, but the pickup is somewhere on the estuary, see? That way, no one in Freetown knows."

Phillipe shifted, drawing Diccon's attention. "The six who've gone to the coast—do they go and return via that path?" He pointed at the path they'd been following, which lay not that far away through the palms.

A pertinent point. Caleb looked at Diccon—and was relieved to see the boy shake his head.

"That path just goes to Kale's camp." Diccon's eyes grew flat, and his expression shuttered. "You don't want to go that way."

"Kale's not there anymore," Caleb said. "He's…left. Along with all his men."

"Yeah?" Diccon studied Caleb's face, then his eyes grew round as the implication registered.

Before he could ask the eager questions clearly bubbling on his tongue, Phillipe intervened. "Which route do the mercenaries take to the coast, then?"

"There's another path—well, there's several leave the compound. One goes to the lake where we get our water, and there's this one, where all of us came in from. Then there's another that divides into two not far from the gate. Those who go to drop off the diamonds take the northwest branch, and we reckon it also eventually leads to Freetown. They *could* get to Freetown through Kale's camp, but Dubois—he's the leader—he mostly sends his men to get ordinary things like food and stuff that we know must come from Freetown when they go to drop off the diamonds."

Caleb nodded, a map taking shape in his brain. "You said that path divides into two—where does the other branch go?"

"Far as we know, it leads dead north. We think there's nothing but jungle that way, all the way to the coast." Diccon paused, then added, "Maybe some natives. There's a chief that owns this land, see, and Dubois pays him to let the mine be. We think he—the chief—lives that way. That's why the track's there, but no one from the mine uses it."

Phillipe caught Caleb's eye. Caleb nodded fractionally. That little-used path sounded like the one they should fall back along. He refocused on Diccon. "Tell us more about the mercenaries."

"Well, like I said, there's thirty of them all up, including the cook and his helper, who are just as fierce as the others. And there's Dubois. He's in charge, and they all mind him. He has two…lieutenants, I suppose you'd say. Arsene—he's Dubois's second-in-command—and Cripps is the other. The mercenaries are all big and tough, and they carry swords, lots of knives, and some have pistols. The ones on the tower and the gates have muskets."

Caleb slowly nodded. Direct observation would be best. But first… "How is it you're allowed out by yourself? You are by yourself, aren't you?"

Diccon's face fell. "Aye. I'm no good in the mine, see. I just cough and cough. Dubois, he was going to kill me—he said I was useless, and he wasn't going to waste food feeding me. But Miss Katherine spoke up for me." Diccon straightened. "She said I wasn't useless and that I could help fetch fruit and berries, and nuts, too, so that the cook could properly feed all us children. And the adults, too. She said that way, we'd all stay healthy and work better—and Dubois went fer it."

Consulting his mental list of the females kidnapped, Caleb asked, "Miss Katherine—is she Miss Fortescue?"

"Aye. That's her. But all us children call her Miss Katherine. She's in charge of us."

And was clearly a lioness if she'd spoken up and saved Diccon.

Diccon heaved a disconsolate sigh. "I wish I could run away, but Dubois said that if'n I ain't back by sundown every day, he'll kill two of me mates." The boy's face paled. "So I don't even dare be late back. He's a devil, Dubois is."

"You believe him?" Phillipe asked the question gently.

Diccon looked him in the eye. "We all believe Dubois's threats. Even Mr. Hillsythe. He says Dubois is one of those villains who enjoys killing, and that we none of us should ever doubt he'll do exactly what he says."

Caleb caught Phillipe's eye. Hillsythe was Wolverstone's man. If that was his assessment of Dubois, they'd be well advised to pay it due heed. "All right." Caleb returned his gaze to Diccon. "I think it's time we took a look at this camp—but first…" As he rose, he glanced at the assembled men, then he looked back at Diccon. "We need to find a place to camp that's close enough to the mine for us to keep watch and study it, but far enough away that no one from the camp is likely to stumble across us. I thought perhaps somewhere along that path to the north—the one no one uses."

Diccon nodded. "I know just the place. There's a good-sized clearing a little way down that track."

Caleb laid a gentle hand on the boy's shoulder. "Can we get to it without going closer to the camp?"

"O' course—I can lead you." Diccon's happy grin returned, and he swiped up his basket. "I know all the places round about. I can go where I like around the camp, and the berries and fruit and nut trees grow everywhere."

"Is it likely anyone from the camp might hear us?" Phillipe asked.

"Nah." As Caleb let his hand fall from Diccon's shoulder, the boy turned and beckoned. "We're still well out, and the trees and leaves and all keep sound in. You often can't hear someone until they're quite close."

Caleb signaled to his men to follow and, with Phillipe on his heels, fell in behind Diccon.

When they reached the path from Kale's camp, Diccon beckoned them onward. "I'll take you through the jungle and around until we hit the other path."

He proved as good as his word, leading them unerringly on a tacking course around jungle trees and more dense pockets of vegetation. He waved them to caution as they approached another path. When Caleb put a hand on Diccon's shoulder and leaned down to breathe in his ear "What?" the boy tipped his head back and whispered, "This is the northwest path they use to drop off the diamonds and go to Freetown. I don't think they'll be on their way back yet, but..."

Caleb released his shoulder with a pat. "Good lad. Always play safe."

They crept to the edge of the path and strained their ears, but heard nothing. Swiftly, they crossed over the beaten track and plunged back into the jungle. Ten yards on, Caleb glanced back and could see nothing but jungle foliage. Finding a guide had been a stroke of luck. Without Diccon to lead them, they would have been stumbling around—very possibly into the mercenaries' clutches.

But Fate had smiled and sent the boy to them.

When they came upon the next path, Diccon walked confidently on to it. "That place I told you about—the nice clearing—is just along here." He led them down what was clearly a very much less well-traveled track. There were small saplings springing up, and vines laced across the path. Phillipe muttered, then told the men to work on keeping their passing as undetectable as possible. So they avoided the saplings and ducked under the vines, all of which Diccon whisked light-footed around.

Then he turned off the path onto a narrow animal track. Fifteen yards on, it descended into a clearing that—as Diccon had promised—was perfect for their needs. Big enough to comfortably house all of them and with a tiny stream trickling past on one side.

"Here you go." Grinning, the boy spun, holding his arms wide.

Caleb grinned back. "Thank you—this is just what we need."

Phillipe smiled at Diccon and patted his shoulder as he passed. "You're an excellent scout, my friend."

The other men made approving noises as they filed into the space.

Diccon positively glowed.

It took only a moment for Caleb and Phillipe to organize the establishment of their camp, then, summoning their quartermasters—Caleb's Quilley and Phillipe's Ducasse—they presented themselves before Diccon.

The boy looked at them expectantly.

"First question," Caleb said. "Have you got enough fruit in your basket to satisfy the cook?"

Diccon lifted the floppy basket, opened it, and examined the pile of fruit inside. "Almost." He looked up and around, then pointed to a small tree with dangling yellow fruit. "If I got some more of those, I'd have enough."

Two captains and two quartermasters dutifully gathered several handfuls of the ripe fruit.

Diccon smiled as they filled his basket, then he clamped the handles together and looked at Caleb. "More than enough."

"Excellent. What we need next," Caleb said, "is for you to lead us to a place where we can see into the camp, all without alerting any guards. Do you know of such a spot?"

Diccon snapped off a salute. "I know just the place, Capt'n." He'd heard Caleb's men using his rank.

"In that case"—Caleb gestured toward where he assumed the mine must be—"lead on."

Diccon did. He lived up to their expectations, leading them first along the disused path again, then cutting left into the untrammeled jungle. He looked back at Caleb and whispered, "This will be safest. We're moving away from the other paths and into the space between that northward path and the one leading to the lake. The mercenaries take some of the men to the lake to fetch water every day, but they do that in the morning. There shouldn't be anyone at the lake now."

Caleb nodded, and they forged on, increasingly slowly as Diccon took the order to be careful to heart.

Eventually, he halted behind a clump of palms. Using hand signals, he intimated that they should crouch down and be extra careful while following him on to the next concealing clump.

Then he slipped like an eel through the shadows.

Caleb followed and instantly saw why Diccon had urged extra caution. The compound's palisade lay ten yards away, separated from the jungle by a beaten, well-maintained perimeter clearing—a cleared space to ensure no one could approach the palisade under cover. The compound's double gates were five yards to their right. And the gates stood wide open with two armed guards slouched against the posts on either side. Both guards' attention was fixed on the activity inside the camp, but any untoward noise would alert them.

Given the gates were propped open, Caleb surmised that the real purpose of the guards—and, indeed, the fence, the gates, and the guard tower in the middle of the compound—was to keep people in; the mercenaries had grown sufficiently complacent that they didn't expect any threat to emerge from the jungle.

Well and good.

They watched in silence for more than half an hour. Caleb noticed that heavily armed guards appeared to be patrolling randomly through the compound, but the attitude of all the mercenaries was transparently one of supreme boredom. They were very far from alert; the impression they gave was that they were perfectly sure there would be no challenge to their authority.

Against that, however, he saw some of the captives—he had no idea which ones, but both male and female—walking freely back and forth. More, some met and stopped to chat, apparently without attracting the attention of the guards.

Curious.

Then he noticed Diccon peering up at the sky. The sun was angling from the west. Remembering the boy's concern over returning in good time, Caleb tapped him on the shoulder, caught Phillipe and the other men's eyes, then tipped his head back, into the relative safety of the area behind them.

Diccon retreated first. One by one, the rest of them followed.

They gathered again well out of hearing of the guards on the gates. Caleb dropped his hand on Diccon's shoulder and met the boy's gaze. "Thank you for all your help. Now, we have to tread warily. Who is the person you trust most inside the camp?"

"Miss Katherine."

Caleb blinked. He'd expected the boy to name one of the men, but his answer had come so rapidly and definitely that there was no real way to argue with his choice. Slowly, Caleb nodded.

"Very well. I want you to tell Miss Katherine all we've told you. Can you remember the important bits?"

Diccon nodded eagerly. "I remember everything. I'm good like that."

Caleb had to grin. "Excellent. So tell Miss Katherine, but no one else, and see what she says. Then tomorrow, when you come out, go and look for fruit in this area—between our camp and the lake. Behave as you usually do and gather fruit, and we'll come and find you. We'll be waiting to hear what Miss Katherine, and any others she thinks fit to tell, say."

Diccon's face brightened. "So I'm like…what is it? A courier?"

"Exactly." Phillipe smiled at the boy. "But remember—the mark of a good courier is that he tells only those he's supposed to tell. Not a word of this to anyone else, all right?"

Diccon nodded. "Mum's the word, except for Miss Katherine."

"Good." Caleb released the boy. "I would suggest you circle around and come in from some other direction."

"I'll go to the lake and walk in from there—that way, if you keep watching, you'll see where that path comes out a-ways to the left."

Caleb's approving smile was entirely genuine. "You're taking to this like a duck to water." He nodded in farewell. "Off you go, then."

With a brisk salute and a grin for them all, Diccon melted into the jungle; in seconds, they'd lost sight of him.

"He is very good." Phillipe turned toward the gates. "But I'll feel happier when he's back inside where he belongs." He waved toward their previous hideaway. "Shall we?"

They returned to the spot. Five minutes later, Diccon appeared out of the jungle to their left. He passed their position without a glance and, basket swinging, all but skipped back through the gates. He headed to the right, vanishing into an area of the compound that from their position they had no view of.

Caleb consulted his memory. "He must have gone to deliver his haul to the cook—he said the kitchen was that way."

He'd barely breathed the words. Phillipe merely nodded in reply.

Sure enough, ten minutes later, they saw Diccon, no longer carrying the basket, cross the area inside the gates, right to left. He appeared to be scanning the far left quadrant of the compound—but then he whirled as if responding to a hail from somewhere out of their sight to the right.

Even from where they crouched, they saw his face light up. Diccon all but jigged on the spot, clearly waiting…

A young woman appeared. Brown-haired, pale skinned, she moved with a grace that marked her as well bred. Smiling, she came up to Diccon and held out her hands. Diccon readily placed his hands in hers, all but wriggling with impatience and excitement.

Closing her hands about the boy's, her gaze on his face, the woman crouched as Caleb had done.

Immediately, the boy started talking, although from the way the woman leaned toward him, he was keeping his voice down.

"Miss Katherine, obviously." Caleb scanned all of the area around the pair that he could see, but there were no guards or, indeed, anyone else close enough to hear the exchange.

As Diccon poured out his news, Caleb saw the woman—younger than he'd expected by more than a decade; he'd had no idea a governess could be that young—start to tense. Clearly, she'd realized the import of what the boy was telling her—and she believed his tale.

That last was verified when she glanced out of the gates—not directly at them but in their direction.

Immediately, she caught herself and refocused on Diccon again.

But Caleb had seen that look, had caught her expression. However fleeting, that look had been a visual cry for help that had also held a flaring of something even more precious—hope.

By some trick of the light, of that moment in eternity, he'd felt that hope—fragile, but real—reaching out to him, something so indescribably precious he'd instinctively wanted to grasp it. To hold and protect it.

Then she'd clamped down on the emotion, but he no longer harbored the slightest concern that the adults in the camp wouldn't believe Diccon's tale. She—Miss Katherine—did, and even though Caleb had yet to exchange so much as a word with her, he felt certain a woman brave enough to stand up to a mercenary captain in order to save an urchin's life would have the backbone to carry her point with the English officers in the camp.

Diccon finished his tale. Her gaze fixed firmly on his face, Miss Katherine slowly rose to her feet. Then she released one of his hands, but retained her clasp on the other. Drawing him around, she set off with a purposeful stride, heading in the direction of the mine. In just a few paces, she and Diccon had passed out of their sight.

They continued to watch for several minutes, but no alarm was raised, and there was nothing of particular interest to see.

Caleb frowned. He leaned toward Phillipe and whispered, "We need to see *into* the compound—we need a much more comprehensive view."

"I was thinking the same, and it just so happens"—without raising his arm, Phillipe pointed, directing Caleb's gaze upward—"the compound is nestled into a curve in the hillside, and if you look very closely just there…"

Caleb looked. His eyes were accustomed to reading ships' flags at considerable distance; he quickly picked out the rock formation Phillipe had spied. "Perfect." Caleb grinned. He glanced back at Quilley and Ducasse. "We've plenty of time before the light fades to find our way to that shelf."

They did and discovered it to be the perfect vantage point from which to survey the compound. The rock shelf was wide enough for all four of them to sit comfortably, sufficiently back from the edge that the shifting leaves of trees growing up from below screened them from anyone on the ground. They spent another half hour observing the movements of the guards and the captives, thus confirming and acquainting themselves with the uses of the different structures in the compound. Diccon had given them an excellent orientation, but it seemed that most of the adult males were down in the mine and not presently available to be viewed.

There was a large circular fire pit in the space between the entrance to the mine, the barrack-like building that from Diccon's description was the men's sleeping quarters, and the large central barracks that housed the mercenaries. Ringed with logs for seats, the fire pit was situated well away from all three structures. A small fire burned at the pit's center, doubtless more for light and the comfort imparted by the leaping flames than for warmth, and the women were already gathering about it. Miss Katherine sat with five others, but from the relaxed postures of the other women, she had not—yet—shared Diccon's news. Instead, she glanced frequently toward the entrance to the mine.

"She's waiting for the men to join them," Phillipe said. "She's waiting to tell whoever's in charge."

Caleb nodded. "I wish we could stay and identify who that is, but we should get down and back to our camp before night falls."

Night in the jungle was the definition of black; scrambling about on an unfamiliar hillside above an encampment of hostile armed mercenaries in the dark would be the definition of irresponsible.

Phillipe pulled a face, but nodded, and the four of them rose and scrambled back onto the animal track along which they'd climbed up. Once they reached the jungle floor, despite the fading light, they skirted wide through the deepening shadows. Giving the open gates of the compound and the well-armed guards a wide berth, they made their way back to their camp.

For alerts as new books are released,
plus information on upcoming books,
sign up for Stephanie's Private Email Newsletter,
either on her website,
or at: http://eepurl.com/gLgPj

Or if you're a member of Goodreads,
join the discussion of Stephanie's books
at the Fans of Stephanie Laurens group.

You can email Stephanie at
stephanie@stephanielaurens.com

Or find her on Facebook at
http://www.facebook.com/AuthorStephanieLaurens

You can find detailed information on all
Stephanie's published books, including covers,
descriptions, and excerpts, on her website at
http://www.stephanielaurens.com